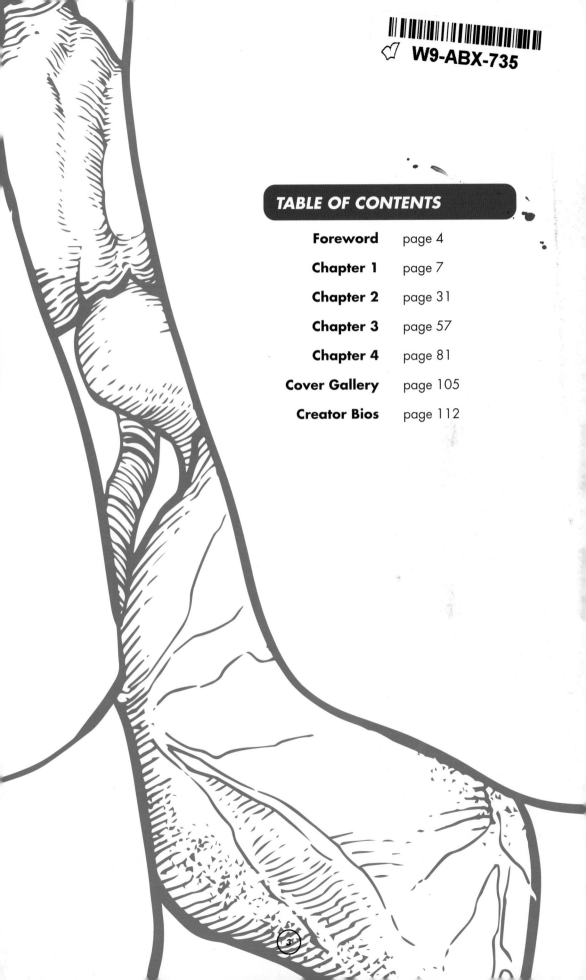

W9-ABX-735

TABLE OF CONTENTS

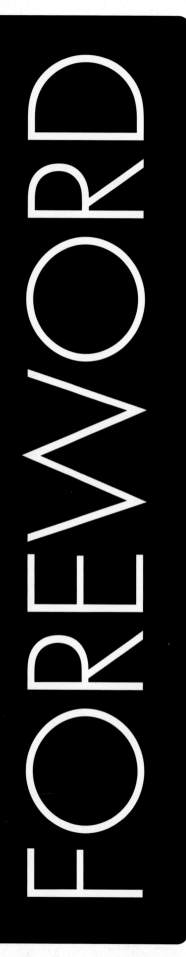

THE QUESTION

This isn't a sob story.

Every month, I walk up to the counter at my local pharmacy and pay a significant percentage of my income for the medication I need to breathe. It tends to go pretty much how it goes for Scout in the opening scene of *Breathless*. Pharmacists, even ones that have helped me before, always squint at the price, as if they know something just can't be right. I've gotten some version of "Are you aware of the co-pay on this?" more times than I can count.

I'm aware.

Breathless is about *that*. The idea that there are people out there who have to pay to breathe. And, more than that, so much more than that, pay to *live*. I wanted to dig into the pharmaceutical industry and try to look at the people who enable this system. It's so easy to make them out to be monsters, because then they're Not Us ™ ©. They're all us, though. All of the monsters are us.

I wanted to look at the people who are caught up in the healthcare industry's wake and try to understand what this kind of lifestyle can do to people. In a society where it's normal to go bankrupt in order to not die, does that change the way that we understand humanity? Empathy?

Also? Let's keep it 100. I paired with Renzo Rodriguez on this because I knew he would draw some gnarly ass creatures. In the real world, the monsters might all be people, but Renzo and I wanted to populate this world with *both* varieties – just to see who comes off worse in the end.

Breathless isn't preaching at anyone, though. It's a question. In fact, it was inspired by a question asked to notorious pharma-bro Martin Shkreli by Charlamagne tha God. I heard this bit on Charlamagne's radio show, *The Breakfast Club*, and I was stunned. It was the exact question I wanted to ask, put into words in a way that blew my fucking mind. Charlamagne sat across from Shkreli, who had gained infamy by jacking up the price of a drug treating HIV/AIDS by an incredible percentage, and he asked:

"First question. Are you a privileged, entitled prick?"

And then, Charlamagne sat back and let Shkreli answer the question.

Breathless isn't a sob story. *Breathless* isn't preaching to you. Or anyone.

Breathless is asking a question. A different question than the one that inspired the series, but a question no less pointed.

The answer is up to us.

- **Pat Shand**, 3/02/2018

BLISS

CODA

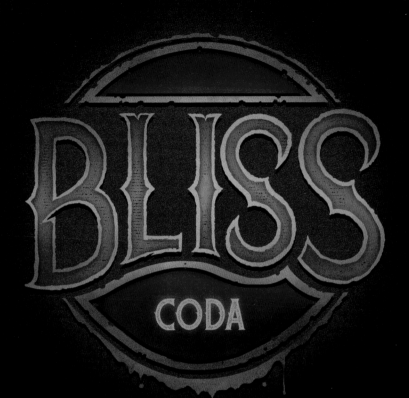

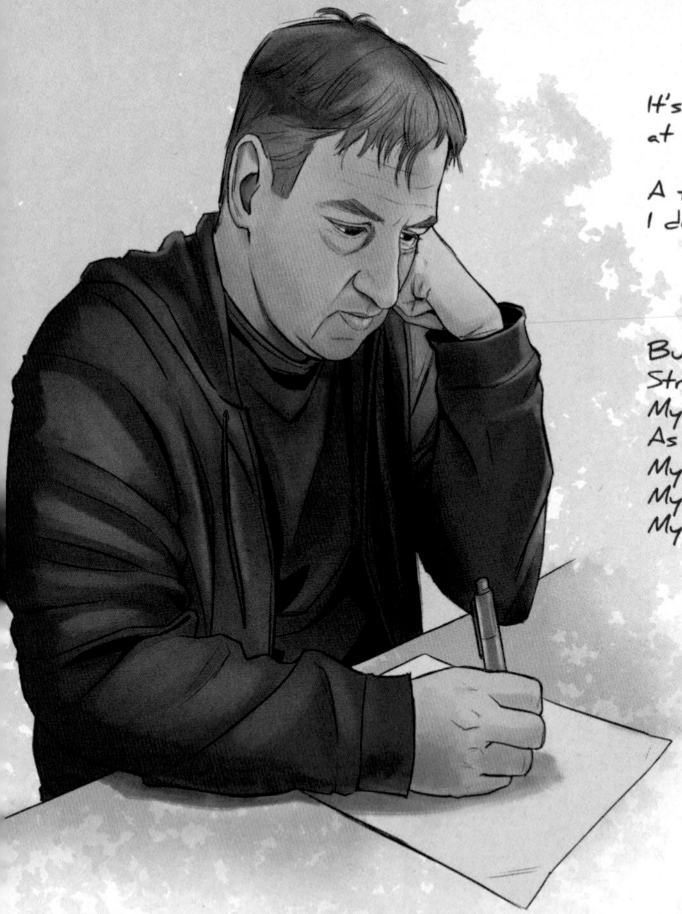

It's strange to write about forgiveness
at a time when no one wants to forgive.

A time when maybe no one should.
I don't really know.

But writing this book has been
Strangely personal.
My dad
As Benton.
Myself as Perry.
Myself as Benton.
My son... as Perry?

I have a son named Eamon.
And lately he's been asking me about my dad.
His "dead" grandpa.
And memories come back.

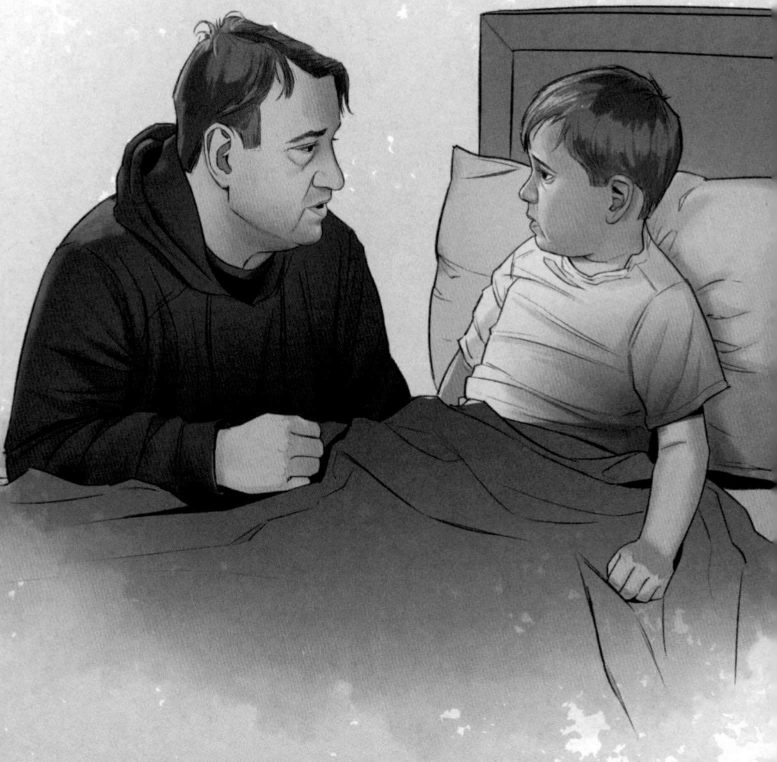

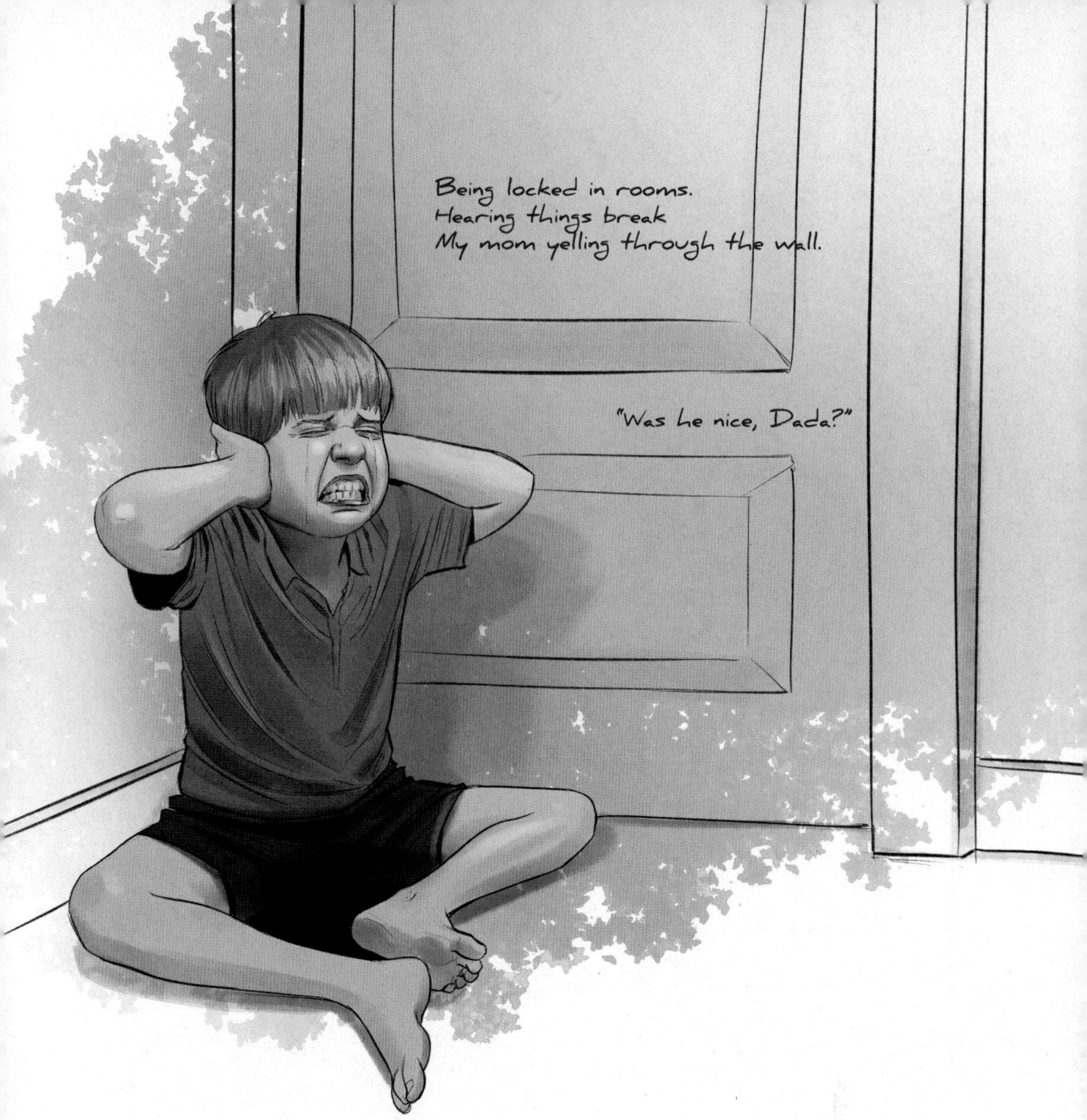
Being locked in rooms.
Hearing things break
My mom yelling through the wall.
"Was he nice, Dada?"

His girlfriends who talked sex with me before I was a teen.
Who kissed me
And at his funeral told me how much I looked like him
Their former lover.

"How'd he die?"

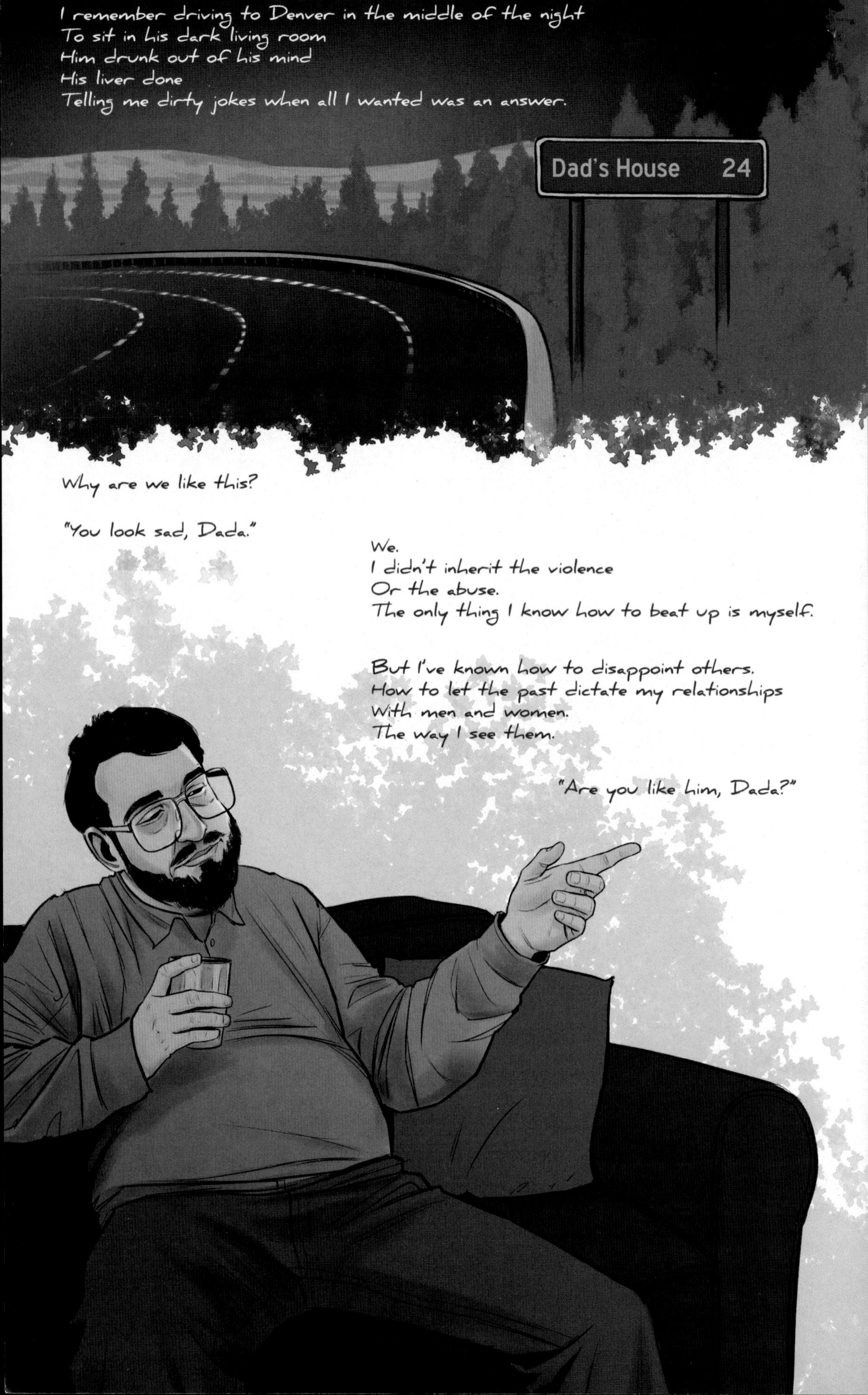
I remember driving to Denver in the middle of the night
To sit in his dark living room
Him drunk out of his mind
His liver done
Telling me dirty jokes when all I wanted was an answer.
Dad's House 24
Why are we like this?
"You look sad, Dada."
We.
I didn't inherit the violence
Or the abuse.
The only thing I know how to beat up is myself.
But I've known how to disappoint others.
How to let the past dictate my relationships
With men and women.
The way I see them.
"Are you like him, Dada?"

And every day
I have to fight against it
So I don't become him.

I write heroes. Cause I need them.

And I look at my own son
And that boy, he looks at me with so much trust.
His eyes so wide and he says-

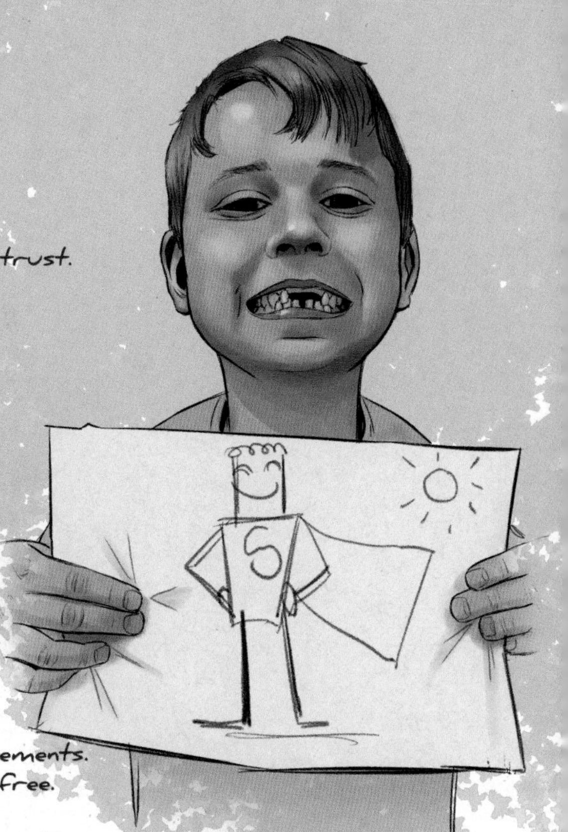

"Dada?"

"Yeah buddy?"

"I'm drawing a comic just like you."

Sometimes I see my son when he lashes out.
A moment of cruelty.
And I can see on his face fear.
Fear he can be so destructive.
That it's in him. He has moments of it.

I had years of it.

And maybe that's the best we can do.
Each generation undoing this pain in little increments.
Getting better each round. Till finally, we're free.

And when he gets scared and shocked and says "I'm a bad boy"

I take him in my arms and say the only thing I know to be true.
There are no Saints.
You'll hurt people.
They'll hurt you.
You'll be better than your father.

And you'll fall.
A lot.

What's important is not only that you get up.
But how.

"If I do it the right way
what will it feel like?" he asks.

"It'll feel perfect," I tell him.

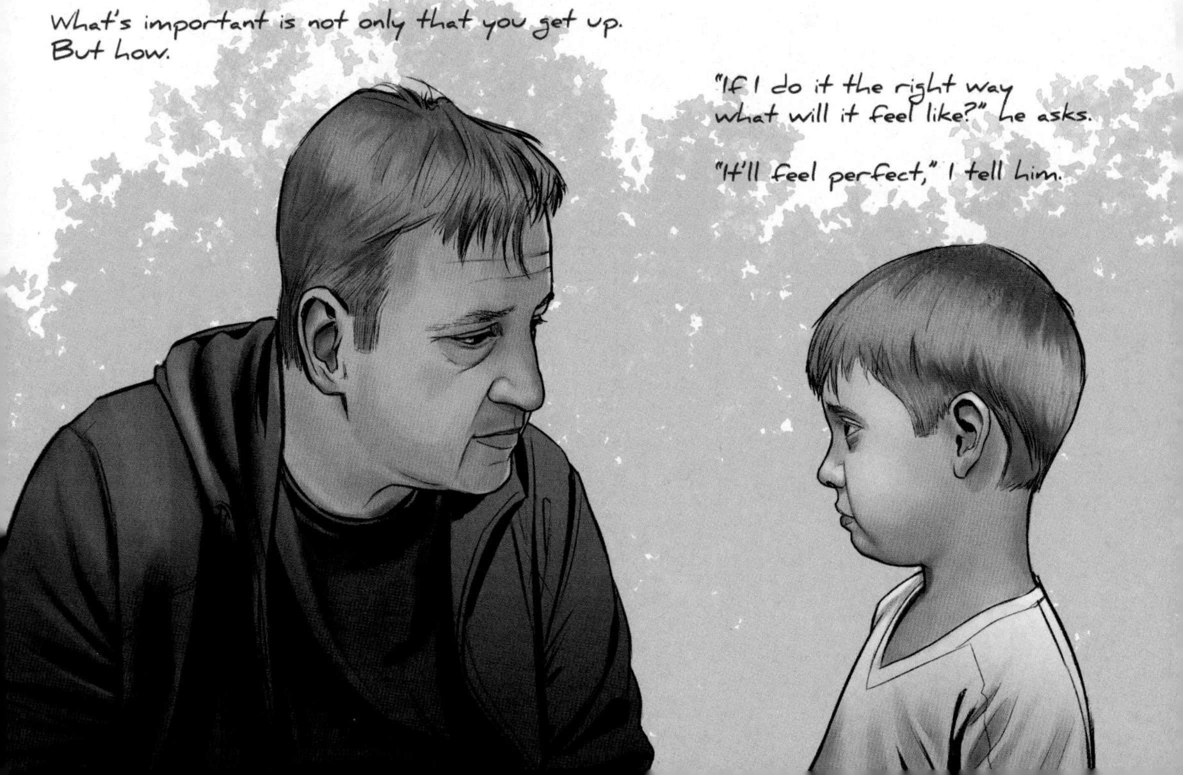

"It will be bliss."

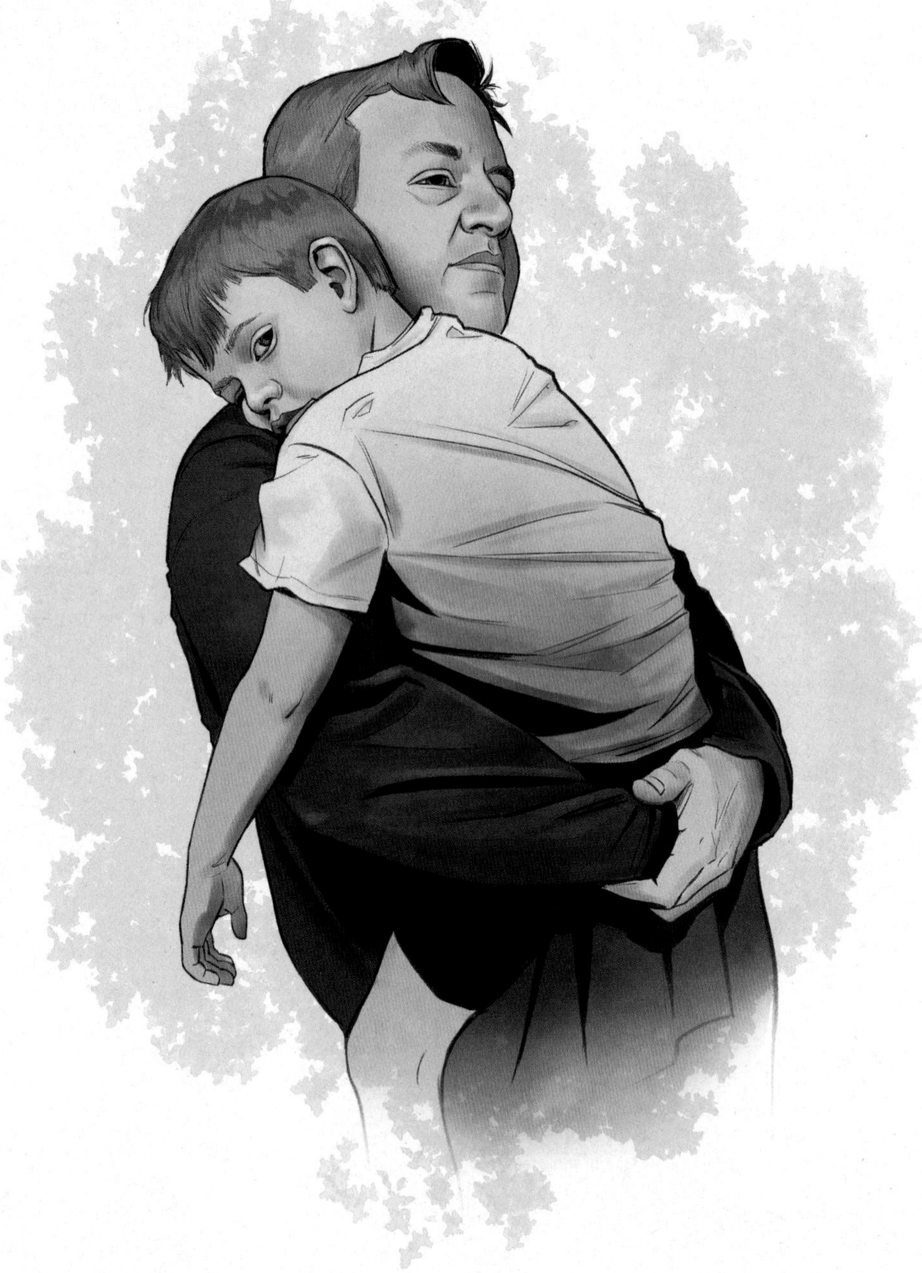

SPECIAL THANKS TO THE CAST!

LEADS

BENTON- MATT KOLACKI

MABEL- JACKIE DAVIS

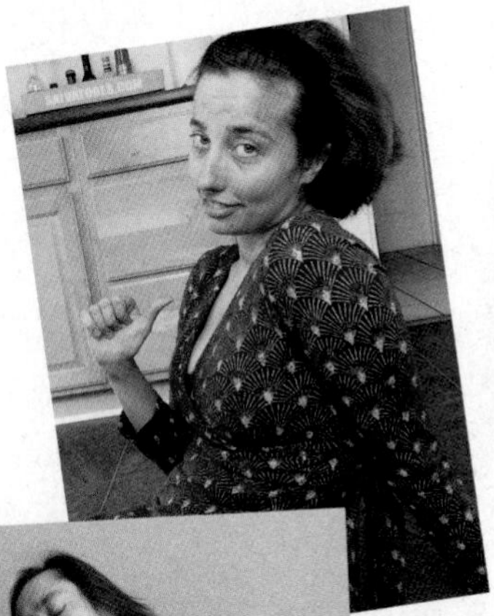
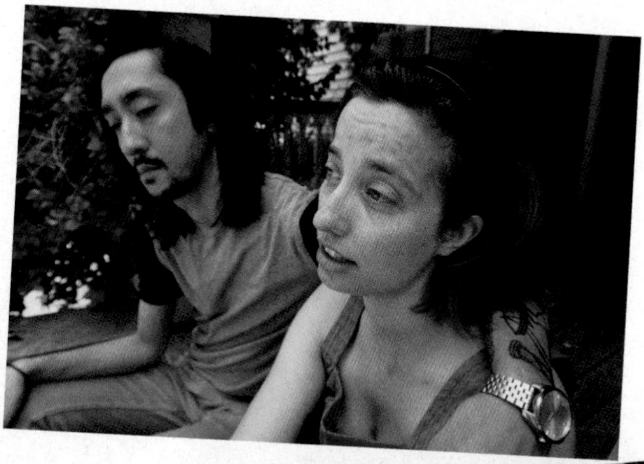
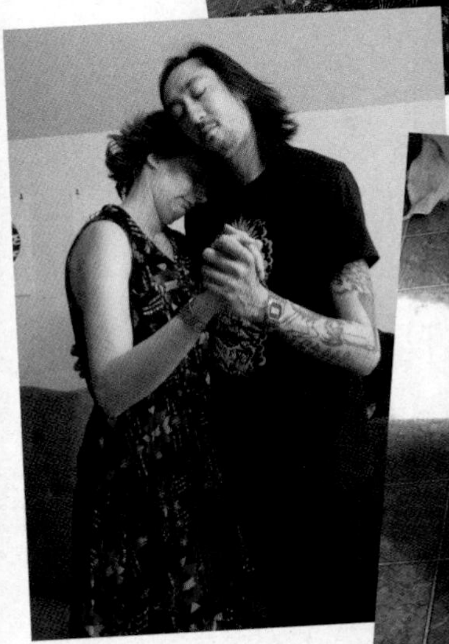
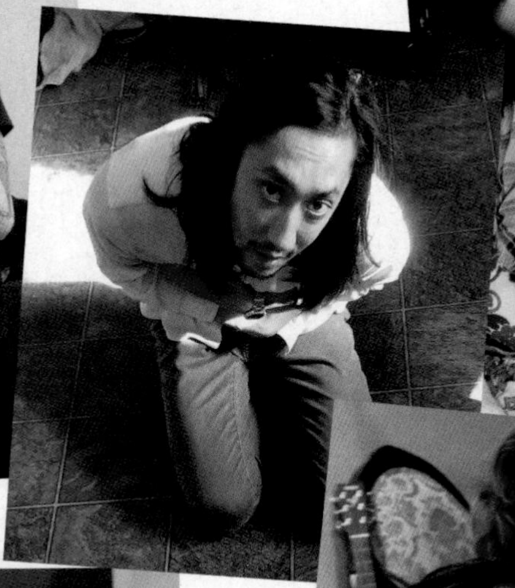
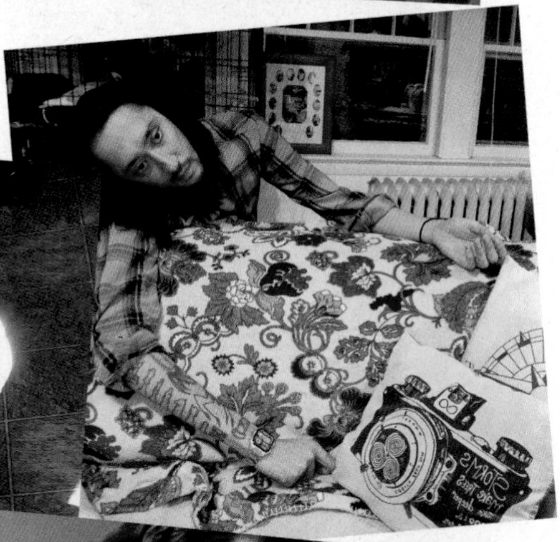
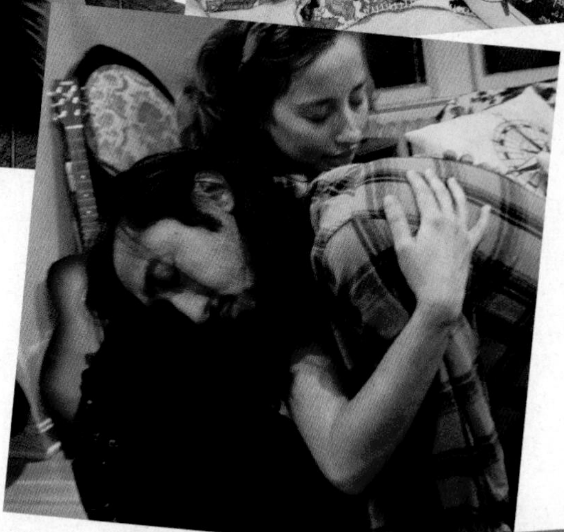
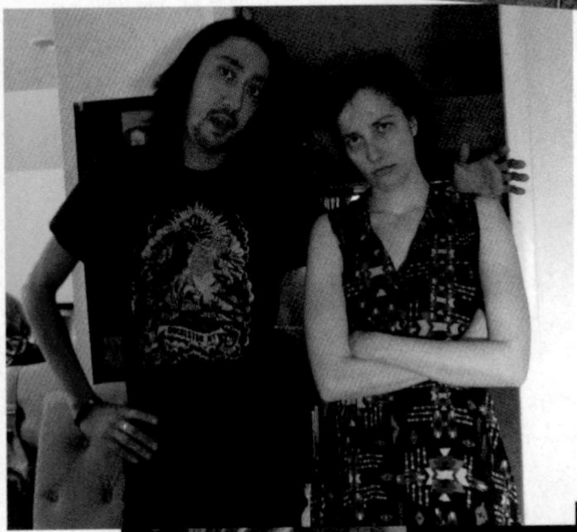
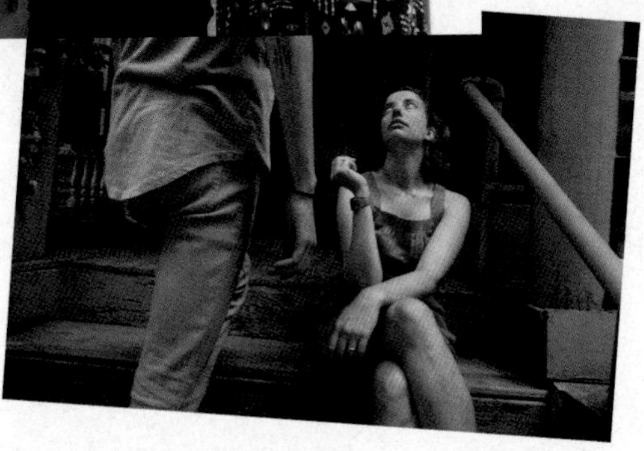
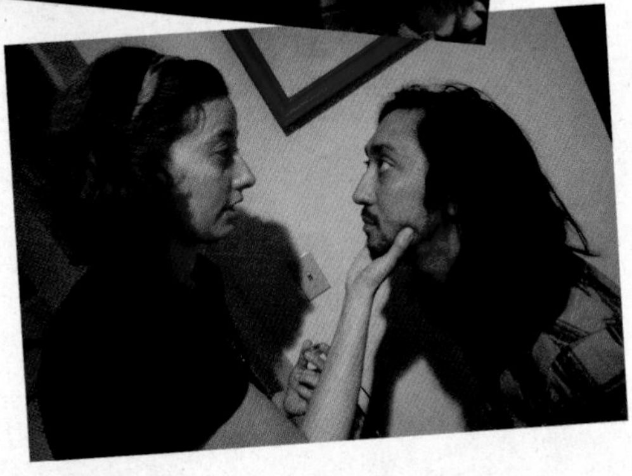

SUPPORTING ROLES

LETHE- KATHLEEN O'NEILL
JUDGE- CALVIN DRAKE
MABEL'S DAD- MATTÉ
WREN'S MOM- KATHRYN DEFEO
GUARD1- BRYAN WILLIAMS
GUARD2- KENT FAIRMAN WILSON
MULTIPLE- MAGNUS CHAMPLIN
REILLY SOLOMON COOK
CLAYTON COWLES
SEAN EDGAR
JENNIE OSBORNE
CAMMY ENAHARO

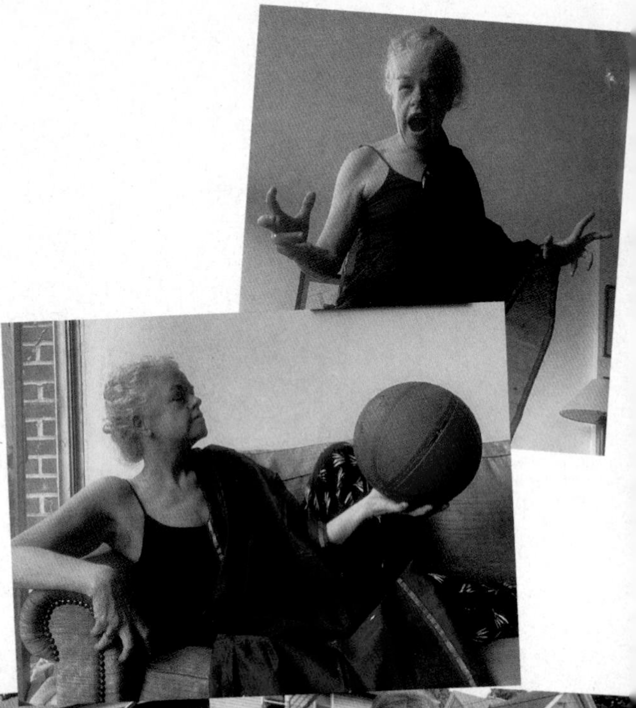

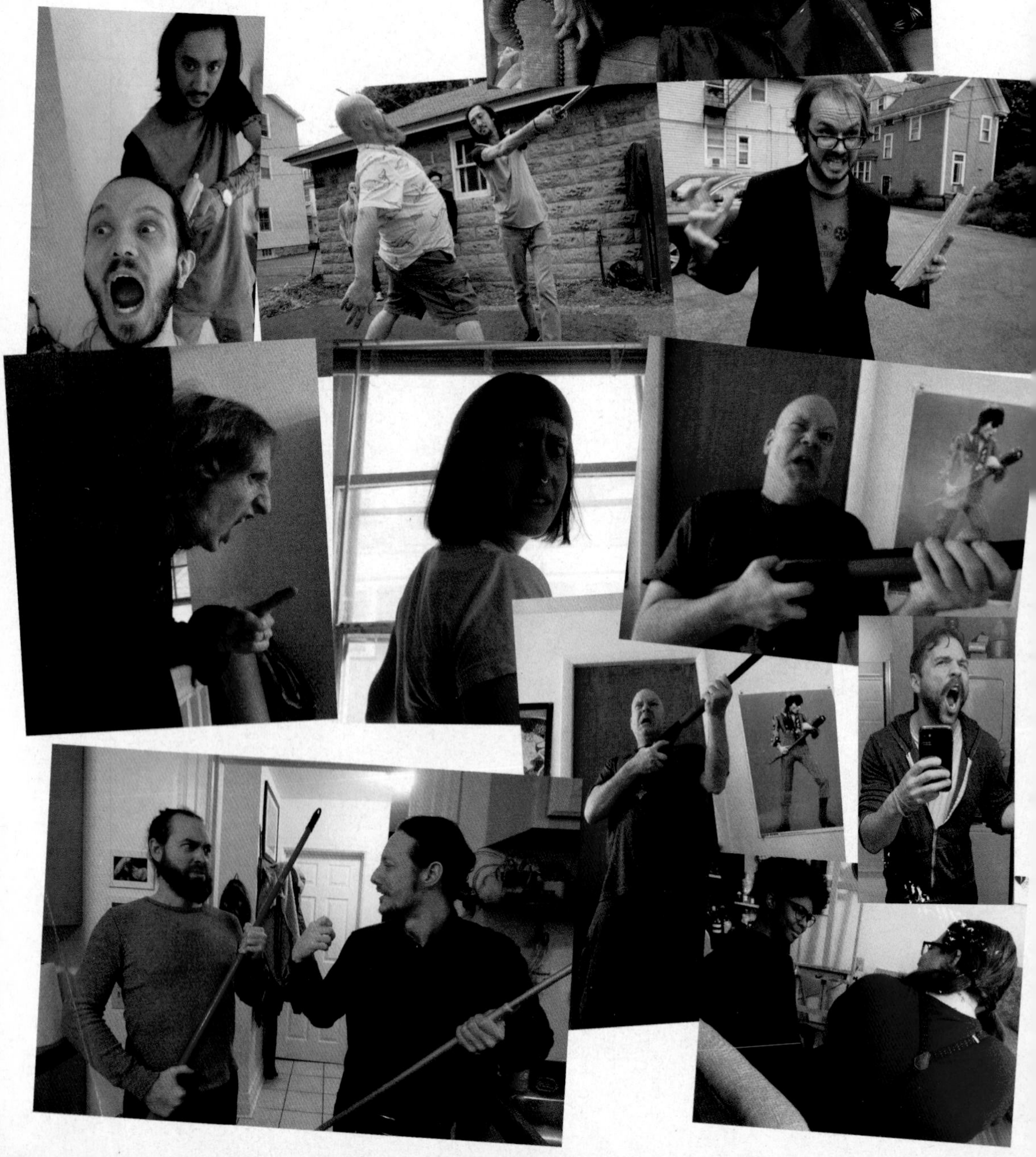

PAY

TO

LIVE

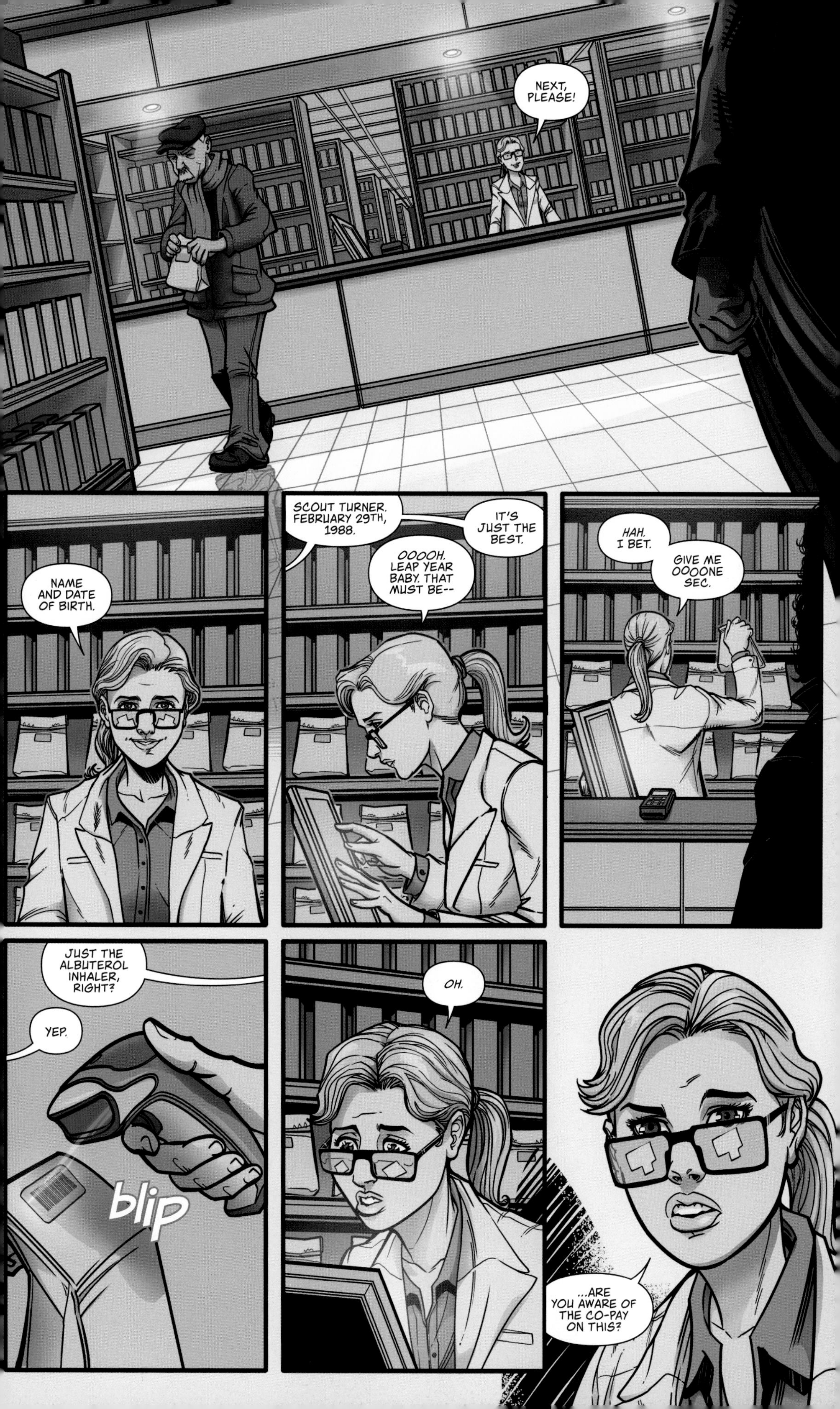
NEXT, PLEASE!
NAME AND DATE OF BIRTH.
SCOUT TURNER. FEBRUARY 29TH, 1988.
OOOOH. LEAP YEAR BABY. THAT MUST BE--
IT'S JUST THE BEST.
HAH. I BET.
GIVE ME OOOONE SEC.
JUST THE ALBUTEROL INHALER, RIGHT?
YEP.
blip
OH.
...ARE YOU AWARE OF THE CO-PAY ON THIS?

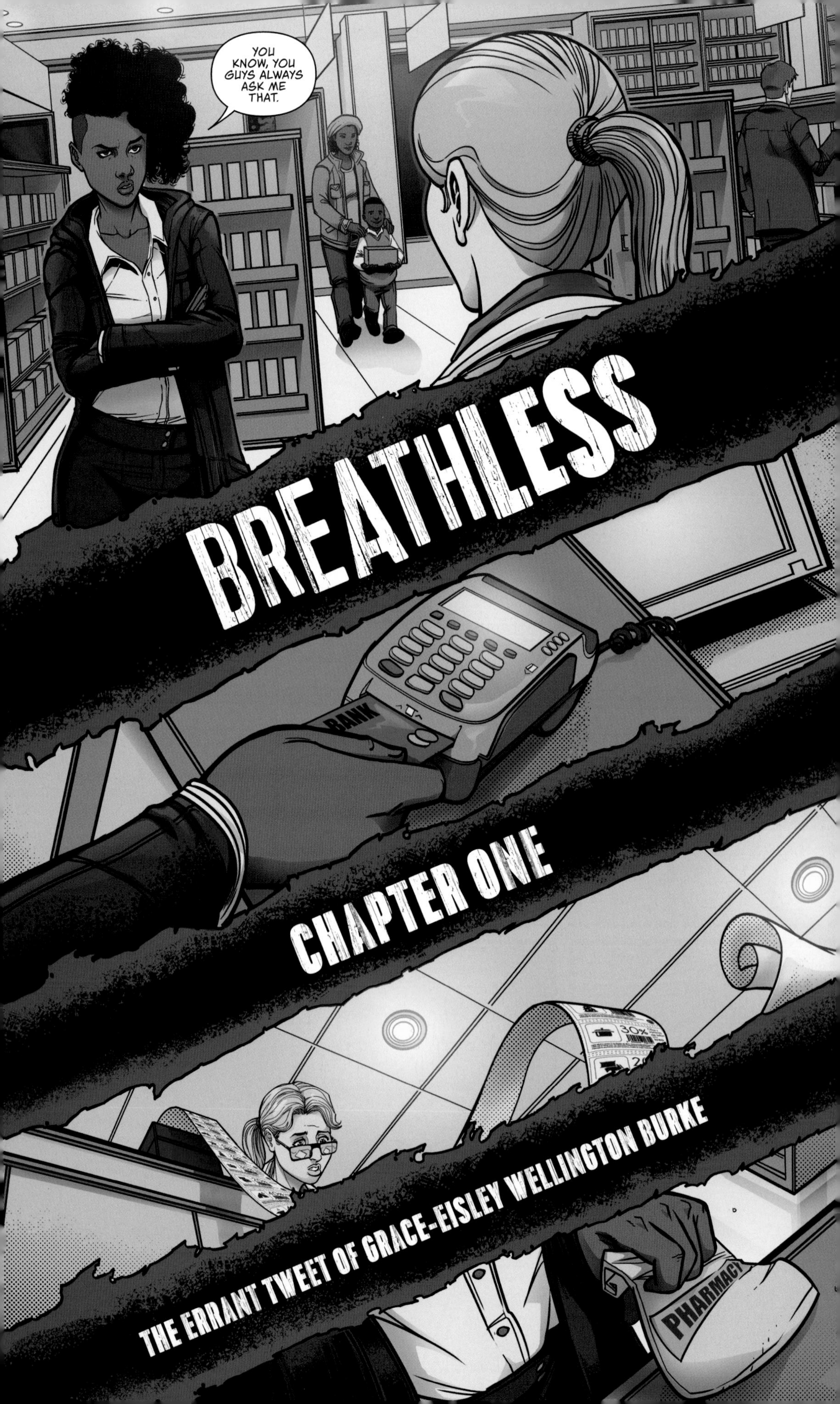
YOU KNOW, YOU GUYS ALWAYS ASK ME THAT.
BREATHLESS
CHAPTER ONE
THE ERRANT TWEET OF GRACE-EISLEY WELLINGTON BURKE
BANK
30%
PHARMACY

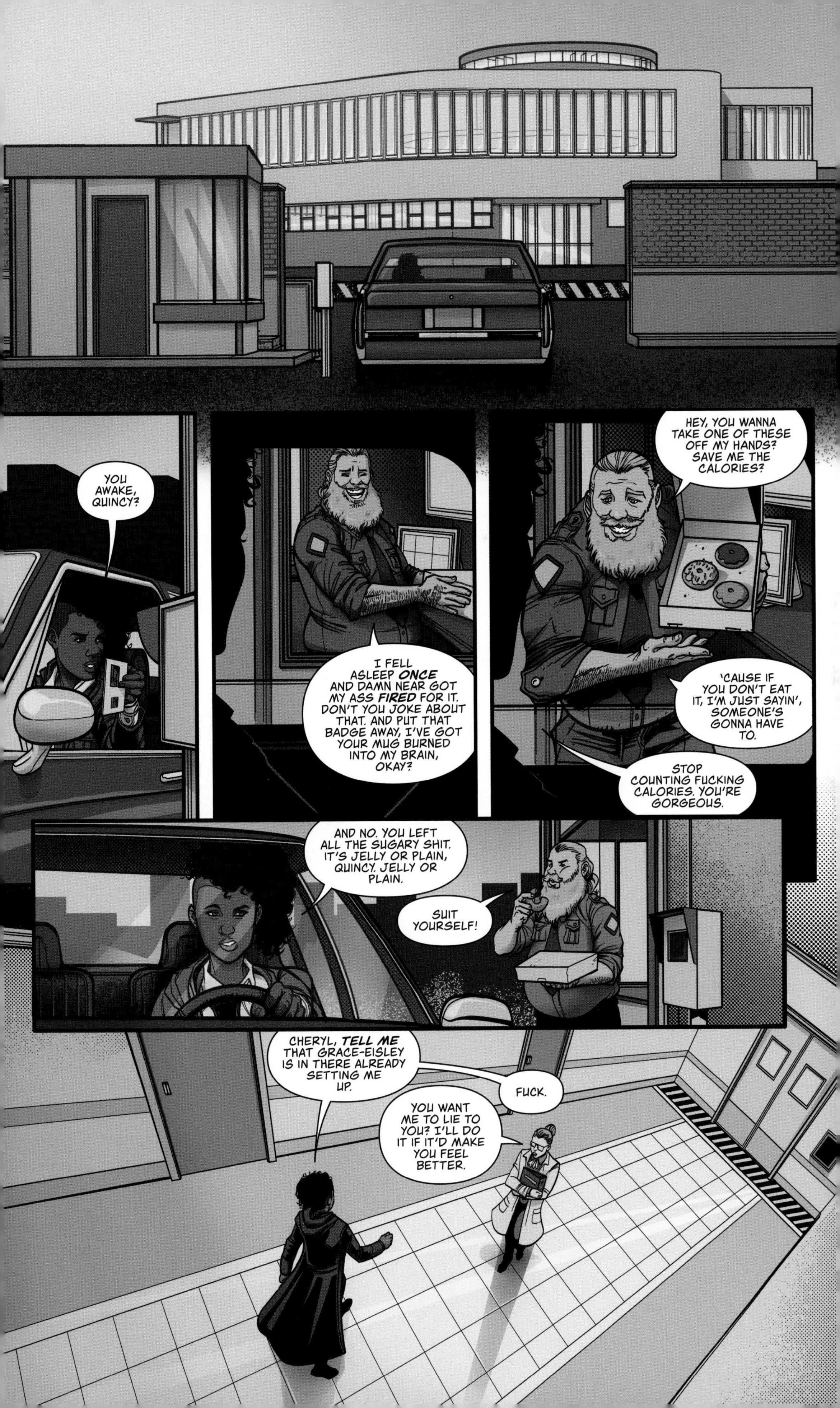
YOU AWAKE, QUINCY?
I FELL ASLEEP ONCE AND DAMN NEAR GOT MY ASS FIRED FOR IT. DON'T YOU JOKE ABOUT THAT. AND PUT THAT BADGE AWAY, I'VE GOT YOUR MUG BURNED INTO MY BRAIN, OKAY?
HEY, YOU WANNA TAKE ONE OF THESE OFF MY HANDS? SAVE ME THE CALORIES?
'CAUSE IF YOU DON'T EAT IT, I'M JUST SAYIN', SOMEONE'S GONNA HAVE TO.
STOP COUNTING FUCKING CALORIES. YOU'RE GORGEOUS.
AND NO. YOU LEFT ALL THE SUGARY SHIT. IT'S JELLY OR PLAIN, QUINCY. JELLY OR PLAIN.
SUIT YOURSELF!
CHERYL, TELL ME THAT GRACE-EISLEY IS IN THERE ALREADY SETTING ME UP.
FUCK.
YOU WANT ME TO LIE TO YOU? I'LL DO IT IF IT'D MAKE YOU FEEL BETTER.

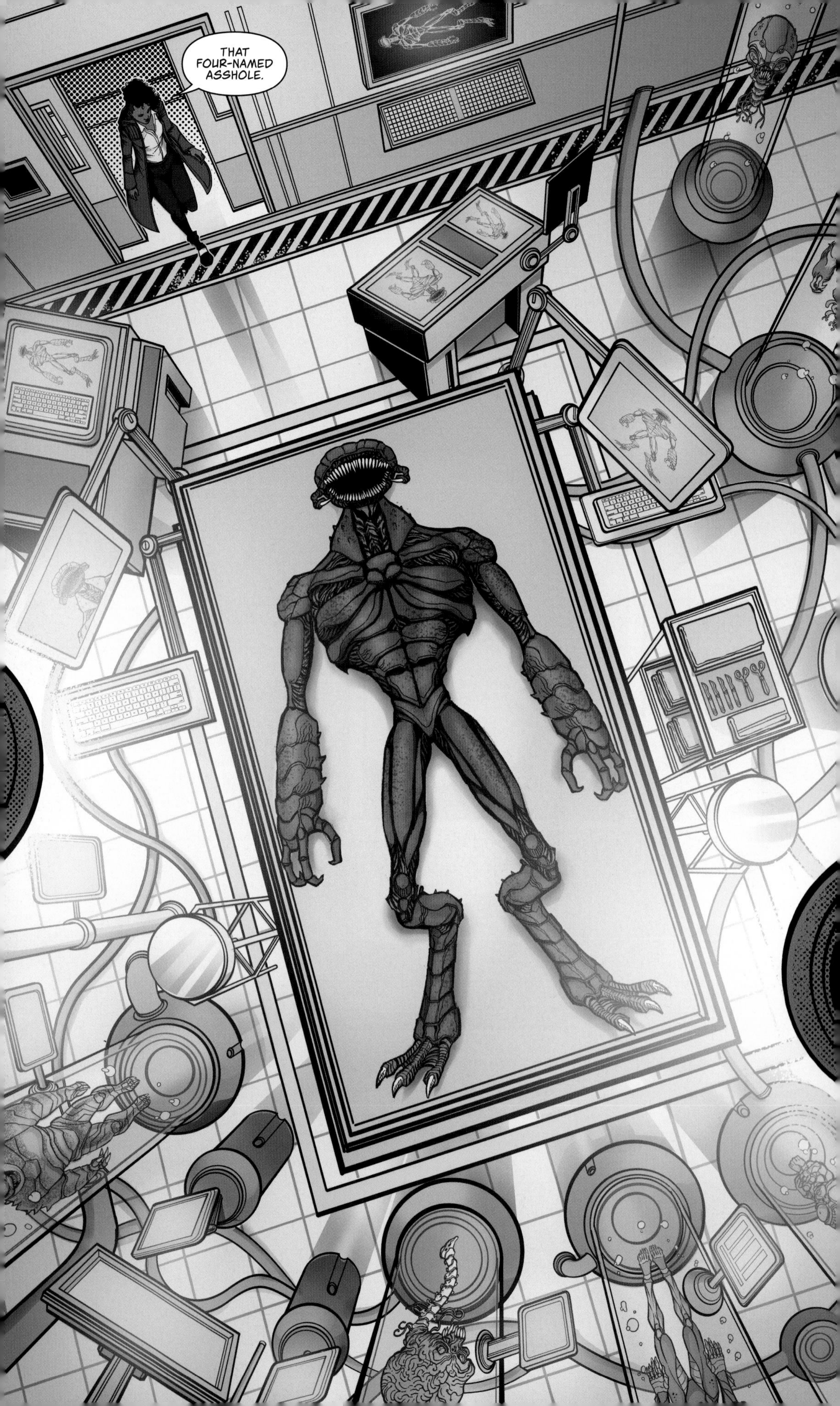
THAT FOUR-NAMED ASSHOLE.

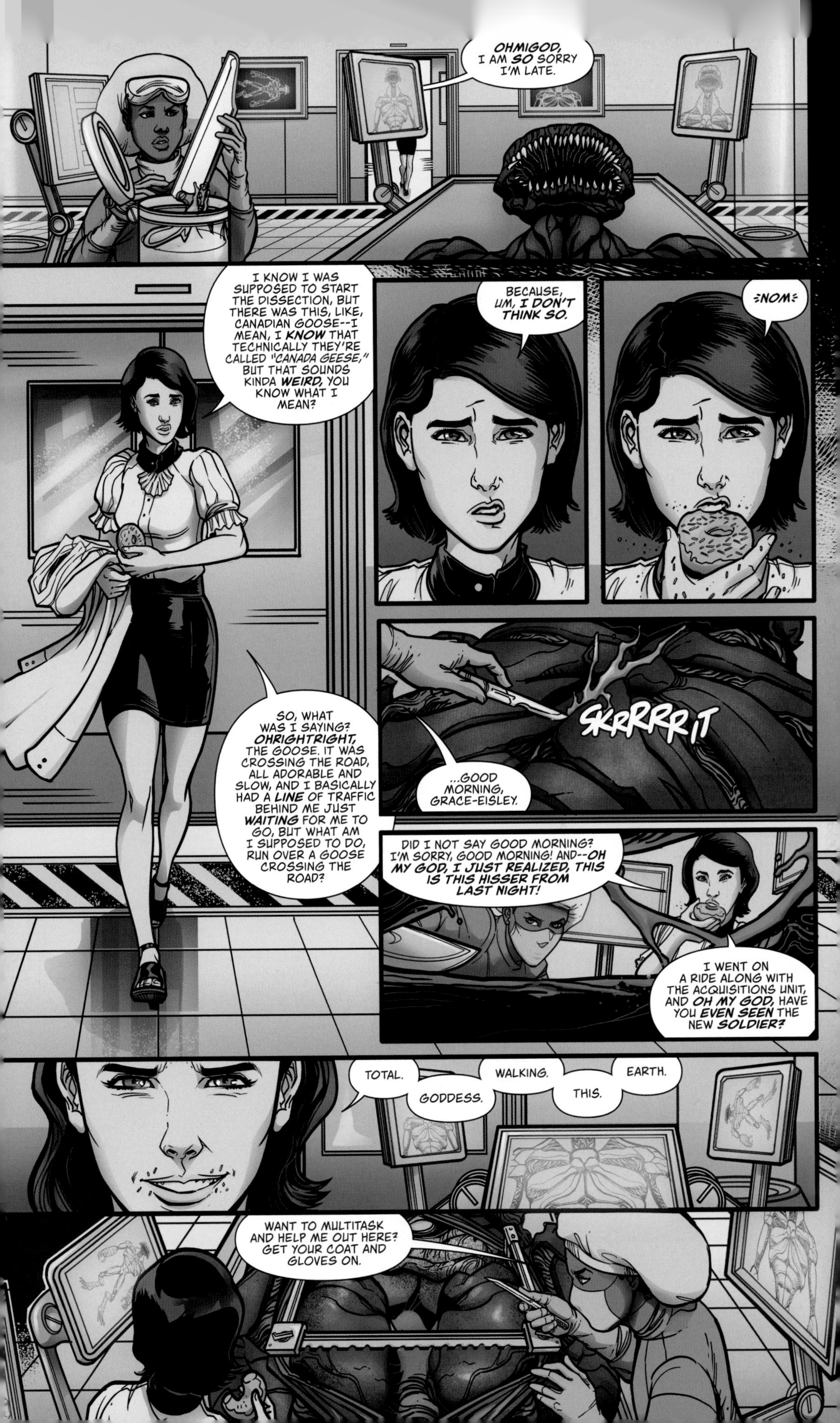

OHMIGOD, I AM SO SORRY I'M LATE.
I KNOW I WAS SUPPOSED TO START THE DISSECTION, BUT THERE WAS THIS, LIKE, CANADIAN GOOSE--I MEAN, I KNOW THAT TECHNICALLY THEY'RE CALLED "CANADA GEESE," BUT THAT SOUNDS KINDA WEIRD, YOU KNOW WHAT I MEAN?
BECAUSE, UM, I DON'T THINK SO.
NOM
SO, WHAT WAS I SAYING? OHRIGHTRIGHT, THE GOOSE. IT WAS CROSSING THE ROAD, ALL ADORABLE AND SLOW, AND I BASICALLY HAD A LINE OF TRAFFIC BEHIND ME JUST WAITING FOR ME TO GO, BUT WHAT AM I SUPPOSED TO DO, RUN OVER A GOOSE CROSSING THE ROAD?
SKRRRRIT
...GOOD MORNING, GRACE-EISLEY.
DID I NOT SAY GOOD MORNING? I'M SORRY, GOOD MORNING! AND--OH MY GOD, I JUST REALIZED, THIS IS THIS HISSER FROM LAST NIGHT!
I WENT ON A RIDE ALONG WITH THE ACQUISITIONS UNIT, AND OH MY GOD, HAVE YOU EVEN SEEN THE NEW SOLDIER?
TOTAL.
GODDESS.
WALKING.
THIS.
EARTH.
WANT TO MULTITASK AND HELP ME OUT HERE? GET YOUR COAT AND GLOVES ON.

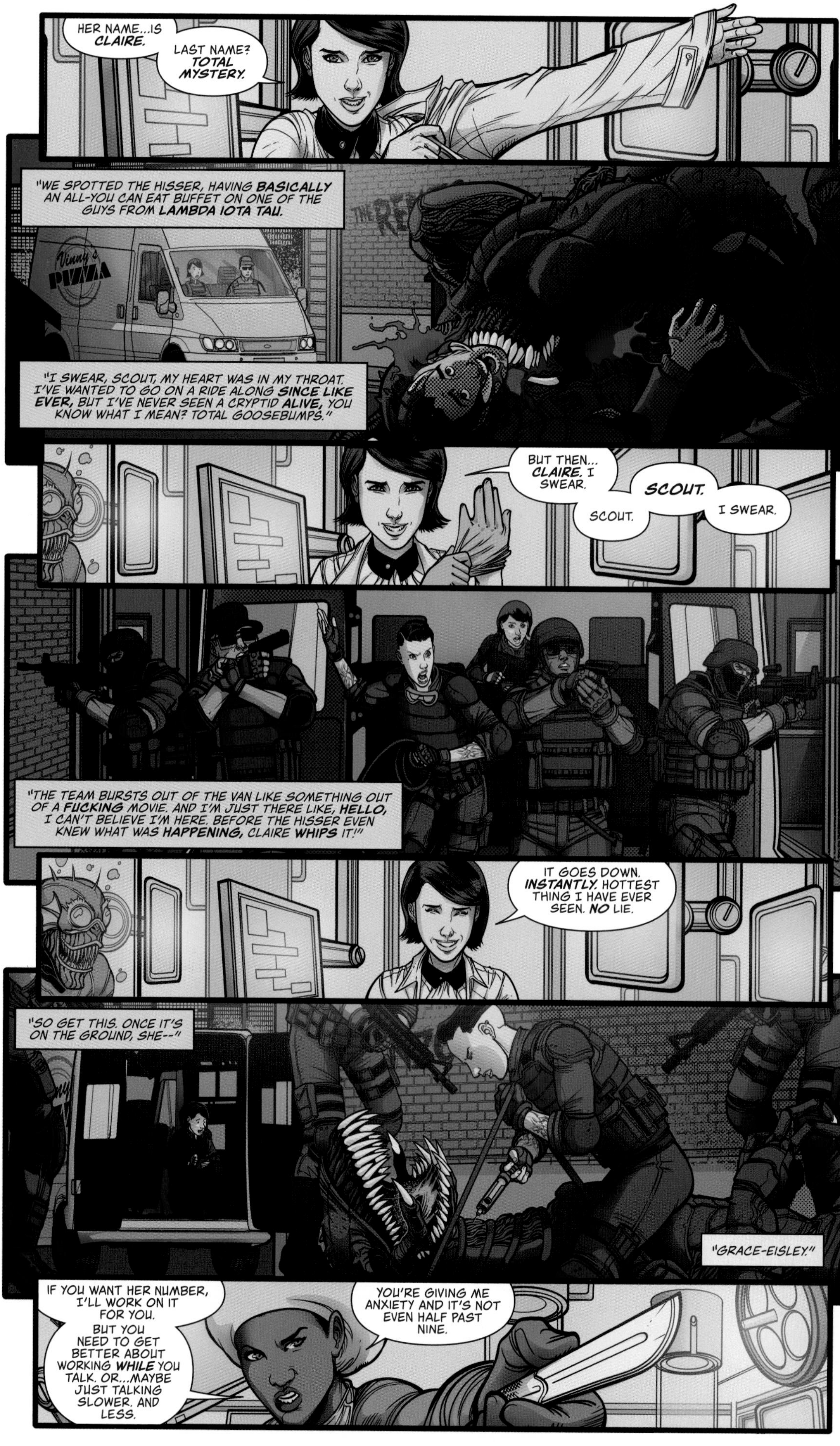

HER NAME...IS **CLAIRE.**
LAST NAME? **TOTAL MYSTERY.**
"WE SPOTTED THE HISSER, HAVING **BASICALLY** AN ALL-YOU CAN EAT BUFFET ON ONE OF THE GUYS FROM **LAMBDA IOTA TAU.**
Vinny's PIZZA
"I SWEAR, SCOUT, MY HEART WAS IN MY THROAT. I'VE WANTED TO GO ON A RIDE ALONG **SINCE LIKE EVER,** BUT I'VE NEVER SEEN A CRYPTID **ALIVE,** YOU KNOW WHAT I MEAN? TOTAL GOOSEBUMPS."
BUT THEN... **CLAIRE.** I SWEAR.
SCOUT.
SCOUT.
I SWEAR.
"THE TEAM BURSTS OUT OF THE VAN LIKE SOMETHING OUT OF A **FUCKING** MOVIE. AND I'M JUST THERE LIKE, **HELLO,** I CAN'T BELIEVE I'M HERE. BEFORE THE HISSER EVEN KNEW WHAT WAS **HAPPENING,** CLAIRE **WHIPS** IT!"
IT GOES DOWN. **INSTANTLY.** HOTTEST THING I HAVE EVER SEEN. **NO** LIE.
"SO GET THIS. ONCE IT'S ON THE GROUND, SHE--"
"GRACE-EISLEY."
IF YOU WANT HER NUMBER, I'LL WORK ON IT FOR YOU.
BUT YOU NEED TO GET BETTER ABOUT WORKING **WHILE** YOU TALK. OR...MAYBE JUST TALKING SLOWER. AND LESS.
YOU'RE GIVING ME ANXIETY AND IT'S NOT EVEN HALF PAST NINE.

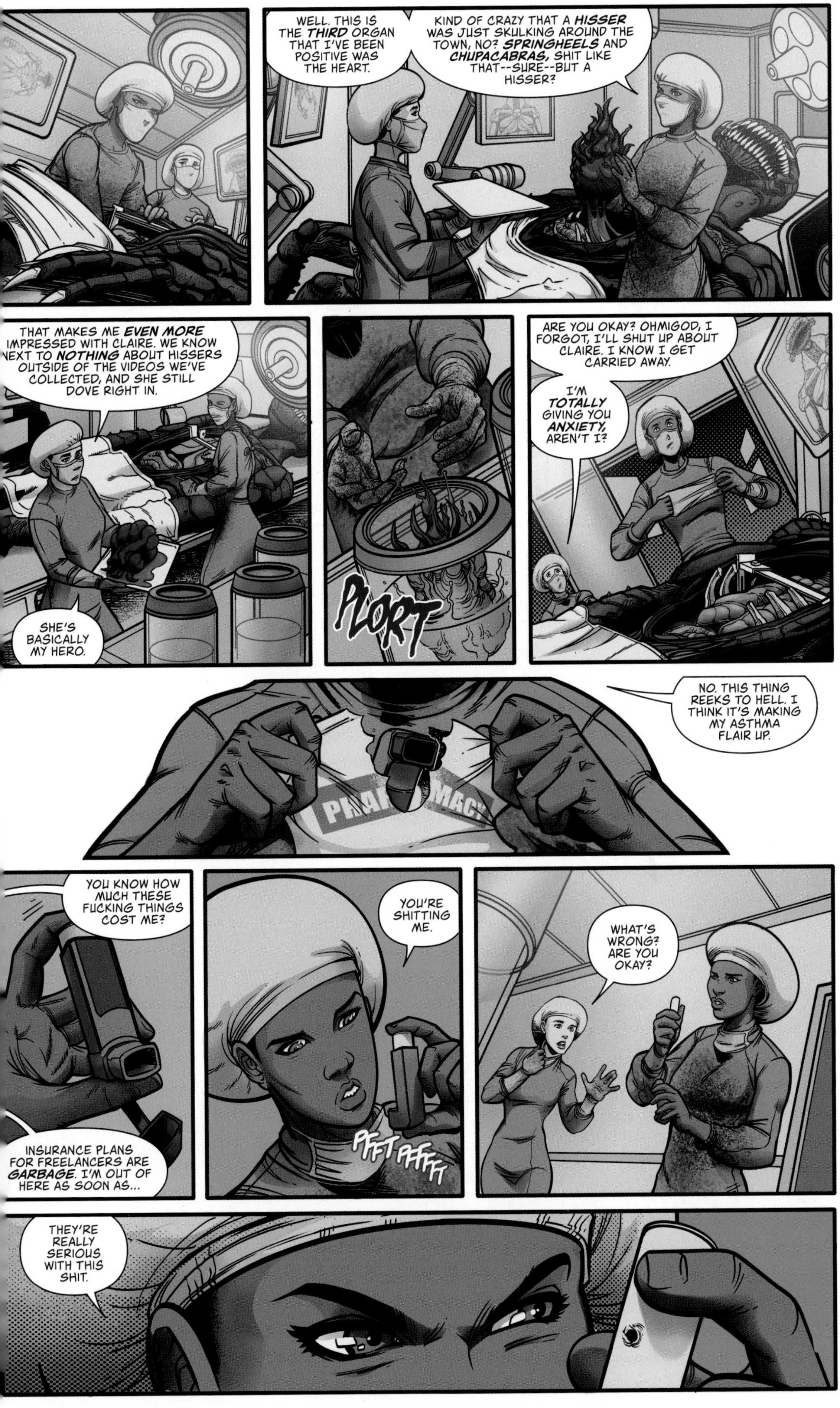
WELL. THIS IS THE THIRD ORGAN THAT I'VE BEEN POSITIVE WAS THE HEART.
KIND OF CRAZY THAT A HISSER WAS JUST SKULKING AROUND THE TOWN, NO? SPRINGHEELS AND CHUPACABRAS, SHIT LIKE THAT--SURE--BUT A HISSER?
THAT MAKES ME EVEN MORE IMPRESSED WITH CLAIRE. WE KNOW NEXT TO NOTHING ABOUT HISSERS OUTSIDE OF THE VIDEOS WE'VE COLLECTED, AND SHE STILL DOVE RIGHT IN.
SHE'S BASICALLY MY HERO.
PLORT
ARE YOU OKAY? OHMIGOD, I FORGOT, I'LL SHUT UP ABOUT CLAIRE. I KNOW I GET CARRIED AWAY.
I'M TOTALLY GIVING YOU ANXIETY, AREN'T I?
NO. THIS THING REEKS TO HELL. I THINK IT'S MAKING MY ASTHMA FLAIR UP.
YOU KNOW HOW MUCH THESE FUCKING THINGS COST ME?
INSURANCE PLANS FOR FREELANCERS ARE GARBAGE. I'M OUT OF HERE AS SOON AS...
YOU'RE SHITTING ME.
PFFFT PFFFFT
WHAT'S WRONG? ARE YOU OKAY?
THEY'RE REALLY SERIOUS WITH THIS SHIT.

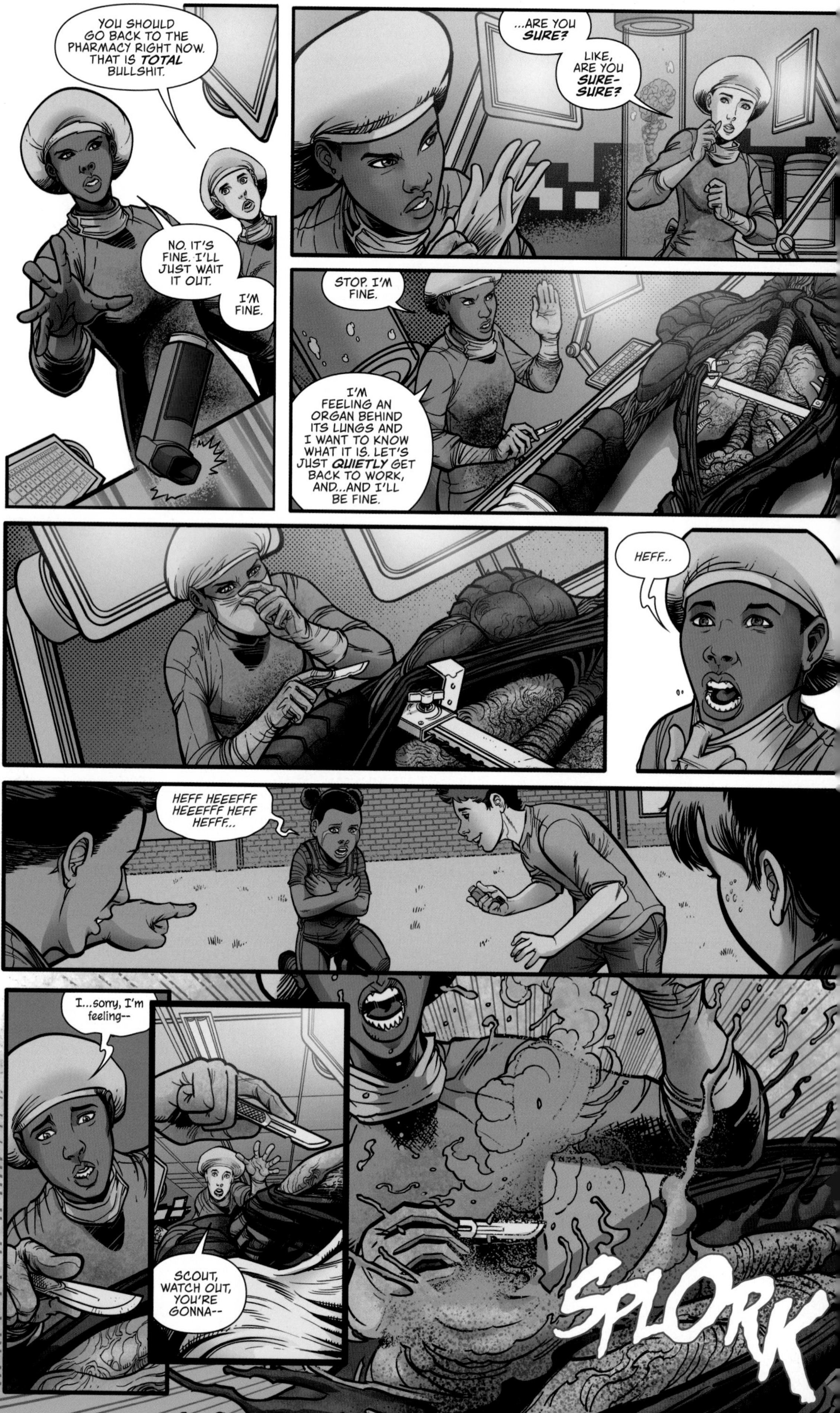
YOU SHOULD GO BACK TO THE PHARMACY RIGHT NOW. THAT IS TOTAL BULLSHIT.
NO. IT'S FINE. I'LL JUST WAIT IT OUT.
I'M FINE.
...ARE YOU SURE?
LIKE, ARE YOU SURE-SURE?
STOP. I'M FINE.
I'M FEELING AN ORGAN BEHIND ITS LUNGS AND I WANT TO KNOW WHAT IT IS. LET'S JUST QUIETLY GET BACK TO WORK, AND...AND I'LL BE FINE.
HEFF...
HEFF HEEEFFF HEEEFFF HEFF HEFFF...
I...sorry, I'm feeling--
SCOUT, WATCH OUT, YOU'RE GONNA--
SPLORK

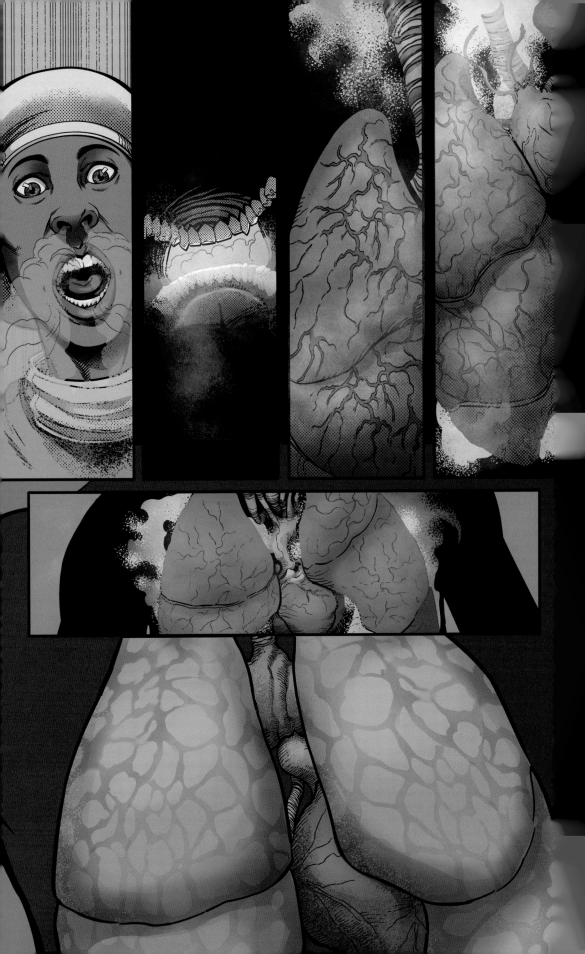

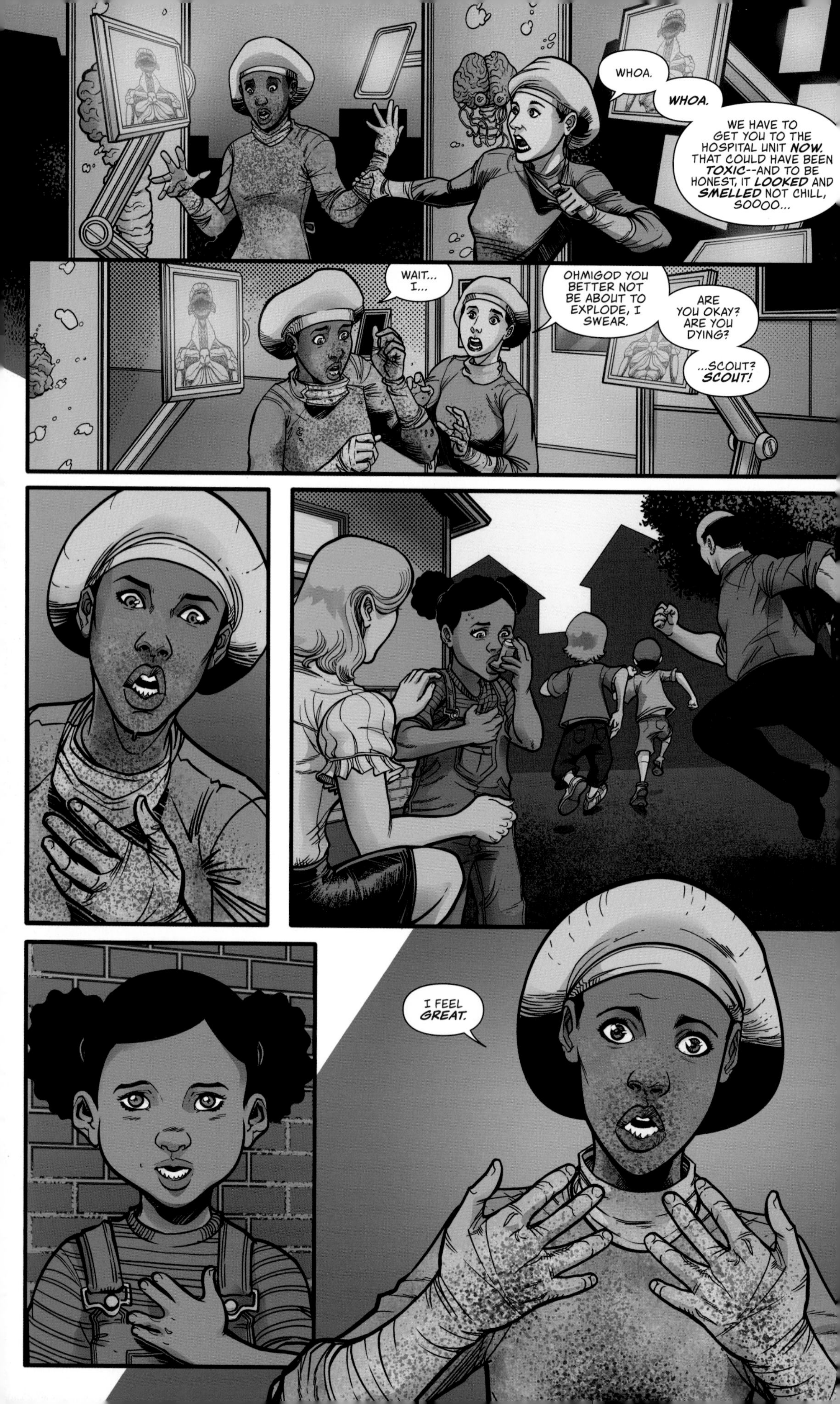
WHOA.
WHOA.
WE HAVE TO GET YOU TO THE HOSPITAL UNIT NOW. THAT COULD HAVE BEEN TOXIC--AND TO BE HONEST, IT LOOKED AND SMELLED NOT CHILL, SOOOO...
WAIT... I...
OHMIGOD YOU BETTER NOT BE ABOUT TO EXPLODE, I SWEAR.
ARE YOU OKAY? ARE YOU DYING?
...SCOUT? SCOUT!
I FEEL GREAT.

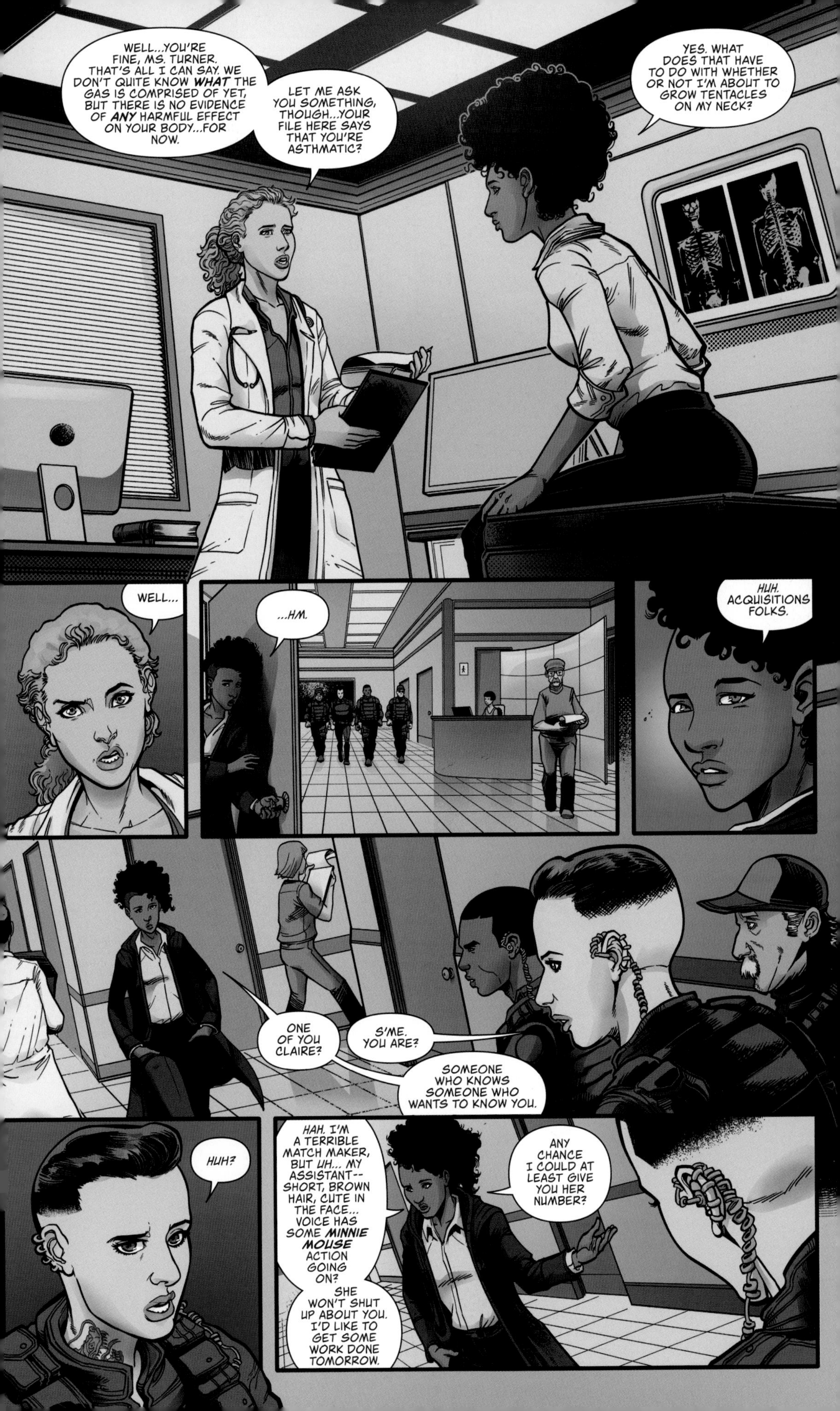

WELL...YOU'RE FINE, MS. TURNER. THAT'S ALL I CAN SAY. WE DON'T QUITE KNOW *WHAT* THE GAS IS COMPRISED OF YET, BUT THERE IS NO EVIDENCE OF *ANY* HARMFUL EFFECT ON YOUR BODY...FOR NOW.
LET ME ASK YOU SOMETHING, THOUGH...YOUR FILE HERE SAYS THAT YOU'RE ASTHMATIC?
YES. WHAT DOES THAT HAVE TO DO WITH WHETHER OR NOT I'M ABOUT TO GROW TENTACLES ON MY NECK?
WELL...
...HM.
HUH. ACQUISITIONS FOLKS.
ONE OF YOU CLAIRE?
S'ME. YOU ARE?
SOMEONE WHO KNOWS SOMEONE WHO WANTS TO KNOW YOU.
HUH?
HAH. I'M A TERRIBLE MATCH MAKER, BUT UH... MY ASSISTANT-- SHORT, BROWN HAIR, CUTE IN THE FACE... VOICE HAS SOME *MINNIE MOUSE* ACTION GOING ON?
SHE WON'T SHUT UP ABOUT YOU. I'D LIKE TO GET SOME WORK DONE TOMORROW.
ANY CHANCE I COULD AT LEAST GIVE YOU HER NUMBER?

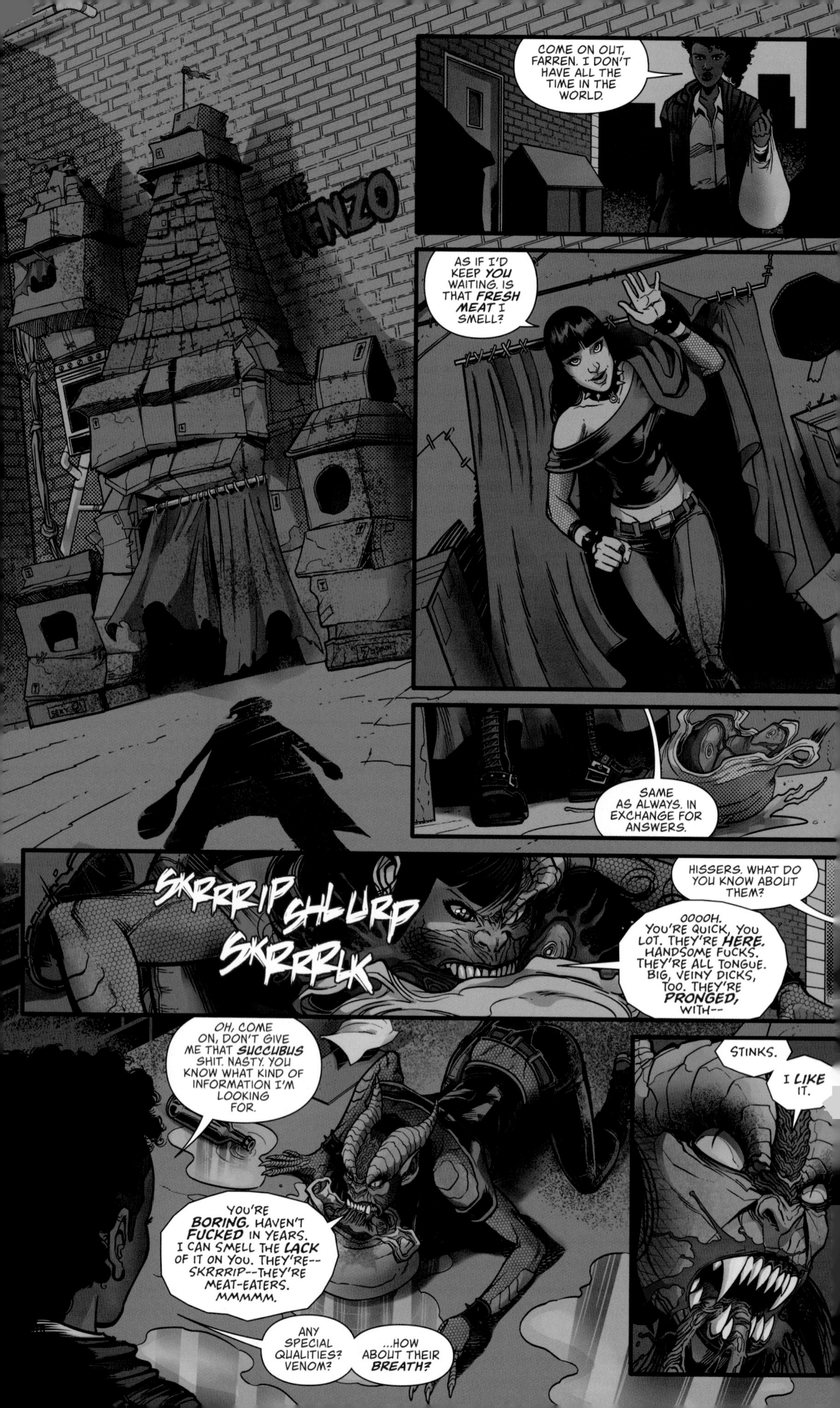
THE RENZO
COME ON OUT, FARREN. I DON'T HAVE ALL THE TIME IN THE WORLD.
AS IF I'D KEEP YOU WAITING. IS THAT FRESH MEAT I SMELL?
SAME AS ALWAYS. IN EXCHANGE FOR ANSWERS.
SKRRRIP SHLURP SKRRRLK
HISSERS. WHAT DO YOU KNOW ABOUT THEM?
OOOOH. YOU'RE QUICK, YOU LOT. THEY'RE HERE. HANDSOME FUCKS. THEY'RE ALL TONGUE. BIG, VEINY DICKS, TOO. THEY'RE PRONGED, WITH--
OH, COME ON, DON'T GIVE ME THAT SUCCUBUS SHIT. NASTY. YOU KNOW WHAT KIND OF INFORMATION I'M LOOKING FOR.
YOU'RE BORING. HAVEN'T FUCKED IN YEARS. I CAN SMELL THE LACK OF IT ON YOU. THEY'RE-- SKRRRIP--THEY'RE MEAT-EATERS. MMMMM.
ANY SPECIAL QUALITIES? VENOM?
...HOW ABOUT THEIR BREATH?
STINKS.
I LIKE IT.

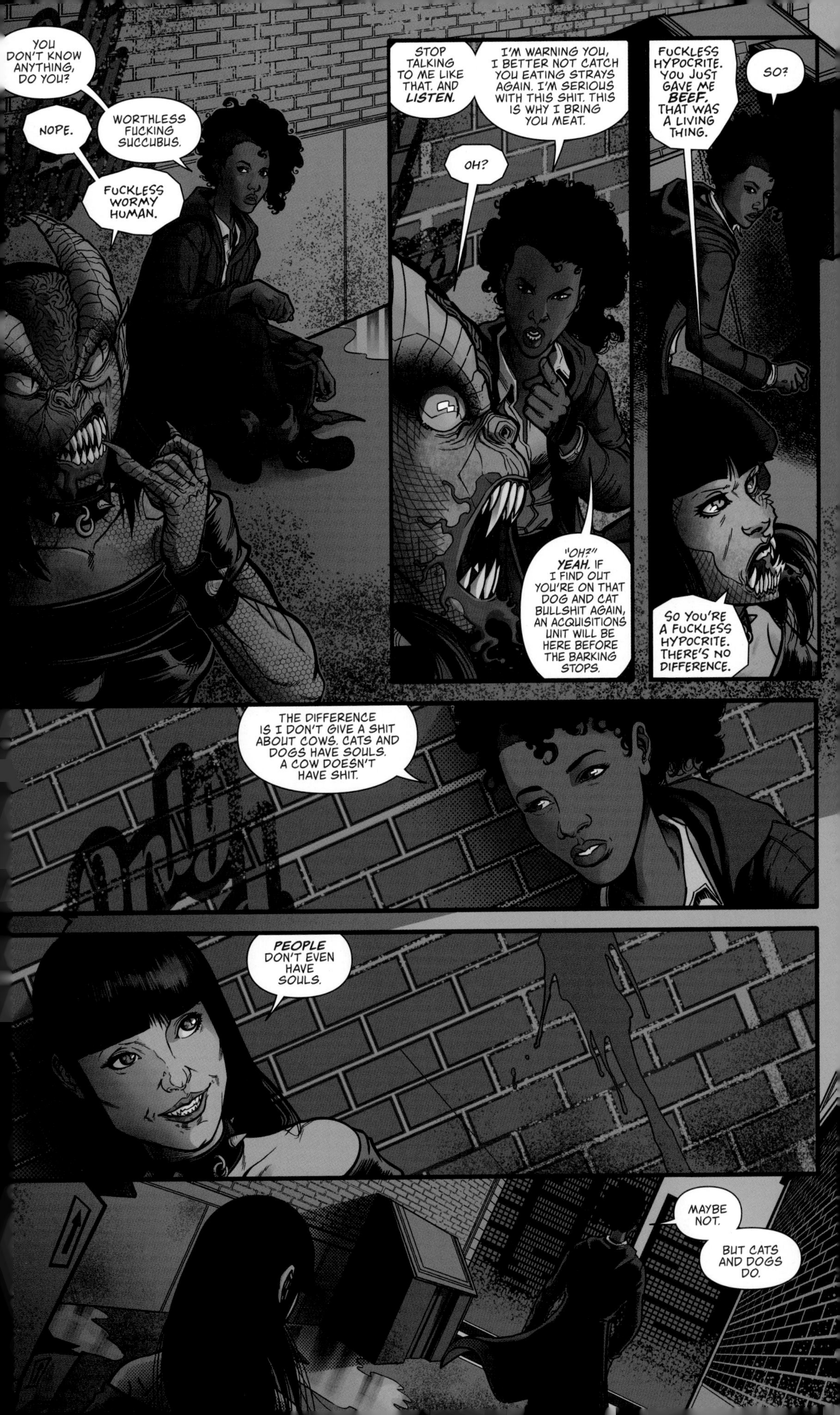
YOU DON'T KNOW ANYTHING, DO YOU?
NOPE.
WORTHLESS FUCKING SUCCUBUS.
FUCKLESS WORMY HUMAN.
STOP TALKING TO ME LIKE THAT. AND LISTEN.
I'M WARNING YOU, I BETTER NOT CATCH YOU EATING STRAYS AGAIN. I'M SERIOUS WITH THIS SHIT. THIS IS WHY I BRING YOU MEAT.
OH?
"OH?" YEAH. IF I FIND OUT YOU'RE ON THAT DOG AND CAT BULLSHIT AGAIN, AN ACQUISITIONS UNIT WILL BE HERE BEFORE THE BARKING STOPS.
FUCKLESS HYPOCRITE. YOU JUST GAVE ME BEEF. THAT WAS A LIVING THING.
SO?
SO YOU'RE A FUCKLESS HYPOCRITE. THERE'S NO DIFFERENCE.
THE DIFFERENCE IS I DON'T GIVE A SHIT ABOUT COWS. CATS AND DOGS HAVE SOULS. A COW DOESN'T HAVE SHIT.
PEOPLE DON'T EVEN HAVE SOULS.
MAYBE NOT.
BUT CATS AND DOGS DO.

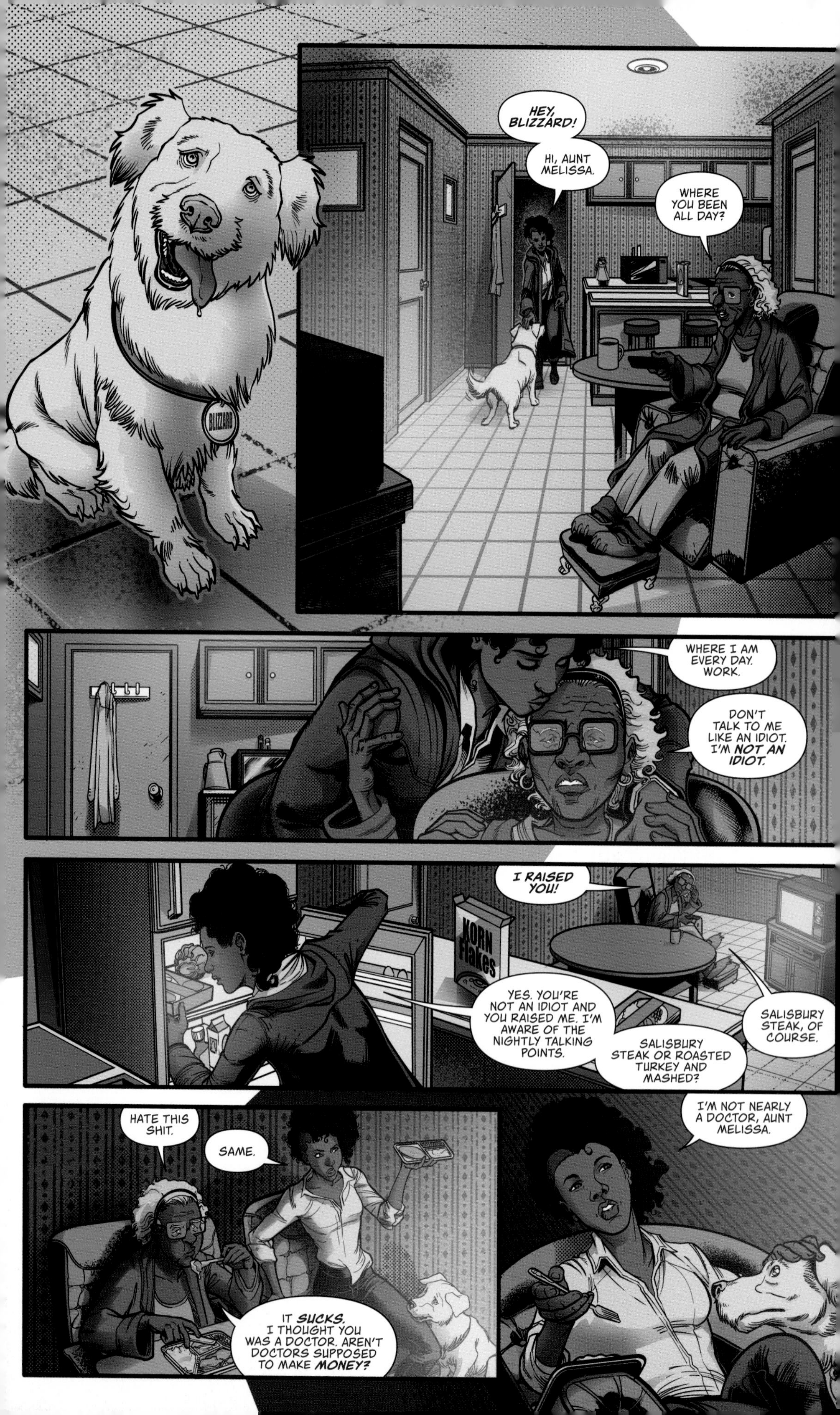
BLIZZARD
HEY, BLIZZARD!
HI, AUNT MELISSA.
WHERE YOU BEEN ALL DAY?
WHERE I AM EVERY DAY. WORK.
DON'T TALK TO ME LIKE AN IDIOT. I'M NOT AN IDIOT.
I RAISED YOU!
KORN Flakes
YES. YOU'RE NOT AN IDIOT AND YOU RAISED ME. I'M AWARE OF THE NIGHTLY TALKING POINTS.
SALISBURY STEAK OR ROASTED TURKEY AND MASHED?
SALISBURY STEAK, OF COURSE.
HATE THIS SHIT.
SAME.
IT SUCKS. I THOUGHT YOU WAS A DOCTOR. AREN'T DOCTORS SUPPOSED TO MAKE MONEY?
I'M NOT NEARLY A DOCTOR, AUNT MELISSA.

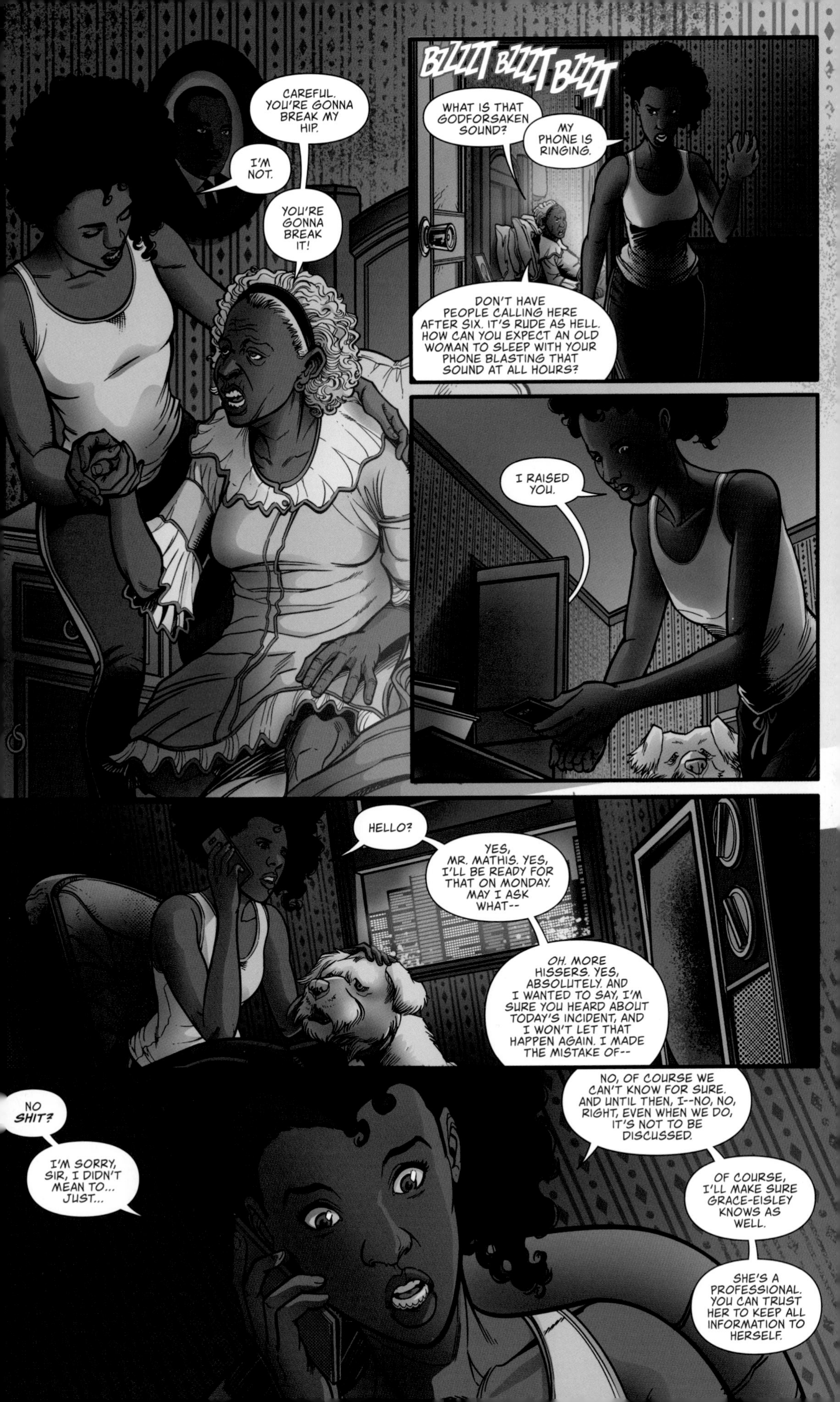
CAREFUL. YOU'RE GONNA BREAK MY HIP.
I'M NOT.
YOU'RE GONNA BREAK IT!
BZZZT BZZZT BZZZT
WHAT IS THAT GODFORSAKEN SOUND?
MY PHONE IS RINGING.
DON'T HAVE PEOPLE CALLING HERE AFTER SIX. IT'S RUDE AS HELL. HOW CAN YOU EXPECT AN OLD WOMAN TO SLEEP WITH YOUR PHONE BLASTING THAT SOUND AT ALL HOURS?
I RAISED YOU.
HELLO?
YES, MR. MATHIS. YES, I'LL BE READY FOR THAT ON MONDAY. MAY I ASK WHAT--
OH. MORE HISSERS. YES, ABSOLUTELY. AND I WANTED TO SAY, I'M SURE YOU HEARD ABOUT TODAY'S INCIDENT, AND I WON'T LET THAT HAPPEN AGAIN. I MADE THE MISTAKE OF--
NO SHIT?
I'M SORRY, SIR, I DIDN'T MEAN TO... JUST...
NO, OF COURSE WE CAN'T KNOW FOR SURE. AND UNTIL THEN, I--NO, NO, RIGHT, EVEN WHEN WE DO, IT'S NOT TO BE DISCUSSED.
OF COURSE, I'LL MAKE SURE GRACE-EISLEY KNOWS AS WELL.
SHE'S A PROFESSIONAL. YOU CAN TRUST HER TO KEEP ALL INFORMATION TO HERSELF.

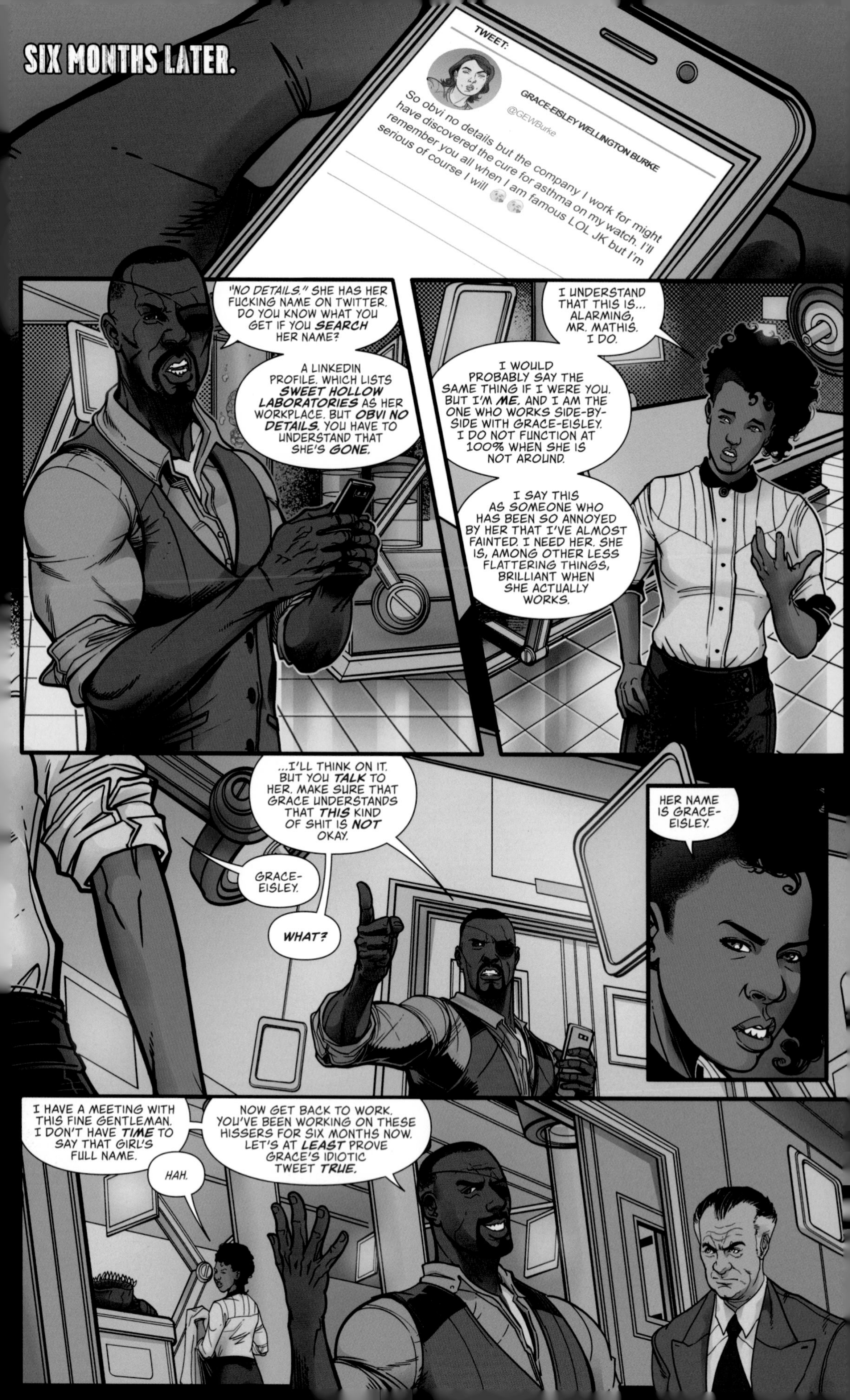
SIX MONTHS LATER.
TWEET:
GRACE-EISLEY WELLINGTON BURKE
@GEWBurke
So obvi no details but the company I work for might have discovered the cure for asthma on my watch. I'll remember you all when I am famous LOL JK but I'm serious of course I will
"NO DETAILS." SHE HAS HER FUCKING NAME ON TWITTER. DO YOU KNOW WHAT YOU GET IF YOU SEARCH HER NAME?
A LINKEDIN PROFILE. WHICH LISTS SWEET HOLLOW LABORATORIES AS HER WORKPLACE. BUT OBVI NO DETAILS. YOU HAVE TO UNDERSTAND THAT SHE'S GONE.
I UNDERSTAND THAT THIS IS... ALARMING, MR. MATHIS. I DO.
I WOULD PROBABLY SAY THE SAME THING IF I WERE YOU. BUT I'M ME. AND I AM THE ONE WHO WORKS SIDE-BY-SIDE WITH GRACE-EISLEY. I DO NOT FUNCTION AT 100% WHEN SHE IS NOT AROUND.
I SAY THIS AS SOMEONE WHO HAS BEEN SO ANNOYED BY HER THAT I'VE ALMOST FAINTED. I NEED HER. SHE IS, AMONG OTHER LESS FLATTERING THINGS, BRILLIANT WHEN SHE ACTUALLY WORKS.
...I'LL THINK ON IT. BUT YOU TALK TO HER. MAKE SURE THAT GRACE UNDERSTANDS THAT THIS KIND OF SHIT IS NOT OKAY.
GRACE-EISLEY.
WHAT?
HER NAME IS GRACE-EISLEY.
I HAVE A MEETING WITH THIS FINE GENTLEMAN. I DON'T HAVE TIME TO SAY THAT GIRL'S FULL NAME.
HAH.
NOW GET BACK TO WORK. YOU'VE BEEN WORKING ON THESE HISSERS FOR SIX MONTHS NOW. LET'S AT LEAST PROVE GRACE'S IDIOTIC TWEET TRUE.

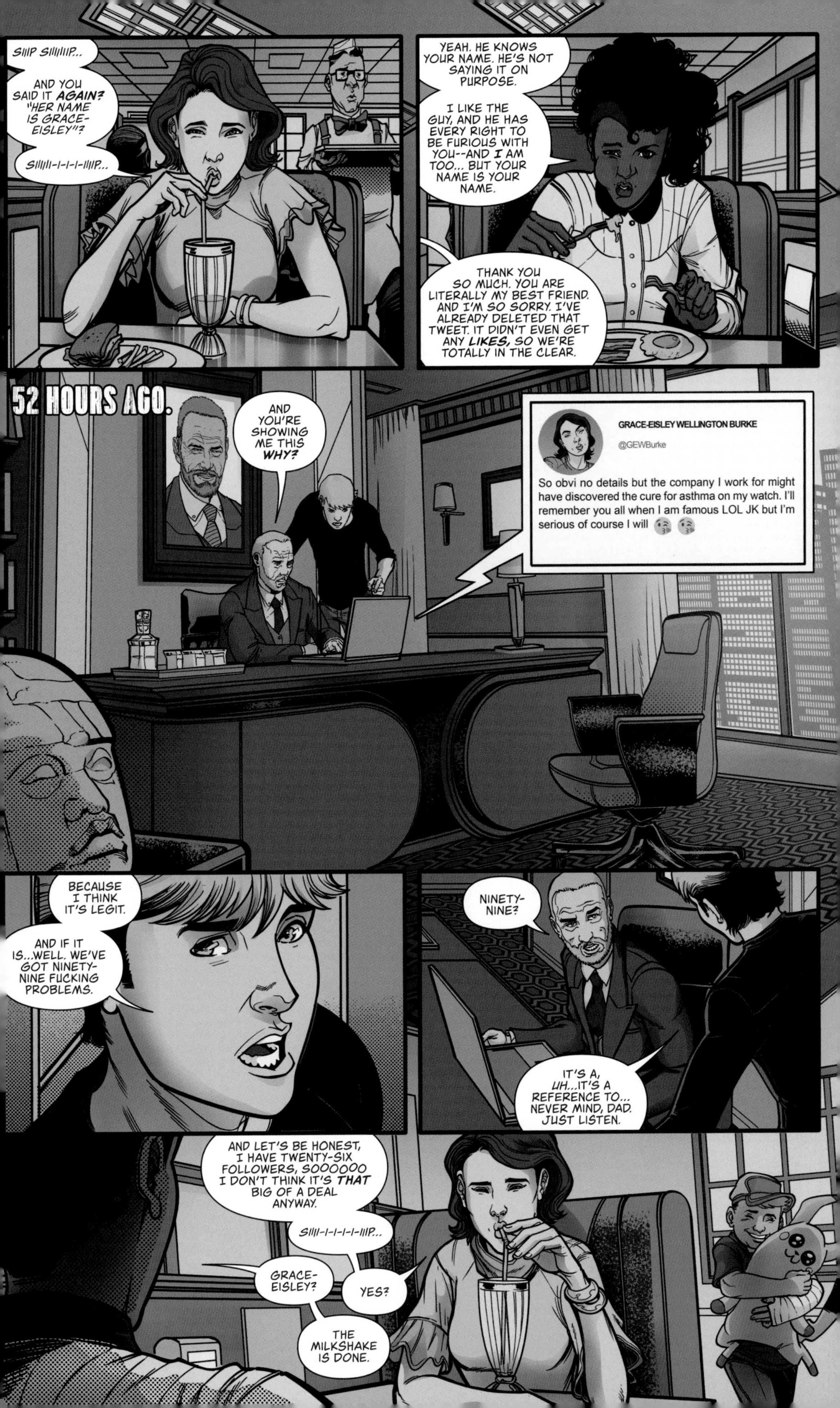

SIIIP SIIIIIIP...
AND YOU SAID IT AGAIN? "HER NAME IS GRACE-EISLEY"?
SIIIIII-I-I-I-IIIIP...
YEAH. HE KNOWS YOUR NAME. HE'S NOT SAYING IT ON PURPOSE.
I LIKE THE GUY, AND HE HAS EVERY RIGHT TO BE FURIOUS WITH YOU--AND I AM TOO... BUT YOUR NAME IS YOUR NAME.
THANK YOU SO MUCH. YOU ARE LITERALLY MY BEST FRIEND. AND I'M SO SORRY. I'VE ALREADY DELETED THAT TWEET. IT DIDN'T EVEN GET ANY LIKES, SO WE'RE TOTALLY IN THE CLEAR.
52 HOURS AGO.
AND YOU'RE SHOWING ME THIS WHY?
GRACE-EISLEY WELLINGTON BURKE
@GEWBurke
So obvi no details but the company I work for might have discovered the cure for asthma on my watch. I'll remember you all when I am famous LOL JK but I'm serious of course I will
BECAUSE I THINK IT'S LEGIT.
AND IF IT IS...WELL. WE'VE GOT NINETY-NINE FUCKING PROBLEMS.
NINETY-NINE?
IT'S A, UH...IT'S A REFERENCE TO... NEVER MIND, DAD. JUST LISTEN.
AND LET'S BE HONEST, I HAVE TWENTY-SIX FOLLOWERS, SOOOOOO I DON'T THINK IT'S THAT BIG OF A DEAL ANYWAY.
SIIII-I-I-I-I-IIIP...
GRACE-EISLEY?
YES?
THE MILKSHAKE IS DONE.

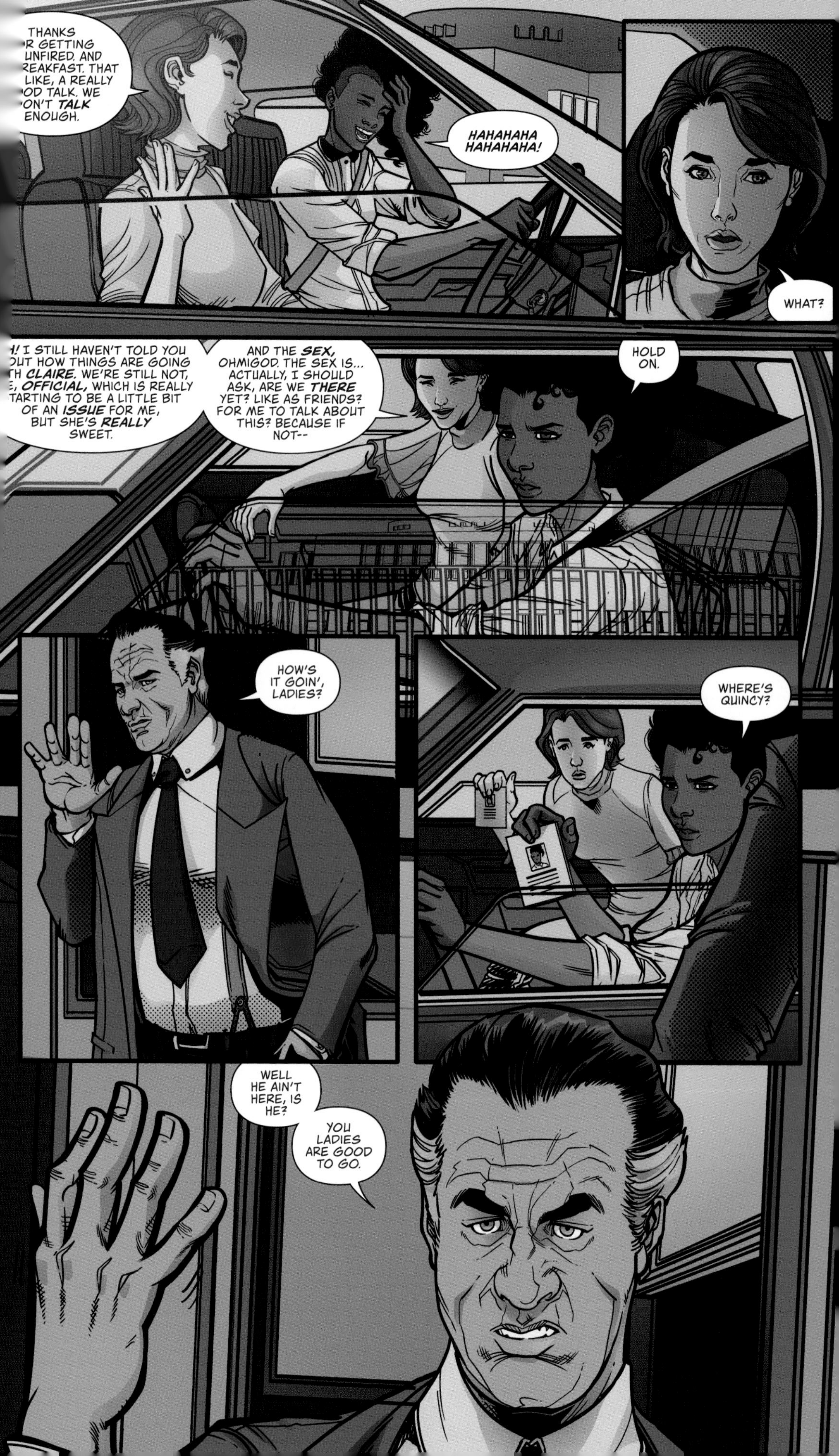
THANKS
R GETTING
UNFIRED. AND
REAKFAST. THAT
LIKE, A REALLY
OD TALK. WE
ON'T TALK
ENOUGH.
HAHAHAHA HAHAHAHA!
WHAT?
! I STILL HAVEN'T TOLD YOU OUT HOW THINGS ARE GOING TH CLAIRE. WE'RE STILL NOT, E, OFFICIAL, WHICH IS REALLY TARTING TO BE A LITTLE BIT OF AN ISSUE FOR ME, BUT SHE'S REALLY SWEET.
AND THE SEX, OHMIGOD. THE SEX IS... ACTUALLY, I SHOULD ASK, ARE WE THERE YET? LIKE AS FRIENDS? FOR ME TO TALK ABOUT THIS? BECAUSE IF NOT--
HOLD ON.
HOW'S IT GOIN', LADIES?
WHERE'S QUINCY?
WELL HE AIN'T HERE, IS HE?
YOU LADIES ARE GOOD TO GO.

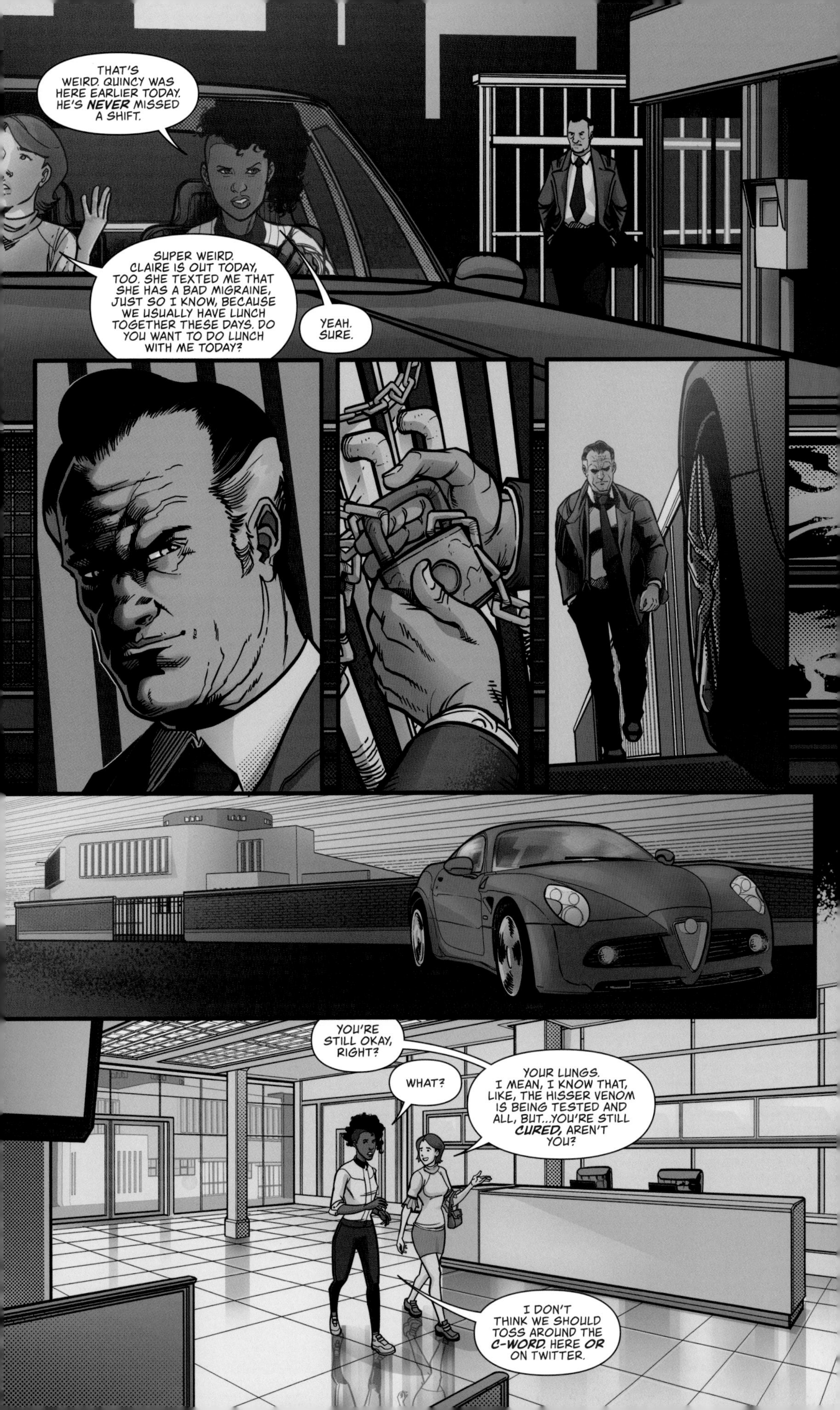
THAT'S WEIRD. QUINCY WAS HERE EARLIER TODAY. HE'S **NEVER** MISSED A SHIFT.
SUPER WEIRD. CLAIRE IS OUT TODAY, TOO. SHE TEXTED ME THAT SHE HAS A BAD MIGRAINE, JUST SO I KNOW, BECAUSE WE USUALLY HAVE LUNCH TOGETHER THESE DAYS. DO YOU WANT TO DO LUNCH WITH ME TODAY?
YEAH. SURE.
YOU'RE STILL OKAY, RIGHT?
WHAT?
YOUR LUNGS. I MEAN, I KNOW THAT, LIKE, THE HISSER VENOM IS BEING TESTED AND ALL, BUT...YOU'RE STILL ***CURED,*** AREN'T YOU?
I DON'T THINK WE SHOULD TOSS AROUND THE ***C-WORD*** HERE ***OR*** ON TWITTER.

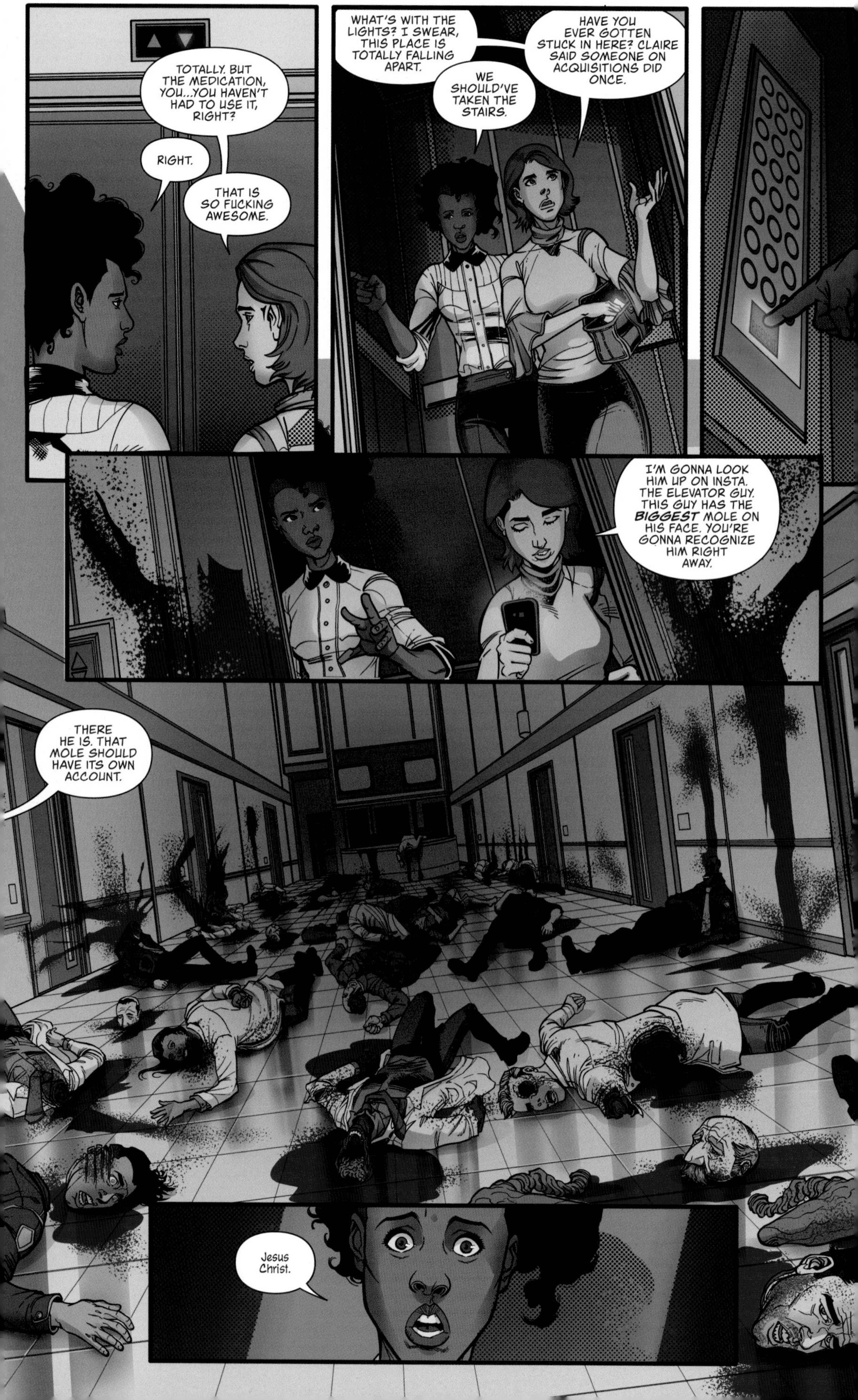
TOTALLY. BUT THE MEDICATION, YOU...YOU HAVEN'T HAD TO USE IT, RIGHT?
RIGHT.
THAT IS SO FUCKING AWESOME.
WHAT'S WITH THE LIGHTS? I SWEAR, THIS PLACE IS TOTALLY FALLING APART.
WE SHOULD'VE TAKEN THE STAIRS.
HAVE YOU EVER GOTTEN STUCK IN HERE? CLAIRE SAID SOMEONE ON ACQUISITIONS DID ONCE.
I'M GONNA LOOK HIM UP ON INSTA. THE ELEVATOR GUY. THIS GUY HAS THE BIGGEST MOLE ON HIS FACE. YOU'RE GONNA RECOGNIZE HIM RIGHT AWAY.
THERE HE IS. THAT MOLE SHOULD HAVE ITS OWN ACCOUNT.
Jesus Christ.

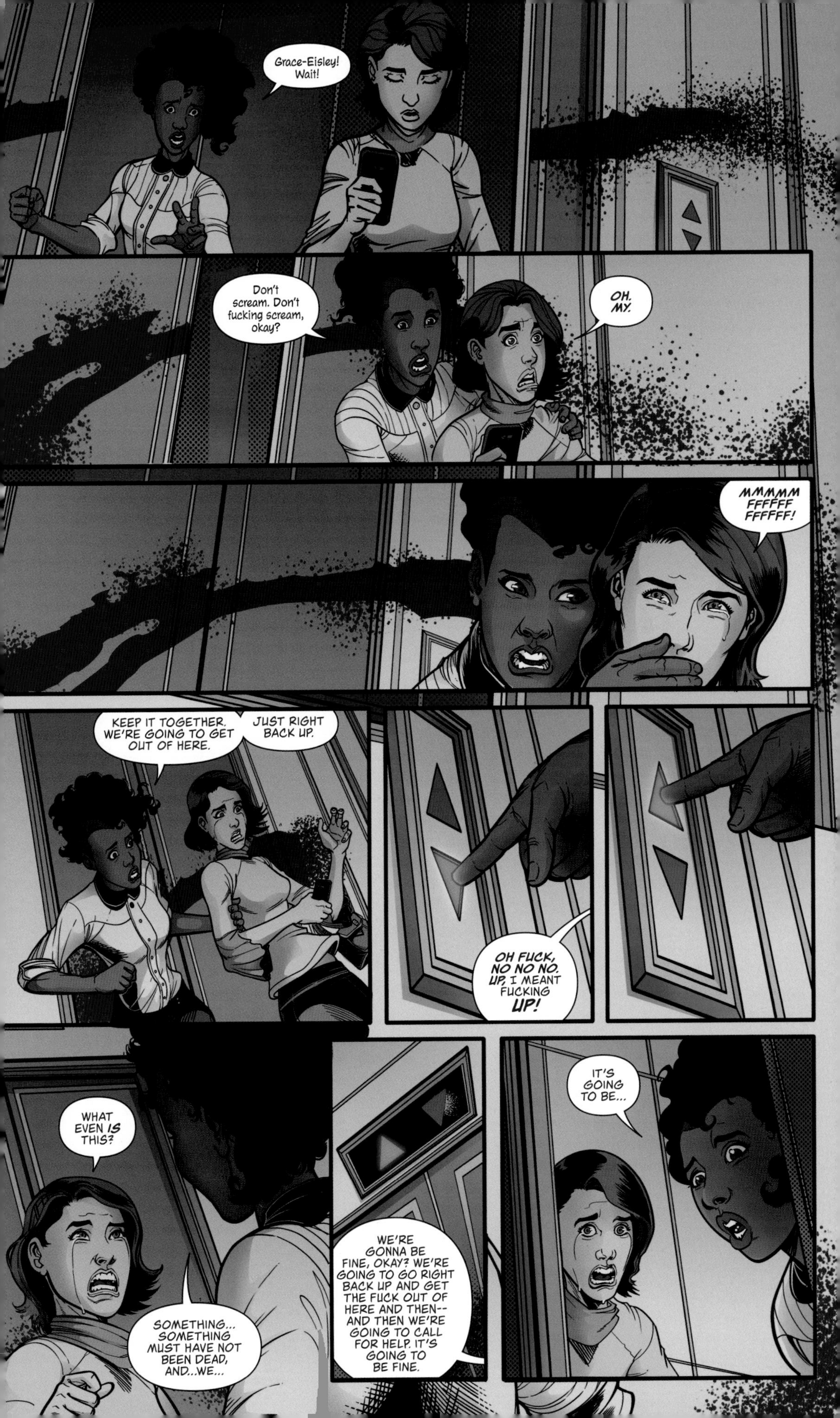
Grace-Eisley! Wait!
Don't scream. Don't fucking scream, okay?
OH. MY.
MMMMM FFFFFF FFFFFF!
KEEP IT TOGETHER. WE'RE GOING TO GET OUT OF HERE.
JUST RIGHT BACK UP.
OH FUCK, NO NO NO. UP, I MEANT FUCKING UP!
WHAT EVEN IS THIS?
SOMETHING... SOMETHING MUST HAVE NOT BEEN DEAD, AND...WE...
WE'RE GONNA BE FINE, OKAY? WE'RE GOING TO GO RIGHT BACK UP AND GET THE FUCK OUT OF HERE AND THEN-- AND THEN WE'RE GOING TO CALL FOR HELP. IT'S GOING TO BE FINE.
IT'S GOING TO BE...

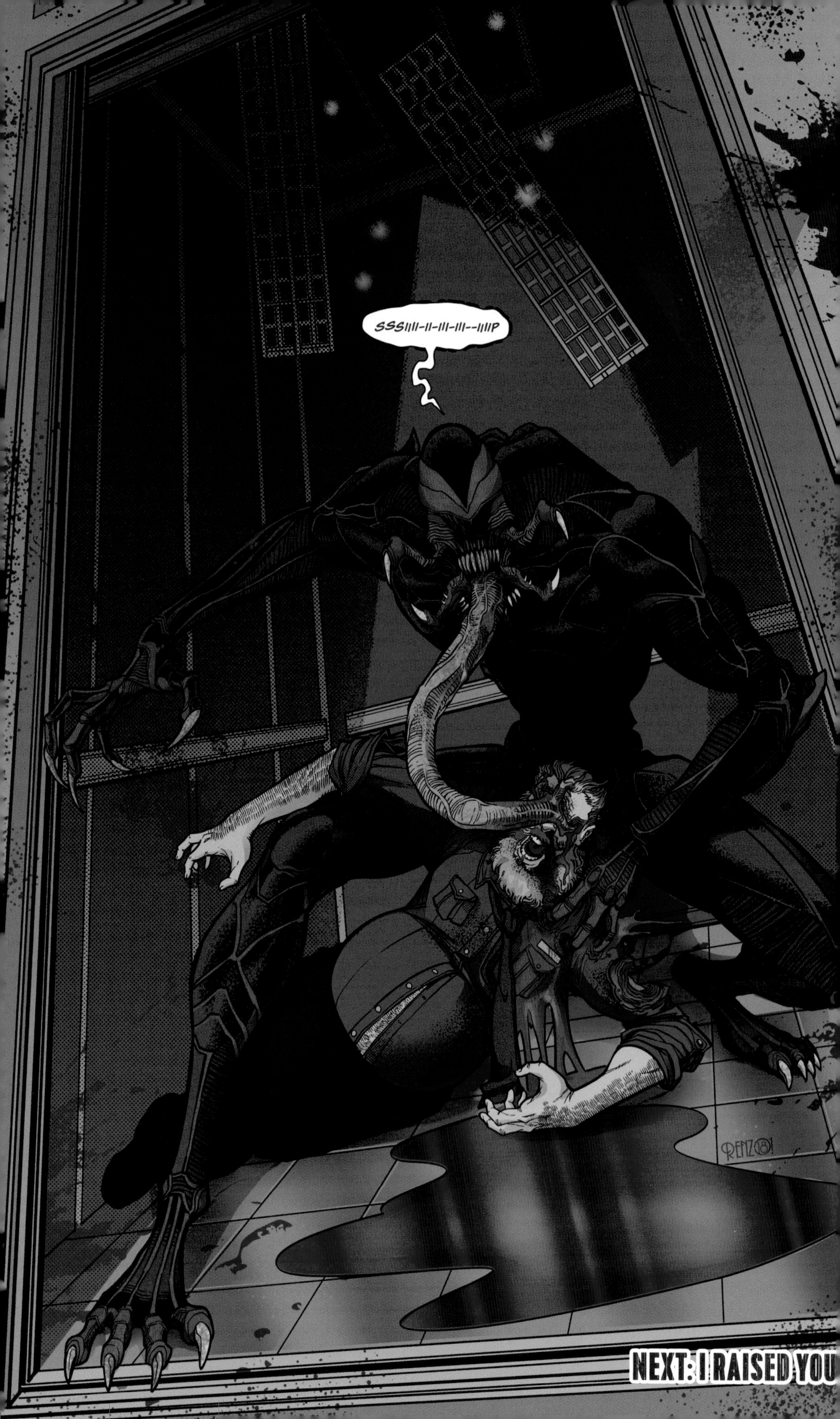
SSSIIII-II-III-III--IIIIP
RENZO 18!
NEXT: I RAISED YOU

PAY

TO

LIVE

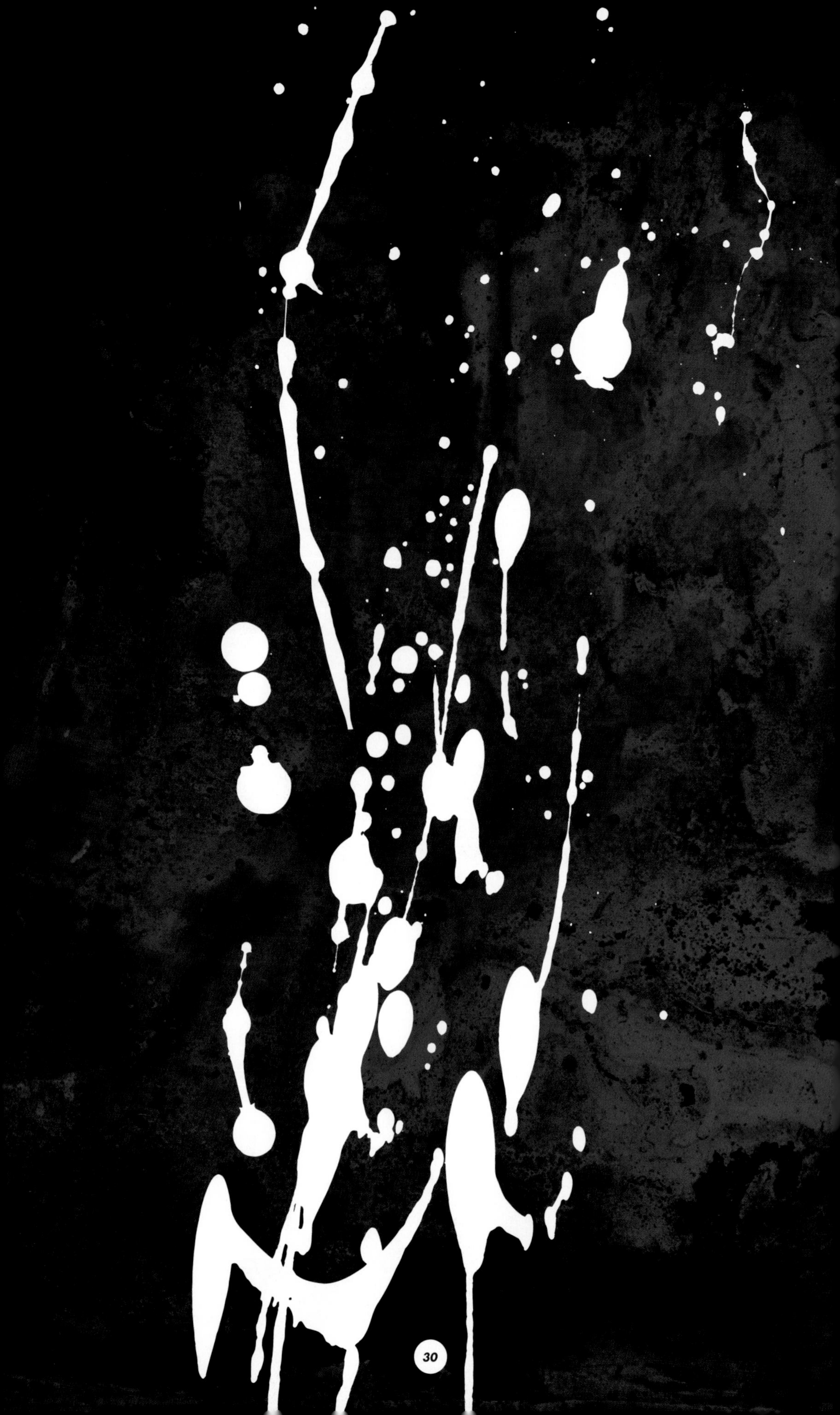

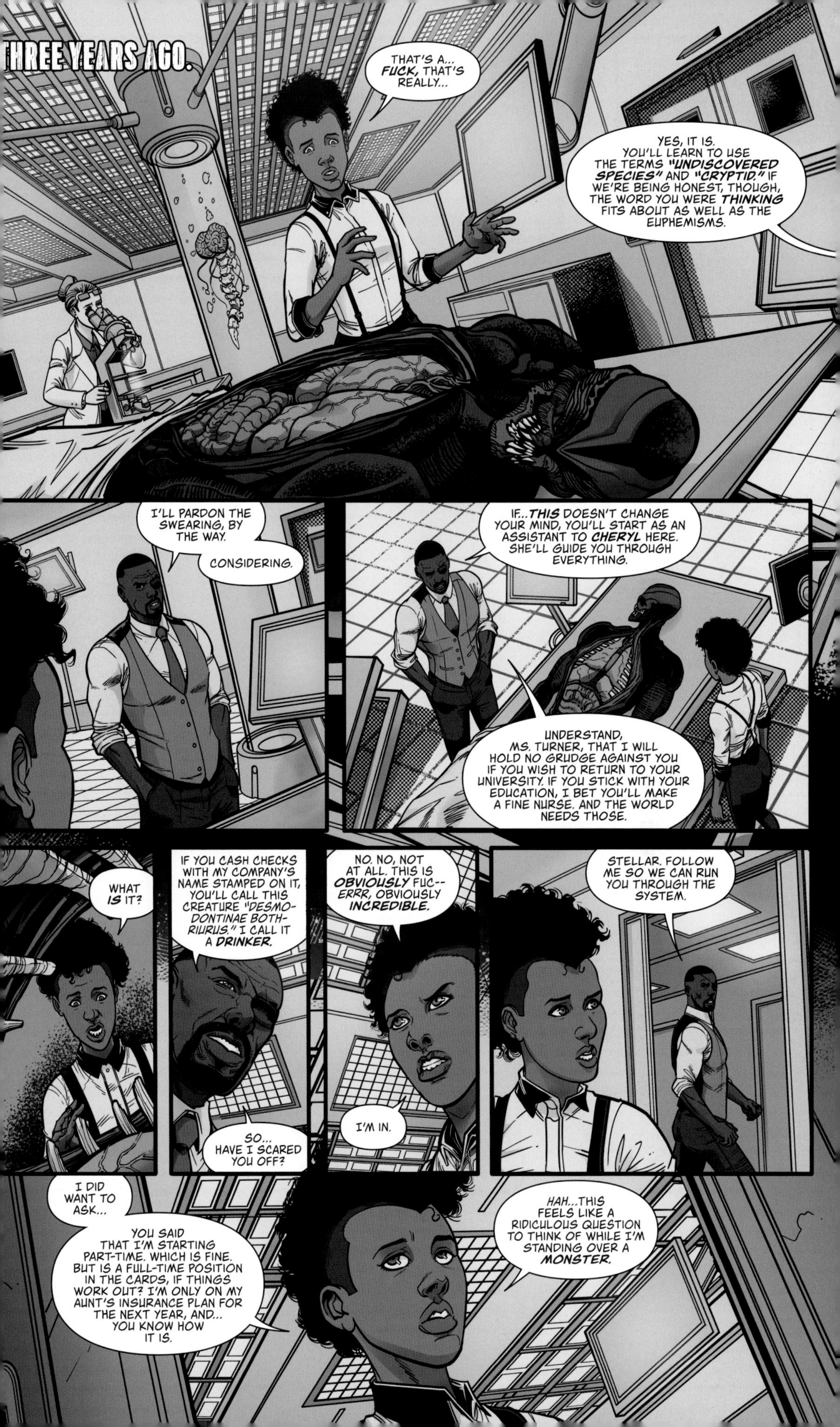
THREE YEARS AGO.
THAT'S A... FUCK, THAT'S REALLY...
YES, IT IS. YOU'LL LEARN TO USE THE TERMS "UNDISCOVERED SPECIES" AND "CRYPTID." IF WE'RE BEING HONEST, THOUGH, THE WORD YOU WERE THINKING FITS ABOUT AS WELL AS THE EUPHEMISMS.
I'LL PARDON THE SWEARING, BY THE WAY.
CONSIDERING.
IF... THIS DOESN'T CHANGE YOUR MIND, YOU'LL START AS AN ASSISTANT TO CHERYL HERE. SHE'LL GUIDE YOU THROUGH EVERYTHING.
UNDERSTAND, MS. TURNER, THAT I WILL HOLD NO GRUDGE AGAINST YOU IF YOU WISH TO RETURN TO YOUR UNIVERSITY. IF YOU STICK WITH YOUR EDUCATION, I BET YOU'LL MAKE A FINE NURSE. AND THE WORLD NEEDS THOSE.
WHAT IS IT?
IF YOU CASH CHECKS WITH MY COMPANY'S NAME STAMPED ON IT, YOU'LL CALL THIS CREATURE "DESMO-DONTINAE BOTH-RIURUS." I CALL IT A DRINKER.
SO... HAVE I SCARED YOU OFF?
NO. NO, NOT AT ALL. THIS IS OBVIOUSLY FUC-- ERRR, OBVIOUSLY INCREDIBLE.
I'M IN.
STELLAR. FOLLOW ME SO WE CAN RUN YOU THROUGH THE SYSTEM.
I DID WANT TO ASK...
YOU SAID THAT I'M STARTING PART-TIME. WHICH IS FINE. BUT IS A FULL-TIME POSITION IN THE CARDS, IF THINGS WORK OUT? I'M ONLY ON MY AUNT'S INSURANCE PLAN FOR THE NEXT YEAR, AND... YOU KNOW HOW IT IS.
HAH... THIS FEELS LIKE A RIDICULOUS QUESTION TO THINK OF WHILE I'M STANDING OVER A MONSTER.

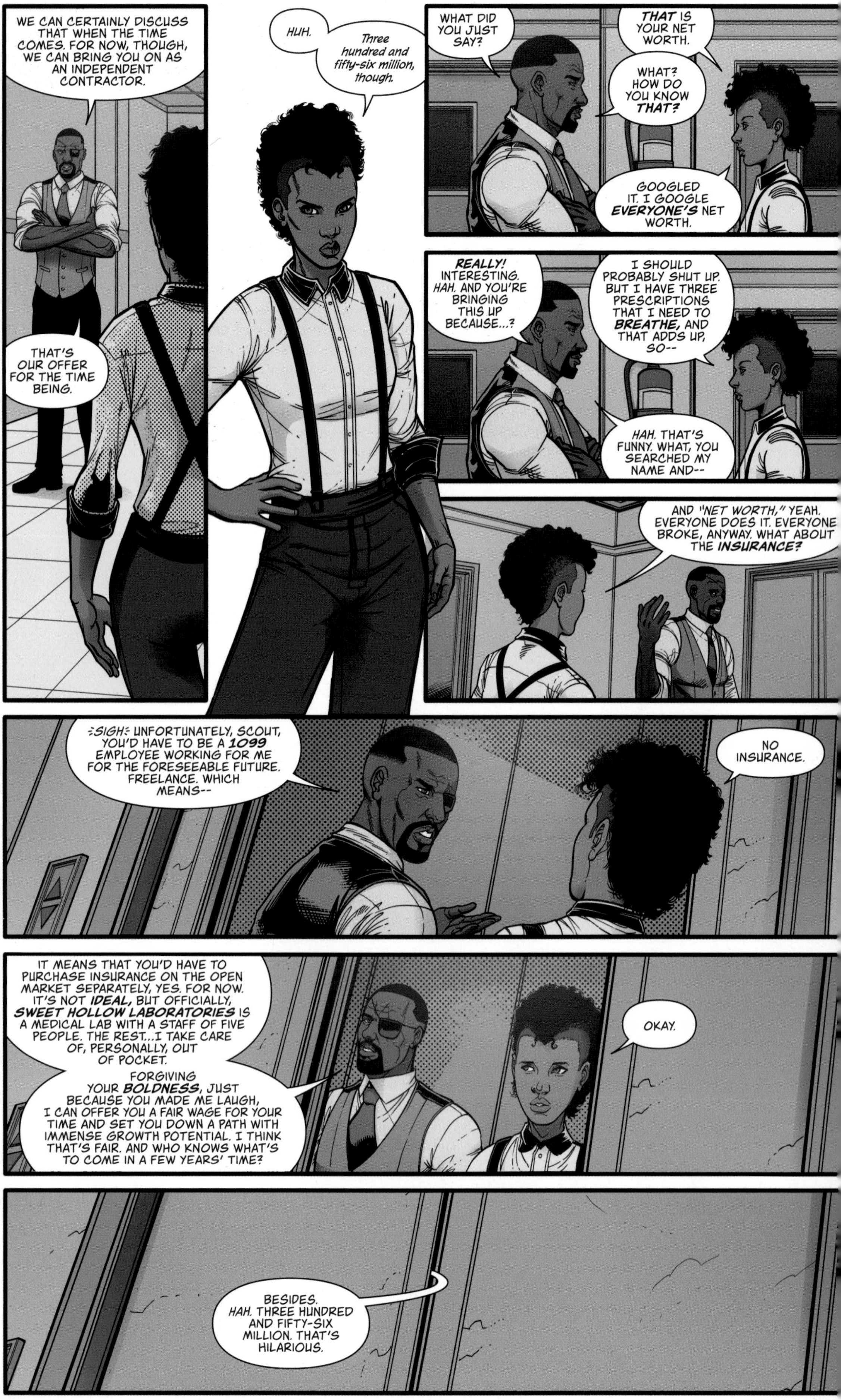
WE CAN CERTAINLY DISCUSS THAT WHEN THE TIME COMES. FOR NOW, THOUGH, WE CAN BRING YOU ON AS AN INDEPENDENT CONTRACTOR.
THAT'S OUR OFFER FOR THE TIME BEING.
HUH.
Three hundred and fifty-six million, though.
WHAT DID YOU JUST SAY?
THAT IS YOUR NET WORTH.
WHAT? HOW DO YOU KNOW THAT?
GOOGLED IT. I GOOGLE EVERYONE'S NET WORTH.
REALLY! INTERESTING. HAH. AND YOU'RE BRINGING THIS UP BECAUSE...?
I SHOULD PROBABLY SHUT UP. BUT I HAVE THREE PRESCRIPTIONS THAT I NEED TO BREATHE, AND THAT ADDS UP, SO--
HAH. THAT'S FUNNY. WHAT, YOU SEARCHED MY NAME AND--
AND "NET WORTH," YEAH. EVERYONE DOES IT. EVERYONE BROKE, ANYWAY. WHAT ABOUT THE INSURANCE?
SIGH UNFORTUNATELY, SCOUT, YOU'D HAVE TO BE A 1099 EMPLOYEE WORKING FOR ME FOR THE FORESEEABLE FUTURE. FREELANCE. WHICH MEANS--
NO INSURANCE.
IT MEANS THAT YOU'D HAVE TO PURCHASE INSURANCE ON THE OPEN MARKET SEPARATELY, YES. FOR NOW. IT'S NOT IDEAL, BUT OFFICIALLY, SWEET HOLLOW LABORATORIES IS A MEDICAL LAB WITH A STAFF OF FIVE PEOPLE. THE REST...I TAKE CARE OF, PERSONALLY, OUT OF POCKET.
FORGIVING YOUR BOLDNESS, JUST BECAUSE YOU MADE ME LAUGH, I CAN OFFER YOU A FAIR WAGE FOR YOUR TIME AND SET YOU DOWN A PATH WITH IMMENSE GROWTH POTENTIAL. I THINK THAT'S FAIR. AND WHO KNOWS WHAT'S TO COME IN A FEW YEARS' TIME?
OKAY.
BESIDES. HAH. THREE HUNDRED AND FIFTY-SIX MILLION. THAT'S HILARIOUS.

"Nobody cares about the truth
when the lie is more entertaining."
—Charlamagne tha God

BREATHLESS

CHAPTER TWO
"I RAISED YOU"
AND OTHER LIES

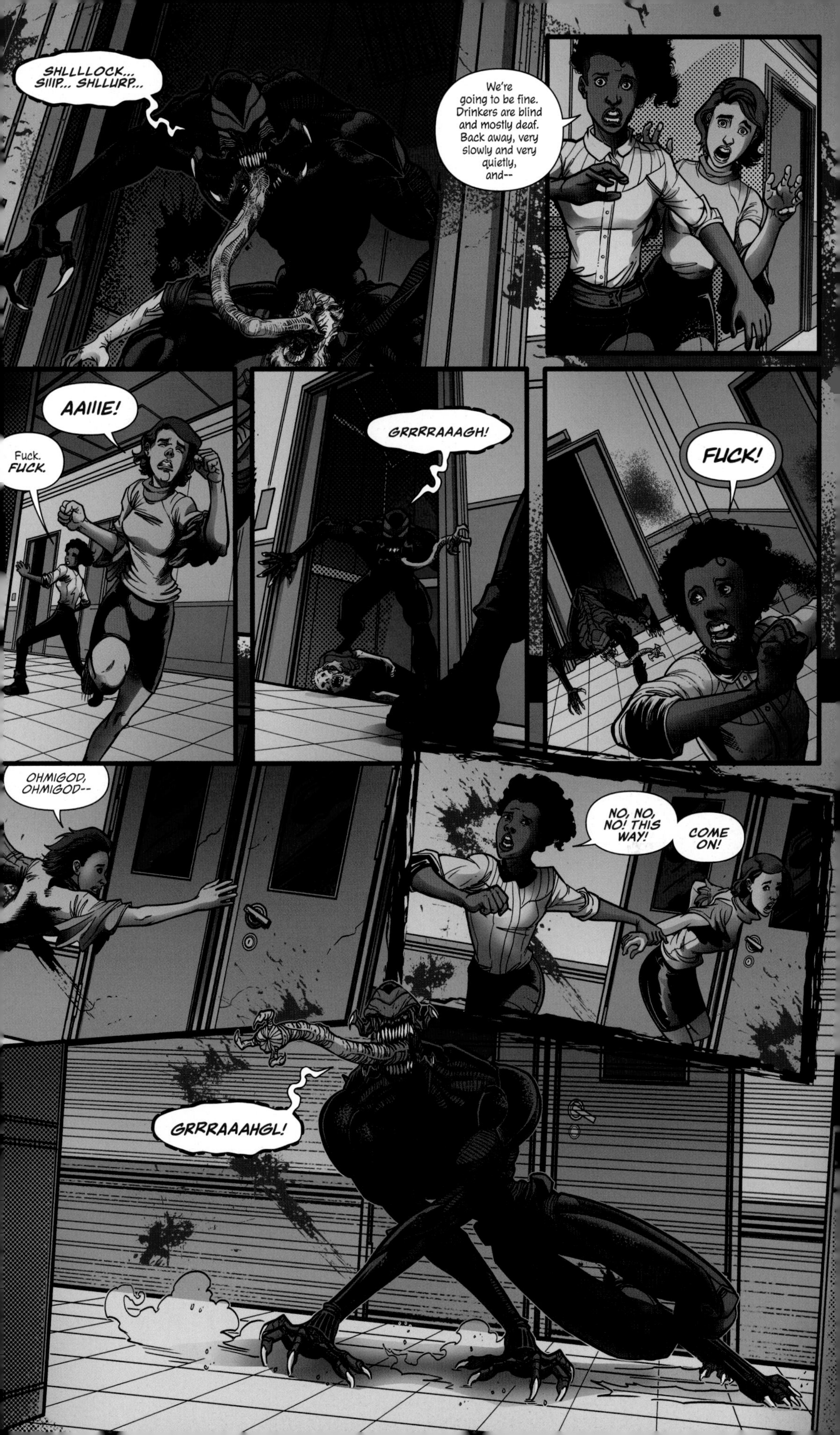
SHLLLLOCK... SIIIP... SHLLURP...
We're going to be fine. Drinkers are blind and mostly deaf. Back away, very slowly and very quietly, and--
AAIIIE!
Fuck. FUCK.
GRRRRAAAGH!
FUCK!
OHMIGOD, OHMIGOD--
NO, NO, NO! THIS WAY!
COME ON!
GRRRAAAHGL!

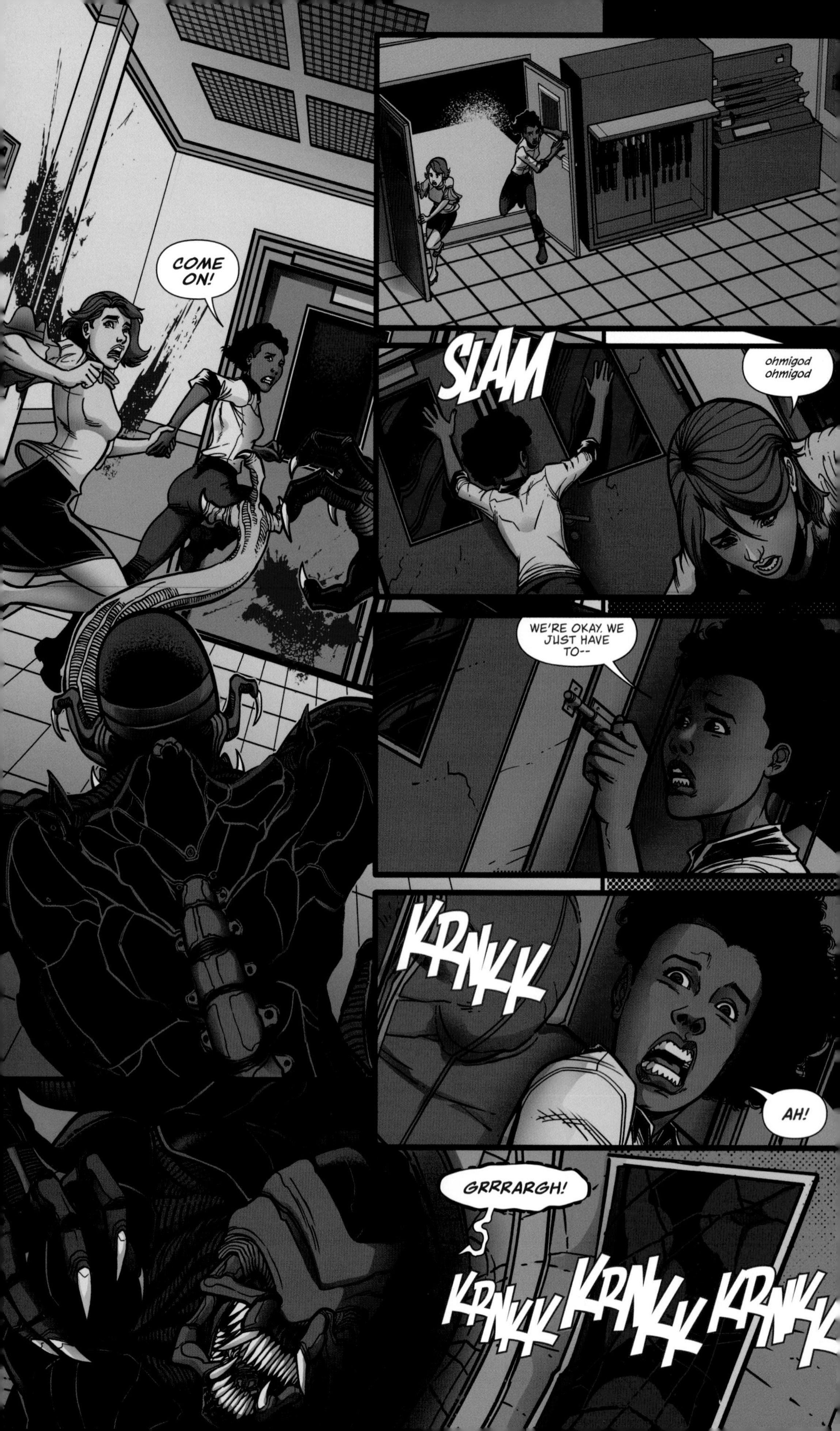
COME ON!
SLAM
ohmigod ohmigod
WE'RE OKAY. WE JUST HAVE TO--
KRNKK
AH!
GRRRARGH!
KRNKK KRNKK KRNKK

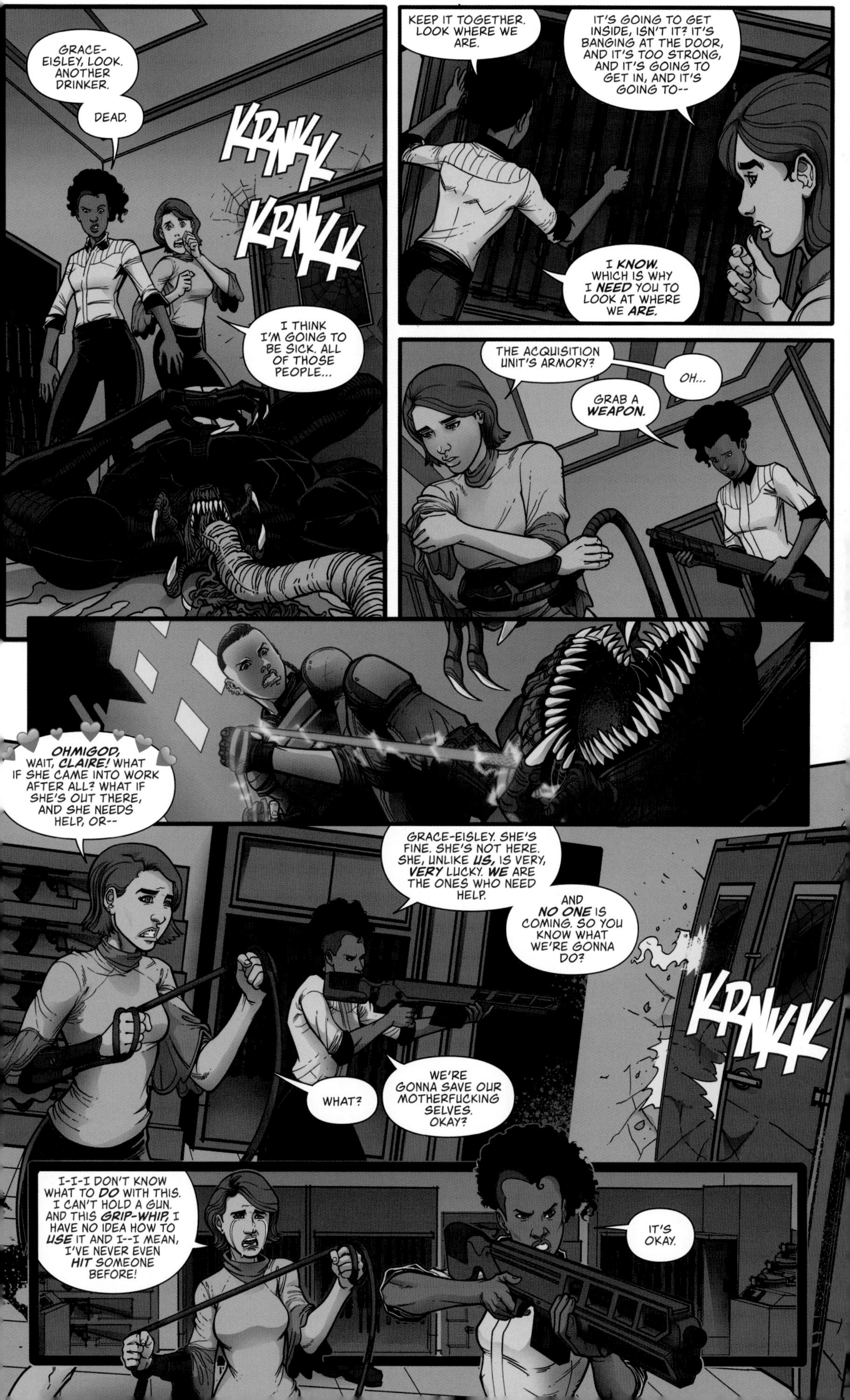

GRACE-EISLEY, LOOK. ANOTHER DRINKER.
DEAD.
KRNKK
KRNKK
I THINK I'M GOING TO BE SICK. ALL OF THOSE PEOPLE...
KEEP IT TOGETHER. LOOK WHERE WE ARE.
IT'S GOING TO GET INSIDE, ISN'T IT? IT'S BANGING AT THE DOOR, AND IT'S TOO STRONG, AND IT'S GOING TO GET IN, AND IT'S GOING TO--
I KNOW. WHICH IS WHY I NEED YOU TO LOOK AT WHERE WE ARE.
THE ACQUISITION UNIT'S ARMORY?
OH...
GRAB A WEAPON.
OHMIGOD, WAIT, CLAIRE! WHAT IF SHE CAME INTO WORK AFTER ALL? WHAT IF SHE'S OUT THERE, AND SHE NEEDS HELP, OR--
GRACE-EISLEY. SHE'S FINE. SHE'S NOT HERE. SHE, UNLIKE US, IS VERY, VERY LUCKY. WE ARE THE ONES WHO NEED HELP.
AND NO ONE IS COMING. SO YOU KNOW WHAT WE'RE GONNA DO?
KRNKK
WHAT?
WE'RE GONNA SAVE OUR MOTHERFUCKING SELVES. OKAY?
I-I-I DON'T KNOW WHAT TO DO WITH THIS. I CAN'T HOLD A GUN. AND THIS GRIP-WHIP, I HAVE NO IDEA HOW TO USE IT AND I--I MEAN, I'VE NEVER EVEN HIT SOMEONE BEFORE!
IT'S OKAY.

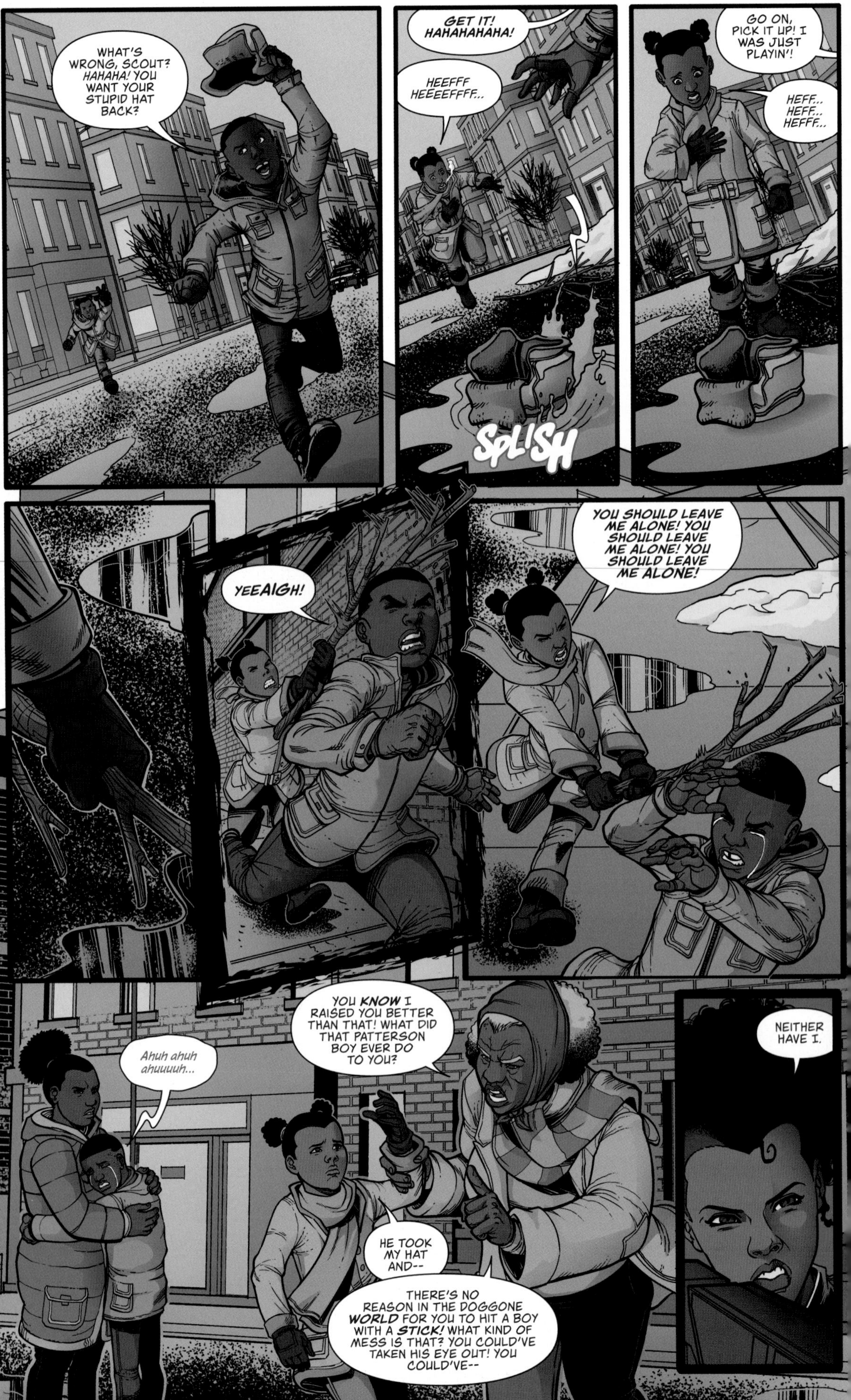
WHAT'S WRONG, SCOUT? HAHAHA! YOU WANT YOUR STUPID HAT BACK?
GET IT! HAHAHAHAHA!
HEEFFF HEEEEFFFF...
SPLISH
GO ON, PICK IT UP! I WAS JUST PLAYIN'!
HEFF... HEFF... HEFFF...
YEEAIGH!
YOU SHOULD LEAVE ME ALONE! YOU SHOULD LEAVE ME ALONE! YOU SHOULD LEAVE ME ALONE!
Ahuh ahuh ahuuuuh...
YOU KNOW I RAISED YOU BETTER THAN THAT! WHAT DID THAT PATTERSON BOY EVER DO TO YOU?
HE TOOK MY HAT AND--
THERE'S NO REASON IN THE DOGGONE WORLD FOR YOU TO HIT A BOY WITH A STICK! WHAT KIND OF MESS IS THAT? YOU COULD'VE TAKEN HIS EYE OUT! YOU COULD'VE--
NEITHER HAVE I.

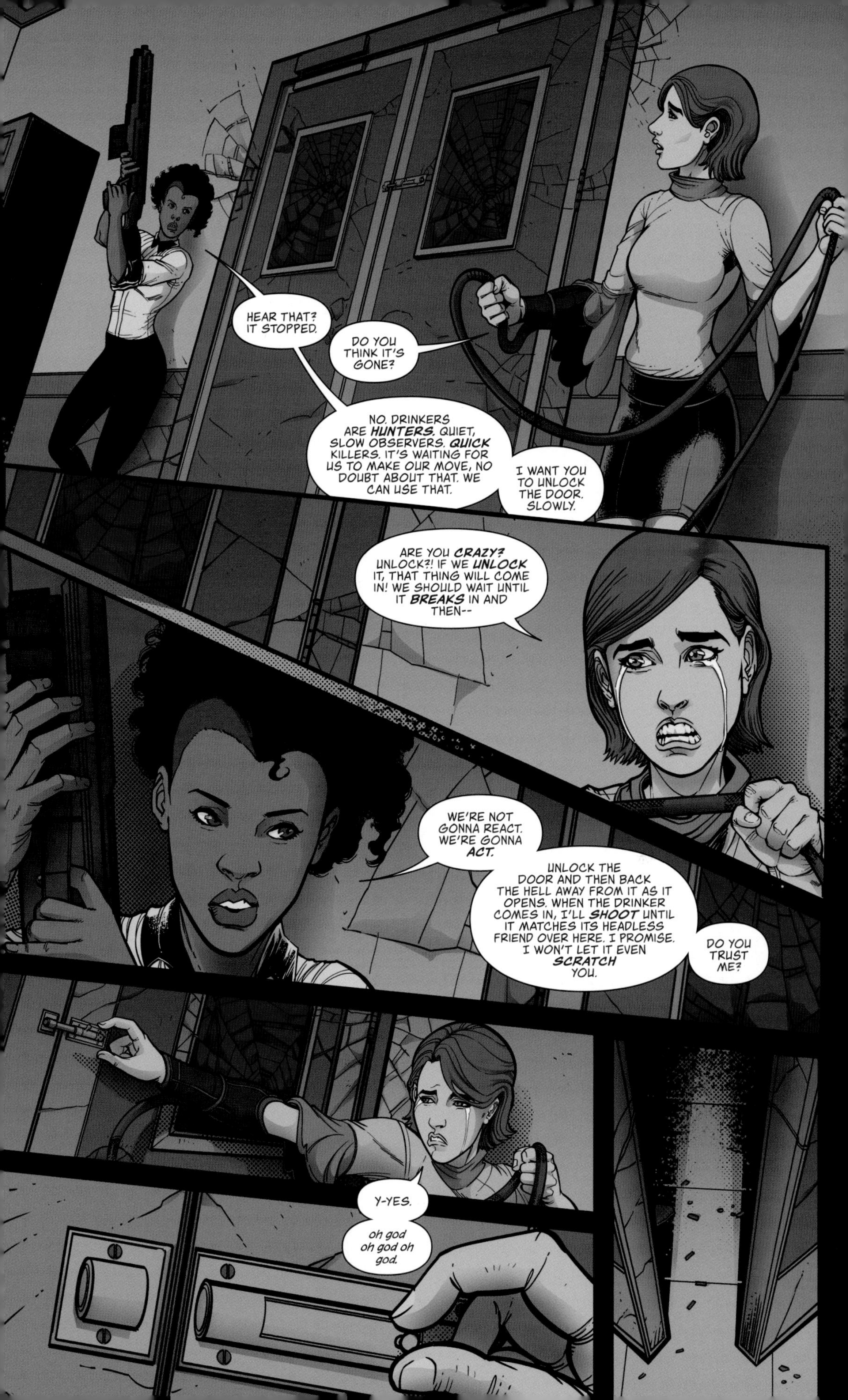
HEAR THAT? IT STOPPED.
DO YOU THINK IT'S GONE?
NO. DRINKERS ARE **HUNTERS**. QUIET, SLOW OBSERVERS. **QUICK** KILLERS. IT'S WAITING FOR US TO MAKE OUR MOVE, NO DOUBT ABOUT THAT. WE CAN USE THAT.
I WANT YOU TO UNLOCK THE DOOR. SLOWLY.
ARE YOU **CRAZY?** UNLOCK?! IF WE **UNLOCK** IT, THAT THING WILL COME IN! WE SHOULD WAIT UNTIL IT **BREAKS** IN AND THEN--
WE'RE NOT GONNA REACT. WE'RE GONNA **ACT**.
UNLOCK THE DOOR AND THEN BACK THE HELL AWAY FROM IT AS IT OPENS. WHEN THE DRINKER COMES IN, I'LL **SHOOT** UNTIL IT MATCHES ITS HEADLESS FRIEND OVER HERE. I PROMISE. I WON'T LET IT EVEN **SCRATCH** YOU.
DO YOU TRUST ME?
Y-YES.
oh god oh god oh god.

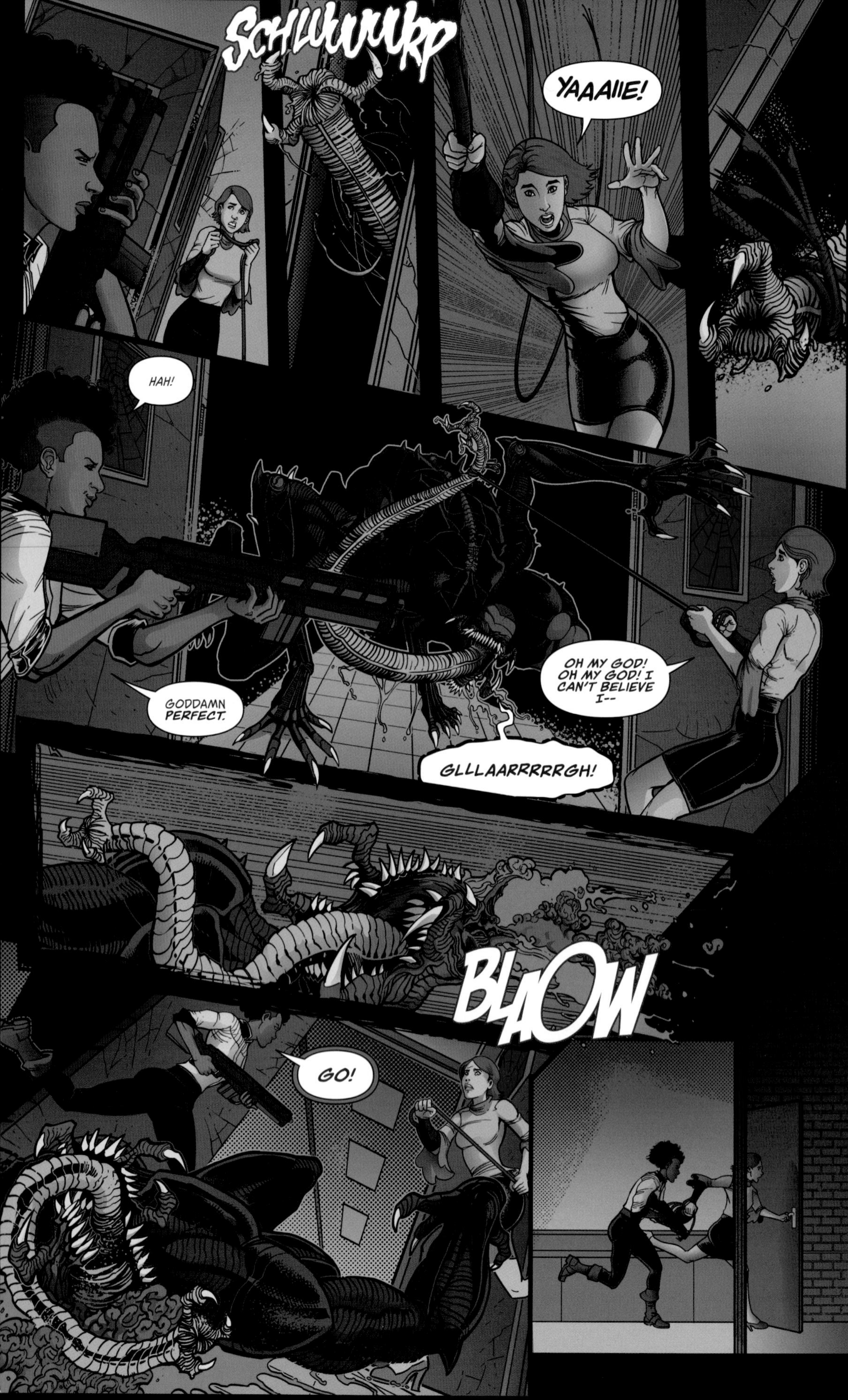
SCHLUUUURP
YAAAIIE!
HAH!
GODDAMN PERFECT.
OH MY GOD! OH MY GOD! I CAN'T BELIEVE I--
GLLLAARRRRRGH!
BLAOW
GO!

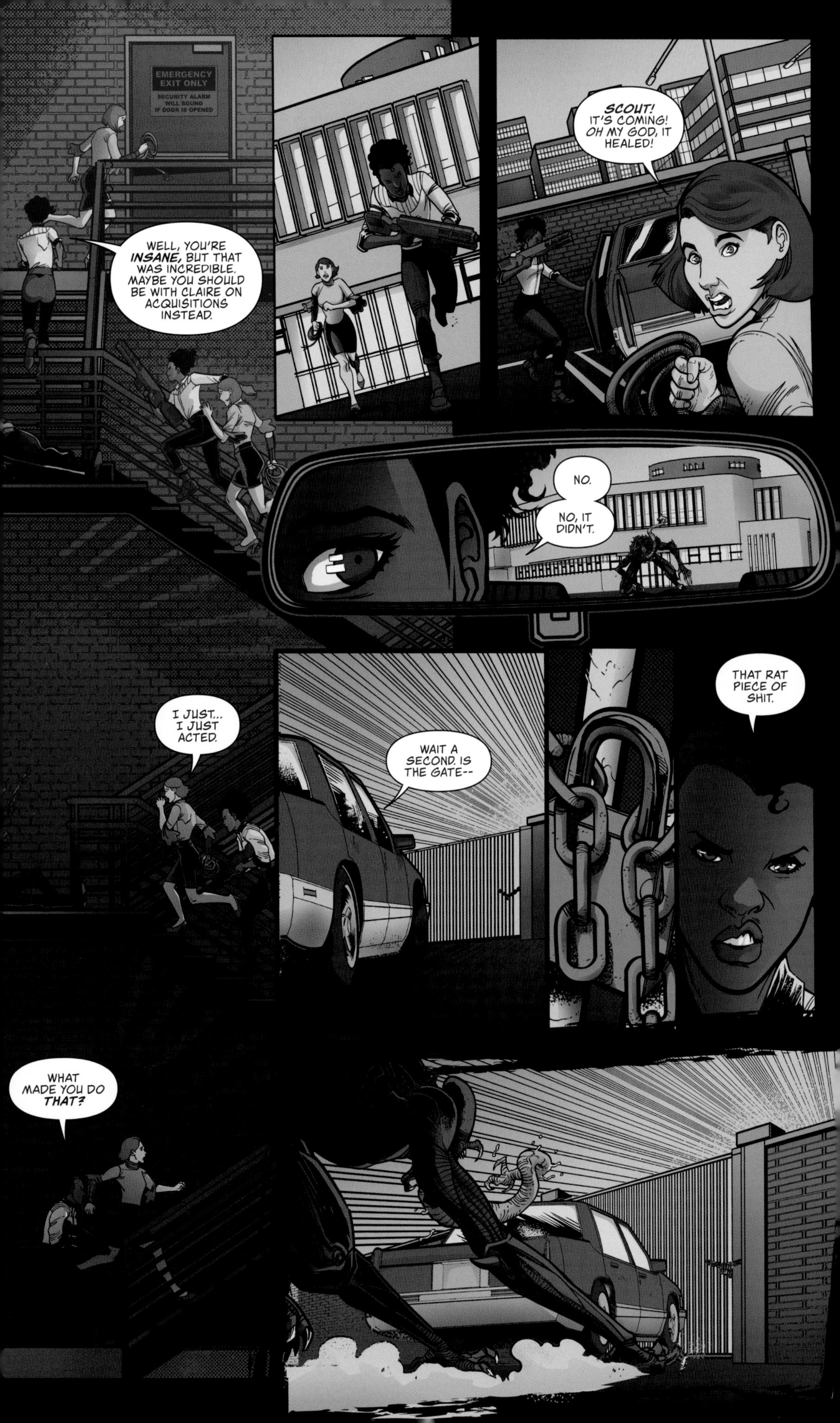
EMERGENCY EXIT ONLY
SECURITY ALARM WILL SOUND IF DOOR IS OPENED
WELL, YOU'RE INSANE, BUT THAT WAS INCREDIBLE. MAYBE YOU SHOULD BE WITH CLAIRE ON ACQUISITIONS INSTEAD.
SCOUT! IT'S COMING! OH MY GOD, IT HEALED!
NO.
NO, IT DIDN'T.
I JUST... I JUST ACTED.
WAIT A SECOND. IS THE GATE--
THAT RAT PIECE OF SHIT.
WHAT MADE YOU DO THAT?

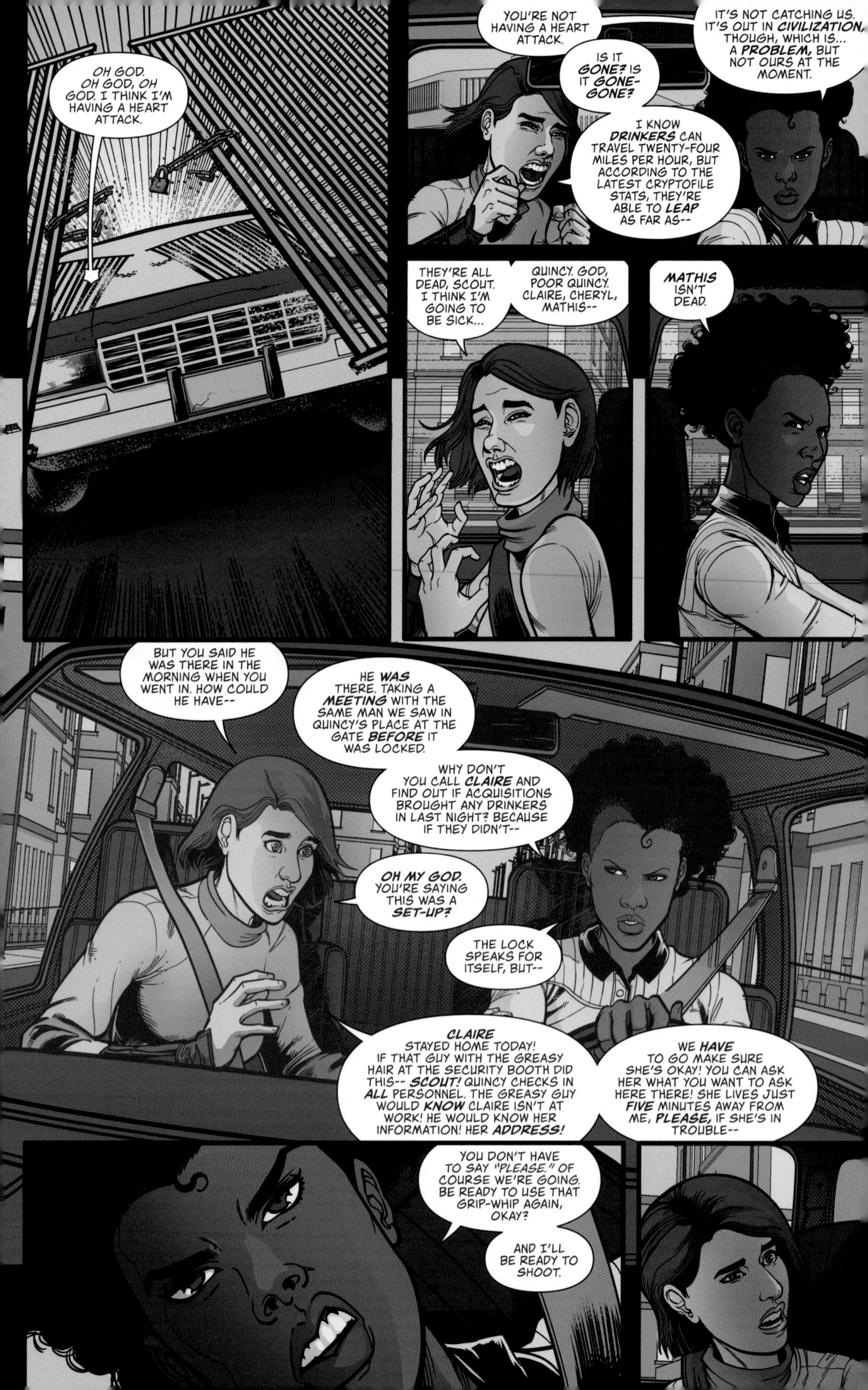
OH GOD. OH GOD, OH GOD. I THINK I'M HAVING A HEART ATTACK.
YOU'RE NOT HAVING A HEART ATTACK.
IS IT GONE? IS IT GONE-GONE?
IT'S NOT CATCHING US. IT'S OUT IN CIVILIZATION, THOUGH, WHICH IS... A PROBLEM, BUT NOT OURS AT THE MOMENT.
I KNOW DRINKERS CAN TRAVEL TWENTY-FOUR MILES PER HOUR, BUT ACCORDING TO THE LATEST CRYPTOFILE STATS, THEY'RE ABLE TO LEAP AS FAR AS--
THEY'RE ALL DEAD, SCOUT. I THINK I'M GOING TO BE SICK...
QUINCY. GOD, POOR QUINCY. CLAIRE, CHERYL, MATHIS--
MATHIS ISN'T DEAD.
BUT YOU SAID HE WAS THERE IN THE MORNING WHEN YOU WENT IN. HOW COULD HE HAVE--
HE WAS THERE. TAKING A MEETING WITH THE SAME MAN WE SAW IN QUINCY'S PLACE AT THE GATE BEFORE IT WAS LOCKED.
WHY DON'T YOU CALL CLAIRE AND FIND OUT IF ACQUISITIONS BROUGHT ANY DRINKERS IN LAST NIGHT? BECAUSE IF THEY DIDN'T--
OH MY GOD. YOU'RE SAYING THIS WAS A SET-UP?
THE LOCK SPEAKS FOR ITSELF, BUT--
CLAIRE STAYED HOME TODAY! IF THAT GUY WITH THE GREASY HAIR AT THE SECURITY BOOTH DID THIS-- SCOUT! QUINCY CHECKS IN ALL PERSONNEL. THE GREASY GUY WOULD KNOW CLAIRE ISN'T AT WORK! HE WOULD KNOW HER INFORMATION! HER ADDRESS!
WE HAVE TO GO MAKE SURE SHE'S OKAY! YOU CAN ASK HER WHAT YOU WANT TO ASK HERE THERE! SHE LIVES JUST FIVE MINUTES AWAY FROM ME, PLEASE, IF SHE'S IN TROUBLE--
YOU DON'T HAVE TO SAY "PLEASE." OF COURSE WE'RE GOING. BE READY TO USE THAT GRIP-WHIP AGAIN, OKAY?
AND I'LL BE READY TO SHOOT.

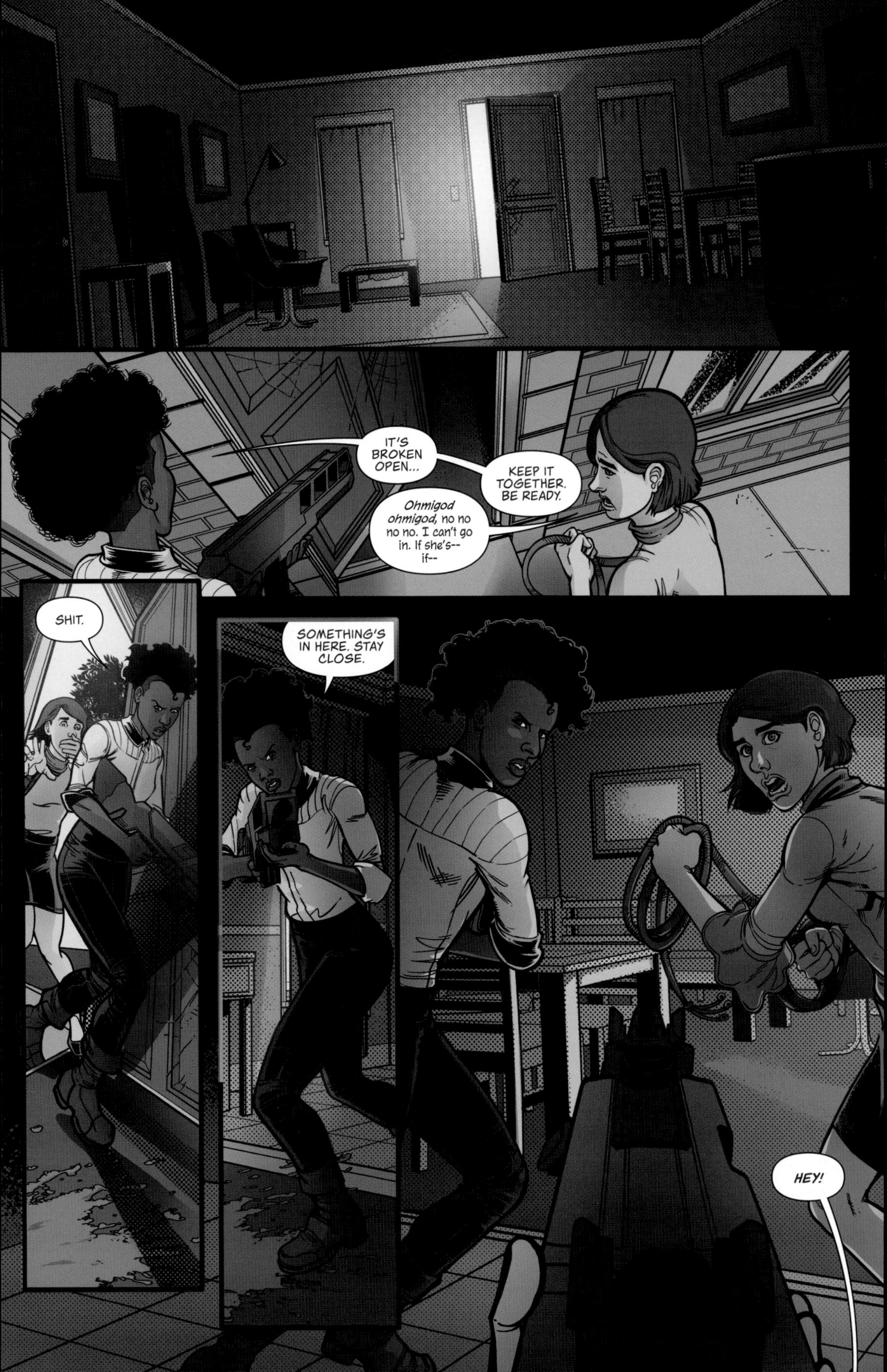
IT'S BROKEN OPEN...
KEEP IT TOGETHER. BE READY.
Ohmigod ohmigod, no no no no. I can't go in. If she's-- if--
SHIT.
SOMETHING'S IN HERE. STAY CLOSE.
HEY!

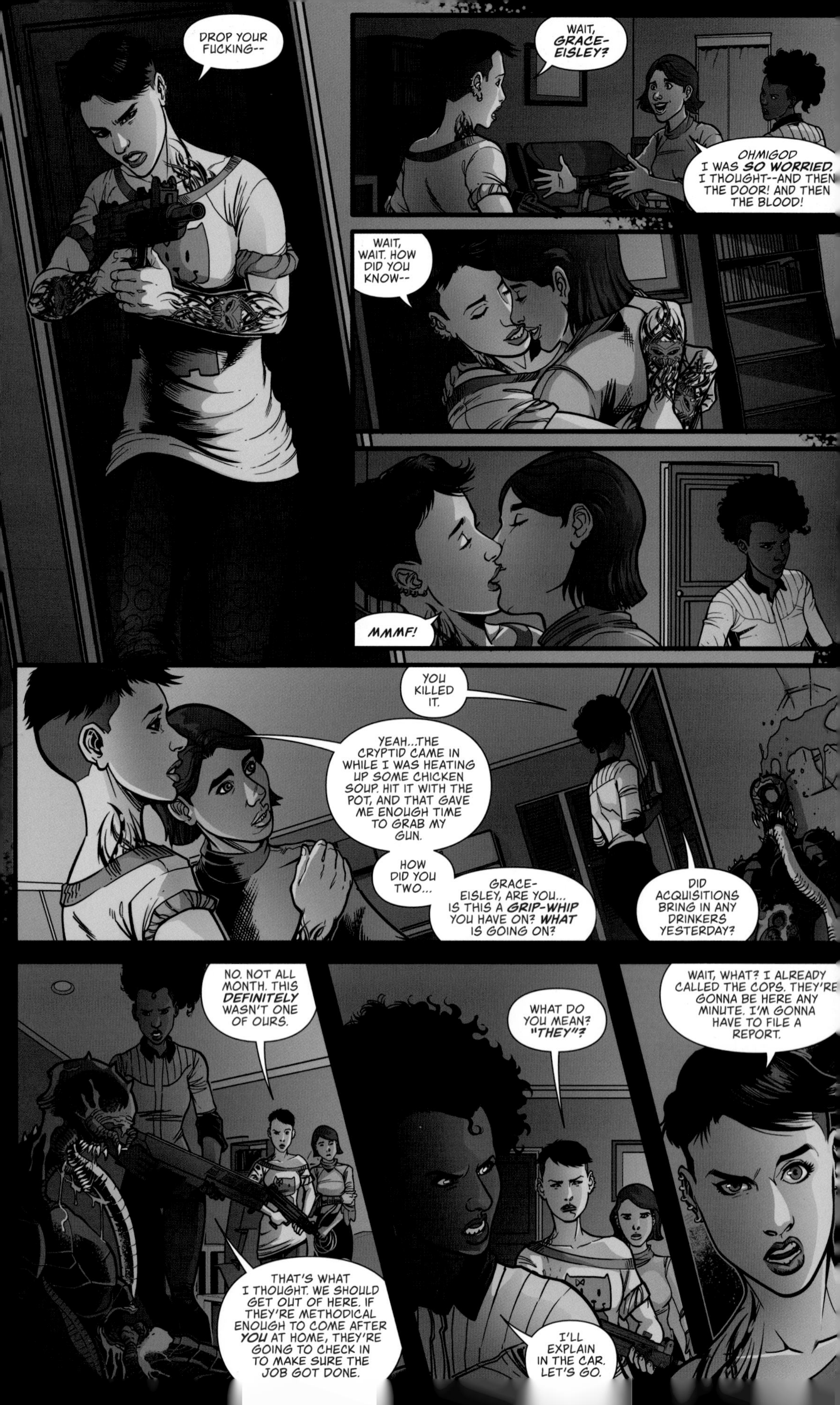
DROP YOUR FUCKING--
WAIT, GRACE-EISLEY?
OHMIGOD I WAS SO WORRIED. I THOUGHT--AND THEN THE DOOR! AND THEN THE BLOOD!
WAIT, WAIT. HOW DID YOU KNOW--
MMMF!
YOU KILLED IT.
YEAH...THE CRYPTID CAME IN WHILE I WAS HEATING UP SOME CHICKEN SOUP. HIT IT WITH THE POT, AND THAT GAVE ME ENOUGH TIME TO GRAB MY GUN.
HOW DID YOU TWO...
GRACE-EISLEY, ARE YOU... IS THIS A GRIP-WHIP YOU HAVE ON? WHAT IS GOING ON?
DID ACQUISITIONS BRING IN ANY DRINKERS YESTERDAY?
NO. NOT ALL MONTH. THIS DEFINITELY WASN'T ONE OF OURS.
THAT'S WHAT I THOUGHT. WE SHOULD GET OUT OF HERE. IF THEY'RE METHODICAL ENOUGH TO COME AFTER YOU AT HOME, THEY'RE GOING TO CHECK IN TO MAKE SURE THE JOB GOT DONE.
WHAT DO YOU MEAN? "THEY"?
I'LL EXPLAIN IN THE CAR. LET'S GO.
WAIT, WHAT? I ALREADY CALLED THE COPS. THEY'RE GONNA BE HERE ANY MINUTE. I'M GONNA HAVE TO FILE A REPORT.

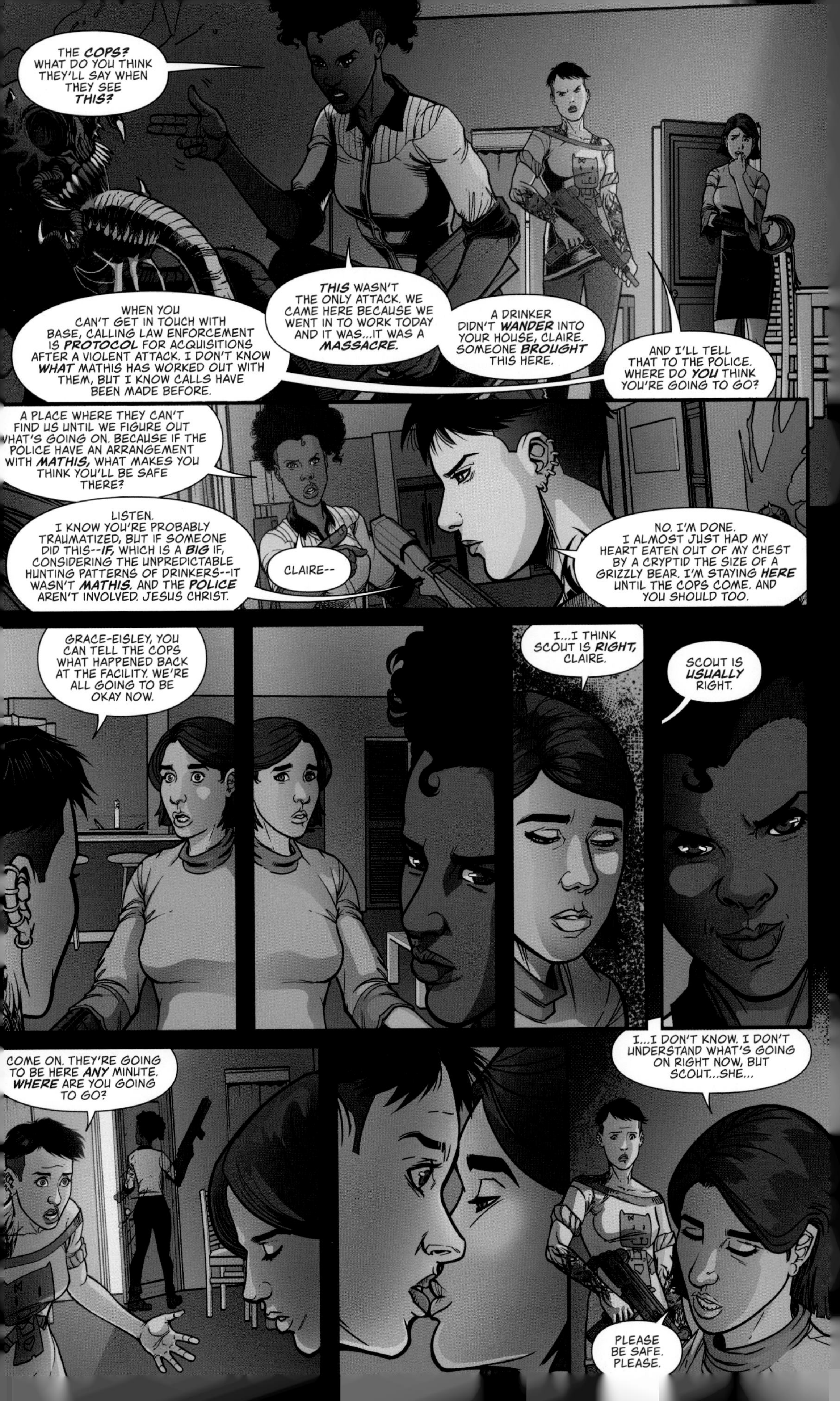
THE COPS? WHAT DO YOU THINK THEY'LL SAY WHEN THEY SEE THIS?
WHEN YOU CAN'T GET IN TOUCH WITH BASE, CALLING LAW ENFORCEMENT IS PROTOCOL FOR ACQUISITIONS AFTER A VIOLENT ATTACK. I DON'T KNOW WHAT MATHIS HAS WORKED OUT WITH THEM, BUT I KNOW CALLS HAVE BEEN MADE BEFORE.
THIS WASN'T THE ONLY ATTACK. WE CAME HERE BECAUSE WE WENT IN TO WORK TODAY AND IT WAS...IT WAS A MASSACRE.
A DRINKER DIDN'T WANDER INTO YOUR HOUSE, CLAIRE. SOMEONE BROUGHT THIS HERE.
AND I'LL TELL THAT TO THE POLICE. WHERE DO YOU THINK YOU'RE GOING TO GO?
A PLACE WHERE THEY CAN'T FIND US UNTIL WE FIGURE OUT WHAT'S GOING ON. BECAUSE IF THE POLICE HAVE AN ARRANGEMENT WITH MATHIS, WHAT MAKES YOU THINK YOU'LL BE SAFE THERE?
LISTEN. I KNOW YOU'RE PROBABLY TRAUMATIZED, BUT IF SOMEONE DID THIS--IF, WHICH IS A BIG IF, CONSIDERING THE UNPREDICTABLE HUNTING PATTERNS OF DRINKERS--IT WASN'T MATHIS. AND THE POLICE AREN'T INVOLVED. JESUS CHRIST.
CLAIRE--
NO. I'M DONE. I ALMOST JUST HAD MY HEART EATEN OUT OF MY CHEST BY A CRYPTID THE SIZE OF A GRIZZLY BEAR. I'M STAYING HERE UNTIL THE COPS COME. AND YOU SHOULD TOO.
GRACE-EISLEY, YOU CAN TELL THE COPS WHAT HAPPENED BACK AT THE FACILITY. WE'RE ALL GOING TO BE OKAY NOW.
I...I THINK SCOUT IS RIGHT, CLAIRE.
SCOUT IS USUALLY RIGHT.
COME ON. THEY'RE GOING TO BE HERE ANY MINUTE. WHERE ARE YOU GOING TO GO?
I...I DON'T KNOW. I DON'T UNDERSTAND WHAT'S GOING ON RIGHT NOW, BUT SCOUT...SHE...
PLEASE BE SAFE. PLEASE.

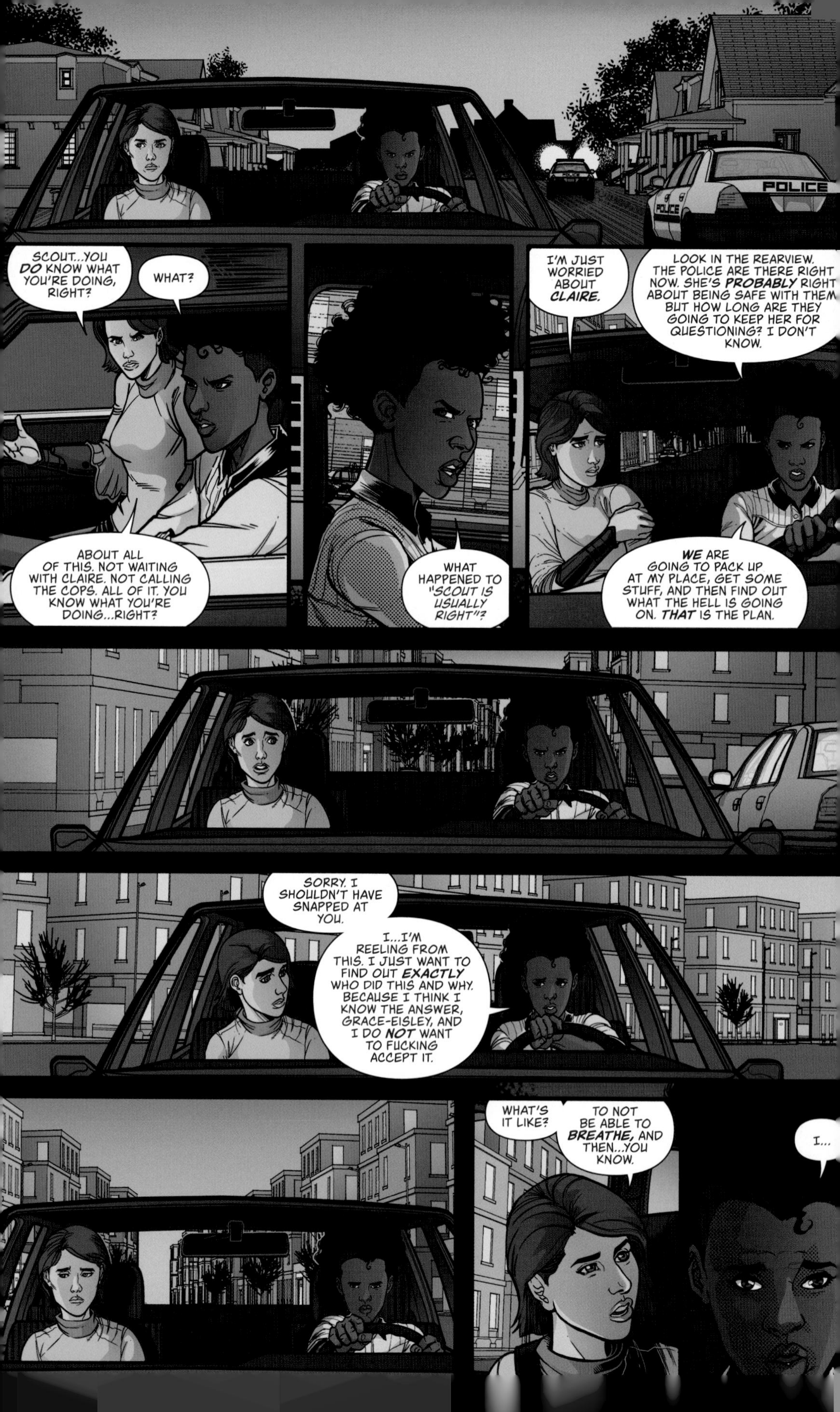
POLICE
POLICE
SCOUT...YOU DO KNOW WHAT YOU'RE DOING, RIGHT?
WHAT?
ABOUT ALL OF THIS. NOT WAITING WITH CLAIRE. NOT CALLING THE COPS. ALL OF IT. YOU KNOW WHAT YOU'RE DOING...RIGHT?
WHAT HAPPENED TO "SCOUT IS USUALLY RIGHT"?
I'M JUST WORRIED ABOUT CLAIRE.
LOOK IN THE REARVIEW. THE POLICE ARE THERE RIGHT NOW. SHE'S PROBABLY RIGHT ABOUT BEING SAFE WITH THEM BUT HOW LONG ARE THEY GOING TO KEEP HER FOR QUESTIONING? I DON'T KNOW.
WE ARE GOING TO PACK UP AT MY PLACE, GET SOME STUFF, AND THEN FIND OUT WHAT THE HELL IS GOING ON. THAT IS THE PLAN.
SORRY. I SHOULDN'T HAVE SNAPPED AT YOU.
I...I'M REELING FROM THIS. I JUST WANT TO FIND OUT EXACTLY WHO DID THIS AND WHY. BECAUSE I THINK I KNOW THE ANSWER, GRACE-EISLEY, AND I DO NOT WANT TO FUCKING ACCEPT IT.
WHAT'S IT LIKE?
TO NOT BE ABLE TO BREATHE, AND THEN...YOU KNOW.
I...

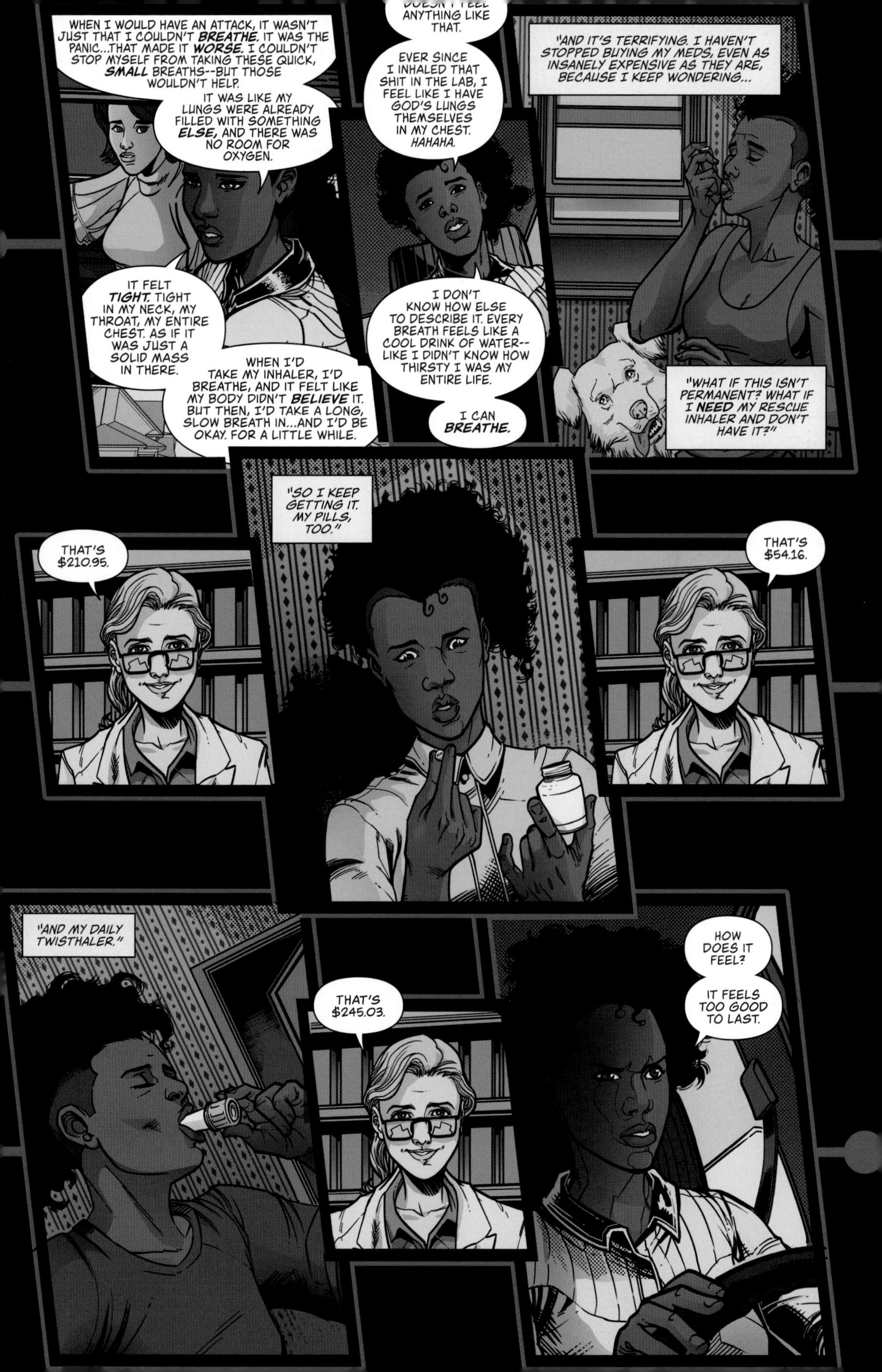

WHEN I WOULD HAVE AN ATTACK, IT WASN'T JUST THAT I COULDN'T BREATHE. IT WAS THE PANIC...THAT MADE IT WORSE. I COULDN'T STOP MYSELF FROM TAKING THESE QUICK, SMALL BREATHS--BUT THOSE WOULDN'T HELP.
IT WAS LIKE MY LUNGS WERE ALREADY FILLED WITH SOMETHING ELSE, AND THERE WAS NO ROOM FOR OXYGEN.
IT FELT TIGHT. TIGHT IN MY NECK, MY THROAT, MY ENTIRE CHEST. AS IF IT WAS JUST A SOLID MASS IN THERE.
WHEN I'D TAKE MY INHALER, I'D BREATHE, AND IT FELT LIKE MY BODY DIDN'T BELIEVE IT. BUT THEN, I'D TAKE A LONG, SLOW BREATH IN...AND I'D BE OKAY. FOR A LITTLE WHILE.
ANYTHING LIKE THAT.
EVER SINCE I INHALED THAT SHIT IN THE LAB, I FEEL LIKE I HAVE GOD'S LUNGS THEMSELVES IN MY CHEST. HAHAHA.
I DON'T KNOW HOW ELSE TO DESCRIBE IT. EVERY BREATH FEELS LIKE A COOL DRINK OF WATER--LIKE I DIDN'T KNOW HOW THIRSTY I WAS MY ENTIRE LIFE.
I CAN BREATHE.
"AND IT'S TERRIFYING. I HAVEN'T STOPPED BUYING MY MEDS, EVEN AS INSANELY EXPENSIVE AS THEY ARE, BECAUSE I KEEP WONDERING...
"WHAT IF THIS ISN'T PERMANENT? WHAT IF I NEED MY RESCUE INHALER AND DON'T HAVE IT?"
THAT'S $210.95.
"SO I KEEP GETTING IT. MY PILLS, TOO."
THAT'S $54.16.
"AND MY DAILY TWISTHALER."
THAT'S $245.03.
HOW DOES IT FEEL?
IT FEELS TOO GOOD TO LAST.

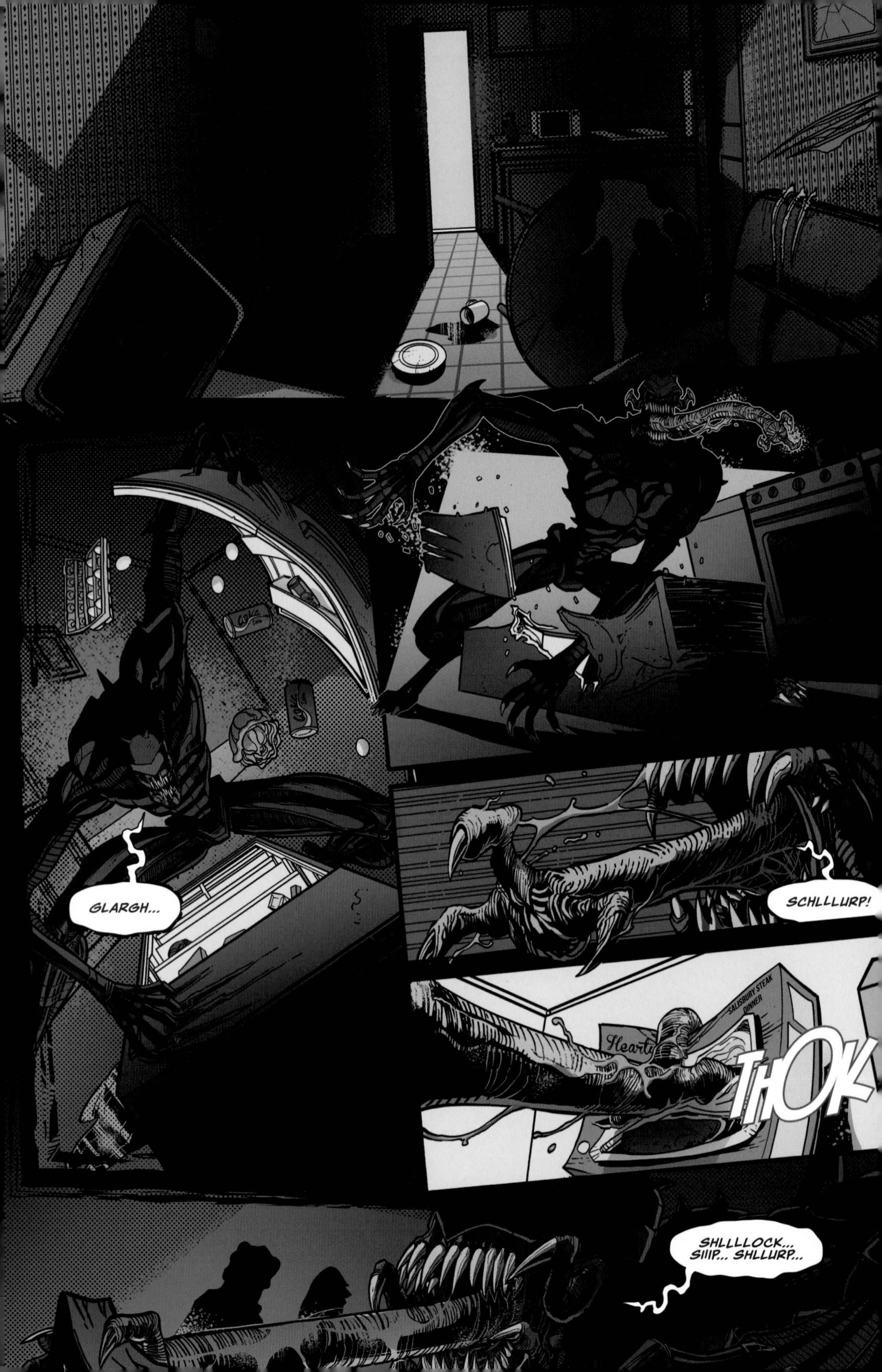
GLARGH...
SCHLLLURP!
SALISBURY STEAK DINNER
THOK
SHLLLLOCK... SIIIP... SHLLURP...

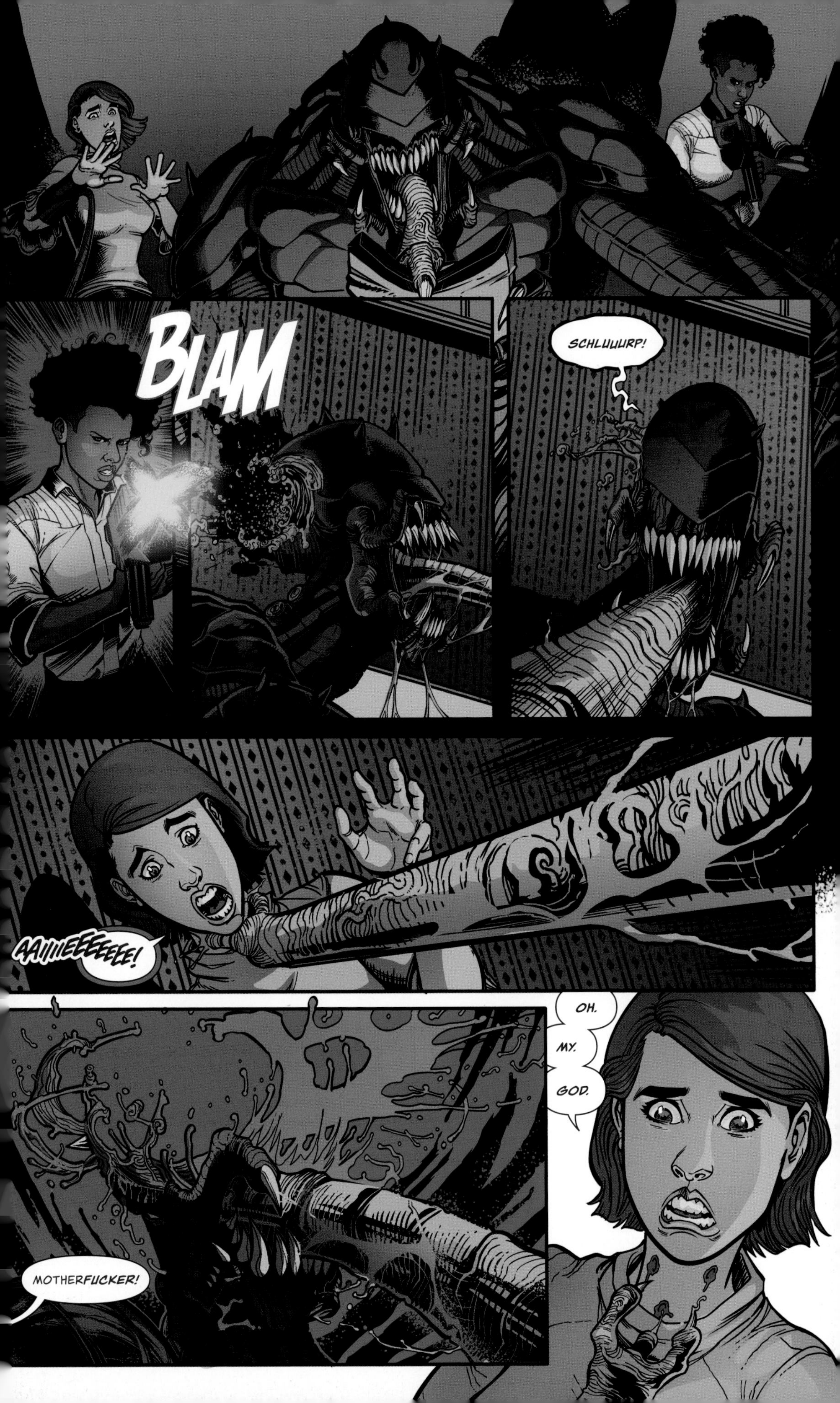
BLAM
SCHLUUURP!
AAIIIIEEEEEEEE!
MOTHERFUCKER!
OH.
MY.
GOD.

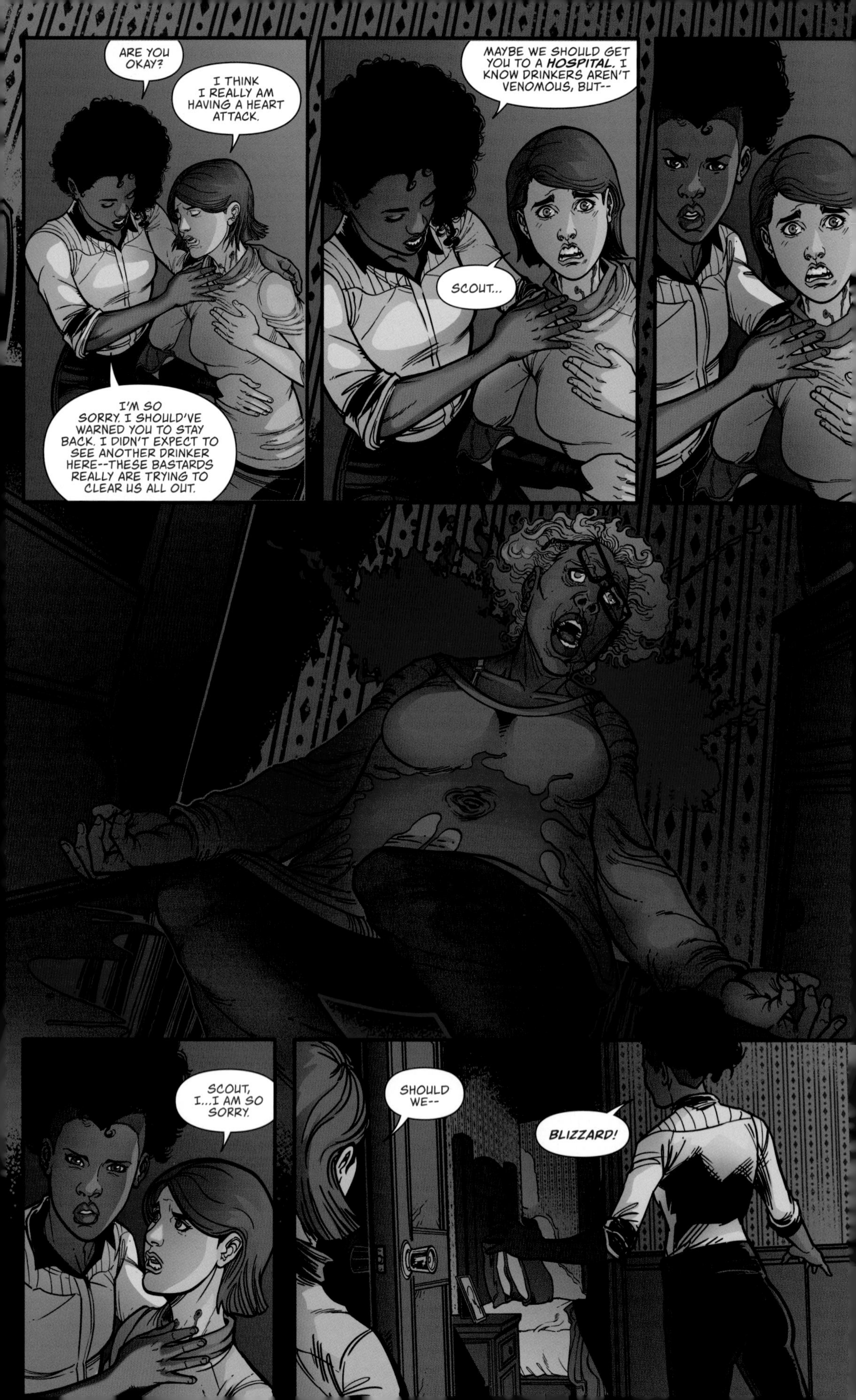
ARE YOU OKAY?
I THINK I REALLY AM HAVING A HEART ATTACK.
I'M SO SORRY. I SHOULD'VE WARNED YOU TO STAY BACK. I DIDN'T EXPECT TO SEE ANOTHER DRINKER HERE--THESE BASTARDS REALLY ARE TRYING TO CLEAR US ALL OUT.
MAYBE WE SHOULD GET YOU TO A HOSPITAL. I KNOW DRINKERS AREN'T VENOMOUS, BUT--
SCOUT...
SCOUT, I...I AM SO SORRY.
SHOULD WE--
BLIZZARD!

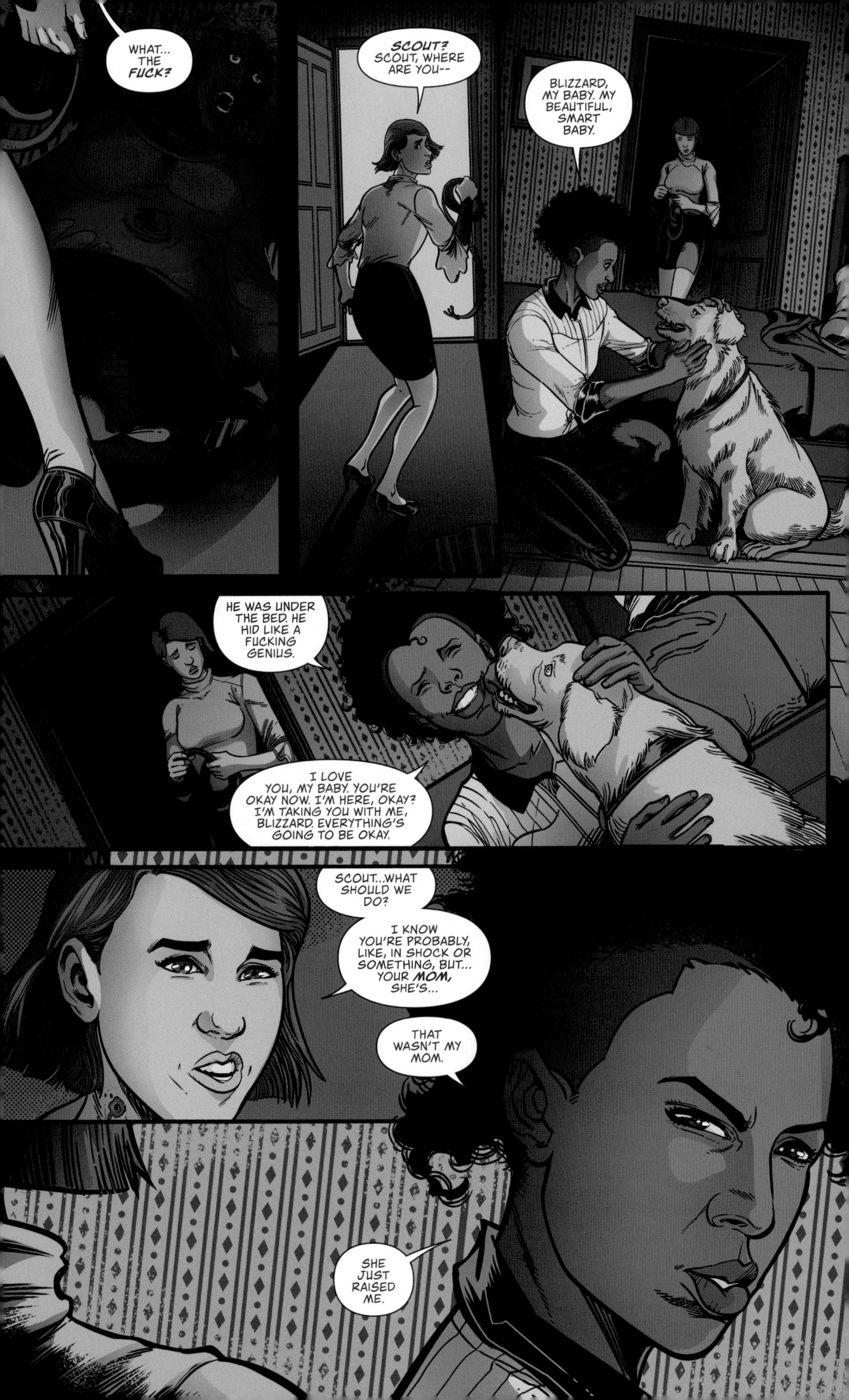
WHAT... THE FUCK?
SCOUT? SCOUT, WHERE ARE YOU--
BLIZZARD, MY BABY. MY BEAUTIFUL, SMART BABY.
HE WAS UNDER THE BED. HE HID LIKE A FUCKING GENIUS.
I LOVE YOU, MY BABY. YOU'RE OKAY NOW. I'M HERE, OKAY? I'M TAKING YOU WITH ME, BLIZZARD. EVERYTHING'S GOING TO BE OKAY.
SCOUT...WHAT SHOULD WE DO?
I KNOW YOU'RE PROBABLY, LIKE, IN SHOCK OR SOMETHING, BUT... YOUR MOM, SHE'S...
THAT WASN'T MY MOM.
SHE JUST RAISED ME.

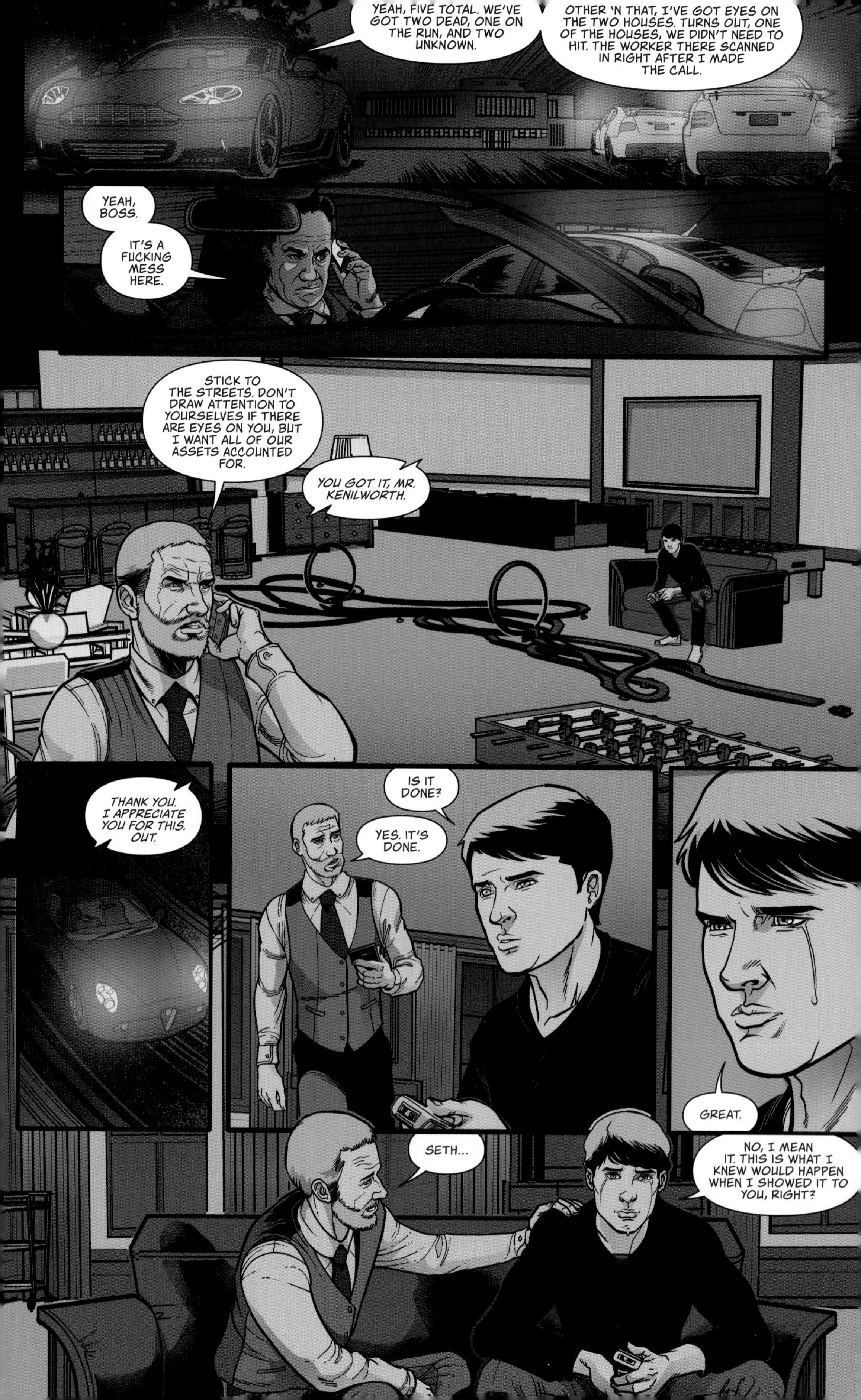
YEAH, FIVE TOTAL. WE'VE GOT TWO DEAD, ONE ON THE RUN, AND TWO UNKNOWN.
OTHER 'N THAT, I'VE GOT EYES ON THE TWO HOUSES. TURNS OUT, ONE OF THE HOUSES, WE DIDN'T NEED TO HIT. THE WORKER THERE SCANNED IN RIGHT AFTER I MADE THE CALL.
YEAH, BOSS.
IT'S A FUCKING MESS HERE.
STICK TO THE STREETS. DON'T DRAW ATTENTION TO YOURSELVES IF THERE ARE EYES ON YOU, BUT I WANT ALL OF OUR ASSETS ACCOUNTED FOR.
YOU GOT IT, MR. KENILWORTH.
THANK YOU. I APPRECIATE YOU FOR THIS. OUT.
IS IT DONE?
YES. IT'S DONE.
GREAT.
SETH...
NO, I MEAN IT. THIS IS WHAT I KNEW WOULD HAPPEN WHEN I SHOWED IT TO YOU, RIGHT?

I KNOW YOU'RE GOING TO FEEL THE WEIGHT OF THIS. WHAT I NEED YOU TO UNDERSTAND, THOUGH, SON, IS WHAT WE'RE BUILDING HERE.

IT'S NOT JUST FOR *US*. IT'S FOR THE FUTURE. IF THESE *PEOPLE* WERE TO INTERFERE WITH THAT...EVERYTHING WE'VE DEDICATED OUR LIVES TO, EVERYTHING THAT *YOU* HELPED REVOLUTIONIZE...

YOU KNOW WHAT WOULD HAPPEN. YOU UNDERSTAND, RIGHT?

HOW MANY OF THEM WERE THERE?

DO YOU REALLY WANT TO KNOW?

I DON'T KNOW... MAYBE. YES.

I DIDN'T ASK.

COME ON, BUD. RACE YA!

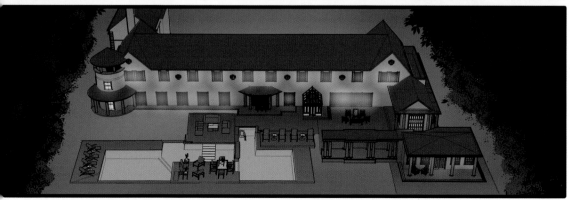

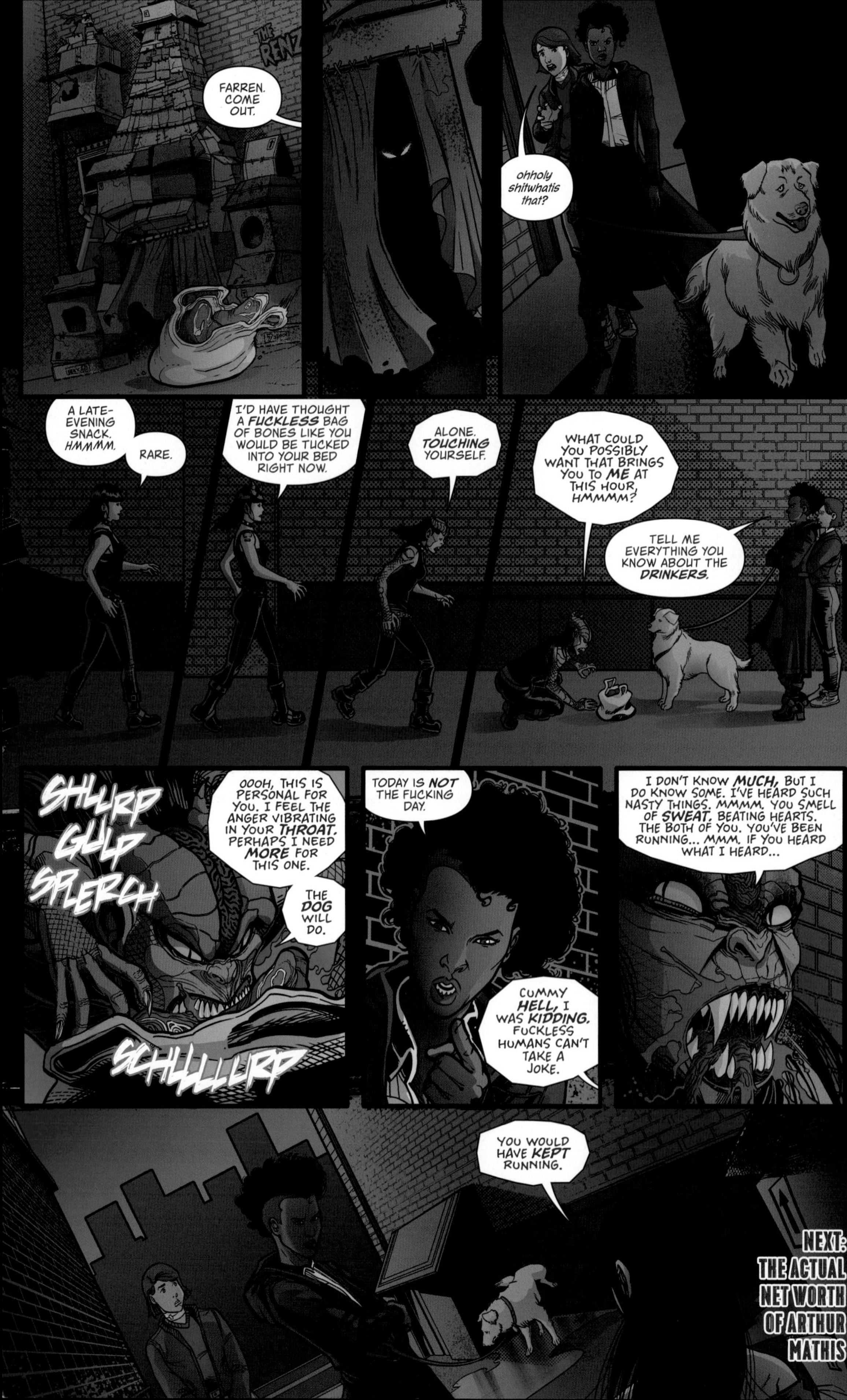
FARREN. COME OUT.
ohholy shitwhatis that?
A LATE-EVENING SNACK. HMMMM.
RARE.
I'D HAVE THOUGHT A FUCKLESS BAG OF BONES LIKE YOU WOULD BE TUCKED INTO YOUR BED RIGHT NOW.
ALONE. TOUCHING YOURSELF.
WHAT COULD YOU POSSIBLY WANT THAT BRINGS YOU TO ME AT THIS HOUR, HMMMM?
TELL ME EVERYTHING YOU KNOW ABOUT THE DRINKERS.
SHLURP
GULP
SPLERCH
OOOH, THIS IS PERSONAL FOR YOU. I FEEL THE ANGER VIBRATING IN YOUR THROAT. PERHAPS I NEED MORE FOR THIS ONE.
THE DOG WILL DO.
SCHLLLLURP
TODAY IS NOT THE FUCKING DAY.
CUMMY HELL, I WAS KIDDING. FUCKLESS HUMANS CAN'T TAKE A JOKE.
I DON'T KNOW MUCH, BUT I DO KNOW SOME. I'VE HEARD SUCH NASTY THINGS. MMMM. YOU SMELL OF SWEAT, BEATING HEARTS. THE BOTH OF YOU. YOU'VE BEEN RUNNING... MMM. IF YOU HEARD WHAT I HEARD...
YOU WOULD HAVE KEPT RUNNING.
NEXT: THE ACTUAL NET WORTH OF ARTHUR MATHIS

PAY TO LIVE

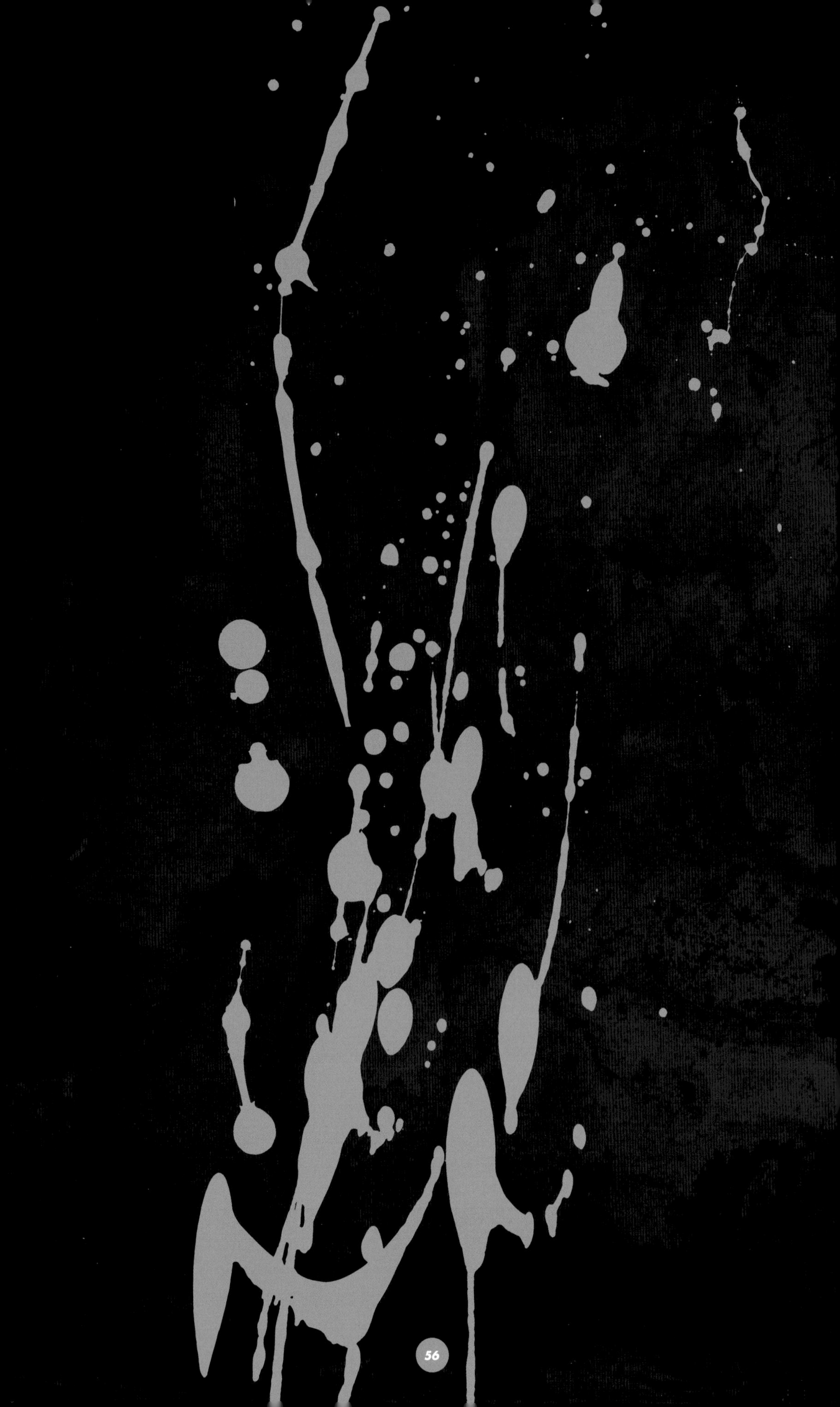

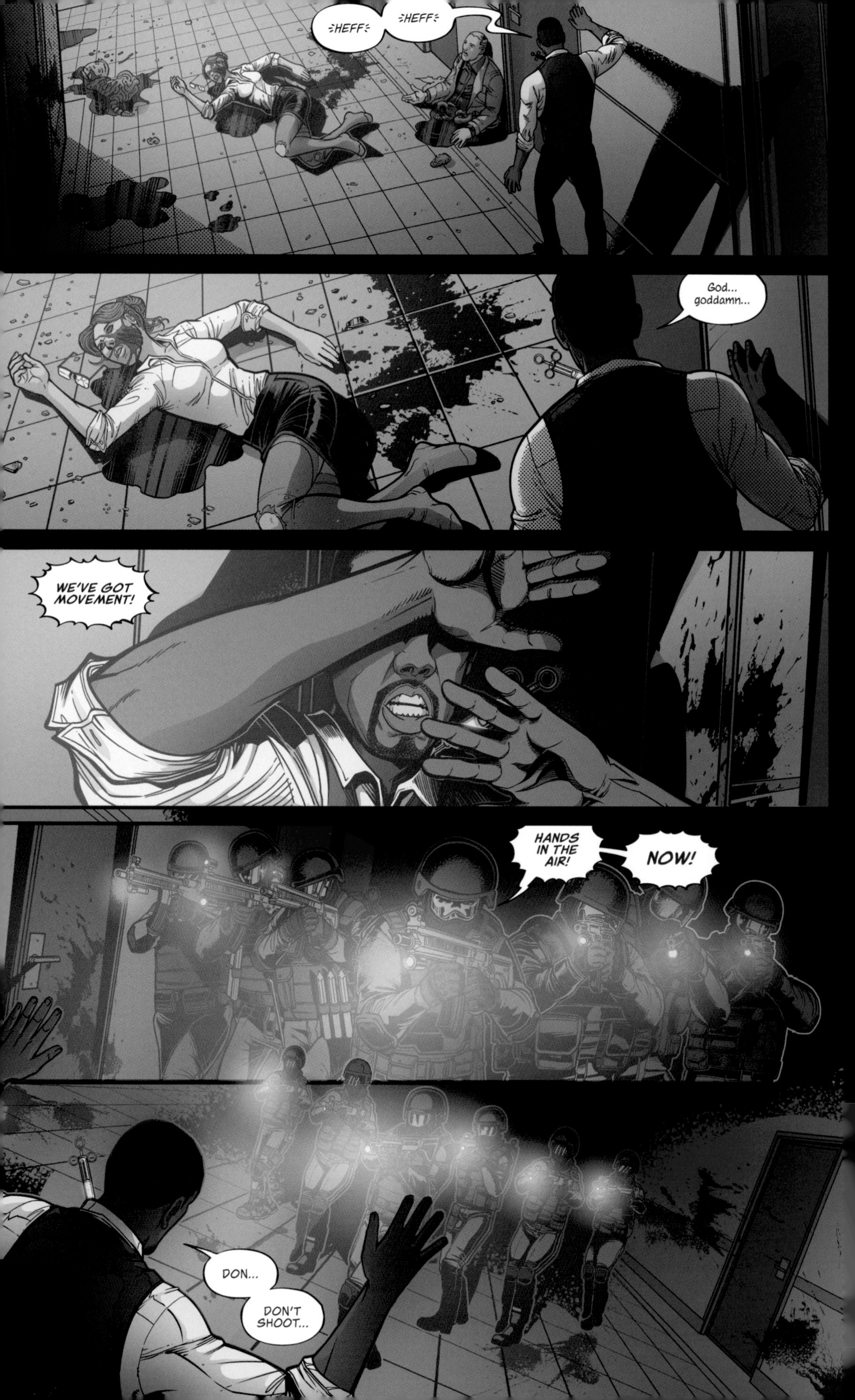
HEFF
HEFF
God... goddamn...
WE'VE GOT MOVEMENT!
HANDS IN THE AIR!
NOW!
DON...
DON'T SHOOT...

BREATHLESS

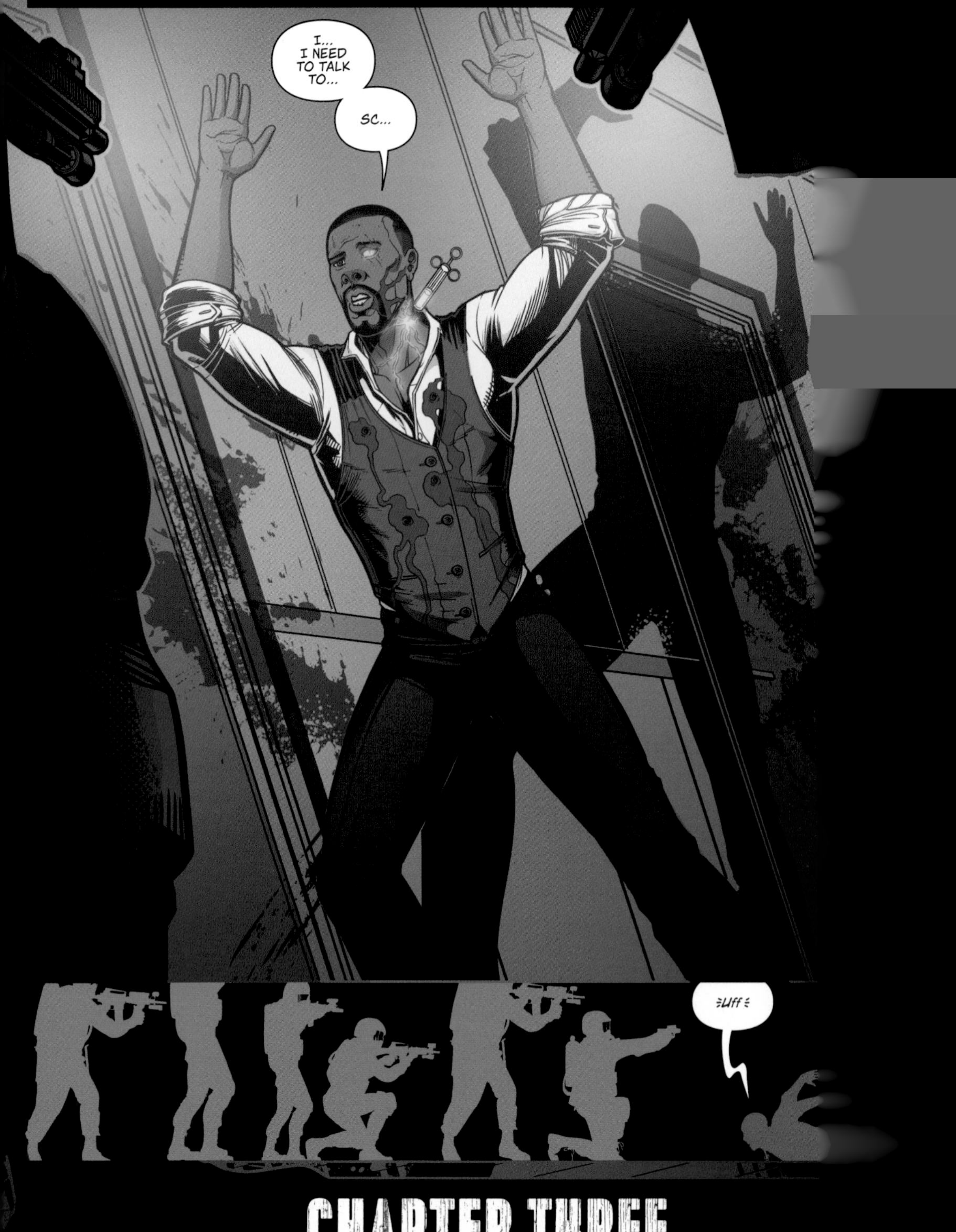
I... I NEED TO TALK TO...
SC...
UFF

CHAPTER THREE
THE ACTUAL NET WORTH OF ARTHUR MATHIS

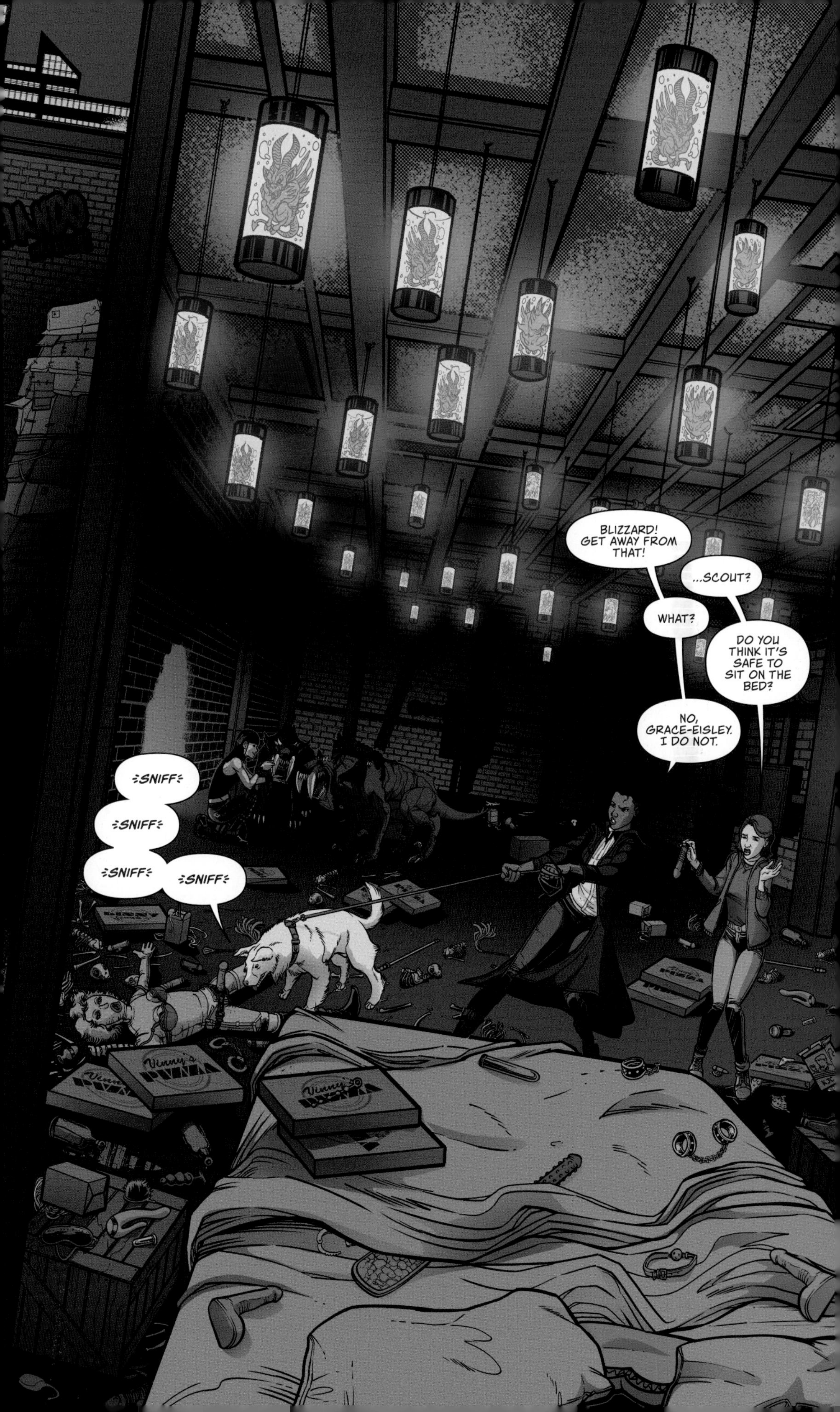
BLIZZARD! GET AWAY FROM THAT!
WHAT?
...SCOUT?
DO YOU THINK IT'S SAFE TO SIT ON THE BED?
NO, GRACE-EISLEY. I DO NOT.
SNIFF
SNIFF
SNIFF
SNIFF

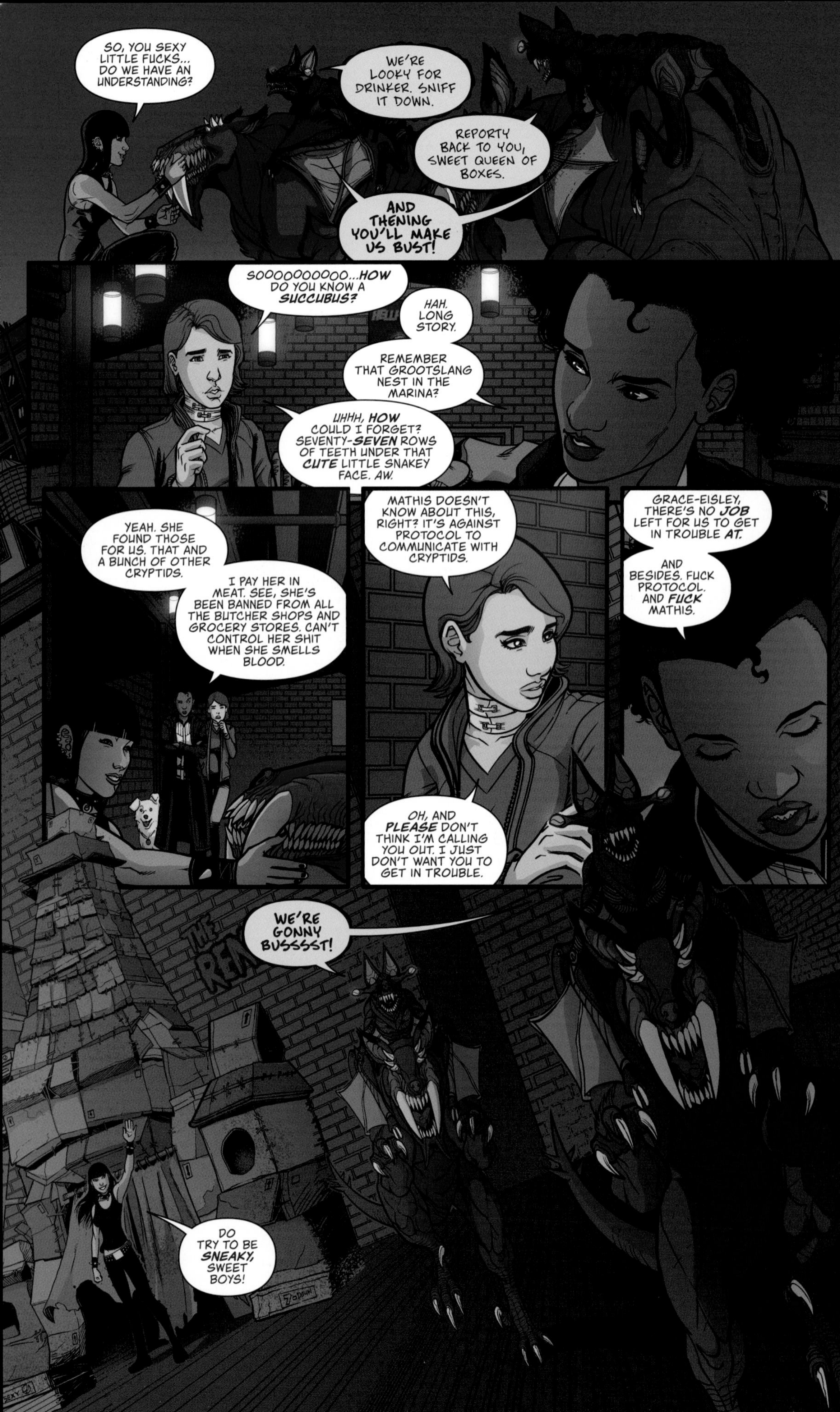
SO, YOU SEXY LITTLE FUCKS... DO WE HAVE AN UNDERSTANDING?
WE'RE LOOKY FOR DRINKER. SNIFF IT DOWN.
REPORTY BACK TO YOU, SWEET QUEEN OF BOXES.
AND THENING YOU'LL MAKE US BUST!
SOOOOOOOOOO...HOW DO YOU KNOW A SUCCUBUS?
HAH. LONG STORY.
REMEMBER THAT GROOTSLANG NEST IN THE MARINA?
UHHH, HOW COULD I FORGET? SEVENTY-SEVEN ROWS OF TEETH UNDER THAT CUTE LITTLE SNAKEY FACE. AW.
YEAH. SHE FOUND THOSE FOR US. THAT AND A BUNCH OF OTHER CRYPTIDS.
I PAY HER IN MEAT. SEE, SHE'S BEEN BANNED FROM ALL THE BUTCHER SHOPS AND GROCERY STORES. CAN'T CONTROL HER SHIT WHEN SHE SMELLS BLOOD.
MATHIS DOESN'T KNOW ABOUT THIS, RIGHT? IT'S AGAINST PROTOCOL TO COMMUNICATE WITH CRYPTIDS.
OH, AND PLEASE DON'T THINK I'M CALLING YOU OUT. I JUST DON'T WANT YOU TO GET IN TROUBLE.
GRACE-EISLEY, THERE'S NO JOB LEFT FOR US TO GET IN TROUBLE AT.
AND BESIDES. FUCK PROTOCOL. AND FUCK MATHIS.
WE'RE GONNY BUSSSST!
DO TRY TO BE SNEAKY, SWEET BOYS!

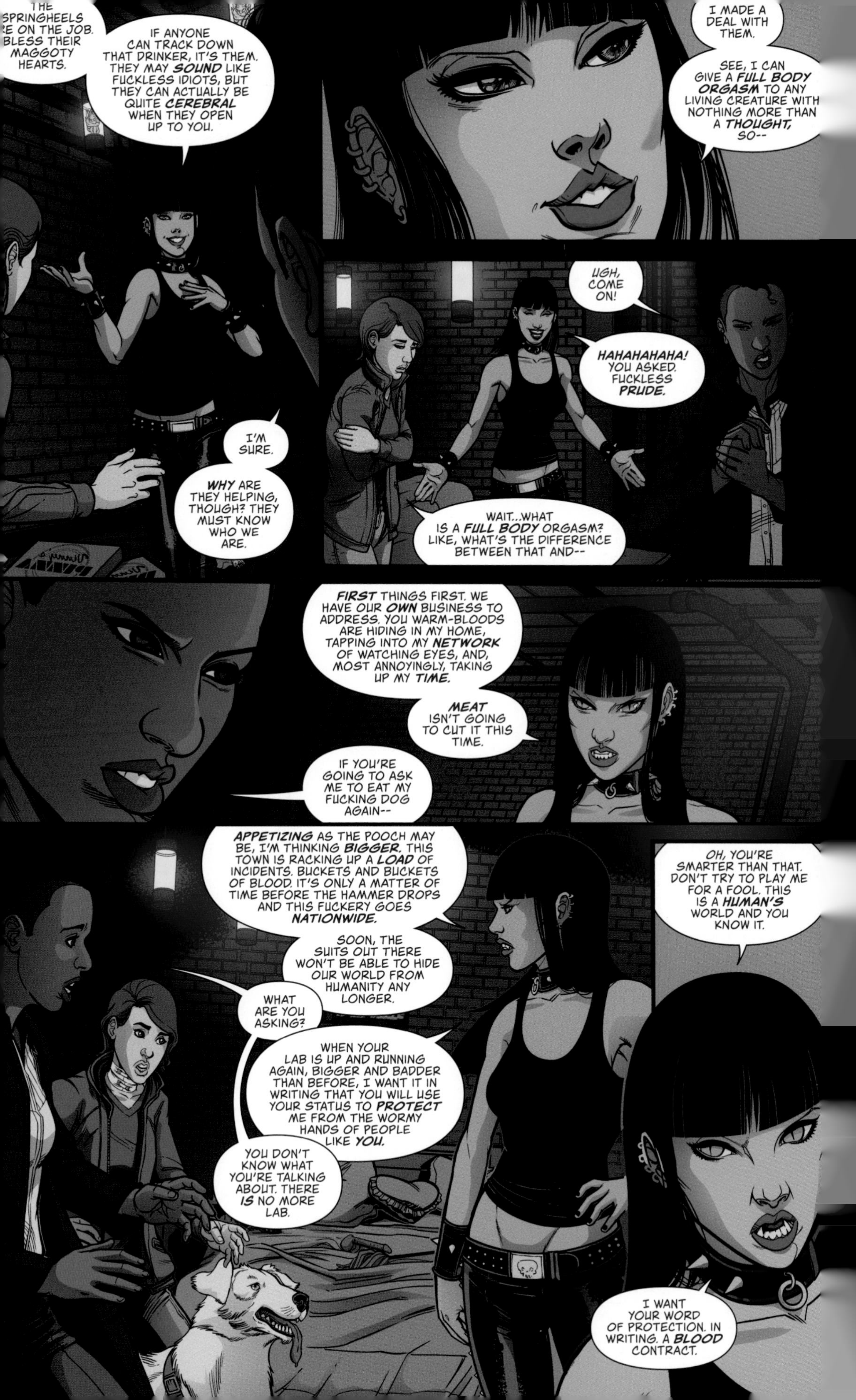
THE SPRINGHEELS E ON THE JOB. BLESS THEIR MAGGOTY HEARTS.
IF ANYONE CAN TRACK DOWN THAT DRINKER, IT'S THEM. THEY MAY SOUND LIKE FUCKLESS IDIOTS, BUT THEY CAN ACTUALLY BE QUITE CEREBRAL WHEN THEY OPEN UP TO YOU.
I'M SURE.
WHY ARE THEY HELPING, THOUGH? THEY MUST KNOW WHO WE ARE.
I MADE A DEAL WITH THEM.
SEE, I CAN GIVE A FULL BODY ORGASM TO ANY LIVING CREATURE WITH NOTHING MORE THAN A THOUGHT, SO--
UGH, COME ON!
HAHAHAHAHA! YOU ASKED. FUCKLESS PRUDE.
WAIT...WHAT IS A FULL BODY ORGASM? LIKE, WHAT'S THE DIFFERENCE BETWEEN THAT AND--
FIRST THINGS FIRST. WE HAVE OUR OWN BUSINESS TO ADDRESS. YOU WARM-BLOODS ARE HIDING IN MY HOME, TAPPING INTO MY NETWORK OF WATCHING EYES, AND, MOST ANNOYINGLY, TAKING UP MY TIME.
MEAT ISN'T GOING TO CUT IT THIS TIME.
IF YOU'RE GOING TO ASK ME TO EAT MY FUCKING DOG AGAIN--
APPETIZING AS THE POOCH MAY BE, I'M THINKING BIGGER. THIS TOWN IS RACKING UP A LOAD OF INCIDENTS. BUCKETS AND BUCKETS OF BLOOD. IT'S ONLY A MATTER OF TIME BEFORE THE HAMMER DROPS AND THIS FUCKERY GOES NATIONWIDE.
SOON, THE SUITS OUT THERE WON'T BE ABLE TO HIDE OUR WORLD FROM HUMANITY ANY LONGER.
WHAT ARE YOU ASKING?
WHEN YOUR LAB IS UP AND RUNNING AGAIN, BIGGER AND BADDER THAN BEFORE, I WANT IT IN WRITING THAT YOU WILL USE YOUR STATUS TO PROTECT ME FROM THE WORMY HANDS OF PEOPLE LIKE YOU.
YOU DON'T KNOW WHAT YOU'RE TALKING ABOUT. THERE IS NO MORE LAB.
OH, YOU'RE SMARTER THAN THAT. DON'T TRY TO PLAY ME FOR A FOOL. THIS IS A HUMAN'S WORLD AND YOU KNOW IT.
I WANT YOUR WORD OF PROTECTION. IN WRITING. A BLOOD CONTRACT.

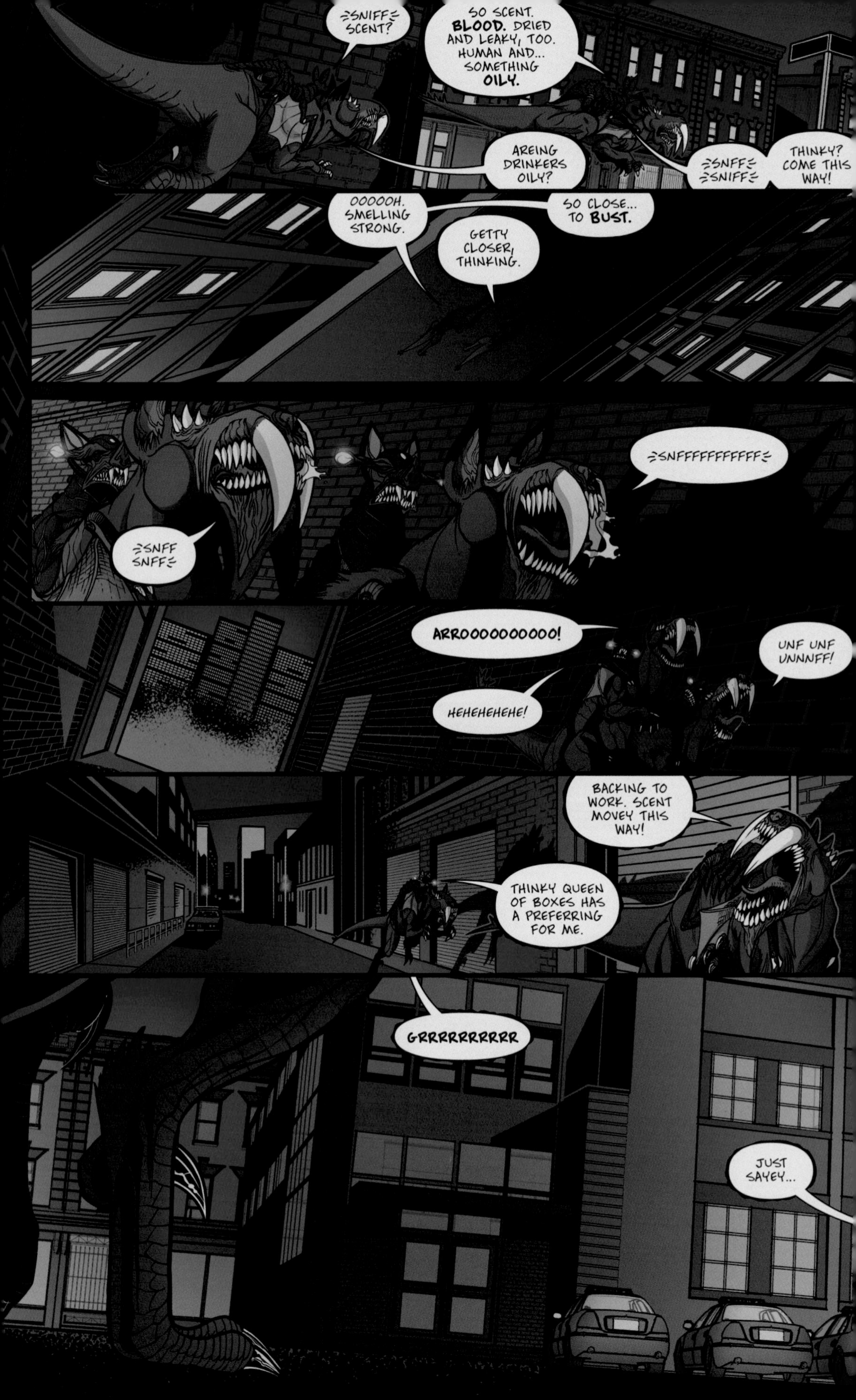

≈SNIFF≈ SCENT?
SO SCENT. BLOOD. DRIED AND LEAKY, TOO. HUMAN AND... SOMETHING OILY.
AREING DRINKERS OILY?
≈SNFF≈ ≈SNIFF≈
THINKY? COME THIS WAY!
OOOOOH. SMELLING STRONG.
SO CLOSE... TO BUST.
GETTY CLOSER, THINKING.
≈SNFFFFFFFFFFF≈
≈SNFF SNFF≈
ARROOOOOOOOOO!
UNF UNF UNNNFF!
HEHEHEHEHE!
BACKING TO WORK. SCENT MOVEY THIS WAY!
THINKY QUEEN OF BOXES HAS A PREFERRING FOR ME.
GRRRRRRRRR
JUST SAYEY...

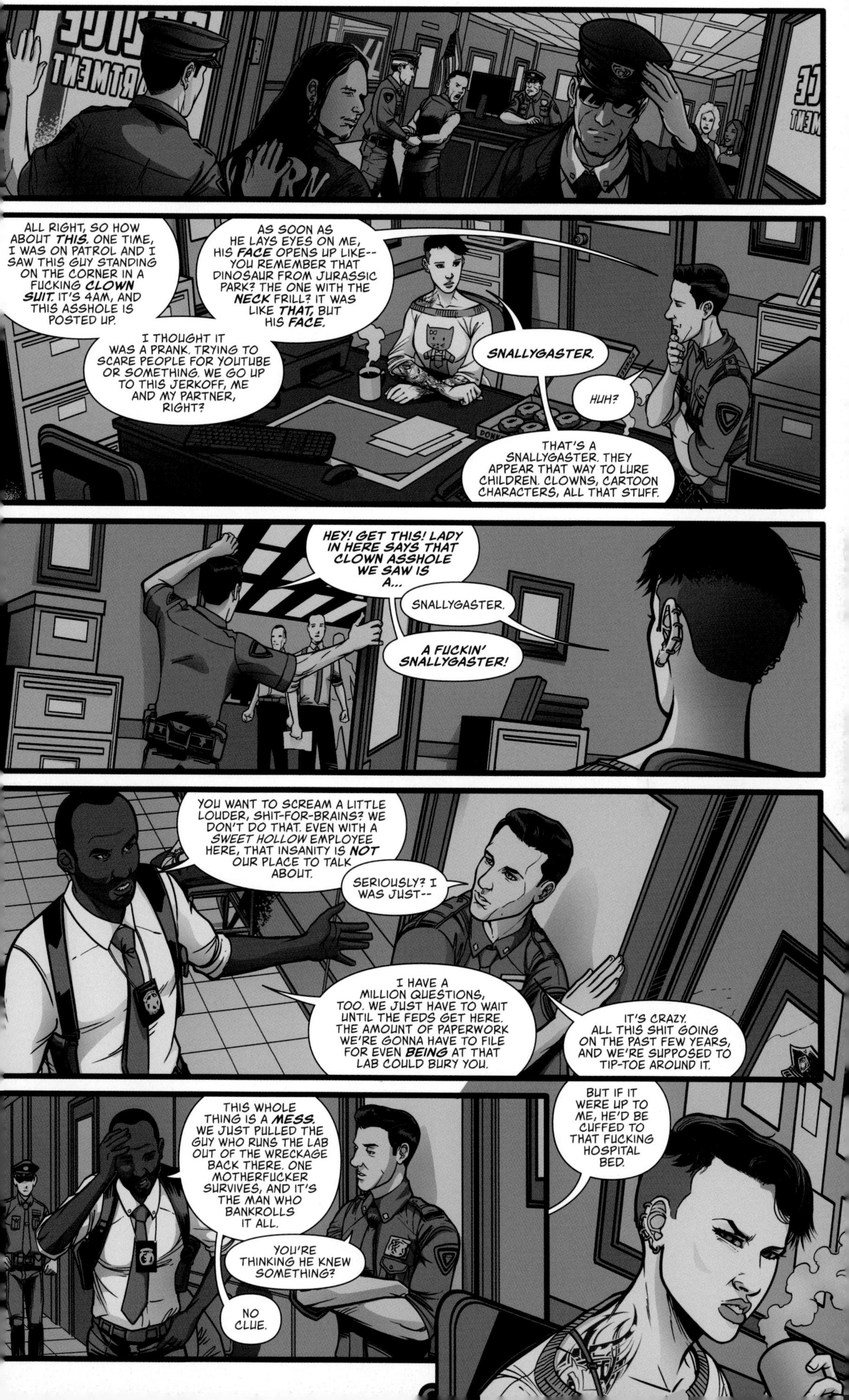

ALL RIGHT, SO HOW ABOUT THIS. ONE TIME, I WAS ON PATROL AND I SAW THIS GUY STANDING ON THE CORNER IN A FUCKING CLOWN SUIT. IT'S 4AM, AND THIS ASSHOLE IS POSTED UP.
I THOUGHT IT WAS A PRANK. TRYING TO SCARE PEOPLE FOR YOUTUBE OR SOMETHING. WE GO UP TO THIS JERKOFF, ME AND MY PARTNER, RIGHT?
AS SOON AS HE LAYS EYES ON ME, HIS FACE OPENS UP LIKE-- YOU REMEMBER THAT DINOSAUR FROM JURASSIC PARK? THE ONE WITH THE NECK FRILL? IT WAS LIKE THAT, BUT HIS FACE.
SNALLYGASTER.
HUH?
THAT'S A SNALLYGASTER. THEY APPEAR THAT WAY TO LURE CHILDREN. CLOWNS, CARTOON CHARACTERS, ALL THAT STUFF.
HEY! GET THIS! LADY IN HERE SAYS THAT CLOWN ASSHOLE WE SAW IS A...
SNALLYGASTER.
A FUCKIN' SNALLYGASTER!
YOU WANT TO SCREAM A LITTLE LOUDER, SHIT-FOR-BRAINS? WE DON'T DO THAT. EVEN WITH A SWEET HOLLOW EMPLOYEE HERE, THAT INSANITY IS NOT OUR PLACE TO TALK ABOUT.
SERIOUSLY? I WAS JUST--
I HAVE A MILLION QUESTIONS, TOO. WE JUST HAVE TO WAIT UNTIL THE FEDS GET HERE. THE AMOUNT OF PAPERWORK WE'RE GONNA HAVE TO FILE FOR EVEN BEING AT THAT LAB COULD BURY YOU.
IT'S CRAZY. ALL THIS SHIT GOING ON THE PAST FEW YEARS, AND WE'RE SUPPOSED TO TIP-TOE AROUND IT.
THIS WHOLE THING IS A MESS. WE JUST PULLED THE GUY WHO RUNS THE LAB OUT OF THE WRECKAGE BACK THERE. ONE MOTHERFUCKER SURVIVES, AND IT'S THE MAN WHO BANKROLLS IT ALL.
YOU'RE THINKING HE KNEW SOMETHING?
NO CLUE.
BUT IF IT WERE UP TO ME, HE'D BE CUFFED TO THAT FUCKING HOSPITAL BED.

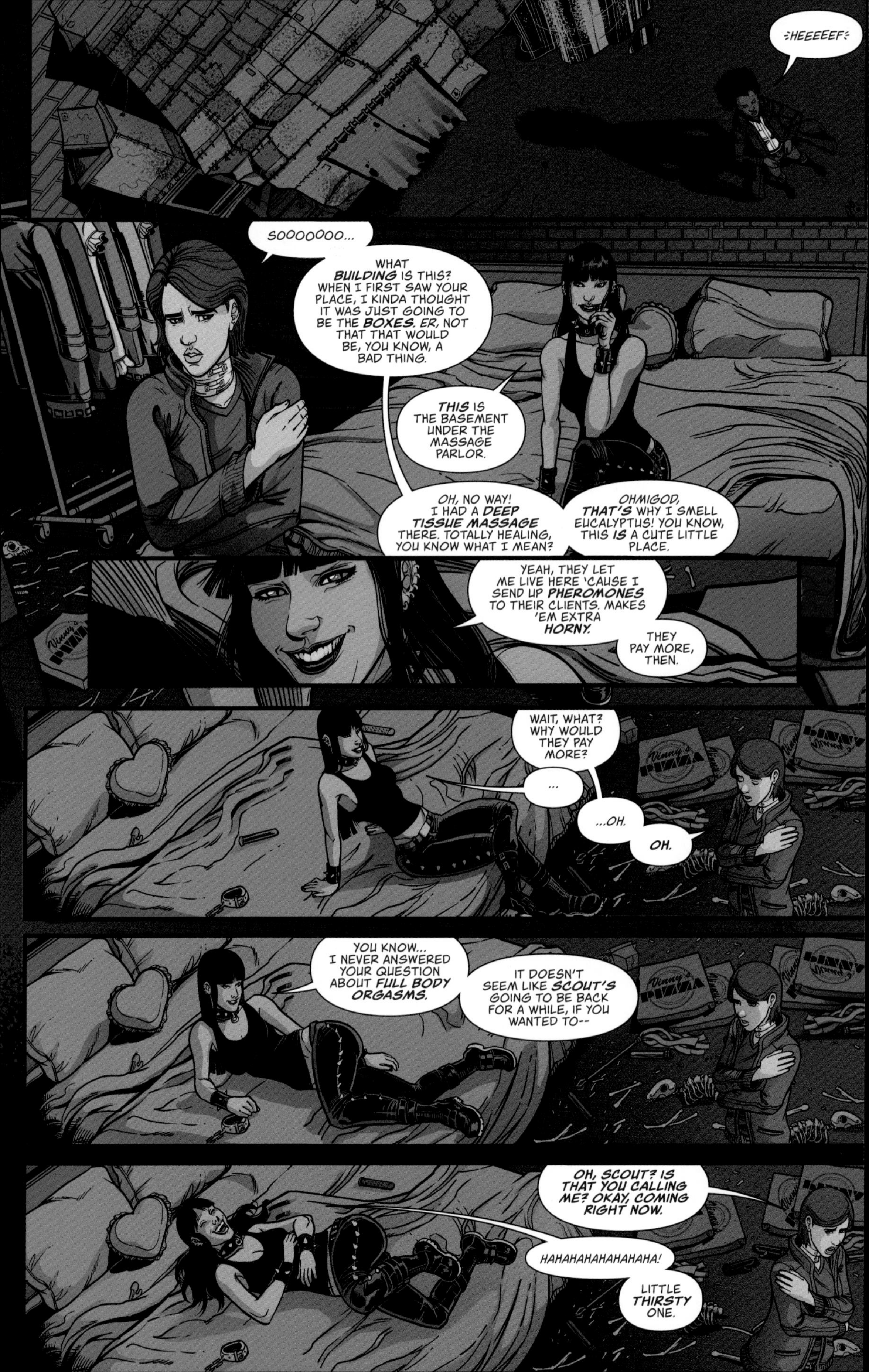

HEEEEEF
SOOOOOOO...
WHAT BUILDING IS THIS? WHEN I FIRST SAW YOUR PLACE, I KINDA THOUGHT IT WAS JUST GOING TO BE THE BOXES. ER, NOT THAT THAT WOULD BE, YOU KNOW, A BAD THING.
THIS IS THE BASEMENT UNDER THE MASSAGE PARLOR.
OH, NO WAY! I HAD A DEEP TISSUE MASSAGE THERE. TOTALLY HEALING, YOU KNOW WHAT I MEAN?
OHMIGOD, THAT'S WHY I SMELL EUCALYPTUS! YOU KNOW, THIS IS A CUTE LITTLE PLACE.
YEAH, THEY LET ME LIVE HERE 'CAUSE I SEND UP PHEROMONES TO THEIR CLIENTS. MAKES 'EM EXTRA HORNY.
THEY PAY MORE, THEN.
WAIT, WHAT? WHY WOULD THEY PAY MORE?
...
...OH.
OH.
YOU KNOW... I NEVER ANSWERED YOUR QUESTION ABOUT FULL BODY ORGASMS.
IT DOESN'T SEEM LIKE SCOUT'S GOING TO BE BACK FOR A WHILE, IF YOU WANTED TO--
OH, SCOUT? IS THAT YOU CALLING ME? OKAY, COMING RIGHT NOW.
HAHAHAHAHAHAHAHA!
LITTLE THIRSTY ONE.

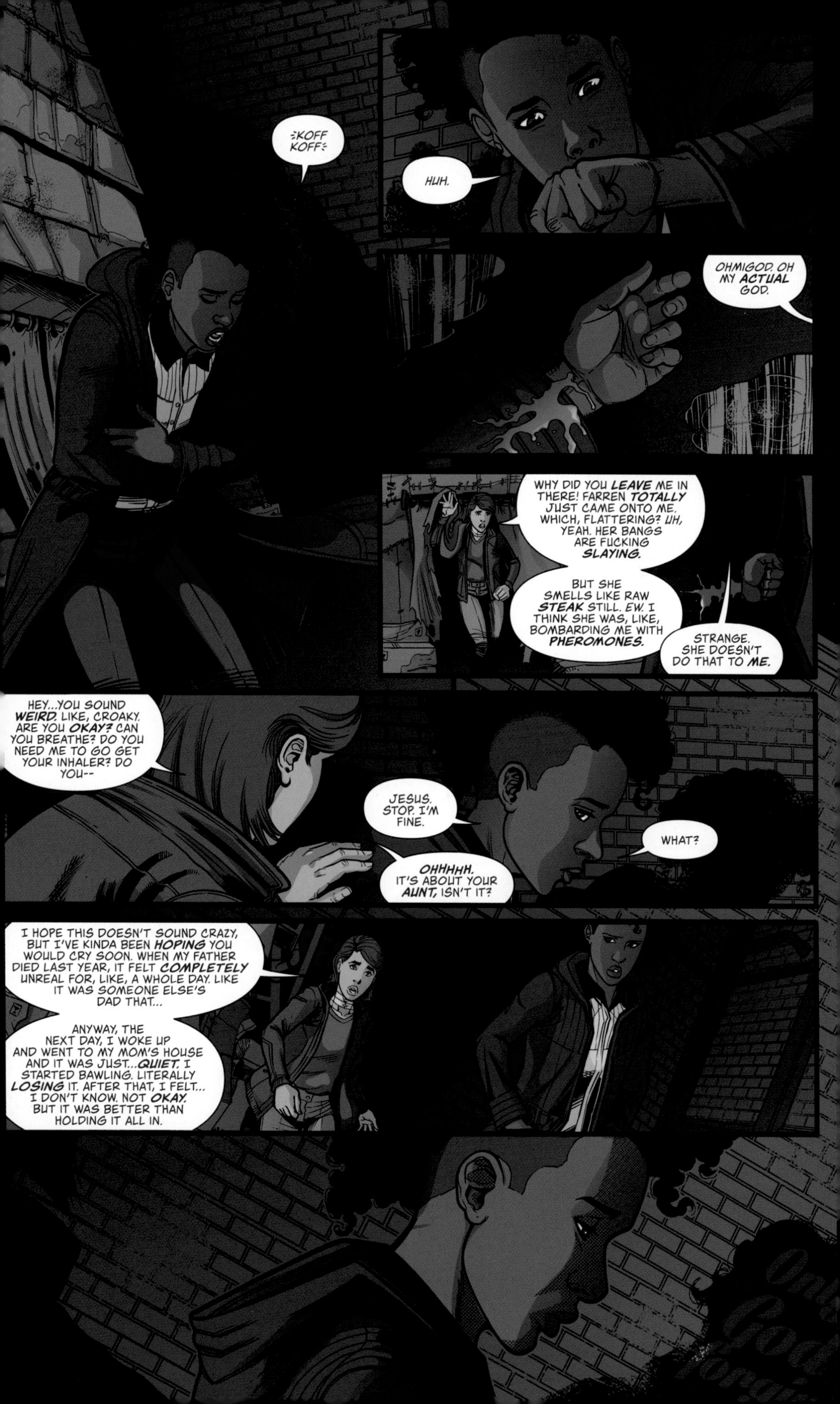

=KOFF KOFF=
HUH.
OHMIGOD. OH MY ACTUAL GOD.
WHY DID YOU LEAVE ME IN THERE! FARREN TOTALLY JUST CAME ONTO ME. WHICH, FLATTERING? UH, YEAH. HER BANGS ARE FUCKING SLAYING.
BUT SHE SMELLS LIKE RAW STEAK STILL. EW. I THINK SHE WAS, LIKE, BOMBARDING ME WITH PHEROMONES.
STRANGE. SHE DOESN'T DO THAT TO ME.
HEY...YOU SOUND WEIRD. LIKE, CROAKY. ARE YOU OKAY? CAN YOU BREATHE? DO YOU NEED ME TO GO GET YOUR INHALER? DO YOU--
JESUS. STOP. I'M FINE.
OHHHHH. IT'S ABOUT YOUR AUNT, ISN'T IT?
WHAT?
I HOPE THIS DOESN'T SOUND CRAZY, BUT I'VE KINDA BEEN HOPING YOU WOULD CRY SOON. WHEN MY FATHER DIED LAST YEAR, IT FELT COMPLETELY UNREAL FOR, LIKE, A WHOLE DAY. LIKE IT WAS SOMEONE ELSE'S DAD THAT...
ANYWAY, THE NEXT DAY, I WOKE UP AND WENT TO MY MOM'S HOUSE AND IT WAS JUST...QUIET. I STARTED BAWLING. LITERALLY LOSING IT. AFTER THAT, I FELT... I DON'T KNOW. NOT OKAY. BUT IT WAS BETTER THAN HOLDING IT ALL IN.

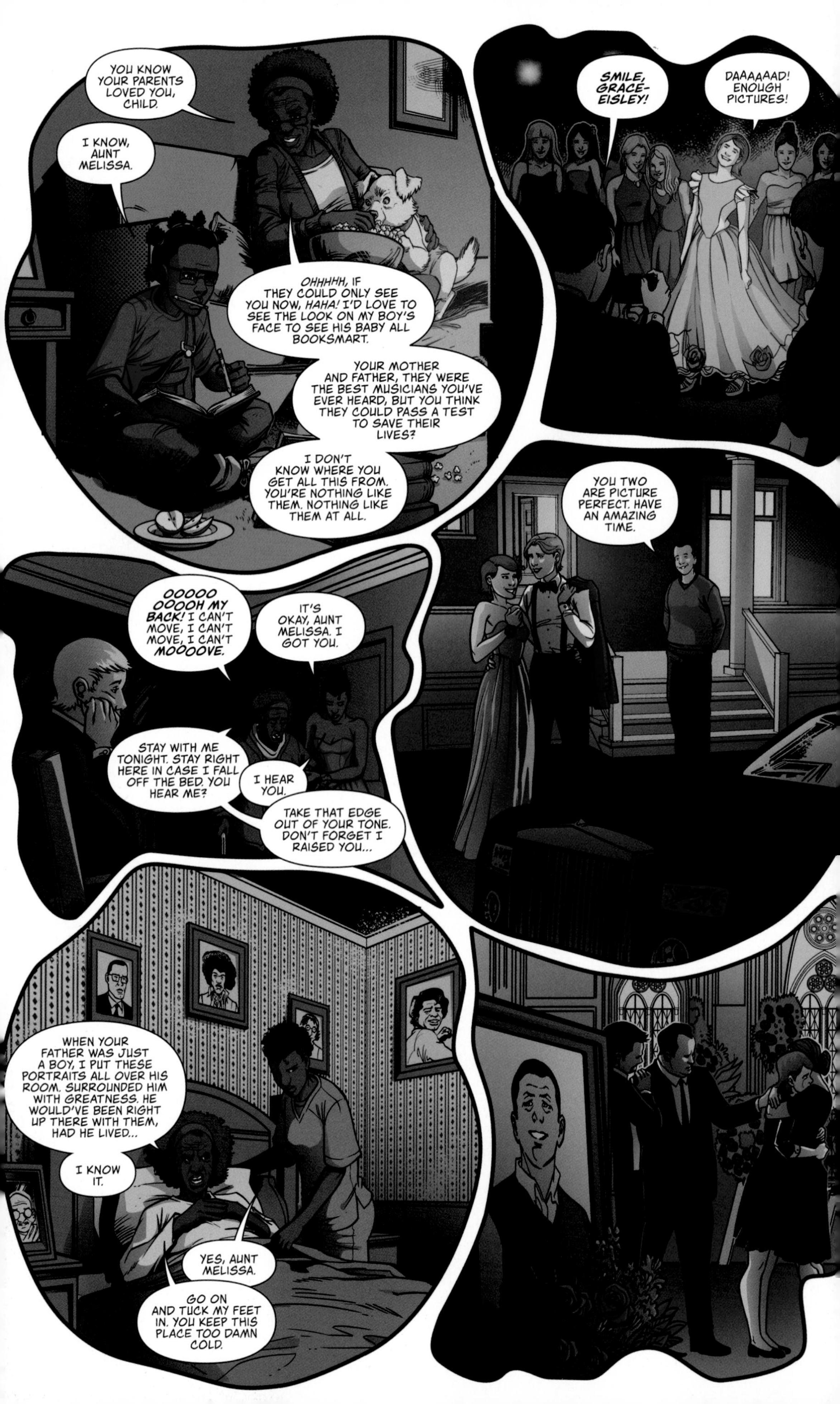

YOU KNOW YOUR PARENTS LOVED YOU, CHILD.
I KNOW, AUNT MELISSA.
OHHHHH, IF THEY COULD ONLY SEE YOU NOW, HAHA! I'D LOVE TO SEE THE LOOK ON MY BOY'S FACE TO SEE HIS BABY ALL BOOKSMART.
YOUR MOTHER AND FATHER, THEY WERE THE BEST MUSICIANS YOU'VE EVER HEARD, BUT YOU THINK THEY COULD PASS A TEST TO SAVE THEIR LIVES?
I DON'T KNOW WHERE YOU GET ALL THIS FROM. YOU'RE NOTHING LIKE THEM. NOTHING LIKE THEM AT ALL.
SMILE, GRACE-EISLEY!
DAAAAAAD! ENOUGH PICTURES!
OOOOO OOOOH MY BACK! I CAN'T MOVE, I CAN'T MOVE, I CAN'T MOOOOVE.
IT'S OKAY, AUNT MELISSA. I GOT YOU.
STAY WITH ME TONIGHT. STAY RIGHT HERE IN CASE I FALL OFF THE BED. YOU HEAR ME?
I HEAR YOU.
TAKE THAT EDGE OUT OF YOUR TONE. DON'T FORGET I RAISED YOU...
YOU TWO ARE PICTURE PERFECT. HAVE AN AMAZING TIME.
WHEN YOUR FATHER WAS JUST A BOY, I PUT THESE PORTRAITS ALL OVER HIS ROOM. SURROUNDED HIM WITH GREATNESS. HE WOULD'VE BEEN RIGHT UP THERE WITH THEM, HAD HE LIVED...
I KNOW IT.
YES, AUNT MELISSA.
GO ON AND TUCK MY FEET IN. YOU KEEP THIS PLACE TOO DAMN COLD.

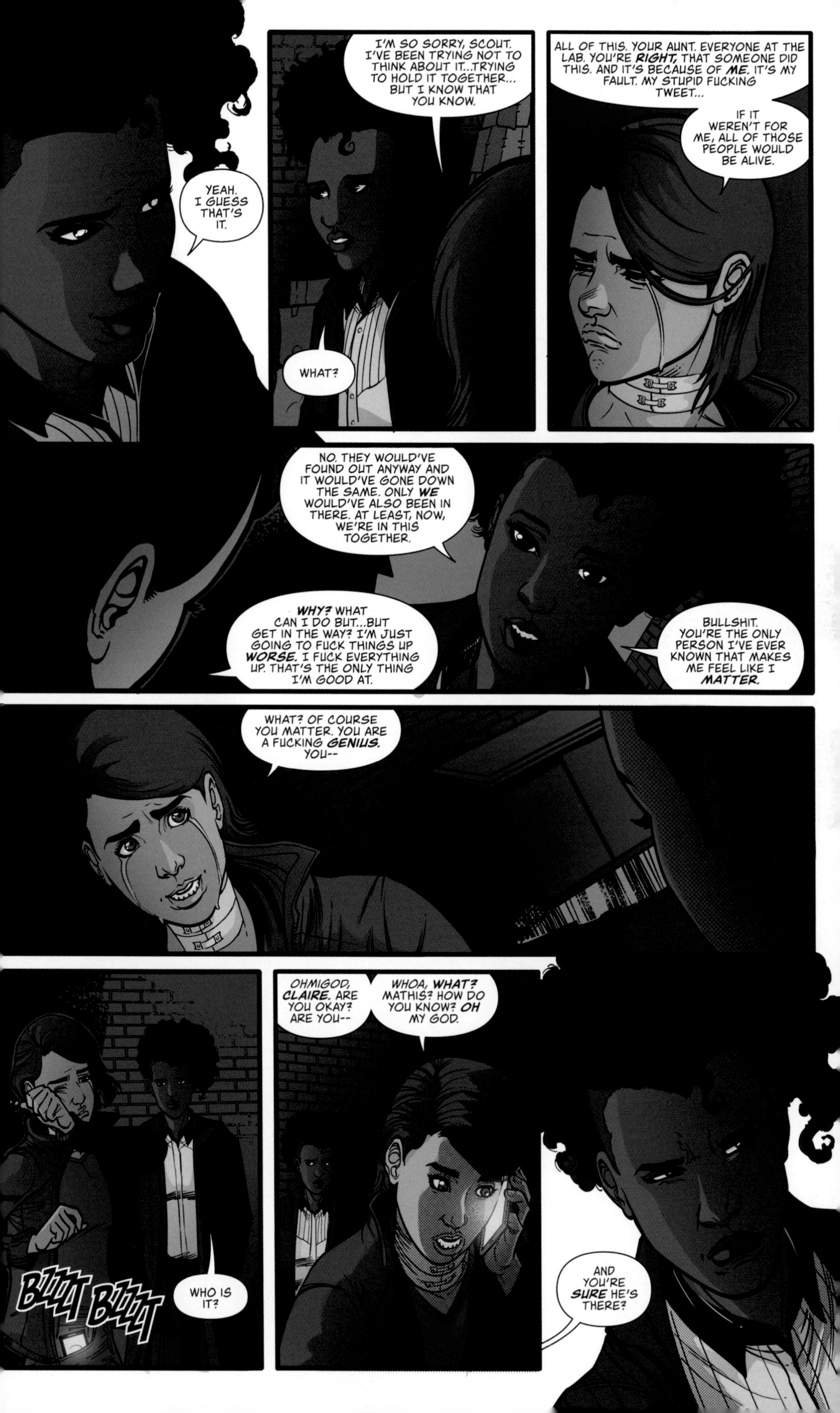
YEAH. I GUESS THAT'S IT.
I'M SO SORRY, SCOUT. I'VE BEEN TRYING NOT TO THINK ABOUT IT...TRYING TO HOLD IT TOGETHER... BUT I KNOW THAT YOU KNOW.
WHAT?
ALL OF THIS. YOUR AUNT. EVERYONE AT THE LAB. YOU'RE RIGHT, THAT SOMEONE DID THIS. AND IT'S BECAUSE OF ME. IT'S MY FAULT. MY STUPID FUCKING TWEET...
IF IT WEREN'T FOR ME, ALL OF THOSE PEOPLE WOULD BE ALIVE.
NO. THEY WOULD'VE FOUND OUT ANYWAY AND IT WOULD'VE GONE DOWN THE SAME. ONLY WE WOULD'VE ALSO BEEN IN THERE. AT LEAST, NOW, WE'RE IN THIS TOGETHER.
WHY? WHAT CAN I DO BUT...BUT GET IN THE WAY? I'M JUST GOING TO FUCK THINGS UP WORSE. I FUCK EVERYTHING UP. THAT'S THE ONLY THING I'M GOOD AT.
BULLSHIT. YOU'RE THE ONLY PERSON I'VE EVER KNOWN THAT MAKES ME FEEL LIKE I MATTER.
WHAT? OF COURSE YOU MATTER. YOU ARE A FUCKING GENIUS. YOU--
BZZT BZZT
WHO IS IT?
OHMIGOD, CLAIRE. ARE YOU OKAY? ARE YOU--
WHOA, WHAT? MATHIS? HOW DO YOU KNOW? OH MY GOD.
AND YOU'RE SURE HE'S THERE?

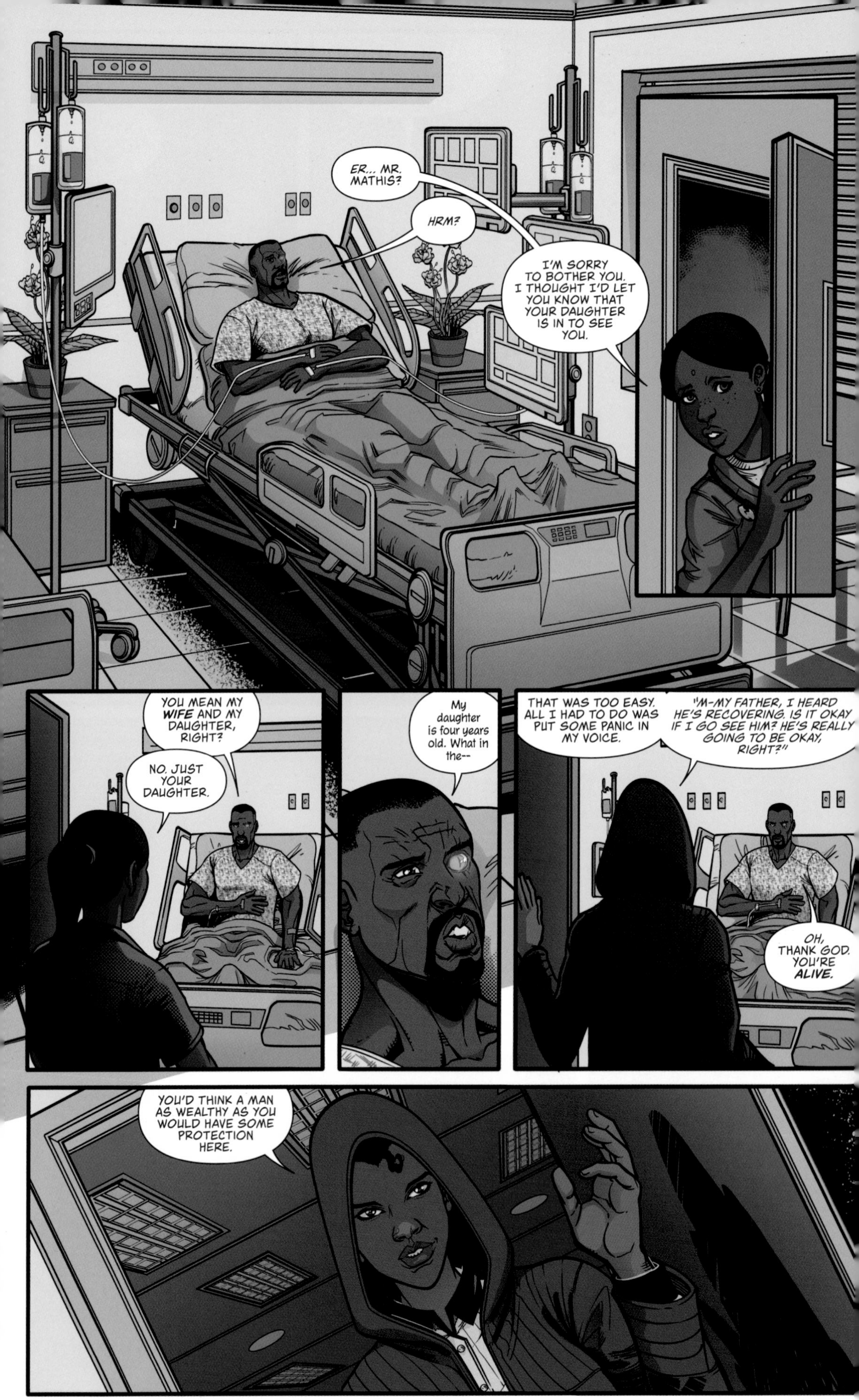
ER... MR. MATHIS?
HRM?
I'M SORRY TO BOTHER YOU. I THOUGHT I'D LET YOU KNOW THAT YOUR DAUGHTER IS IN TO SEE YOU.
YOU MEAN MY WIFE AND MY DAUGHTER, RIGHT?
NO. JUST YOUR DAUGHTER.
My daughter is four years old. What in the--
THAT WAS TOO EASY. ALL I HAD TO DO WAS PUT SOME PANIC IN MY VOICE.
"M-MY FATHER, I HEARD HE'S RECOVERING. IS IT OKAY IF I GO SEE HIM? HE'S REALLY GOING TO BE OKAY, RIGHT?"
OH, THANK GOD. YOU'RE ALIVE.
YOU'D THINK A MAN AS WEALTHY AS YOU WOULD HAVE SOME PROTECTION HERE.

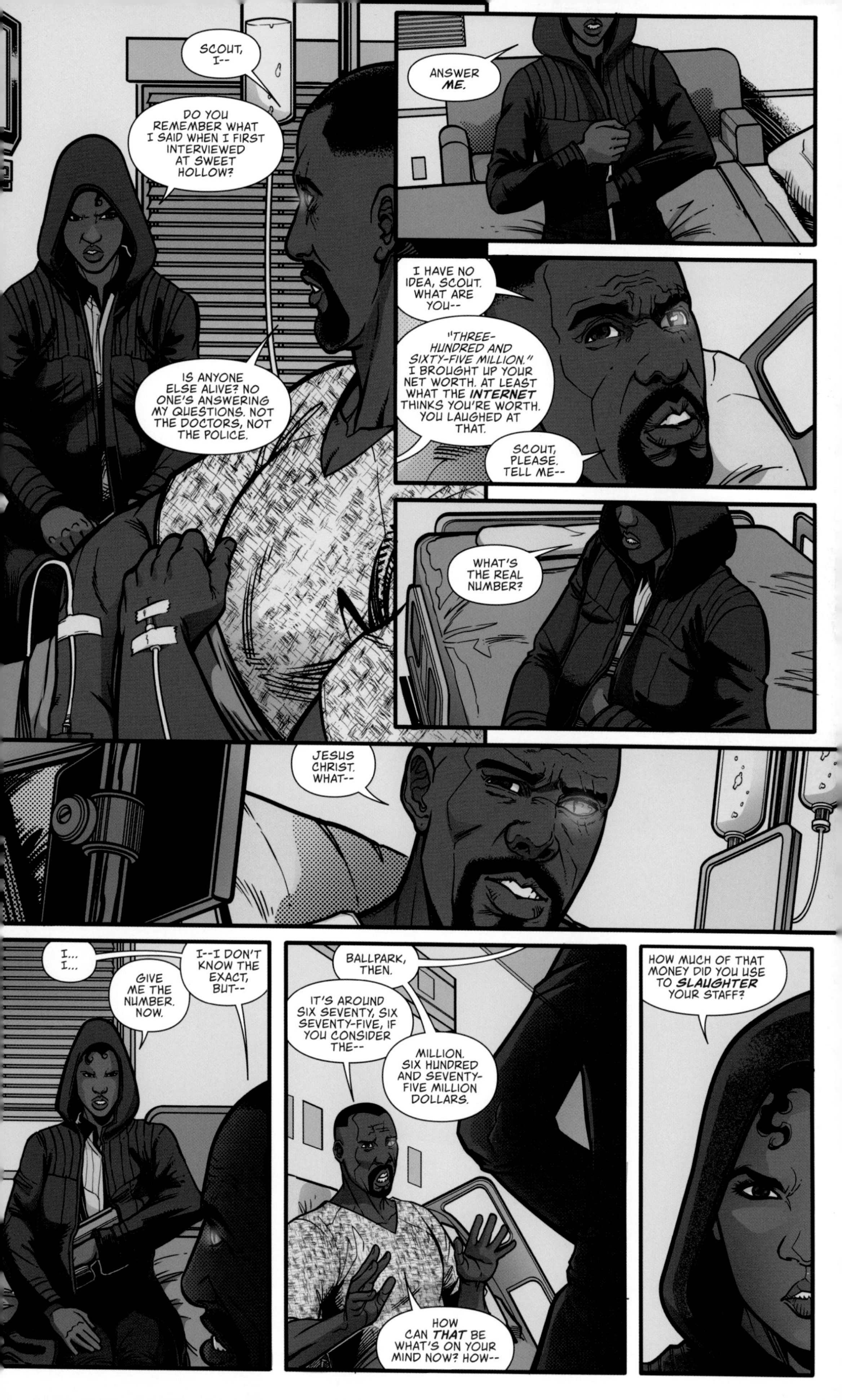
SCOUT, I--
DO YOU REMEMBER WHAT I SAID WHEN I FIRST INTERVIEWED AT SWEET HOLLOW?
IS ANYONE ELSE ALIVE? NO ONE'S ANSWERING MY QUESTIONS. NOT THE DOCTORS, NOT THE POLICE.
ANSWER ME.
I HAVE NO IDEA, SCOUT. WHAT ARE YOU--
"THREE-HUNDRED AND SIXTY-FIVE MILLION." I BROUGHT UP YOUR NET WORTH. AT LEAST WHAT THE INTERNET THINKS YOU'RE WORTH. YOU LAUGHED AT THAT.
SCOUT, PLEASE. TELL ME--
WHAT'S THE REAL NUMBER?
JESUS CHRIST. WHAT--
I... I...
GIVE ME THE NUMBER. NOW.
I--I DON'T KNOW THE EXACT, BUT--
BALLPARK, THEN.
IT'S AROUND SIX SEVENTY, SIX SEVENTY-FIVE, IF YOU CONSIDER THE--
MILLION. SIX HUNDRED AND SEVENTY-FIVE MILLION DOLLARS.
HOW CAN THAT BE WHAT'S ON YOUR MIND NOW? HOW--
HOW MUCH OF THAT MONEY DID YOU USE TO SLAUGHTER YOUR STAFF?

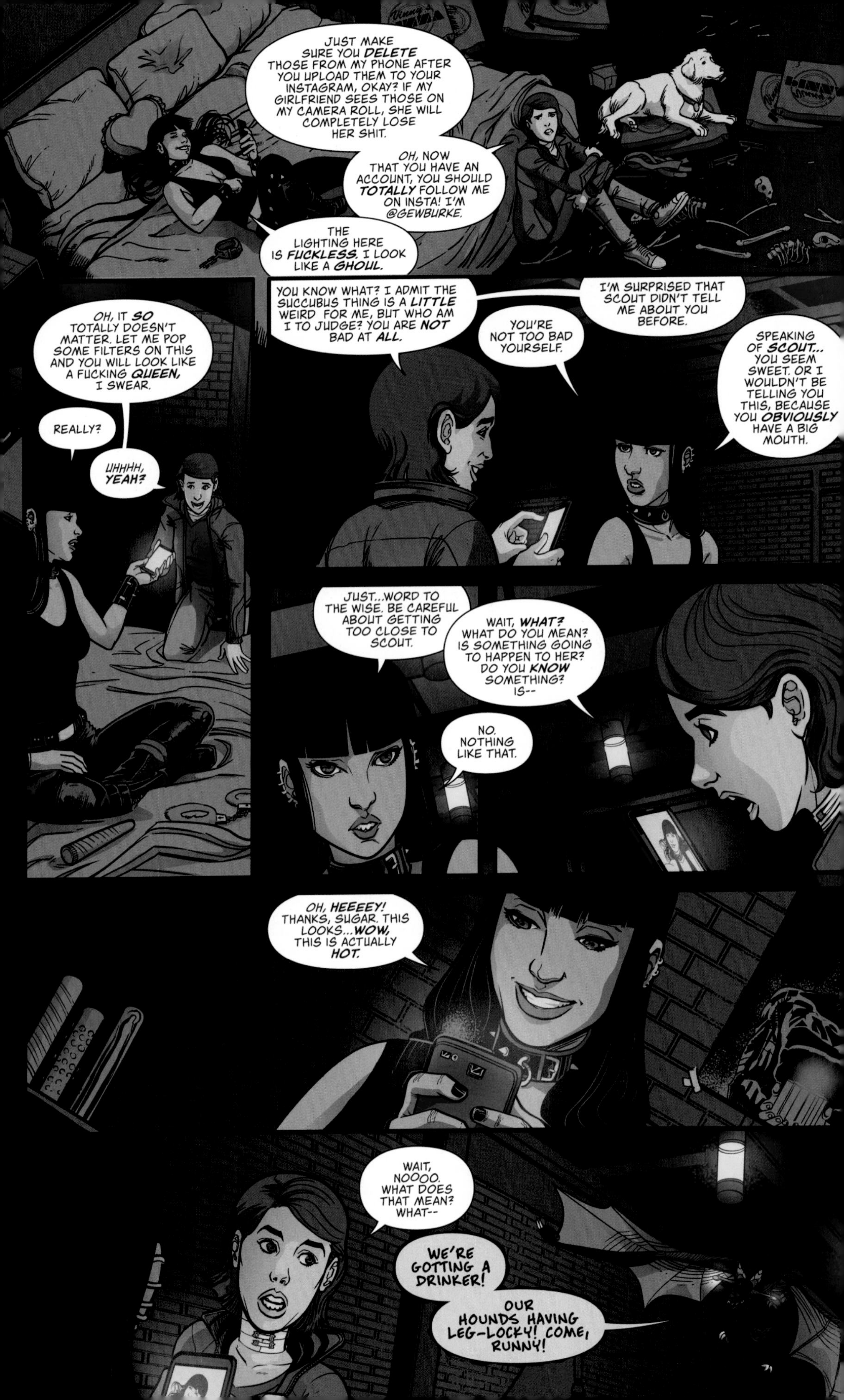
JUST MAKE SURE YOU DELETE THOSE FROM MY PHONE AFTER YOU UPLOAD THEM TO YOUR INSTAGRAM, OKAY? IF MY GIRLFRIEND SEES THOSE ON MY CAMERA ROLL, SHE WILL COMPLETELY LOSE HER SHIT.
OH, NOW THAT YOU HAVE AN ACCOUNT, YOU SHOULD TOTALLY FOLLOW ME ON INSTA! I'M @GEWBURKE.
THE LIGHTING HERE IS FUCKLESS. I LOOK LIKE A GHOUL.
OH, IT SO TOTALLY DOESN'T MATTER. LET ME POP SOME FILTERS ON THIS AND YOU WILL LOOK LIKE A FUCKING QUEEN, I SWEAR.
REALLY?
UHHHH, YEAH?
YOU KNOW WHAT? I ADMIT THE SUCCUBUS THING IS A LITTLE WEIRD FOR ME, BUT WHO AM I TO JUDGE? YOU ARE NOT BAD AT ALL.
I'M SURPRISED THAT SCOUT DIDN'T TELL ME ABOUT YOU BEFORE.
YOU'RE NOT TOO BAD YOURSELF.
SPEAKING OF SCOUT... YOU SEEM SWEET. OR I WOULDN'T BE TELLING YOU THIS, BECAUSE YOU OBVIOUSLY HAVE A BIG MOUTH.
JUST...WORD TO THE WISE. BE CAREFUL ABOUT GETTING TOO CLOSE TO SCOUT.
WAIT, WHAT? WHAT DO YOU MEAN? IS SOMETHING GOING TO HAPPEN TO HER? DO YOU KNOW SOMETHING? IS--
NO. NOTHING LIKE THAT.
OH, HEEEEY! THANKS, SUGAR. THIS LOOKS...WOW, THIS IS ACTUALLY HOT.
WAIT, NOOOO. WHAT DOES THAT MEAN? WHAT--
WE'RE GOTTING A DRINKER!
OUR HOUNDS HAVING LEG-LOCKY! COME, RUNNY!

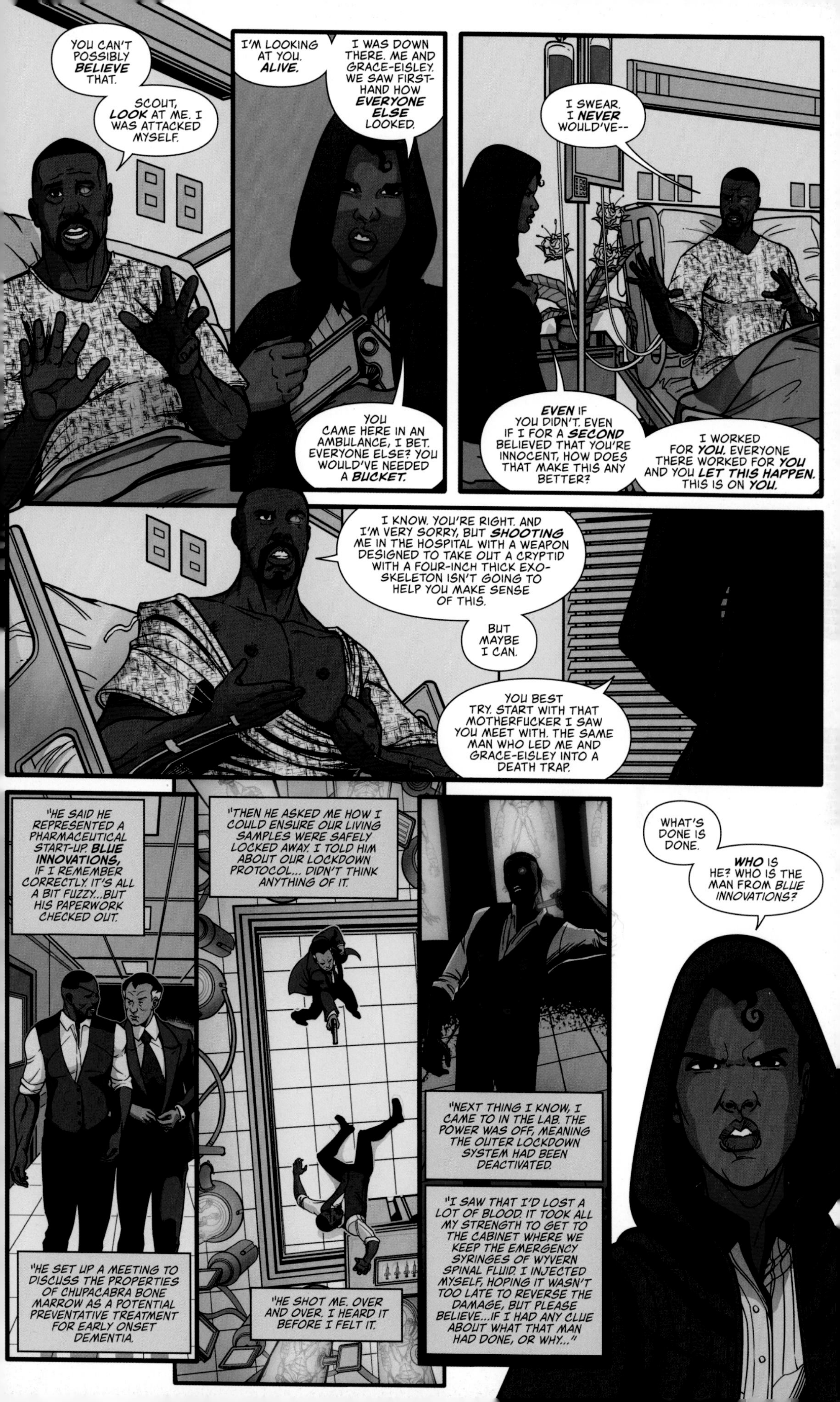

YOU CAN'T POSSIBLY **BELIEVE** THAT.
SCOUT, **LOOK** AT ME. I WAS ATTACKED MYSELF.
I'M LOOKING AT YOU. **ALIVE.**
I WAS DOWN THERE. ME AND GRACE-EISLEY. WE SAW FIRST-HAND HOW **EVERYONE ELSE** LOOKED.
YOU CAME HERE IN AN AMBULANCE, I BET. EVERYONE ELSE? YOU WOULD'VE NEEDED A **BUCKET.**
I SWEAR. I **NEVER** WOULD'VE--
EVEN IF YOU DIDN'T. EVEN IF I FOR A **SECOND** BELIEVED THAT YOU'RE INNOCENT, HOW DOES THAT MAKE THIS ANY BETTER?
I WORKED FOR **YOU.** EVERYONE THERE WORKED FOR **YOU** AND YOU **LET THIS HAPPEN.** THIS IS ON **YOU.**
I KNOW. YOU'RE RIGHT. AND I'M VERY SORRY, BUT **SHOOTING** ME IN THE HOSPITAL WITH A WEAPON DESIGNED TO TAKE OUT A CRYPTID WITH A FOUR-INCH THICK EXO-SKELETON ISN'T GOING TO HELP YOU MAKE SENSE OF THIS.
BUT MAYBE I CAN.
YOU BEST TRY. START WITH THAT MOTHERFUCKER I SAW YOU MEET WITH. THE SAME MAN WHO LED ME AND GRACE-EISLEY INTO A DEATH TRAP.
"HE SAID HE REPRESENTED A PHARMACEUTICAL START-UP. **BLUE INNOVATIONS,** IF I REMEMBER CORRECTLY. IT'S ALL A BIT FUZZY...BUT HIS PAPERWORK CHECKED OUT.
"HE SET UP A MEETING TO DISCUSS THE PROPERTIES OF CHUPACABRA BONE MARROW AS A POTENTIAL PREVENTATIVE TREATMENT FOR EARLY ONSET DEMENTIA.
"THEN HE ASKED ME HOW I COULD ENSURE OUR LIVING SAMPLES WERE SAFELY LOCKED AWAY. I TOLD HIM ABOUT OUR LOCKDOWN PROTOCOL... DIDN'T THINK ANYTHING OF IT.
"HE SHOT ME. OVER AND OVER. I HEARD IT BEFORE I FELT IT.
"NEXT THING I KNOW, I CAME TO IN THE LAB. THE POWER WAS OFF, MEANING THE OUTER LOCKDOWN SYSTEM HAD BEEN DEACTIVATED.
"I SAW THAT I'D LOST A LOT OF BLOOD. IT TOOK ALL MY STRENGTH TO GET TO THE CABINET WHERE WE KEEP THE EMERGENCY SYRINGES OF WYVERN SPINAL FLUID. I INJECTED MYSELF, HOPING IT WASN'T TOO LATE TO REVERSE THE DAMAGE, BUT PLEASE BELIEVE...IF I HAD ANY CLUE ABOUT WHAT THAT MAN HAD DONE, OR WHY..."
WHAT'S DONE IS DONE.
WHO IS HE? WHO IS THE MAN FROM *BLUE INNOVATIONS?*

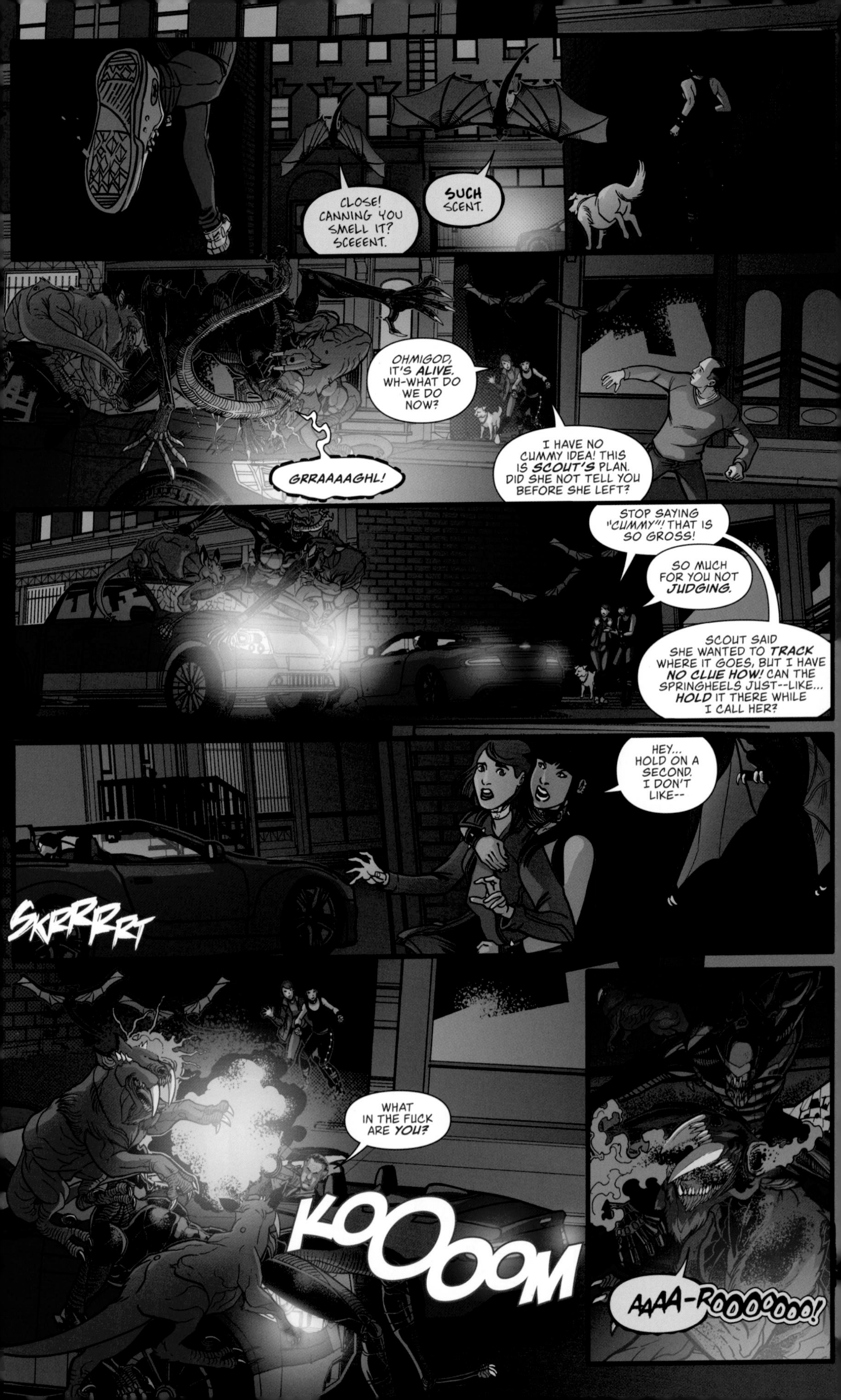
CLOSE! CANNING YOU SMELL IT? SCEEENT.
SUCH SCENT.
OHMIGOD, IT'S ALIVE. WH-WHAT DO WE DO NOW?
GRRAAAAGHL!
I HAVE NO CUMMY IDEA! THIS IS SCOUT'S PLAN. DID SHE NOT TELL YOU BEFORE SHE LEFT?
STOP SAYING "CUMMY"! THAT IS SO GROSS!
SO MUCH FOR YOU NOT JUDGING.
SCOUT SAID SHE WANTED TO TRACK WHERE IT GOES, BUT I HAVE NO CLUE HOW! CAN THE SPRINGHEELS JUST--LIKE... HOLD IT THERE WHILE I CALL HER?
HEY... HOLD ON A SECOND. I DON'T LIKE--
SKRRRRT
WHAT IN THE FUCK ARE YOU?
KOOOOM
AAAA-ROOOOOOOO!

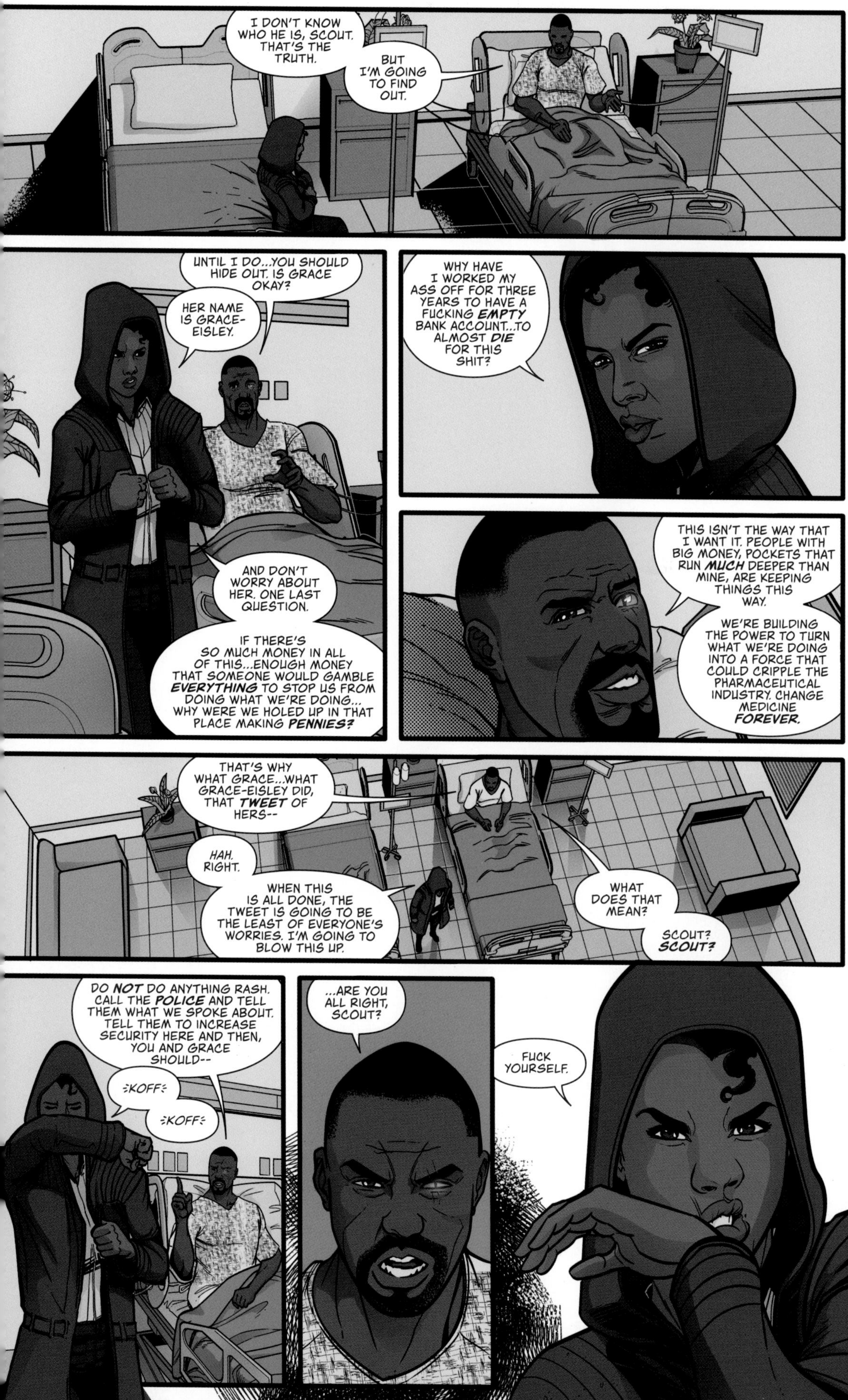
I DON'T KNOW WHO HE IS, SCOUT. THAT'S THE TRUTH.
BUT I'M GOING TO FIND OUT.
UNTIL I DO...YOU SHOULD HIDE OUT. IS GRACE OKAY?
HER NAME IS GRACE-EISLEY.
AND DON'T WORRY ABOUT HER. ONE LAST QUESTION.
IF THERE'S SO MUCH MONEY IN ALL OF THIS...ENOUGH MONEY THAT SOMEONE WOULD GAMBLE EVERYTHING TO STOP US FROM DOING WHAT WE'RE DOING... WHY WERE WE HOLED UP IN THAT PLACE MAKING PENNIES?
WHY HAVE I WORKED MY ASS OFF FOR THREE YEARS TO HAVE A FUCKING EMPTY BANK ACCOUNT...TO ALMOST DIE FOR THIS SHIT?
THIS ISN'T THE WAY THAT I WANT IT. PEOPLE WITH BIG MONEY, POCKETS THAT RUN MUCH DEEPER THAN MINE, ARE KEEPING THINGS THIS WAY.
WE'RE BUILDING THE POWER TO TURN WHAT WE'RE DOING INTO A FORCE THAT COULD CRIPPLE THE PHARMACEUTICAL INDUSTRY. CHANGE MEDICINE FOREVER.
THAT'S WHY WHAT GRACE...WHAT GRACE-EISLEY DID, THAT TWEET OF HERS--
HAH. RIGHT.
WHEN THIS IS ALL DONE, THE TWEET IS GOING TO BE THE LEAST OF EVERYONE'S WORRIES. I'M GOING TO BLOW THIS UP.
WHAT DOES THAT MEAN?
SCOUT? SCOUT?
DO NOT DO ANYTHING RASH. CALL THE POLICE AND TELL THEM WHAT WE SPOKE ABOUT. TELL THEM TO INCREASE SECURITY HERE AND THEN, YOU AND GRACE SHOULD--
KOFF
KOFF
...ARE YOU ALL RIGHT, SCOUT?
FUCK YOURSELF.

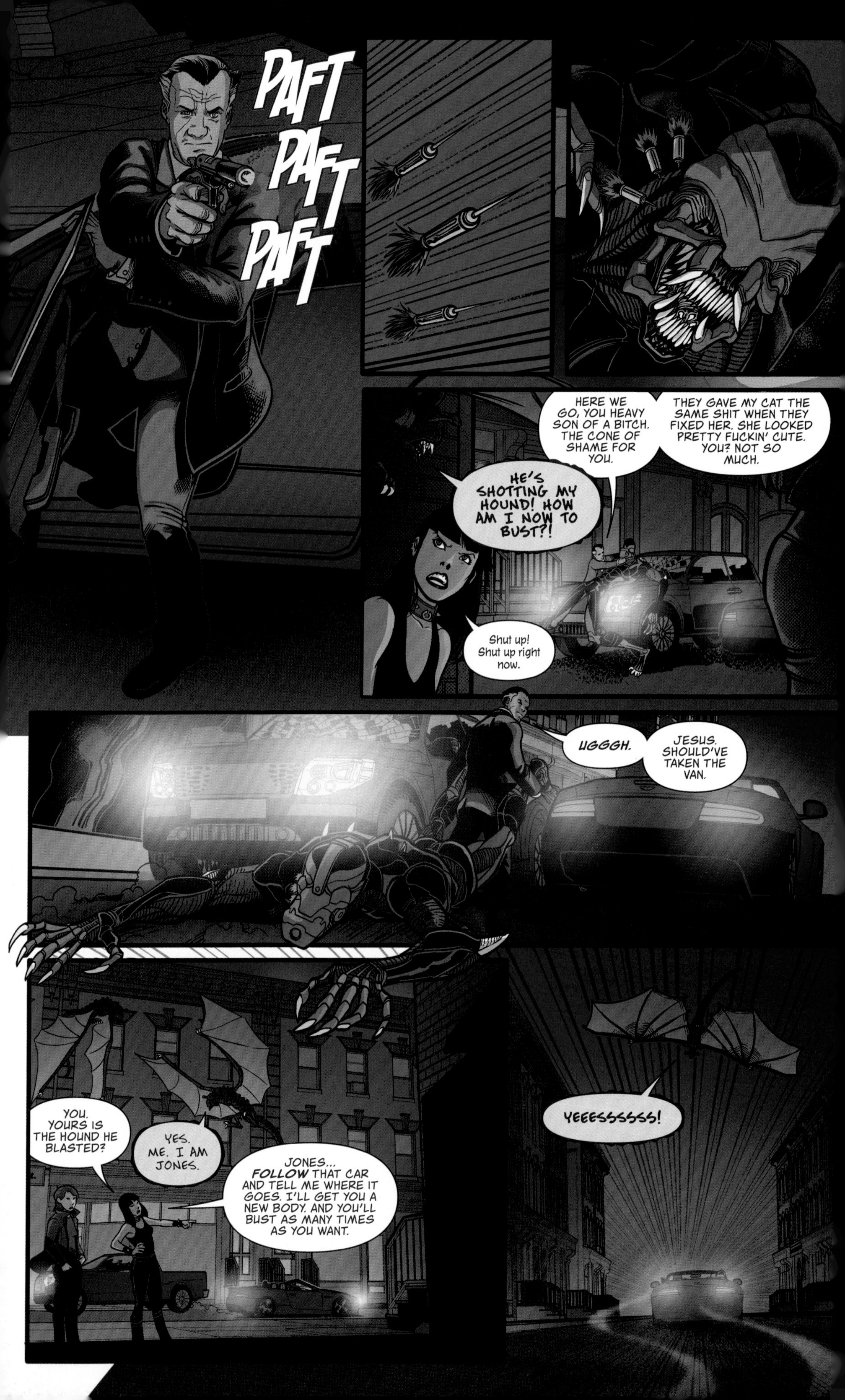
PAFT PAFT PAFT
HE'S SHOTTING MY HOUND! HOW AM I NOW TO BUST?!
HERE WE GO, YOU HEAVY SON OF A BITCH. THE CONE OF SHAME FOR YOU.
THEY GAVE MY CAT THE SAME SHIT WHEN THEY FIXED HER. SHE LOOKED PRETTY FUCKIN' CUTE. YOU? NOT SO MUCH.
Shut up! Shut up right now.
UGGGH.
JESUS. SHOULD'VE TAKEN THE VAN.
YOU. YOURS IS THE HOUND HE BLASTED?
YES. ME. I AM JONES.
JONES... FOLLOW THAT CAR AND TELL ME WHERE IT GOES. I'LL GET YOU A NEW BODY. AND YOU'LL BUST AS MANY TIMES AS YOU WANT.
YEEESSSSSSS!

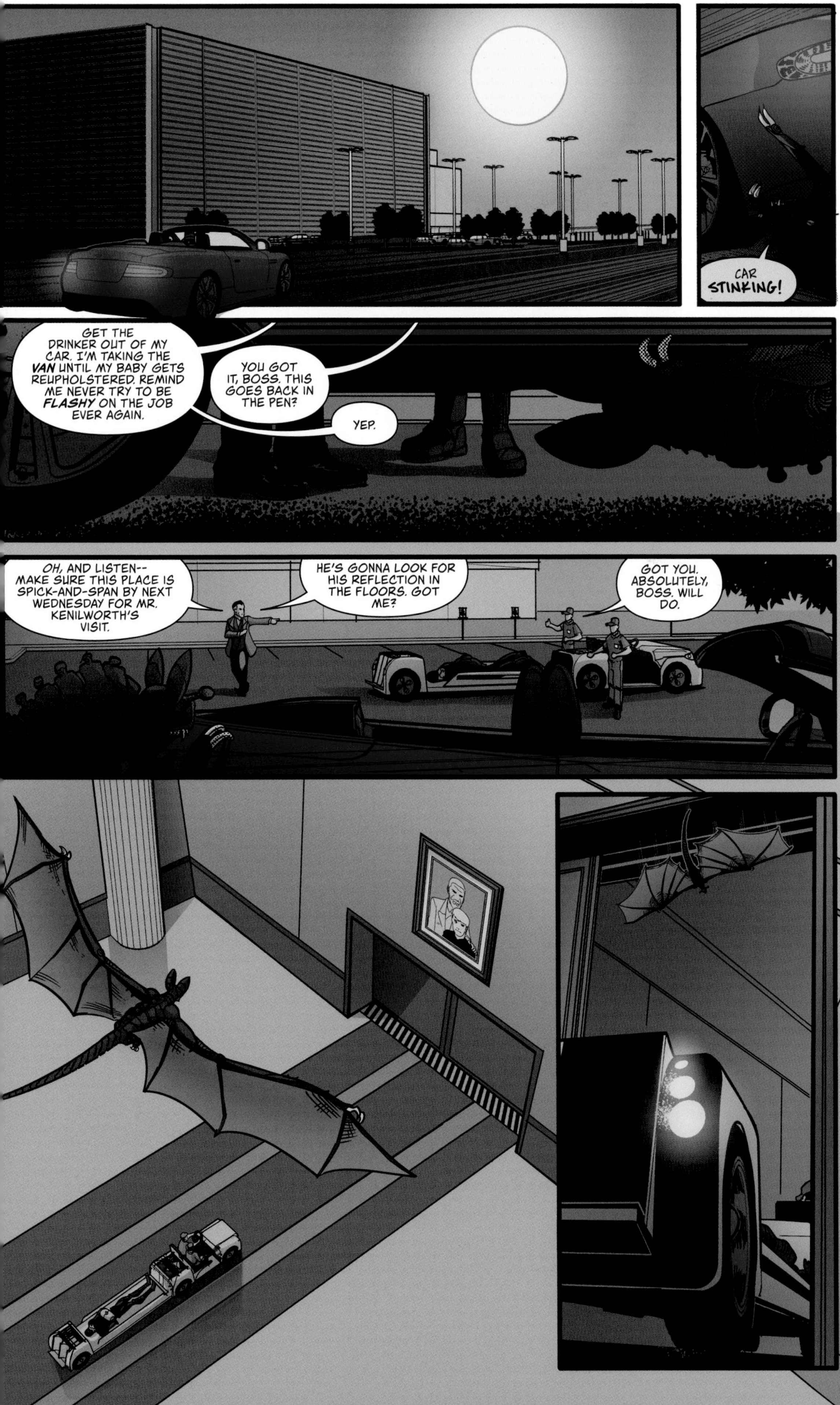
CAR STINKING!
GET THE DRINKER OUT OF MY CAR. I'M TAKING THE VAN UNTIL MY BABY GETS REUPHOLSTERED. REMIND ME NEVER TRY TO BE FLASHY ON THE JOB EVER AGAIN.
YOU GOT IT, BOSS. THIS GOES BACK IN THE PEN?
YEP.
OH, AND LISTEN-- MAKE SURE THIS PLACE IS SPICK-AND-SPAN BY NEXT WEDNESDAY FOR MR. KENILWORTH'S VISIT.
HE'S GONNA LOOK FOR HIS REFLECTION IN THE FLOORS. GOT ME?
GOT YOU. ABSOLUTELY, BOSS. WILL DO.

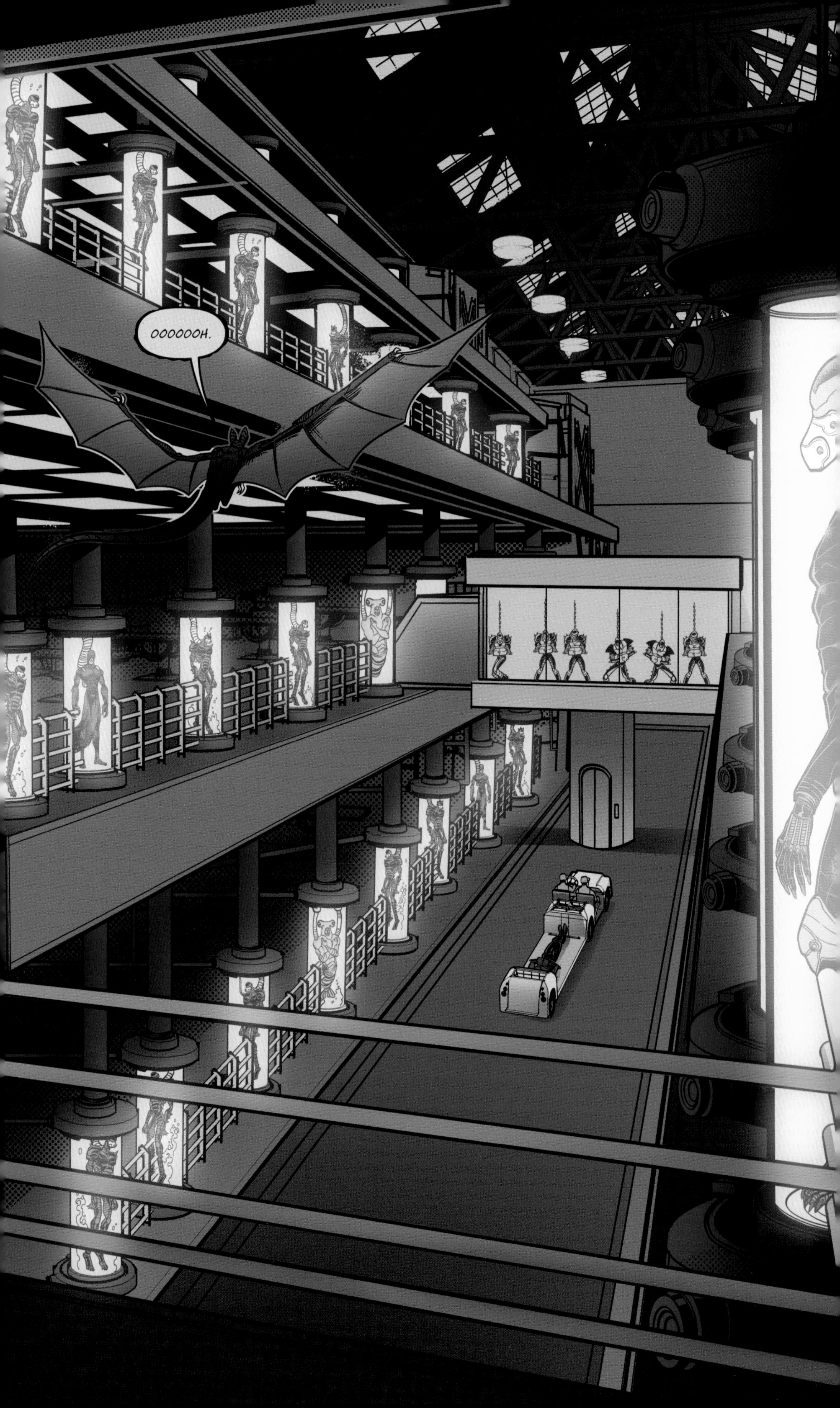
OOOOOOH.

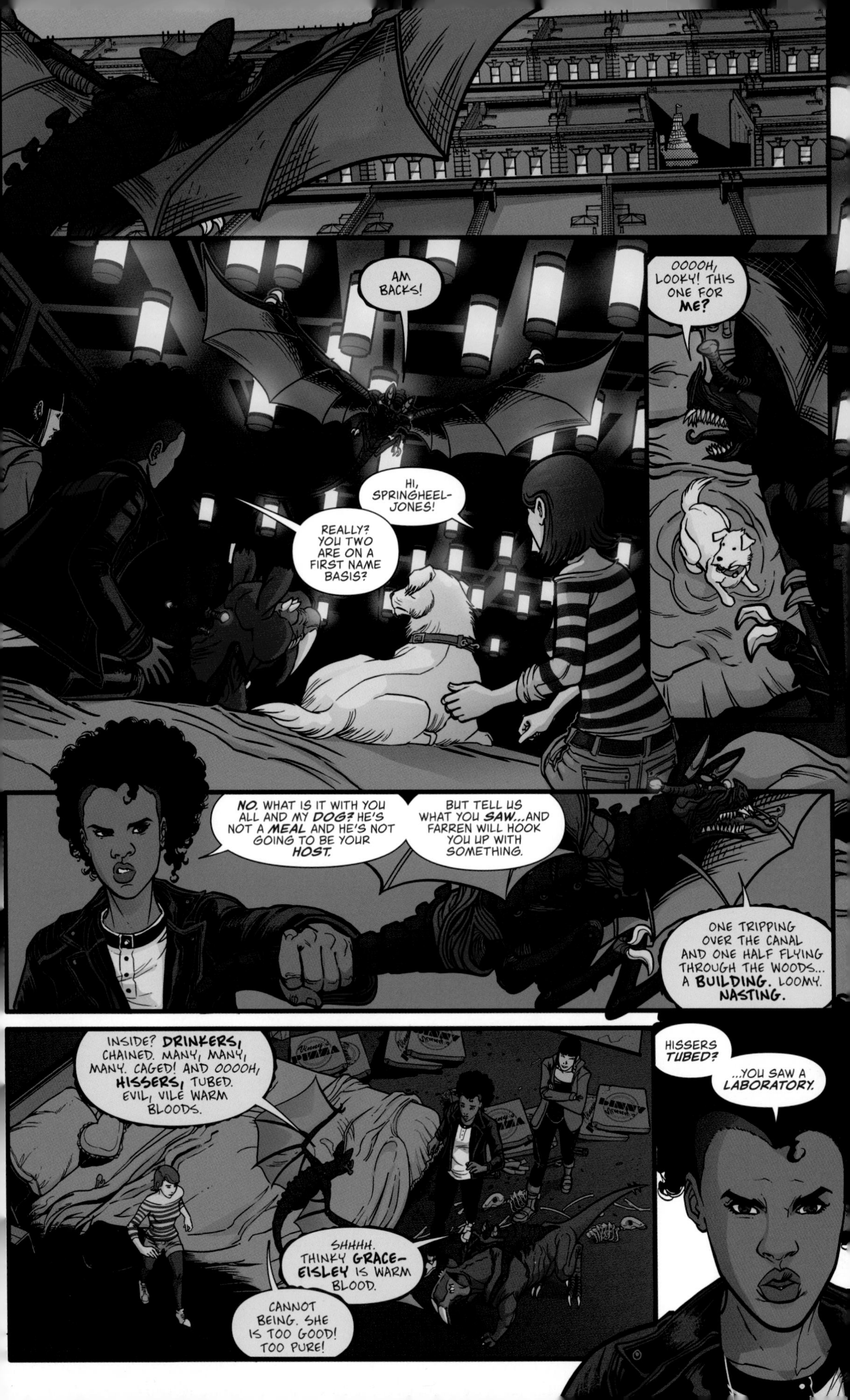
AM BACKS!
OOOOH, LOOKY! THIS ONE FOR **ME?**
HI, SPRINGHEEL-JONES!
REALLY? YOU TWO ARE ON A FIRST NAME BASIS?
NO. WHAT IS IT WITH YOU ALL AND MY ***DOG?*** HE'S NOT A ***MEAL*** AND HE'S NOT GOING TO BE YOUR ***HOST.***
BUT TELL US WHAT YOU ***SAW...*** AND FARREN WILL HOOK YOU UP WITH SOMETHING.
ONE TRIPPING OVER THE CANAL AND ONE HALF FLYING THROUGH THE WOODS... A **BUILDING.** LOOMY. **NASTING.**
INSIDE? **DRINKERS,** CHAINED. MANY, MANY, MANY. CAGED! AND OOOOH, **HISSERS,** TUBED. EVIL, VILE WARM BLOODS.
SHHHH. THINKY **GRACE-EISLEY** IS WARM BLOOD.
CANNOT BEING. SHE IS TOO GOOD! TOO PURE!
HISSERS ***TUBED?***
...YOU SAW A ***LABORATORY.***

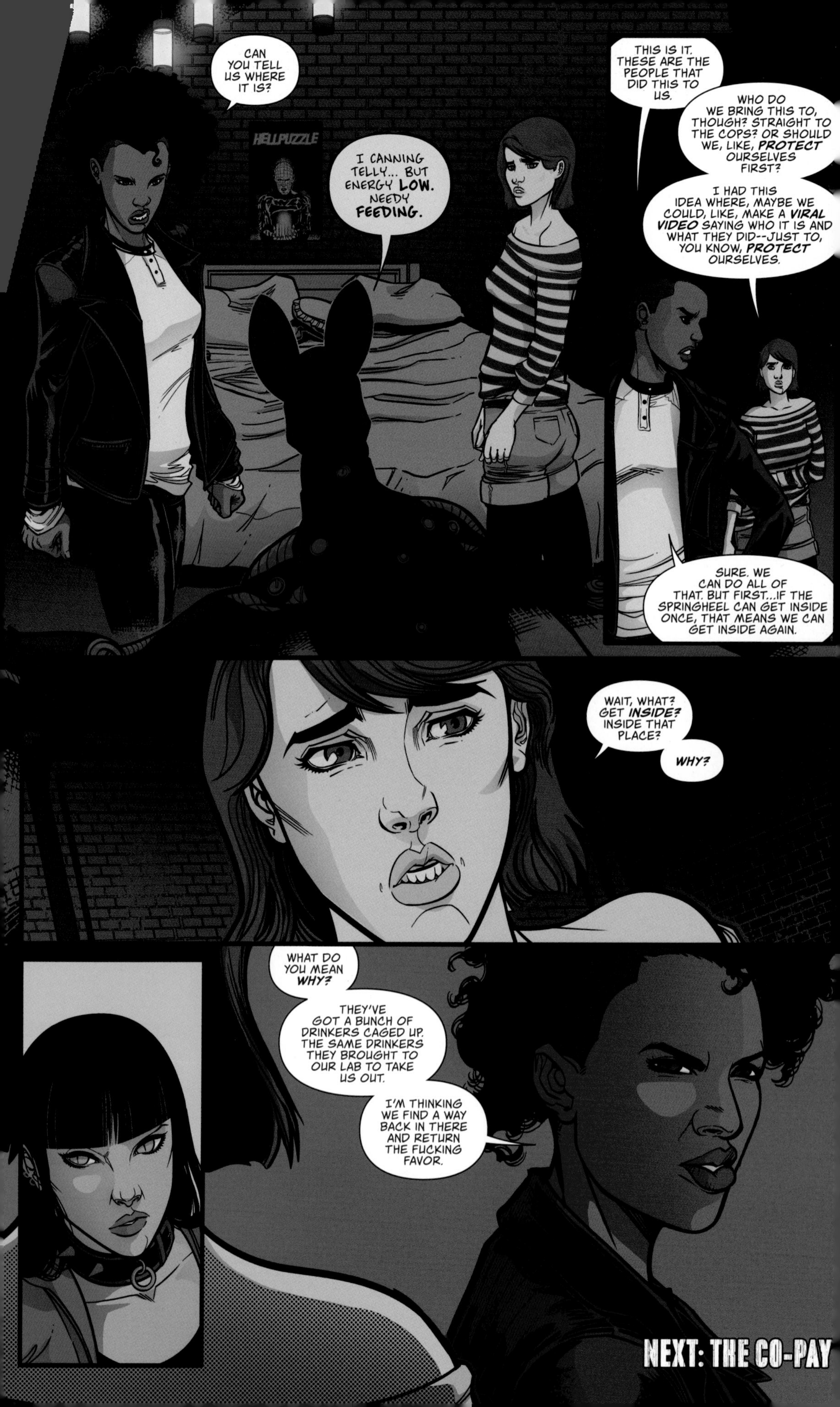
CAN YOU TELL US WHERE IT IS?
HELLPUZZLE
I CANNING TELLY... BUT ENERGY LOW. NEEDY FEEDING.
THIS IS IT. THESE ARE THE PEOPLE THAT DID THIS TO US.
WHO DO WE BRING THIS TO, THOUGH? STRAIGHT TO THE COPS? OR SHOULD WE, LIKE, PROTECT OURSELVES FIRST?
I HAD THIS IDEA WHERE, MAYBE WE COULD, LIKE, MAKE A VIRAL VIDEO SAYING WHO IT IS AND WHAT THEY DID--JUST TO, YOU KNOW, PROTECT OURSELVES.
SURE. WE CAN DO ALL OF THAT. BUT FIRST...IF THE SPRINGHEEL CAN GET INSIDE ONCE, THAT MEANS WE CAN GET INSIDE AGAIN.
WAIT, WHAT? GET INSIDE? INSIDE THAT PLACE?
WHY?
WHAT DO YOU MEAN WHY?
THEY'VE GOT A BUNCH OF DRINKERS CAGED UP. THE SAME DRINKERS THEY BROUGHT TO OUR LAB TO TAKE US OUT.
I'M THINKING WE FIND A WAY BACK IN THERE AND RETURN THE FUCKING FAVOR.
NEXT: THE CO-PAY

PAY

TO

LIVE

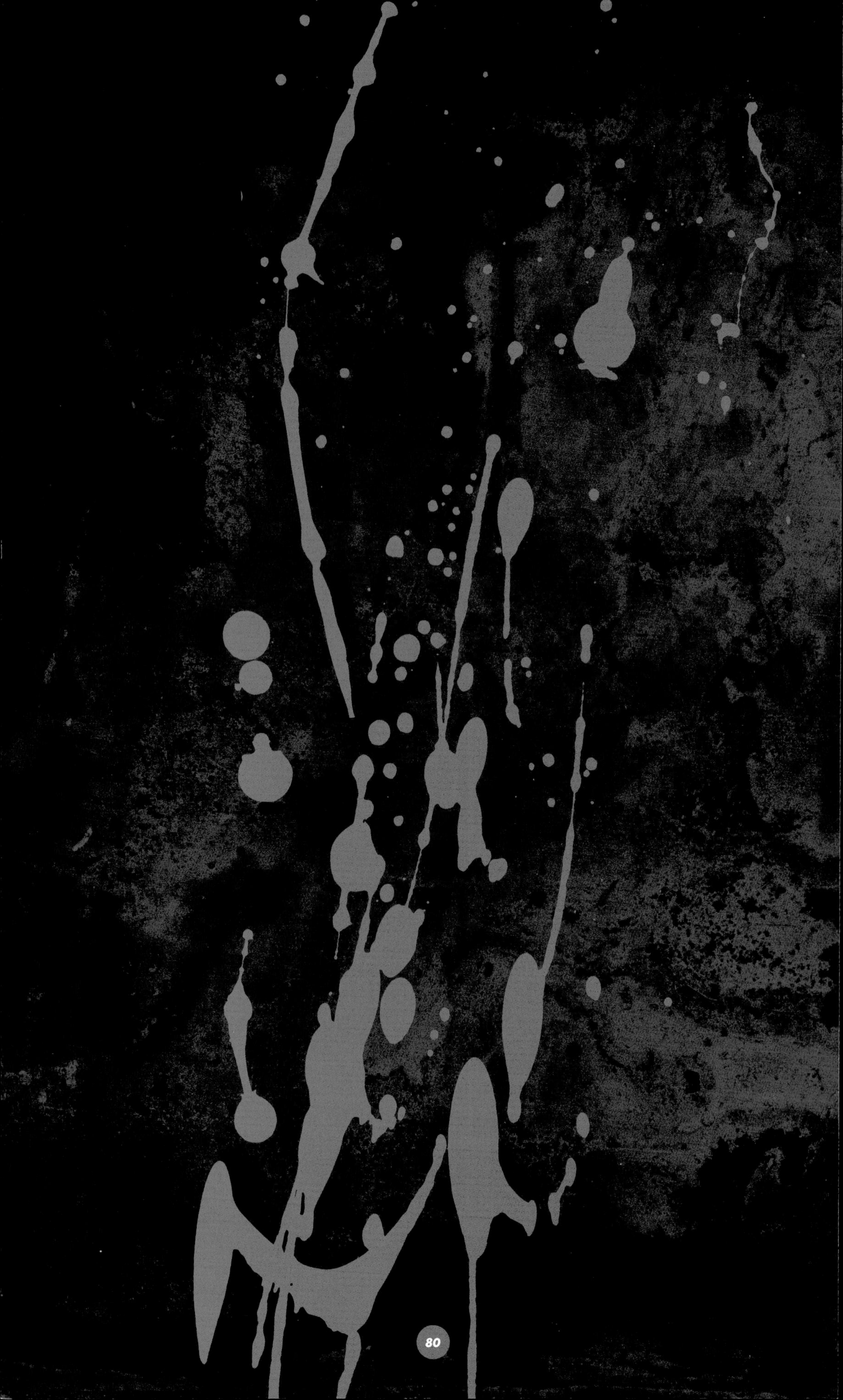

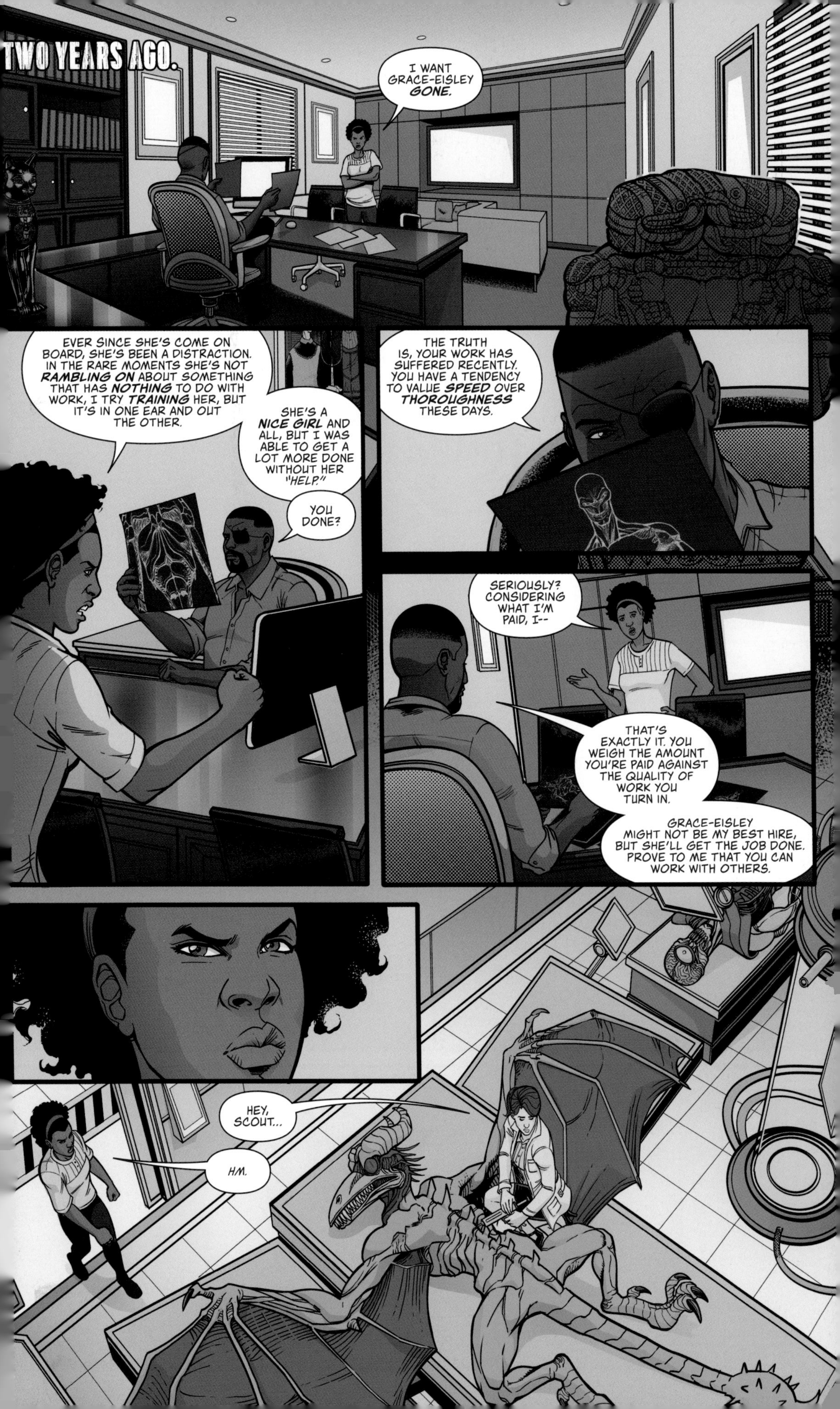
TWO YEARS AGO.
I WANT GRACE-EISLEY GONE.
EVER SINCE SHE'S COME ON BOARD, SHE'S BEEN A DISTRACTION. IN THE RARE MOMENTS SHE'S NOT RAMBLING ON ABOUT SOMETHING THAT HAS NOTHING TO DO WITH WORK, I TRY TRAINING HER, BUT IT'S IN ONE EAR AND OUT THE OTHER.
SHE'S A NICE GIRL AND ALL, BUT I WAS ABLE TO GET A LOT MORE DONE WITHOUT HER "HELP."
YOU DONE?
THE TRUTH IS, YOUR WORK HAS SUFFERED RECENTLY. YOU HAVE A TENDENCY TO VALUE SPEED OVER THOROUGHNESS THESE DAYS.
SERIOUSLY? CONSIDERING WHAT I'M PAID, I--
THAT'S EXACTLY IT. YOU WEIGH THE AMOUNT YOU'RE PAID AGAINST THE QUALITY OF WORK YOU TURN IN.
GRACE-EISLEY MIGHT NOT BE MY BEST HIRE, BUT SHE'LL GET THE JOB DONE. PROVE TO ME THAT YOU CAN WORK WITH OTHERS.
HEY, SCOUT...
HM.

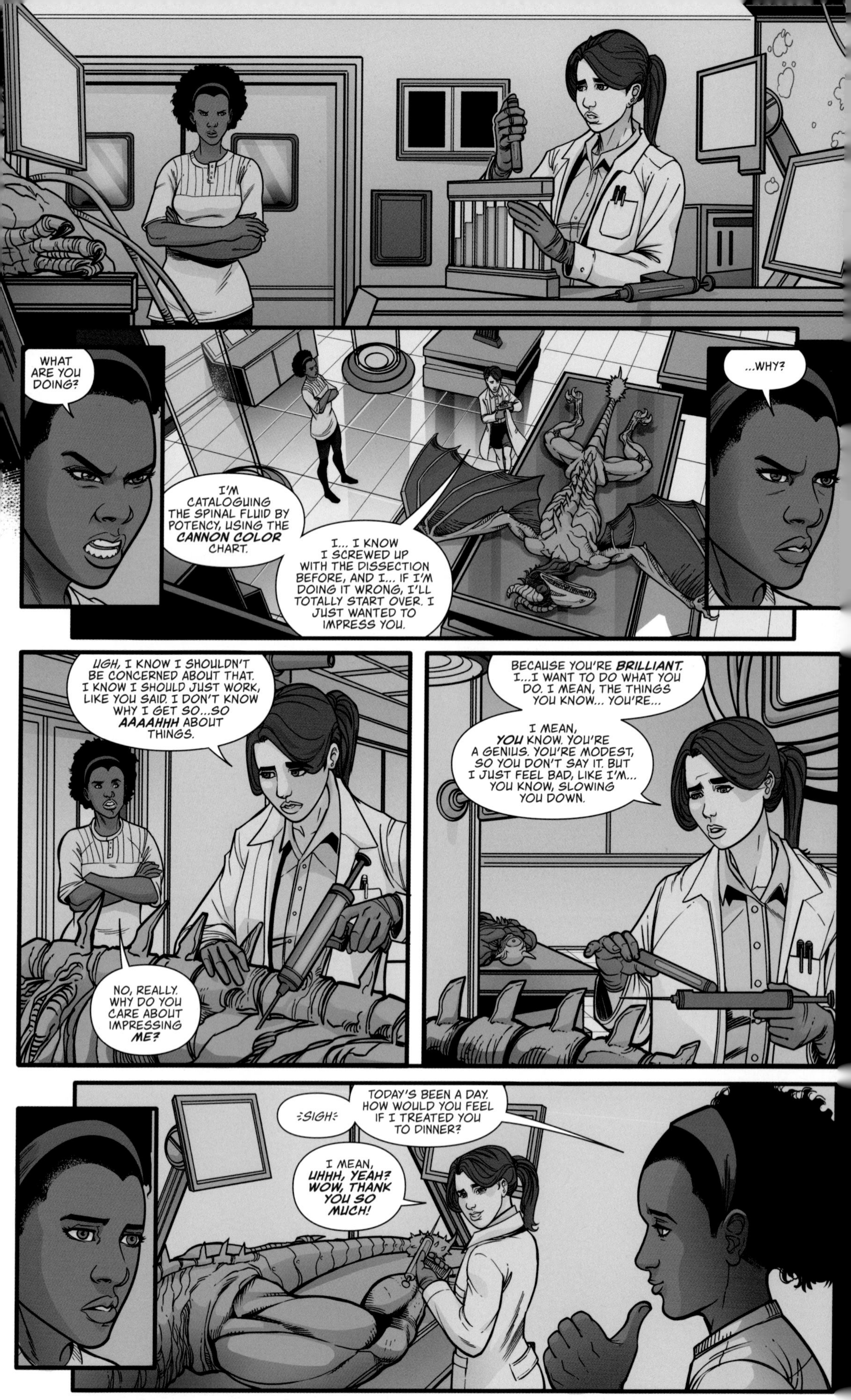

WHAT ARE YOU DOING?
I'M CATALOGUING THE SPINAL FLUID BY POTENCY, USING THE CANNON COLOR CHART.
I... I KNOW I SCREWED UP WITH THE DISSECTION BEFORE, AND I... IF I'M DOING IT WRONG, I'LL TOTALLY START OVER. I JUST WANTED TO IMPRESS YOU.
...WHY?
UGH, I KNOW I SHOULDN'T BE CONCERNED ABOUT THAT. I KNOW I SHOULD JUST WORK, LIKE YOU SAID. I DON'T KNOW WHY I GET SO...SO AAAAHHH ABOUT THINGS.
NO, REALLY. WHY DO YOU CARE ABOUT IMPRESSING ME?
BECAUSE YOU'RE BRILLIANT. I...I WANT TO DO WHAT YOU DO. I MEAN, THE THINGS YOU KNOW... YOU'RE...
I MEAN, YOU KNOW. YOU'RE A GENIUS. YOU'RE MODEST, SO YOU DON'T SAY IT. BUT I JUST FEEL BAD, LIKE I'M... YOU KNOW, SLOWING YOU DOWN.
SIGH
TODAY'S BEEN A DAY. HOW WOULD YOU FEEL IF I TREATED YOU TO DINNER?
I MEAN, UHHH, YEAH? WOW, THANK YOU SO MUCH!

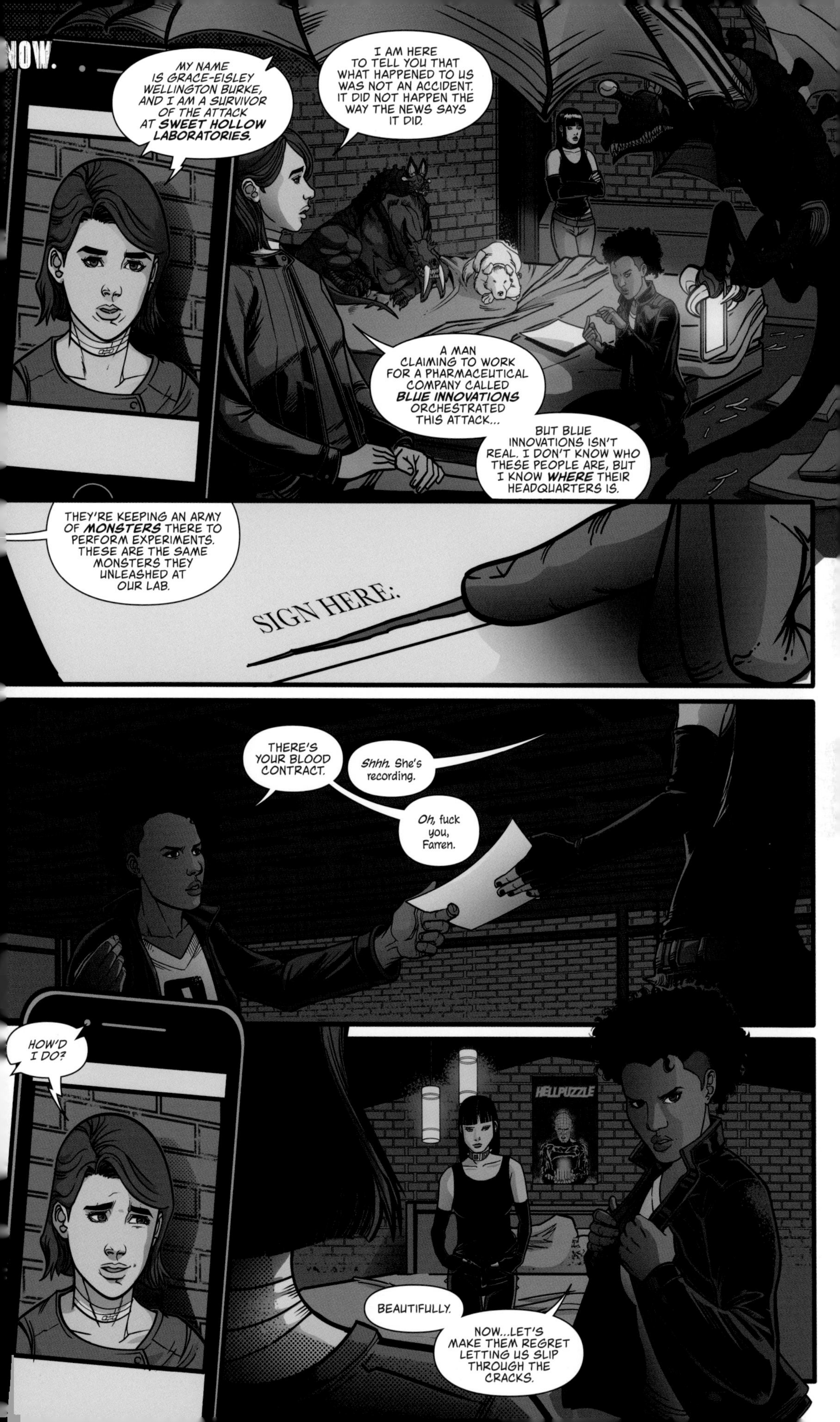
NOW.
MY NAME IS GRACE-EISLEY WELLINGTON BURKE, AND I AM A SURVIVOR OF THE ATTACK AT SWEET HOLLOW LABORATORIES.
I AM HERE TO TELL YOU THAT WHAT HAPPENED TO US WAS NOT AN ACCIDENT. IT DID NOT HAPPEN THE WAY THE NEWS SAYS IT DID.
A MAN CLAIMING TO WORK FOR A PHARMACEUTICAL COMPANY CALLED BLUE INNOVATIONS ORCHESTRATED THIS ATTACK...
BUT BLUE INNOVATIONS ISN'T REAL. I DON'T KNOW WHO THESE PEOPLE ARE, BUT I KNOW WHERE THEIR HEADQUARTERS IS.
THEY'RE KEEPING AN ARMY OF MONSTERS THERE TO PERFORM EXPERIMENTS. THESE ARE THE SAME MONSTERS THEY UNLEASHED AT OUR LAB.
SIGN HERE:
THERE'S YOUR BLOOD CONTRACT.
Shhh. She's recording.
Oh, fuck you, Farren.
HOW'D I DO?
HELLPUZZLE
BEAUTIFULLY.
NOW...LET'S MAKE THEM REGRET LETTING US SLIP THROUGH THE CRACKS.

BREATHLESS

CHAPTER FOUR
THE CO-PAY

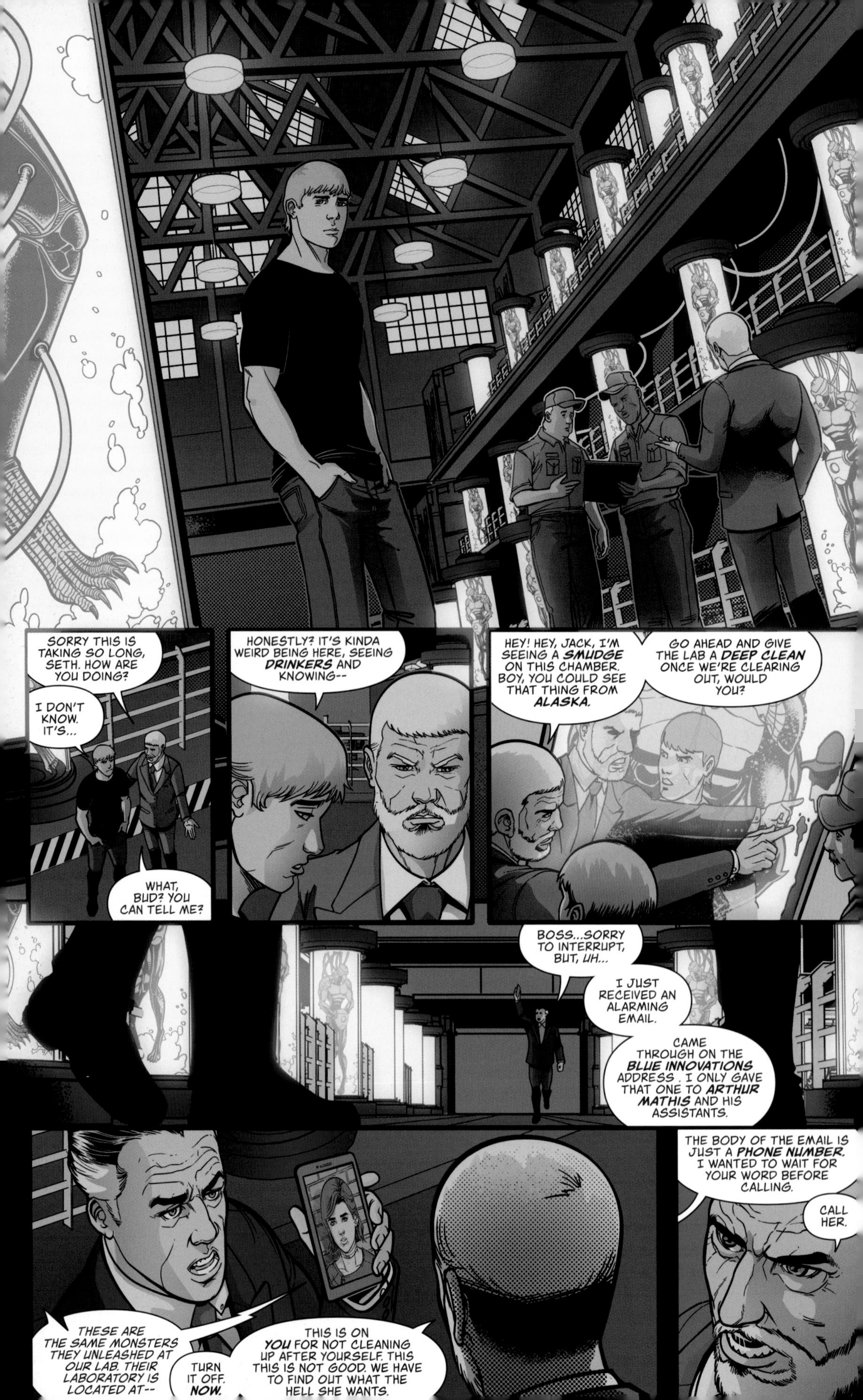
SORRY THIS IS TAKING SO LONG, SETH. HOW ARE YOU DOING?
I DON'T KNOW. IT'S...
WHAT, BUD? YOU CAN TELL ME?
HONESTLY? IT'S KINDA WEIRD BEING HERE, SEEING DRINKERS AND KNOWING--
HEY! HEY, JACK, I'M SEEING A SMUDGE ON THIS CHAMBER. BOY, YOU COULD SEE THAT THING FROM ALASKA.
GO AHEAD AND GIVE THE LAB A DEEP CLEAN ONCE WE'RE CLEARING OUT, WOULD YOU?
BOSS...SORRY TO INTERRUPT, BUT, UH...
I JUST RECEIVED AN ALARMING EMAIL.
CAME THROUGH ON THE BLUE INNOVATIONS ADDRESS . I ONLY GAVE THAT ONE TO ARTHUR MATHIS AND HIS ASSISTANTS.
THESE ARE THE SAME MONSTERS THEY UNLEASHED AT OUR LAB. THEIR LABORATORY IS LOCATED AT--
TURN IT OFF. NOW.
THIS IS ON YOU FOR NOT CLEANING UP AFTER YOURSELF. THIS THIS IS NOT GOOD. WE HAVE TO FIND OUT WHAT THE HELL SHE WANTS.
THE BODY OF THE EMAIL IS JUST A PHONE NUMBER. I WANTED TO WAIT FOR YOUR WORD BEFORE CALLING.
CALL HER.

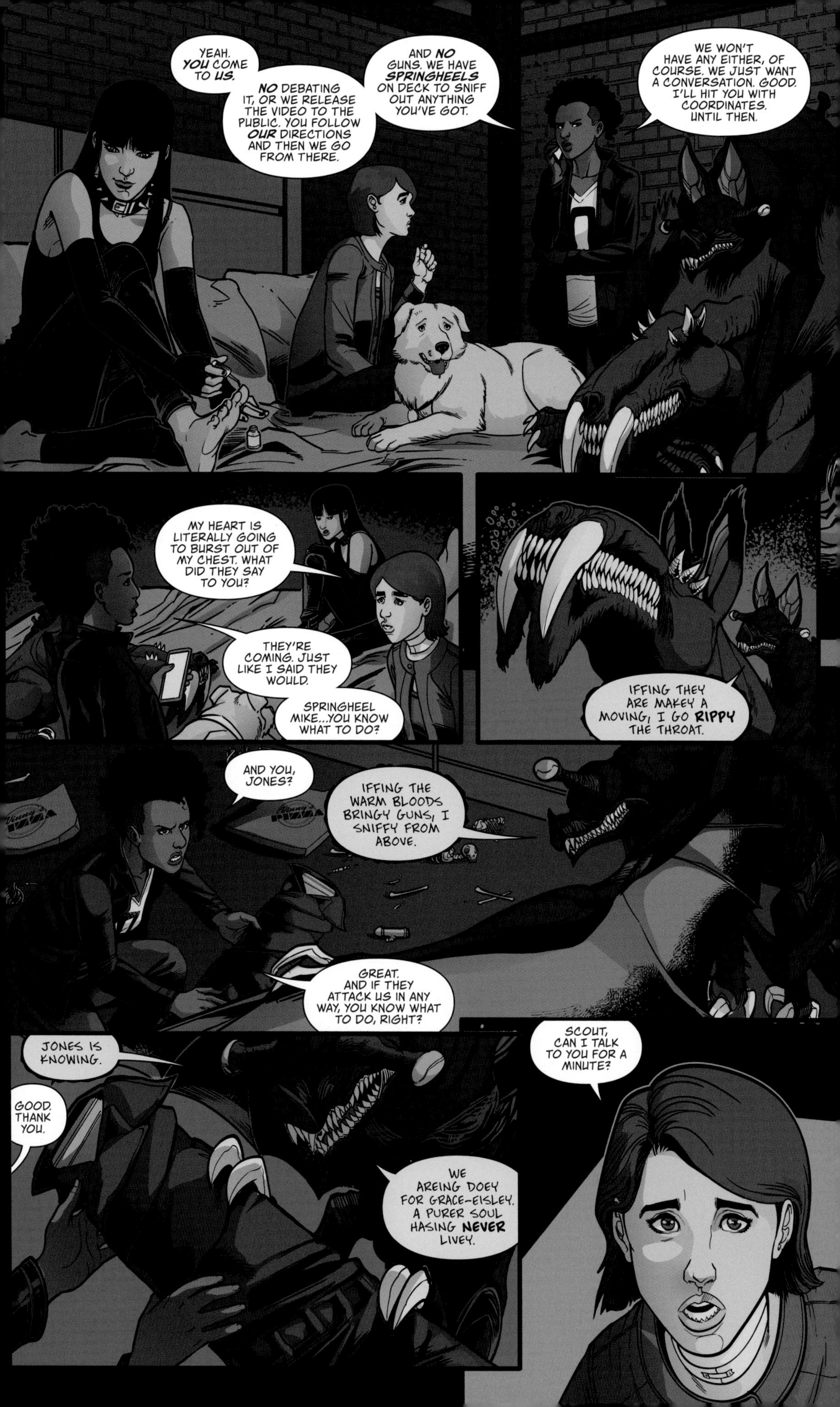
YEAH. YOU COME TO US.
NO DEBATING IT, OR WE RELEASE THE VIDEO TO THE PUBLIC. YOU FOLLOW OUR DIRECTIONS AND THEN WE GO FROM THERE.
AND NO GUNS. WE HAVE SPRINGHEELS ON DECK TO SNIFF OUT ANYTHING YOU'VE GOT.
WE WON'T HAVE ANY EITHER, OF COURSE. WE JUST WANT A CONVERSATION. GOOD. I'LL HIT YOU WITH COORDINATES. UNTIL THEN.
MY HEART IS LITERALLY GOING TO BURST OUT OF MY CHEST. WHAT DID THEY SAY TO YOU?
THEY'RE COMING. JUST LIKE I SAID THEY WOULD.
SPRINGHEEL MIKE...YOU KNOW WHAT TO DO?
IFFING THEY ARE MAKEY A MOVING, I GO RIPPY THE THROAT.
AND YOU, JONES?
IFFING THE WARM BLOODS BRINGY GUNS, I SNIFFY FROM ABOVE.
GREAT. AND IF THEY ATTACK US IN ANY WAY, YOU KNOW WHAT TO DO, RIGHT?
JONES IS KNOWING.
GOOD. THANK YOU.
WE AREING DOEY FOR GRACE-EISLEY. A PURER SOUL HASING NEVER LIVEY.
SCOUT, CAN I TALK TO YOU FOR A MINUTE?

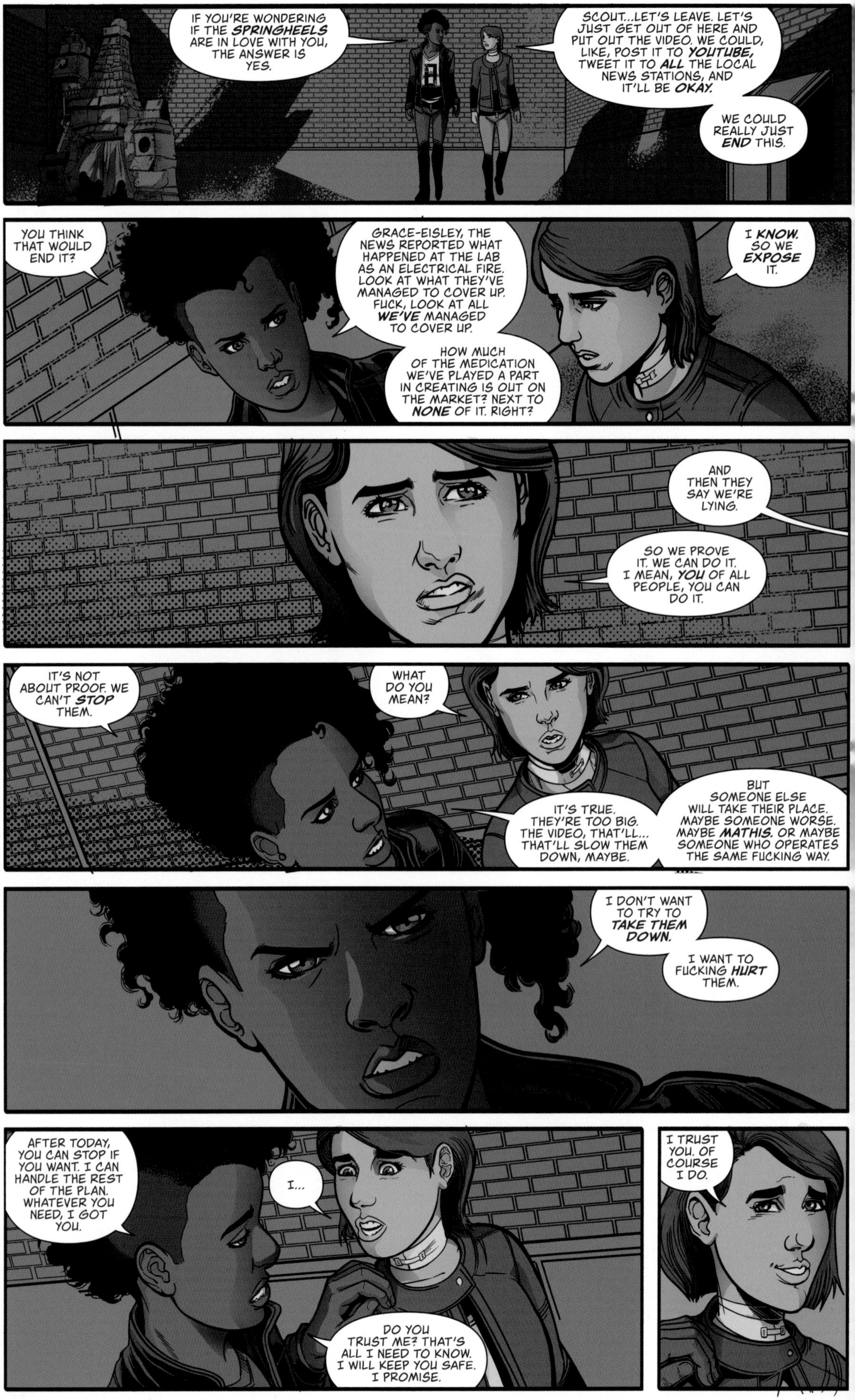

IF YOU'RE WONDERING IF THE SPRINGHEELS ARE IN LOVE WITH YOU, THE ANSWER IS YES.
SCOUT...LET'S LEAVE. LET'S JUST GET OUT OF HERE AND PUT OUT THE VIDEO. WE COULD, LIKE, POST IT TO YOUTUBE, TWEET IT TO ALL THE LOCAL NEWS STATIONS, AND IT'LL BE OKAY.
WE COULD REALLY JUST END THIS.
YOU THINK THAT WOULD END IT?
GRACE-EISLEY, THE NEWS REPORTED WHAT HAPPENED AT THE LAB AS AN ELECTRICAL FIRE. LOOK AT WHAT THEY'VE MANAGED TO COVER UP. FUCK, LOOK AT ALL WE'VE MANAGED TO COVER UP.
HOW MUCH OF THE MEDICATION WE'VE PLAYED A PART IN CREATING IS OUT ON THE MARKET? NEXT TO NONE OF IT. RIGHT?
I KNOW. SO WE EXPOSE IT.
AND THEN THEY SAY WE'RE LYING.
SO WE PROVE IT. WE CAN DO IT. I MEAN, YOU OF ALL PEOPLE, YOU CAN DO IT.
IT'S NOT ABOUT PROOF. WE CAN'T STOP THEM.
WHAT DO YOU MEAN?
IT'S TRUE. THEY'RE TOO BIG. THE VIDEO, THAT'LL... THAT'LL SLOW THEM DOWN, MAYBE.
BUT SOMEONE ELSE WILL TAKE THEIR PLACE. MAYBE SOMEONE WORSE. MAYBE MATHIS. OR MAYBE SOMEONE WHO OPERATES THE SAME FUCKING WAY.
I DON'T WANT TO TRY TO TAKE THEM DOWN.
I WANT TO FUCKING HURT THEM.
AFTER TODAY, YOU CAN STOP IF YOU WANT. I CAN HANDLE THE REST OF THE PLAN. WHATEVER YOU NEED, I GOT YOU.
I...
DO YOU TRUST ME? THAT'S ALL I NEED TO KNOW. I WILL KEEP YOU SAFE. I PROMISE.
I TRUST YOU. OF COURSE I DO.

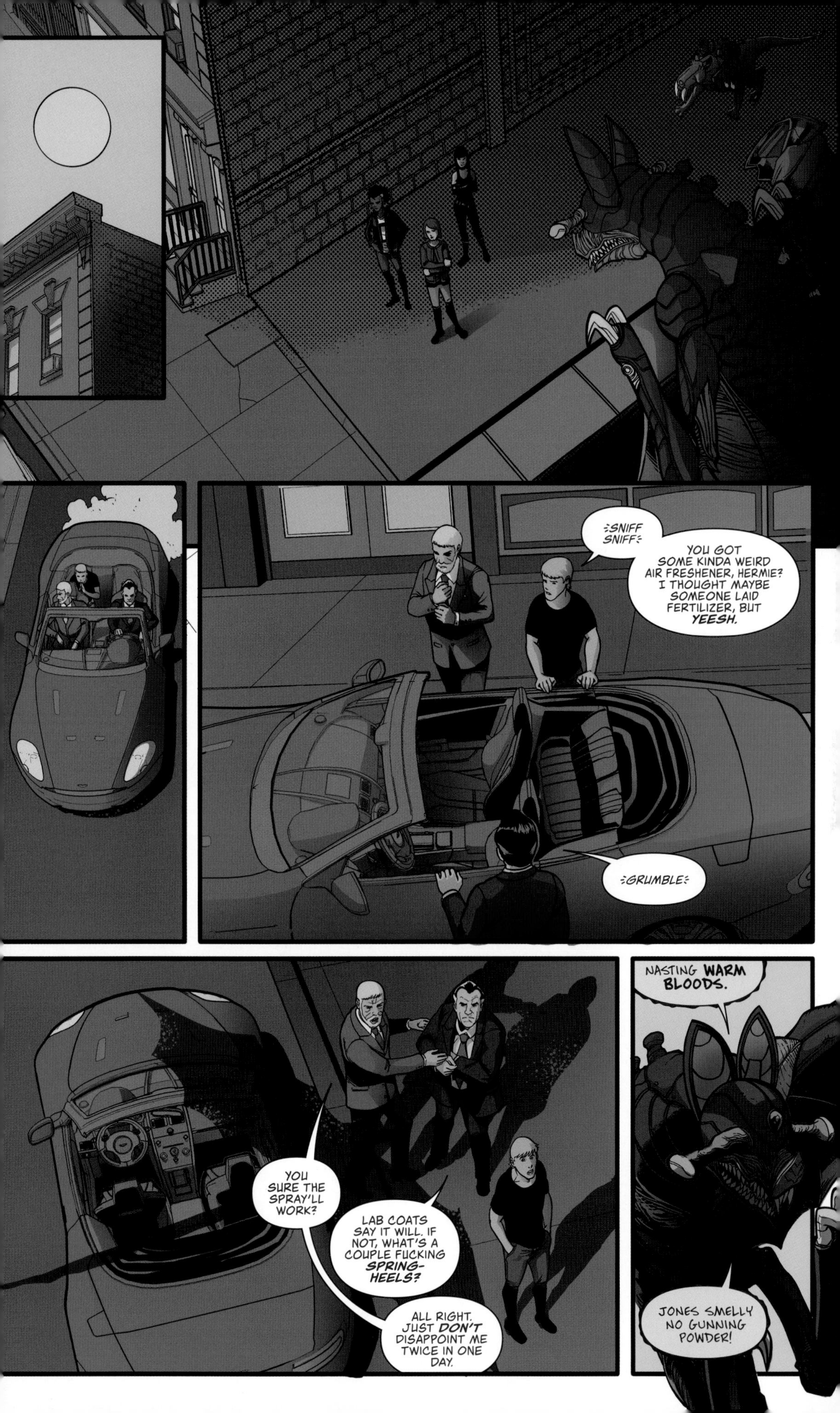

SNIFF SNIFF
YOU GOT SOME KINDA WEIRD AIR FRESHENER, HERMIE? I THOUGHT MAYBE SOMEONE LAID FERTILIZER, BUT **YEESH.**
GRUMBLE
YOU SURE THE SPRAY'LL WORK?
LAB COATS SAY IT WILL. IF NOT, WHAT'S A COUPLE FUCKING **SPRING-HEELS?**
ALL RIGHT. JUST **DON'T** DISAPPOINT ME TWICE IN ONE DAY.
NASTING **WARM BLOODS.**
JONES SMELLY NO GUNNING POWDER!

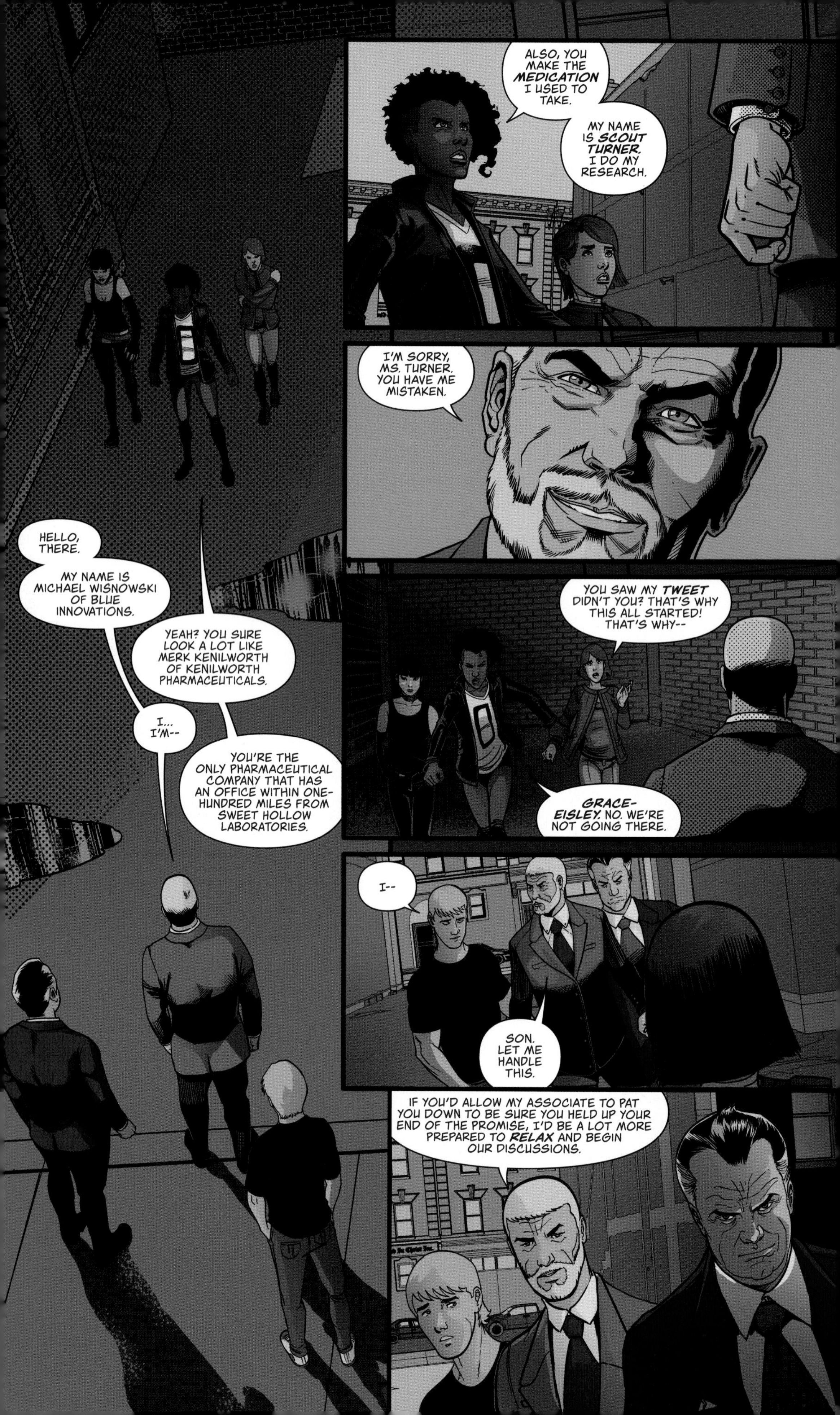
ALSO, YOU MAKE THE MEDICATION I USED TO TAKE.
MY NAME IS SCOUT TURNER. I DO MY RESEARCH.
I'M SORRY, MS. TURNER. YOU HAVE ME MISTAKEN.
HELLO, THERE.
MY NAME IS MICHAEL WISNOWSKI OF BLUE INNOVATIONS.
YEAH? YOU SURE LOOK A LOT LIKE MERK KENILWORTH OF KENILWORTH PHARMACEUTICALS.
I... I'M--
YOU'RE THE ONLY PHARMACEUTICAL COMPANY THAT HAS AN OFFICE WITHIN ONE-HUNDRED MILES FROM SWEET HOLLOW LABORATORIES.
YOU SAW MY TWEET DIDN'T YOU? THAT'S WHY THIS ALL STARTED! THAT'S WHY--
GRACE-EISLEY. NO. WE'RE NOT GOING THERE.
I--
SON. LET ME HANDLE THIS.
IF YOU'D ALLOW MY ASSOCIATE TO PAT YOU DOWN TO BE SURE YOU HELD UP YOUR END OF THE PROMISE, I'D BE A LOT MORE PREPARED TO RELAX AND BEGIN OUR DISCUSSIONS.

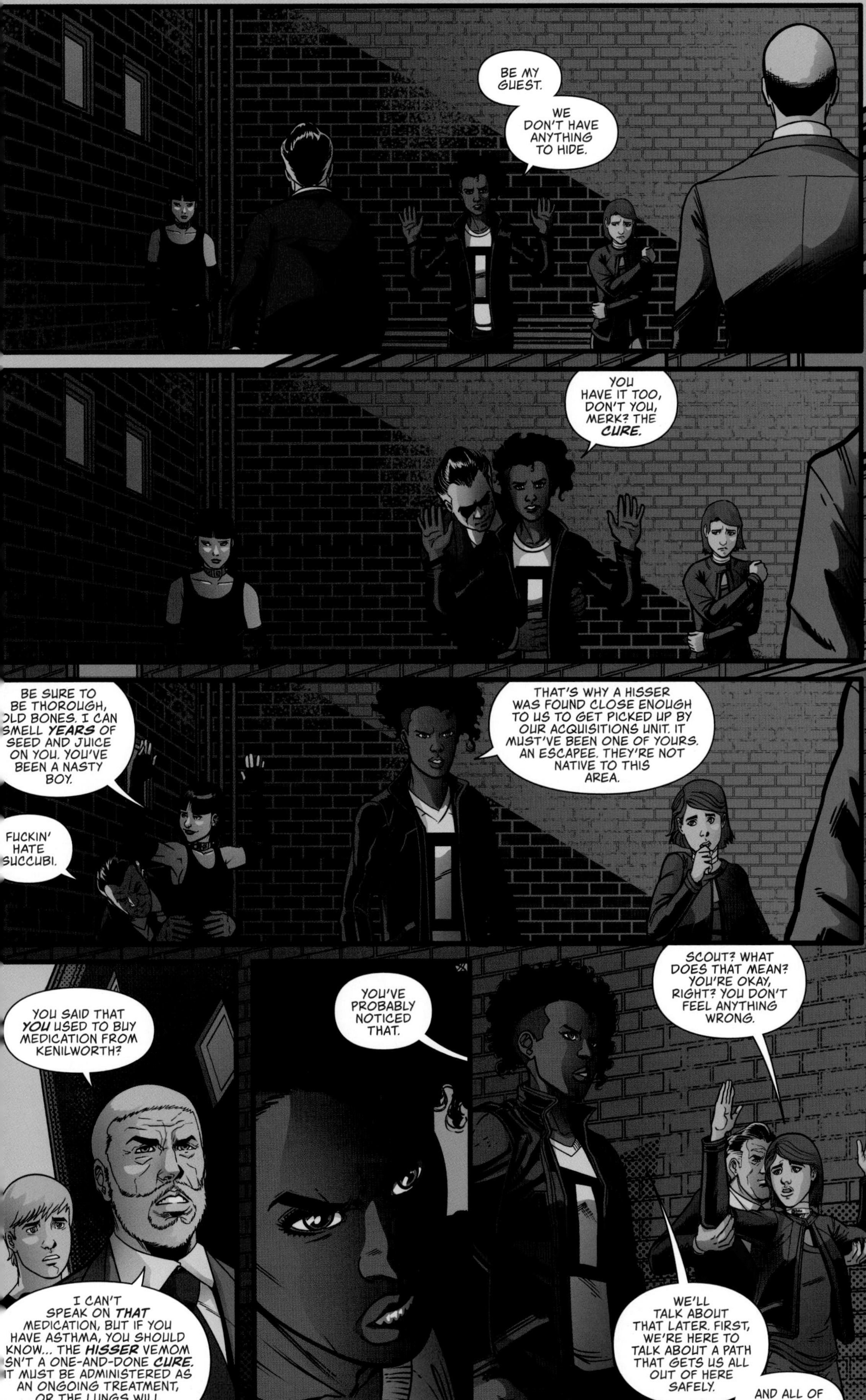
BE MY GUEST.
WE DON'T HAVE ANYTHING TO HIDE.
YOU HAVE IT TOO, DON'T YOU, MERK? THE CURE.
BE SURE TO BE THOROUGH, LD BONES. I CAN SMELL YEARS OF SEED AND JUICE ON YOU. YOU'VE BEEN A NASTY BOY.
FUCKIN' HATE UCCUBI.
THAT'S WHY A HISSER WAS FOUND CLOSE ENOUGH TO US TO GET PICKED UP BY OUR ACQUISITIONS UNIT. IT MUST'VE BEEN ONE OF YOURS. AN ESCAPEE. THEY'RE NOT NATIVE TO THIS AREA.
YOU SAID THAT YOU USED TO BUY MEDICATION FROM KENILWORTH?
I CAN'T SPEAK ON THAT MEDICATION, BUT IF YOU HAVE ASTHMA, YOU SHOULD KNOW... THE HISSER VEMOM SN'T A ONE-AND-DONE CURE. IT MUST BE ADMINISTERED AS AN ONGOING TREATMENT, OR THE LUNGS WILL EVENTUALLY FLOOD.
YOU'VE PROBABLY NOTICED THAT.
SCOUT? WHAT DOES THAT MEAN? YOU'RE OKAY, RIGHT? YOU DON'T FEEL ANYTHING WRONG.
WE'LL TALK ABOUT THAT LATER. FIRST, WE'RE HERE TO TALK ABOUT A PATH THAT GETS US ALL OUT OF HERE SAFELY.
AND ALL OF US GAINFULLY

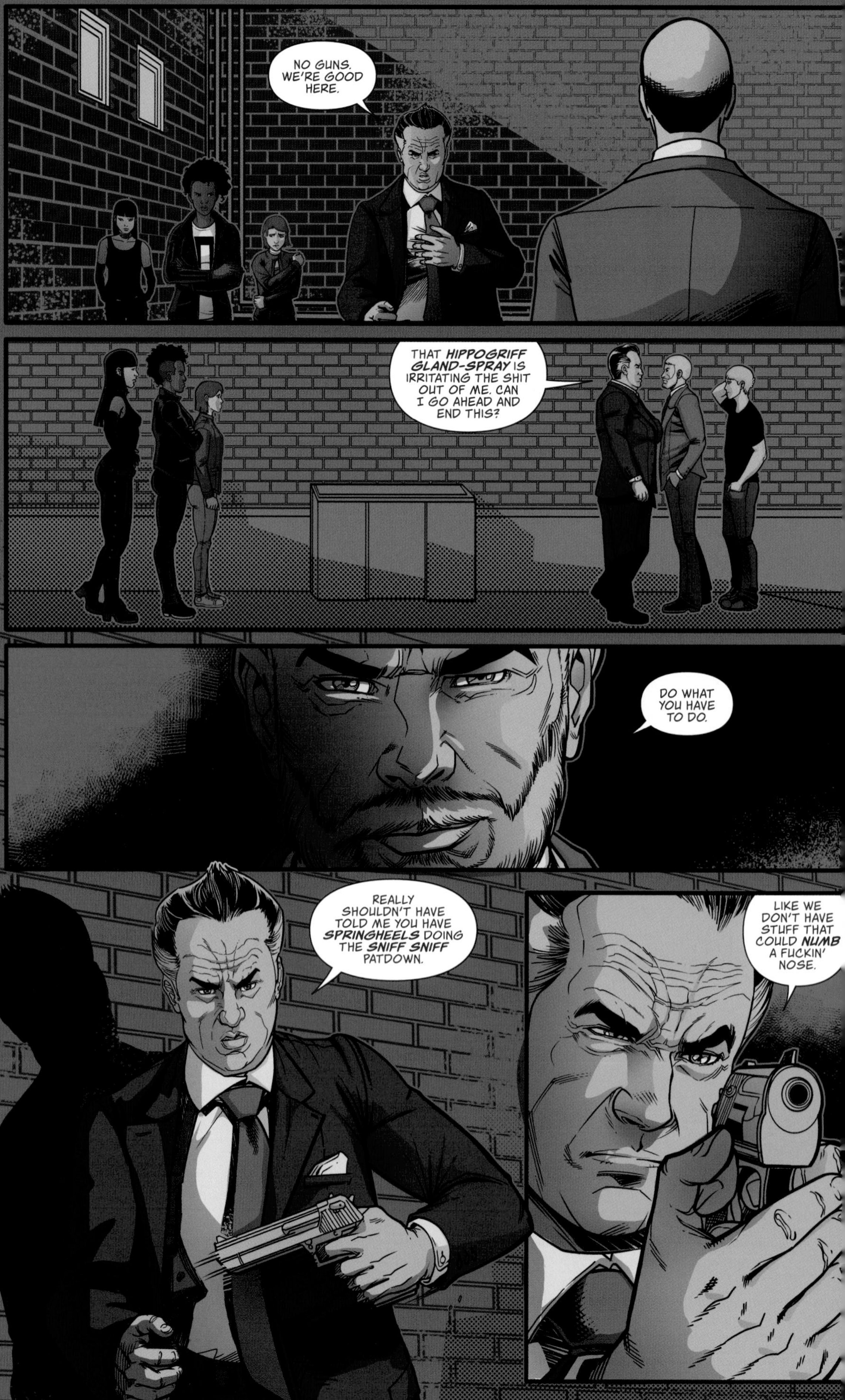
NO GUNS. WE'RE GOOD HERE.
THAT **HIPPOGRIFF GLAND-SPRAY** IS IRRITATING THE SHIT OUT OF ME. CAN I GO AHEAD AND END THIS?
DO WHAT YOU HAVE TO DO.
REALLY SHOULDN'T HAVE TOLD ME YOU HAVE **SPRINGHEELS** DOING THE **SNIFF SNIFF** PATDOWN.
LIKE WE DON'T HAVE STUFF THAT COULD **NUMB** A FUCKIN' NOSE.

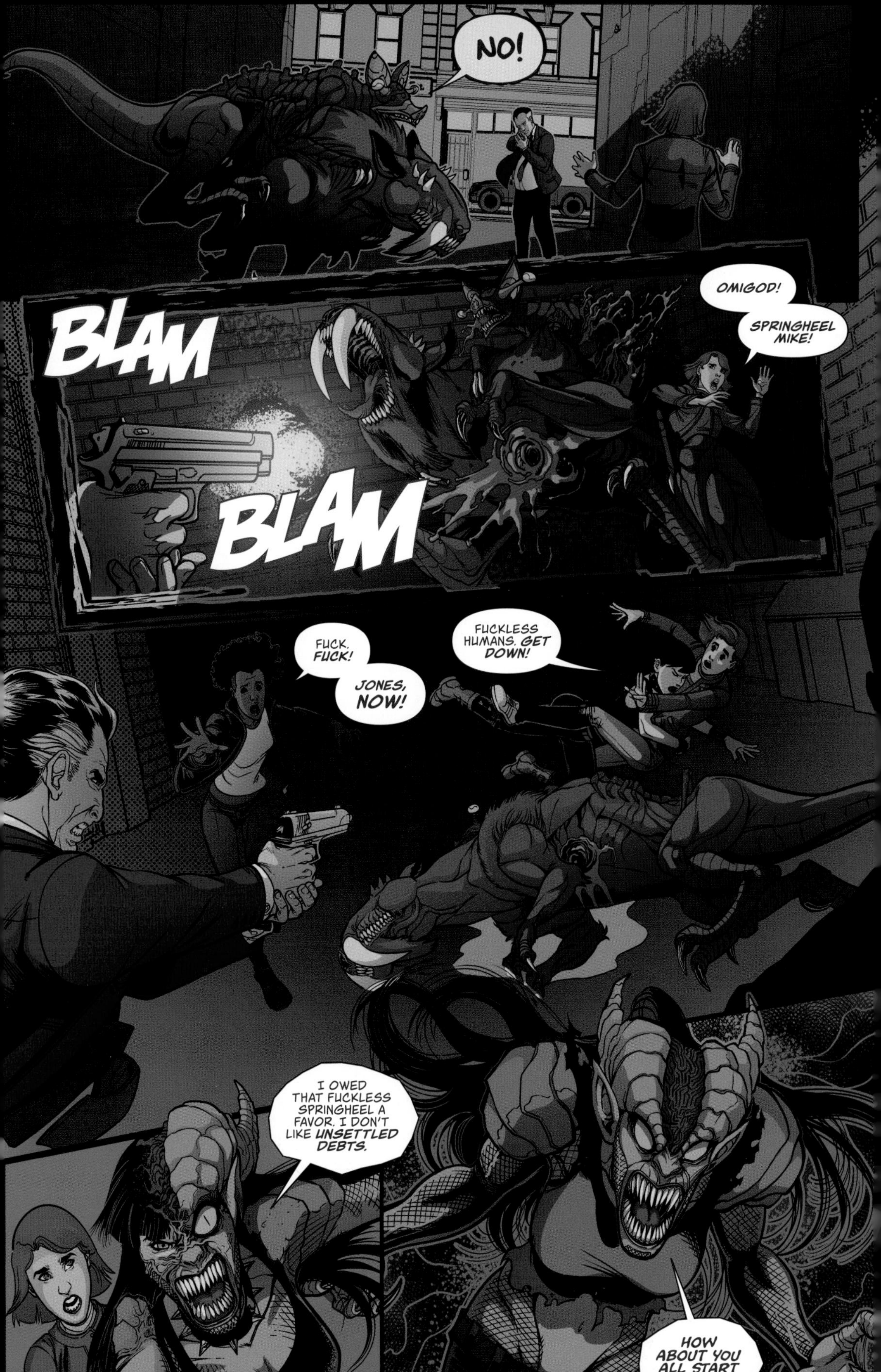
NO!
BLAM
OMIGOD!
SPRINGHEEL MIKE!
BLAM
FUCK. FUCK!
JONES, NOW!
FUCKLESS HUMANS. GET DOWN!
I OWED THAT FUCKLESS SPRINGHEEL A FAVOR. I DON'T LIKE UNSETTLED DEBTS.
HOW ABOUT YOU ALL START BUSTING?

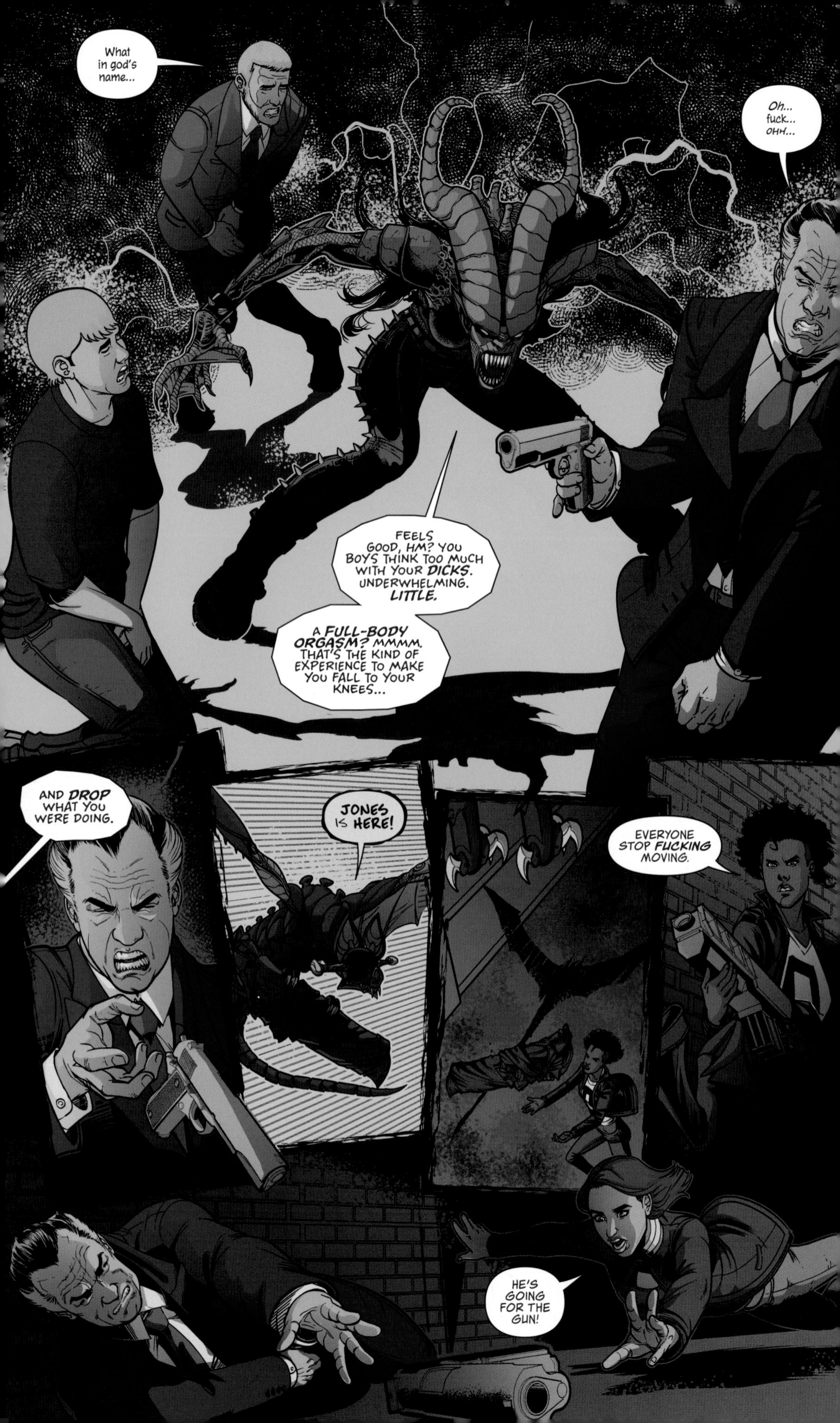
What in god's name...
Oh... fuck... OHH...
FEELS GOOD, HM? YOU BOYS THINK TOO MUCH WITH YOUR DICKS. UNDERWHELMING. LITTLE.
A FULL-BODY ORGASM? MMMM. THAT'S THE KIND OF EXPERIENCE TO MAKE YOU FALL TO YOUR KNEES...
AND DROP WHAT YOU WERE DOING.
JONES IS HERE!
EVERYONE STOP FUCKING MOVING.
HE'S GOING FOR THE GUN!

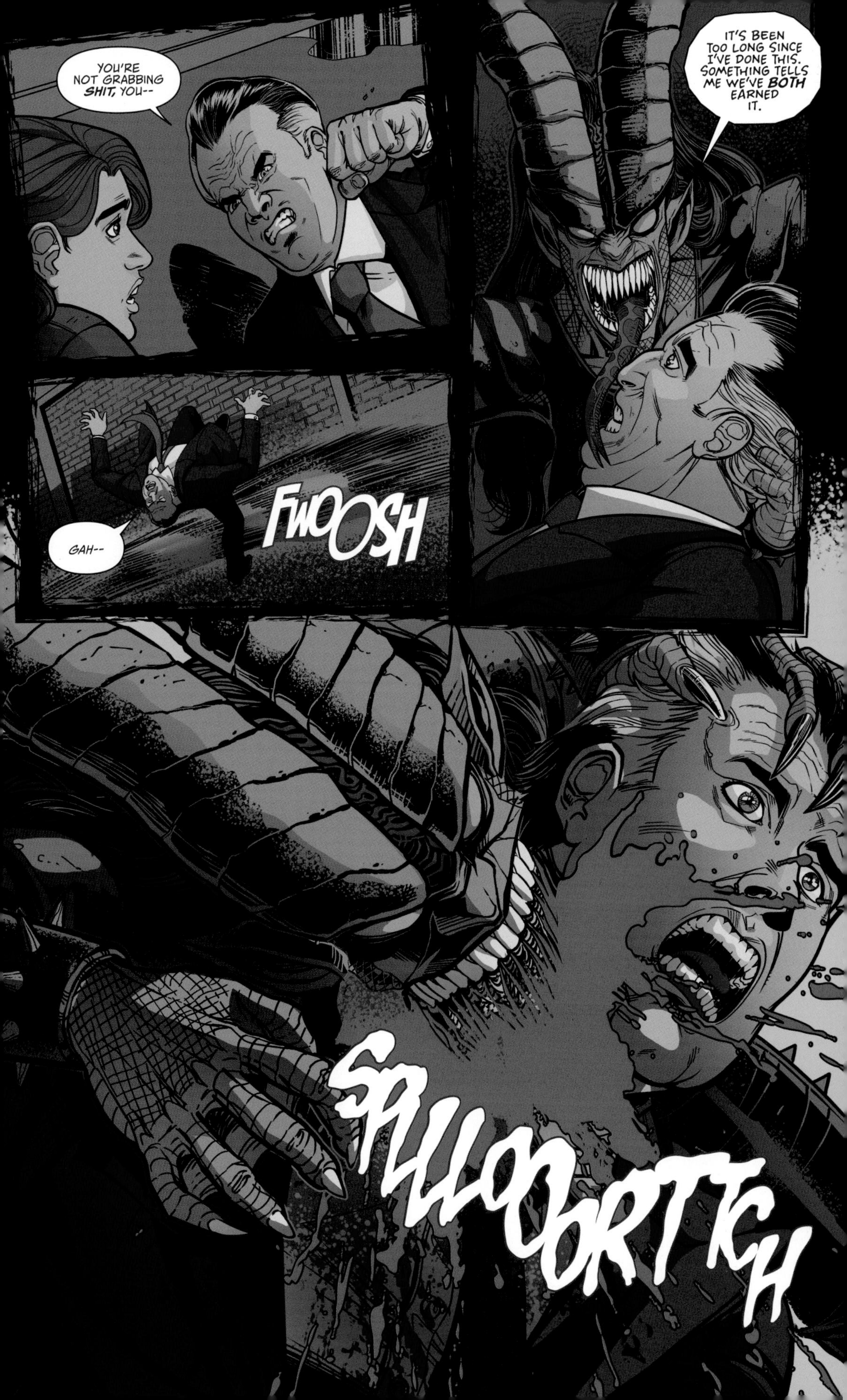
YOU'RE NOT GRABBING SHIT, YOU--
IT'S BEEN TOO LONG SINCE I'VE DONE THIS. SOMETHING TELLS ME WE'VE BOTH EARNED IT.
GAH--
FWOOSH
SPLLOOORTTCH

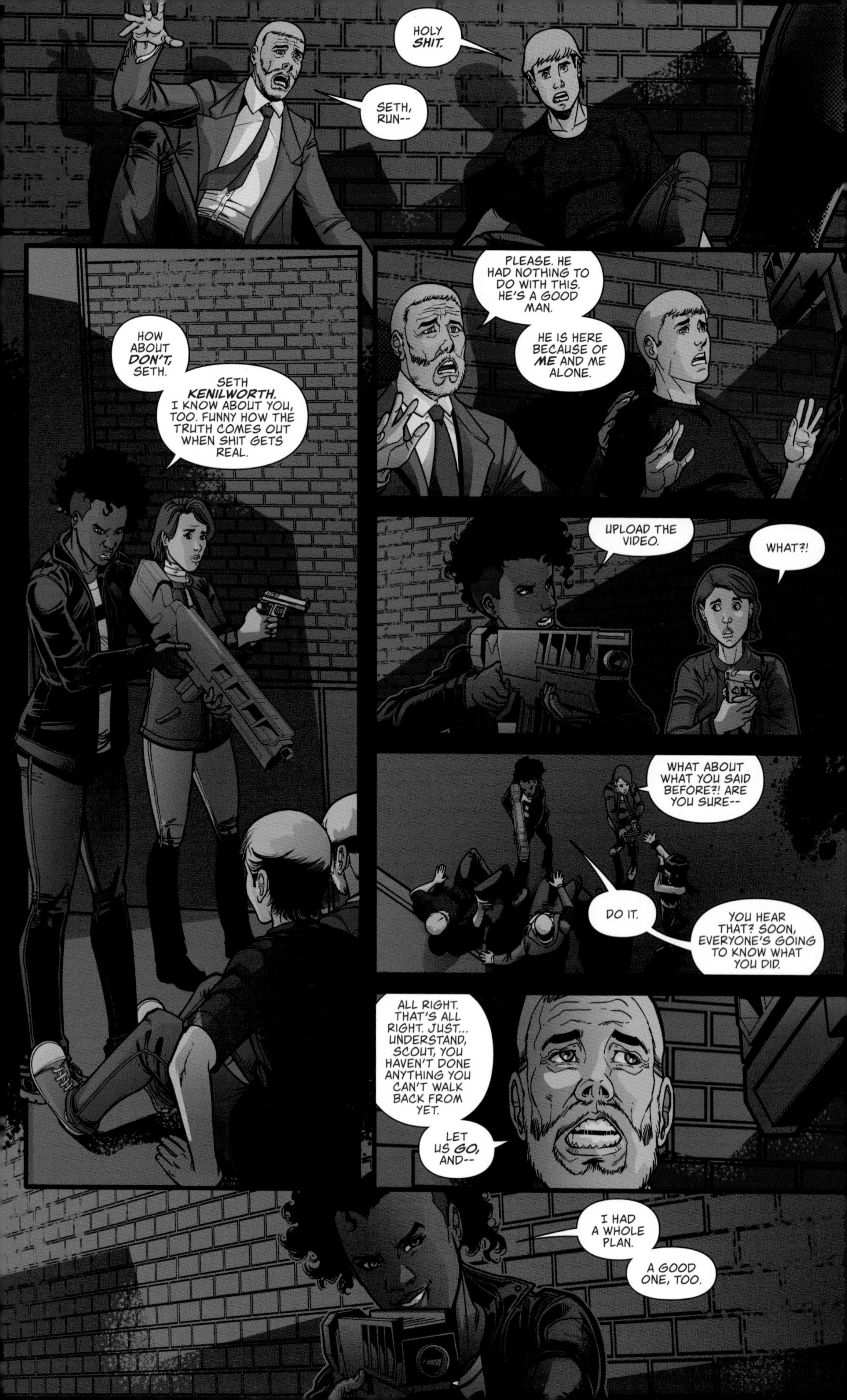
HOLY SHIT.
SETH, RUN--
HOW ABOUT DON'T, SETH.
SETH KENILWORTH. I KNOW ABOUT YOU, TOO. FUNNY HOW THE TRUTH COMES OUT WHEN SHIT GETS REAL.
PLEASE. HE HAD NOTHING TO DO WITH THIS. HE'S A GOOD MAN.
HE IS HERE BECAUSE OF ME AND ME ALONE.
UPLOAD THE VIDEO.
WHAT?!
WHAT ABOUT WHAT YOU SAID BEFORE?! ARE YOU SURE--
DO IT.
YOU HEAR THAT? SOON, EVERYONE'S GOING TO KNOW WHAT YOU DID.
ALL RIGHT. THAT'S ALL RIGHT. JUST... UNDERSTAND, SCOUT, YOU HAVEN'T DONE ANYTHING YOU CAN'T WALK BACK FROM YET.
LET US GO, AND--
I HAD A WHOLE PLAN.
A GOOD ONE, TOO.

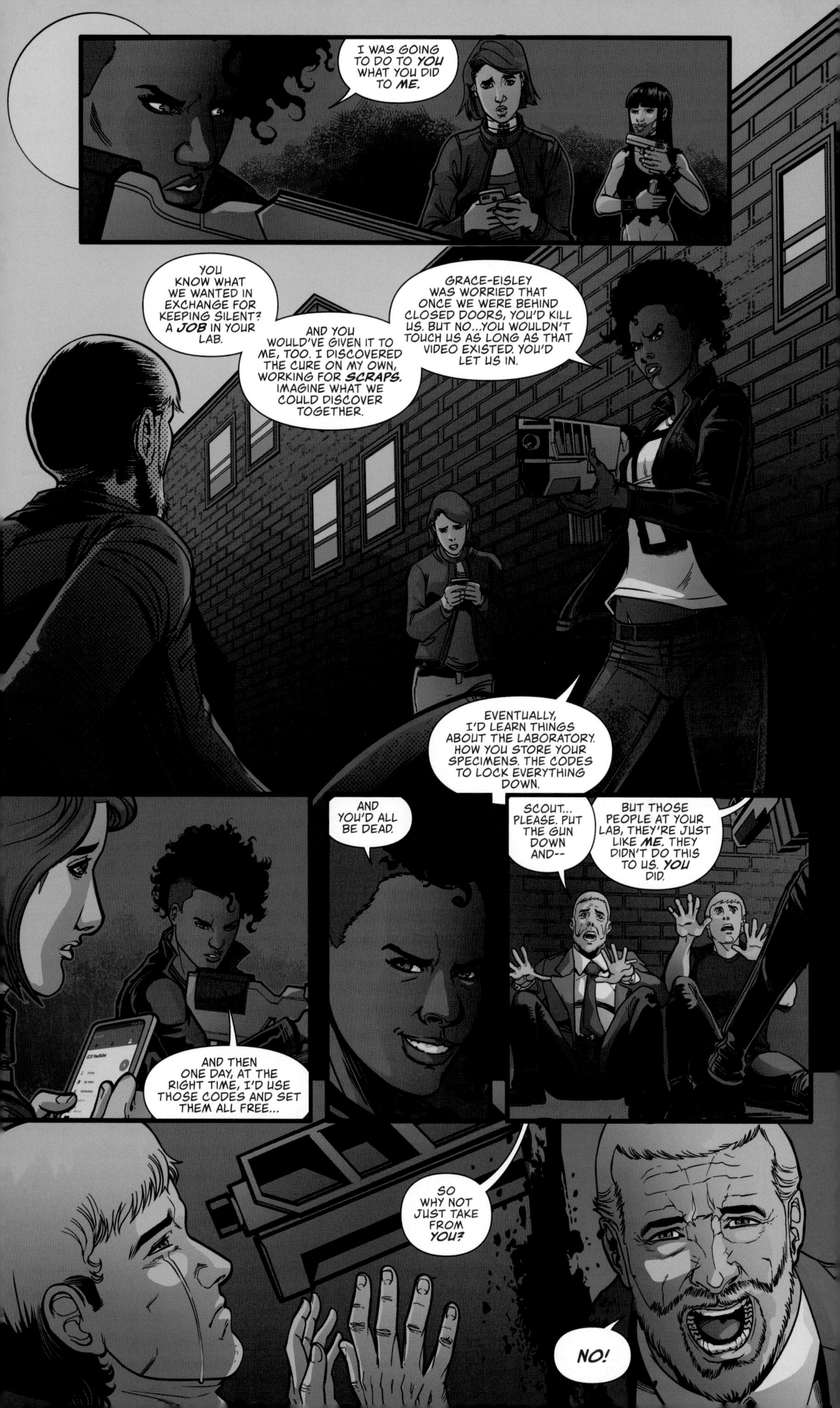
I WAS GOING TO DO TO YOU WHAT YOU DID TO ME.
YOU KNOW WHAT WE WANTED IN EXCHANGE FOR KEEPING SILENT? A JOB IN YOUR LAB.
AND YOU WOULD'VE GIVEN IT TO ME, TOO. I DISCOVERED THE CURE ON MY OWN, WORKING FOR SCRAPS. IMAGINE WHAT WE COULD DISCOVER TOGETHER.
GRACE-EISLEY WAS WORRIED THAT ONCE WE WERE BEHIND CLOSED DOORS, YOU'D KILL US. BUT NO...YOU WOULDN'T TOUCH US AS LONG AS THAT VIDEO EXISTED. YOU'D LET US IN.
EVENTUALLY, I'D LEARN THINGS ABOUT THE LABORATORY. HOW YOU STORE YOUR SPECIMENS. THE CODES TO LOCK EVERYTHING DOWN.
AND THEN ONE DAY, AT THE RIGHT TIME, I'D USE THOSE CODES AND SET THEM ALL FREE...
AND YOU'D ALL BE DEAD.
SCOUT... PLEASE. PUT THE GUN DOWN AND--
BUT THOSE PEOPLE AT YOUR LAB, THEY'RE JUST LIKE ME. THEY DIDN'T DO THIS TO US. YOU DID.
SO WHY NOT JUST TAKE FROM YOU?
NO!

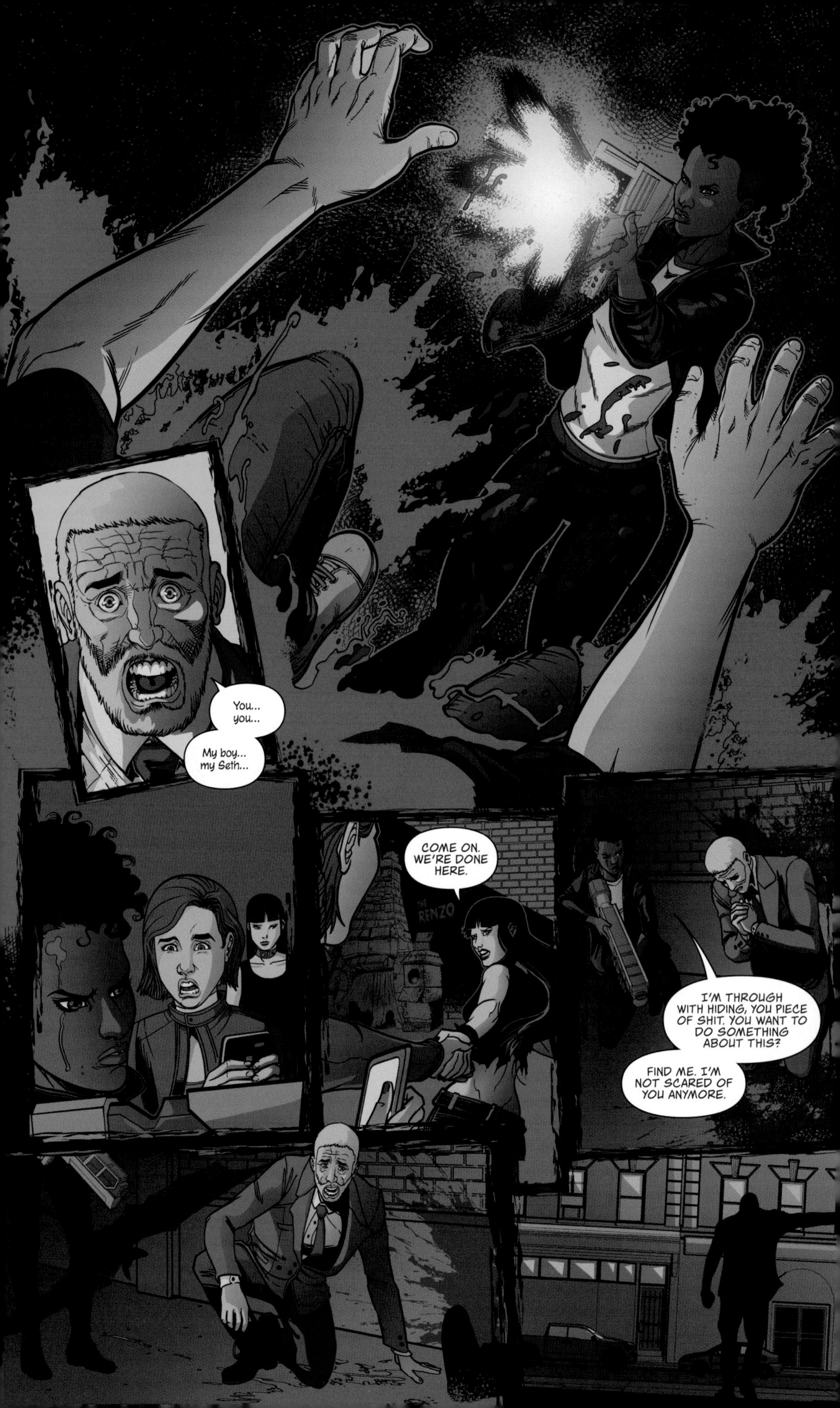
You... you...
My boy... my Seth...
COME ON. WE'RE DONE HERE.
THE RENZO
I'M THROUGH WITH HIDING, YOU PIECE OF SHIT. YOU WANT TO DO SOMETHING ABOUT THIS?
FIND ME. I'M NOT SCARED OF YOU ANYMORE.

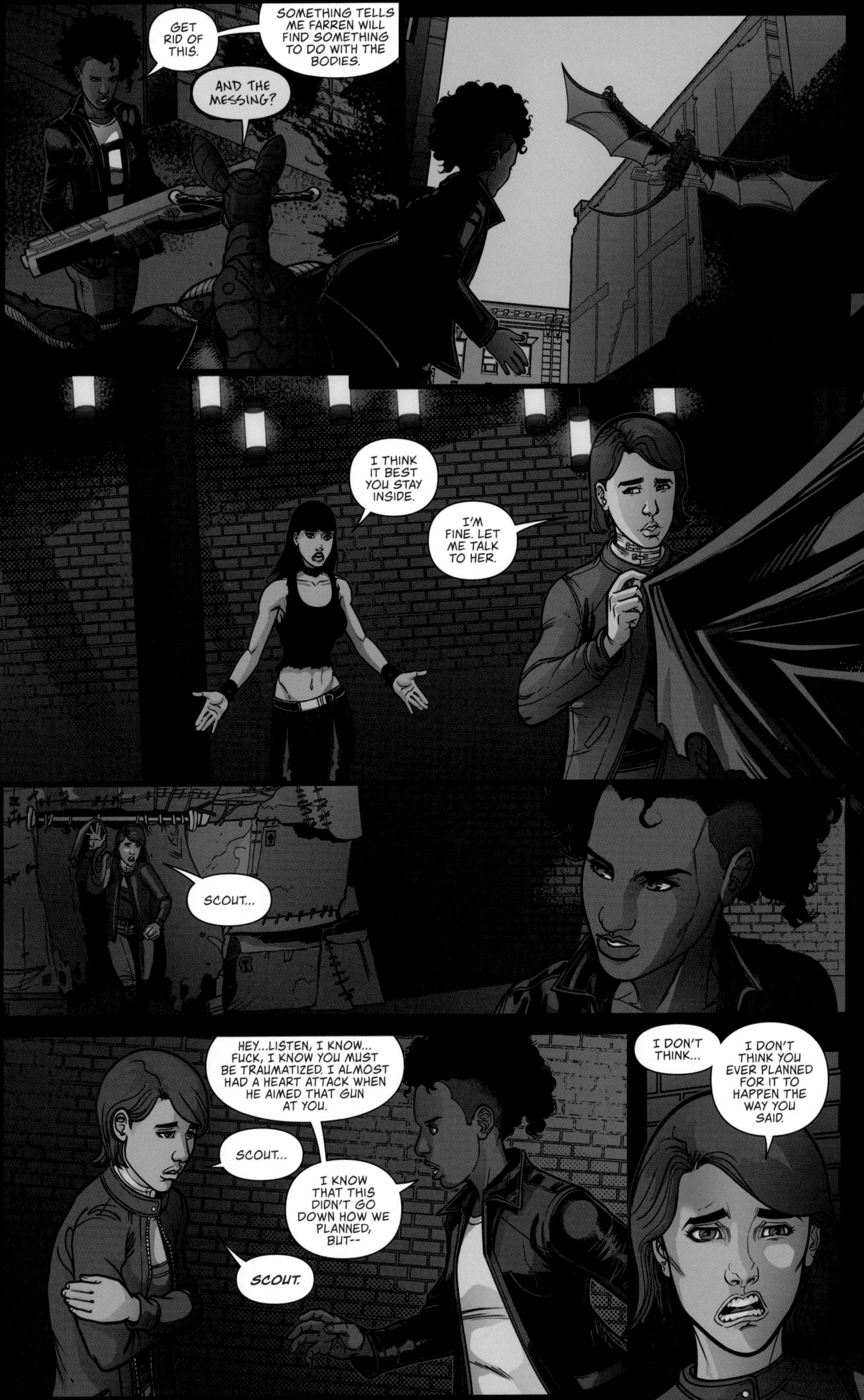

GET RID OF THIS.
SOMETHING TELLS ME FARREN WILL FIND SOMETHING TO DO WITH THE BODIES.
AND THE MESSING?
I THINK IT BEST YOU STAY INSIDE.
I'M FINE. LET ME TALK TO HER.
SCOUT...
HEY...LISTEN, I KNOW... FUCK, I KNOW YOU MUST BE TRAUMATIZED. I ALMOST HAD A HEART ATTACK WHEN HE AIMED THAT GUN AT YOU.
SCOUT...
I KNOW THAT THIS DIDN'T GO DOWN HOW WE PLANNED, BUT--
SCOUT.
I DON'T THINK...
I DON'T THINK YOU EVER PLANNED FOR IT TO HAPPEN THE WAY YOU SAID.

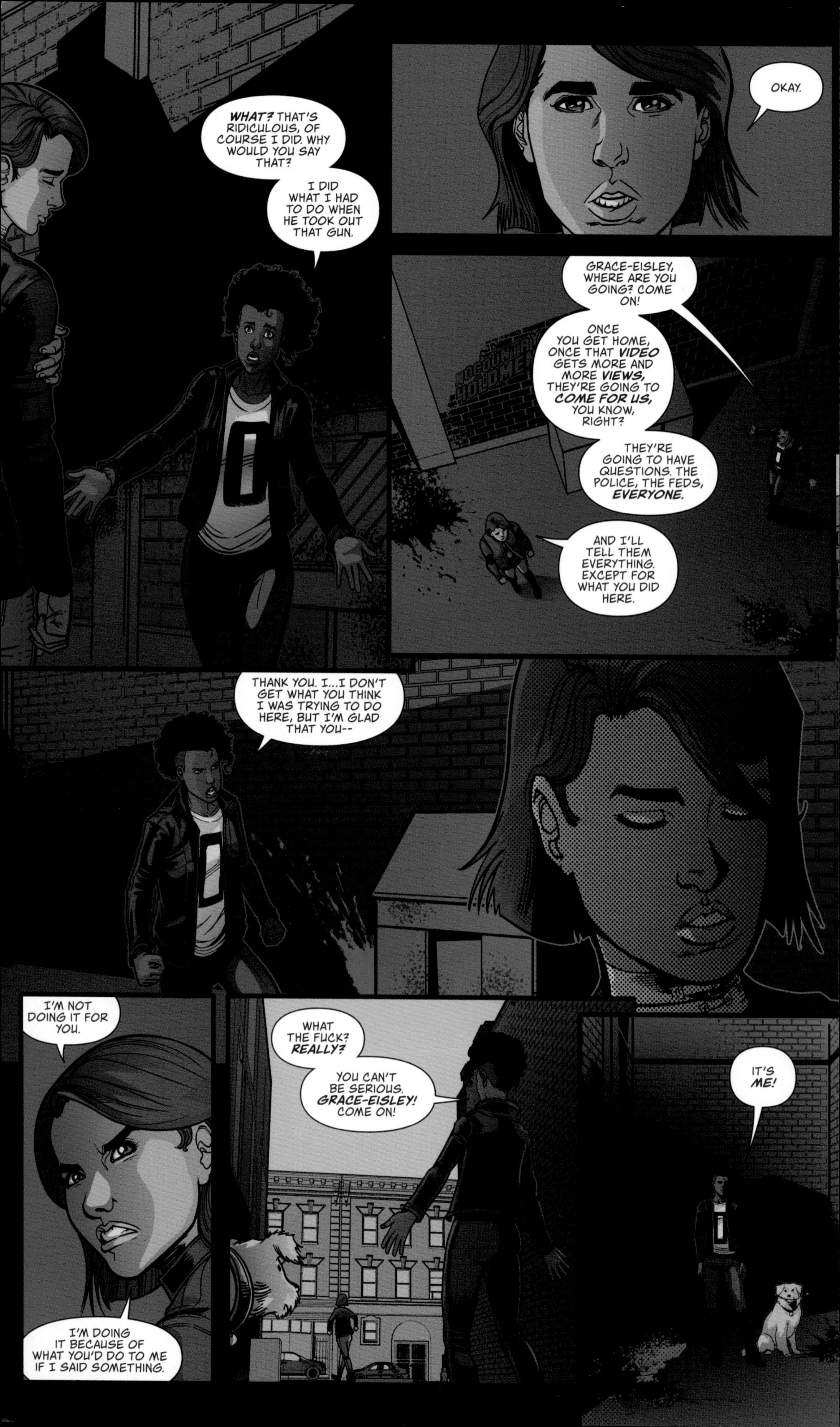

WHAT? THAT'S RIDICULOUS, OF COURSE I DID. WHY WOULD YOU SAY THAT?
I DID WHAT I HAD TO DO WHEN HE TOOK OUT THAT GUN.
OKAY.
GRACE-EISLEY, WHERE ARE YOU GOING? COME ON!
ONCE YOU GET HOME, ONCE THAT VIDEO GETS MORE AND MORE VIEWS, THEY'RE GOING TO COME FOR US, YOU KNOW, RIGHT?
THEY'RE GOING TO HAVE QUESTIONS. THE POLICE, THE FEDS, EVERYONE.
AND I'LL TELL THEM EVERYTHING. EXCEPT FOR WHAT YOU DID HERE.
THANK YOU. I...I DON'T GET WHAT YOU THINK I WAS TRYING TO DO HERE, BUT I'M GLAD THAT YOU--
I'M NOT DOING IT FOR YOU.
I'M DOING IT BECAUSE OF WHAT YOU'D DO TO ME IF I SAID SOMETHING.
WHAT THE FUCK? REALLY?
YOU CAN'T BE SERIOUS. GRACE-EISLEY! COME ON!
IT'S ME!

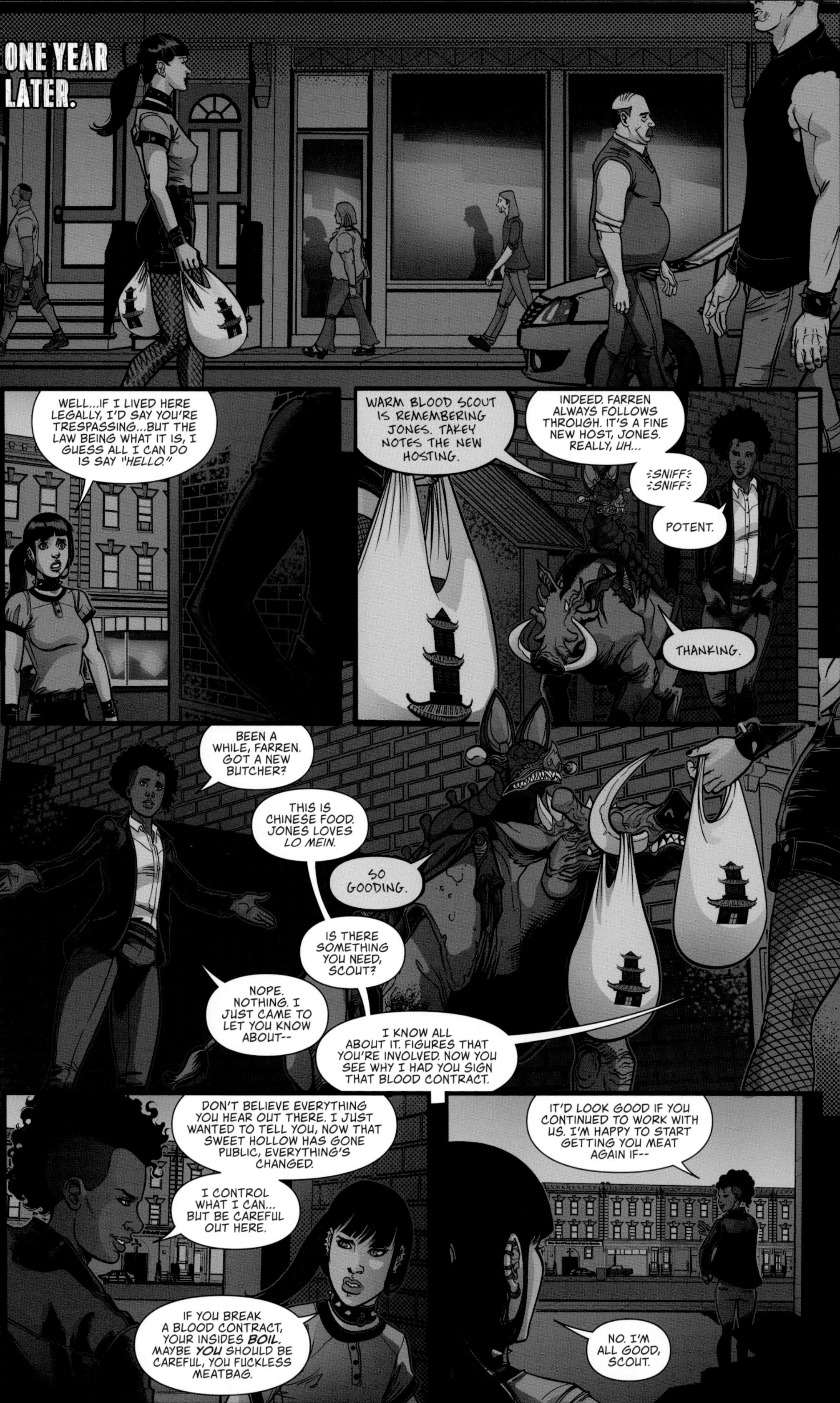
ONE YEAR LATER.
WELL...IF I LIVED HERE LEGALLY, I'D SAY YOU'RE TRESPASSING...BUT THE LAW BEING WHAT IT IS, I GUESS ALL I CAN DO IS SAY "HELLO."
WARM BLOOD SCOUT IS REMEMBERING JONES. TAKEY NOTES THE NEW HOSTING.
INDEED. FARREN ALWAYS FOLLOWS THROUGH. IT'S A FINE NEW HOST, JONES. REALLY, UH...
SNIFF SNIFF
POTENT.
THANKING.
BEEN A WHILE, FARREN. GOT A NEW BUTCHER?
THIS IS CHINESE FOOD. JONES LOVES LO MEIN.
SO GOODING.
IS THERE SOMETHING YOU NEED, SCOUT?
NOPE. NOTHING. I JUST CAME TO LET YOU KNOW ABOUT--
I KNOW ALL ABOUT IT. FIGURES THAT YOU'RE INVOLVED. NOW YOU SEE WHY I HAD YOU SIGN THAT BLOOD CONTRACT.
DON'T BELIEVE EVERYTHING YOU HEAR OUT THERE. I JUST WANTED TO TELL YOU, NOW THAT SWEET HOLLOW HAS GONE PUBLIC, EVERYTHING'S CHANGED.
I CONTROL WHAT I CAN... BUT BE CAREFUL OUT HERE.
IF YOU BREAK A BLOOD CONTRACT, YOUR INSIDES BOIL. MAYBE YOU SHOULD BE CAREFUL, YOU FUCKLESS MEATBAG.
IT'D LOOK GOOD IF YOU CONTINUED TO WORK WITH US. I'M HAPPY TO START GETTING YOU MEAT AGAIN IF--
NO. I'M ALL GOOD, SCOUT.

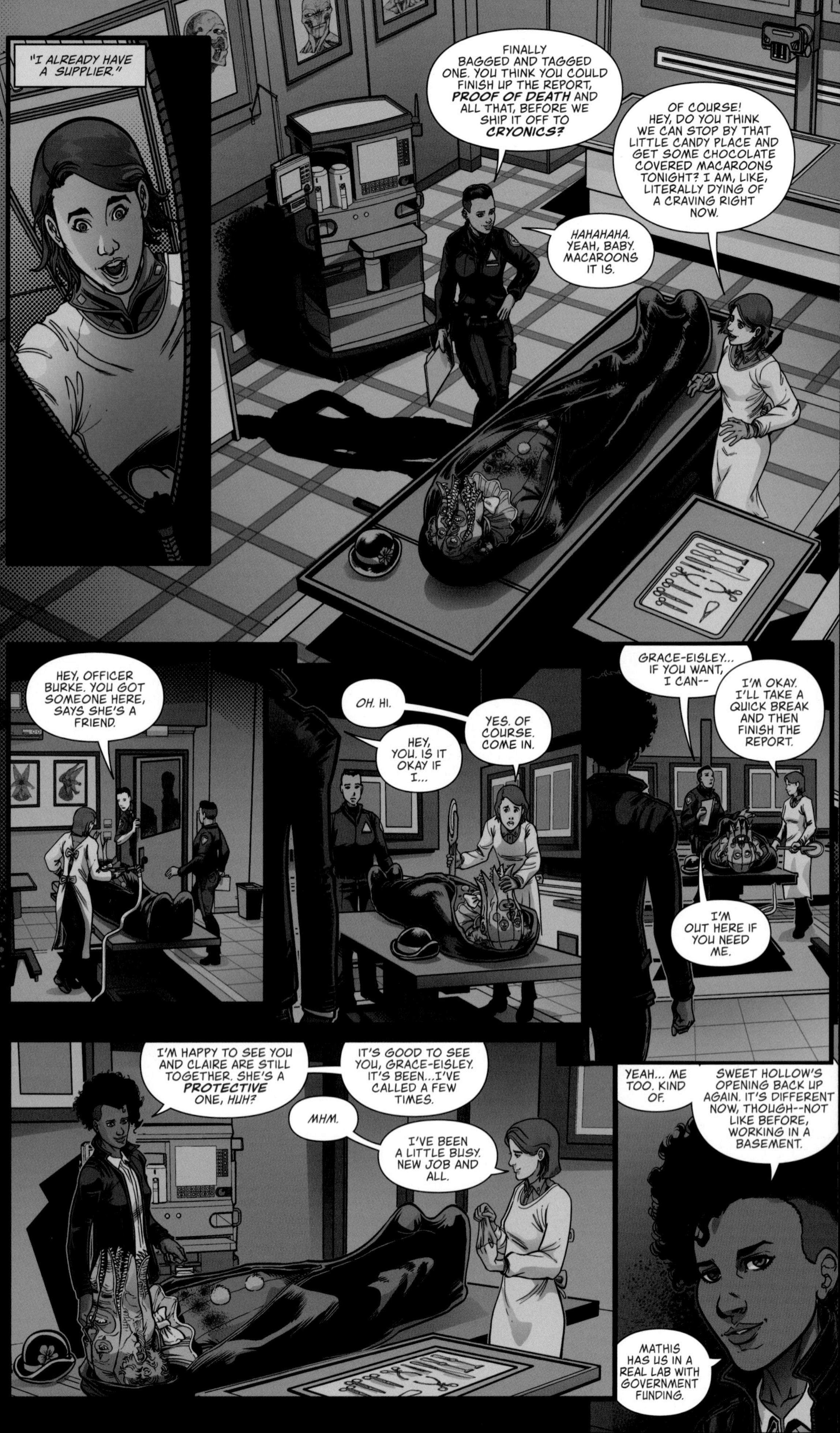

"I ALREADY HAVE A SUPPLIER."
FINALLY BAGGED AND TAGGED ONE. YOU THINK YOU COULD FINISH UP THE REPORT, PROOF OF DEATH AND ALL THAT, BEFORE WE SHIP IT OFF TO CRYONICS?
OF COURSE! HEY, DO YOU THINK WE CAN STOP BY THAT LITTLE CANDY PLACE AND GET SOME CHOCOLATE COVERED MACAROONS TONIGHT? I AM, LIKE, LITERALLY DYING OF A CRAVING RIGHT NOW.
HAHAHAHA. YEAH, BABY. MACAROONS IT IS.
HEY, OFFICER BURKE. YOU GOT SOMEONE HERE, SAYS SHE'S A FRIEND.
OH. HI.
HEY, YOU. IS IT OKAY IF I...
YES. OF COURSE. COME IN.
GRACE-EISLEY... IF YOU WANT, I CAN--
I'M OKAY. I'LL TAKE A QUICK BREAK AND THEN FINISH THE REPORT.
I'M OUT HERE IF YOU NEED ME.
I'M HAPPY TO SEE YOU AND CLAIRE ARE STILL TOGETHER. SHE'S A PROTECTIVE ONE, HUH?
IT'S GOOD TO SEE YOU, GRACE-EISLEY. IT'S BEEN...I'VE CALLED A FEW TIMES.
MHM.
I'VE BEEN A LITTLE BUSY. NEW JOB AND ALL.
YEAH... ME TOO. KIND OF.
SWEET HOLLOW'S OPENING BACK UP AGAIN. IT'S DIFFERENT NOW, THOUGH--NOT LIKE BEFORE, WORKING IN A BASEMENT.
MATHIS HAS US IN A REAL LAB WITH GOVERNMENT FUNDING.

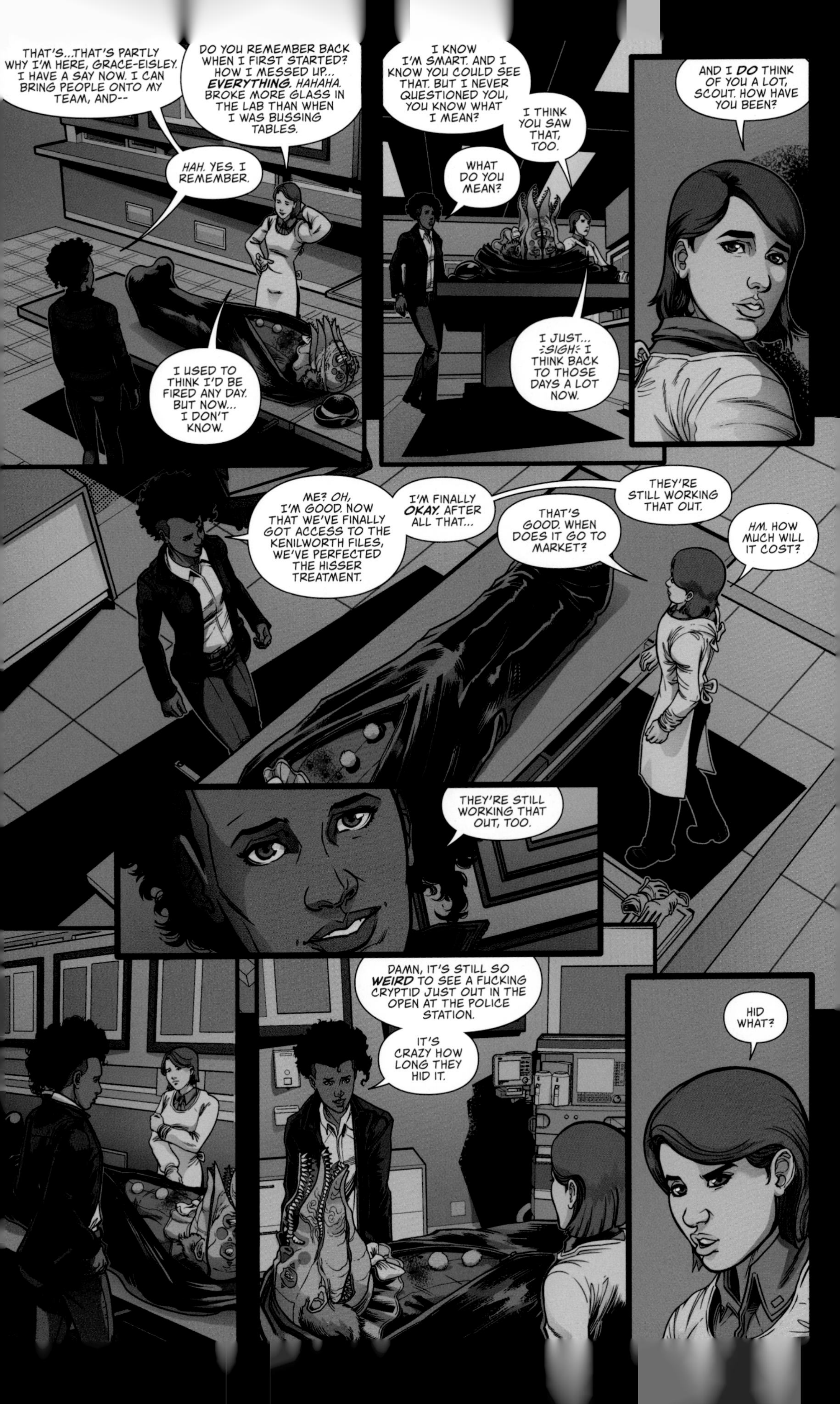
THAT'S...THAT'S PARTLY WHY I'M HERE, GRACE-EISLEY. I HAVE A SAY NOW. I CAN BRING PEOPLE ONTO MY TEAM, AND--
DO YOU REMEMBER BACK WHEN I FIRST STARTED? HOW I MESSED UP... EVERYTHING. HAHAHA. BROKE MORE GLASS IN THE LAB THAN WHEN I WAS BUSSING TABLES.
HAH. YES. I REMEMBER.
I USED TO THINK I'D BE FIRED ANY DAY. BUT NOW... I DON'T KNOW.
I KNOW I'M SMART. AND I KNOW YOU COULD SEE THAT. BUT I NEVER QUESTIONED YOU, YOU KNOW WHAT I MEAN?
I THINK YOU SAW THAT, TOO.
WHAT DO YOU MEAN?
I JUST... SIGH I THINK BACK TO THOSE DAYS A LOT NOW.
AND I DO THINK OF YOU A LOT, SCOUT. HOW HAVE YOU BEEN?
ME? OH, I'M GOOD. NOW THAT WE'VE FINALLY GOT ACCESS TO THE KENILWORTH FILES, WE'VE PERFECTED THE HISSER TREATMENT.
I'M FINALLY OKAY. AFTER ALL THAT...
THAT'S GOOD. WHEN DOES IT GO TO MARKET?
THEY'RE STILL WORKING THAT OUT.
HM. HOW MUCH WILL IT COST?
THEY'RE STILL WORKING THAT OUT, TOO.
DAMN, IT'S STILL SO WEIRD TO SEE A FUCKING CRYPTID JUST OUT IN THE OPEN AT THE POLICE STATION.
IT'S CRAZY HOW LONG THEY HID IT.
HID WHAT?

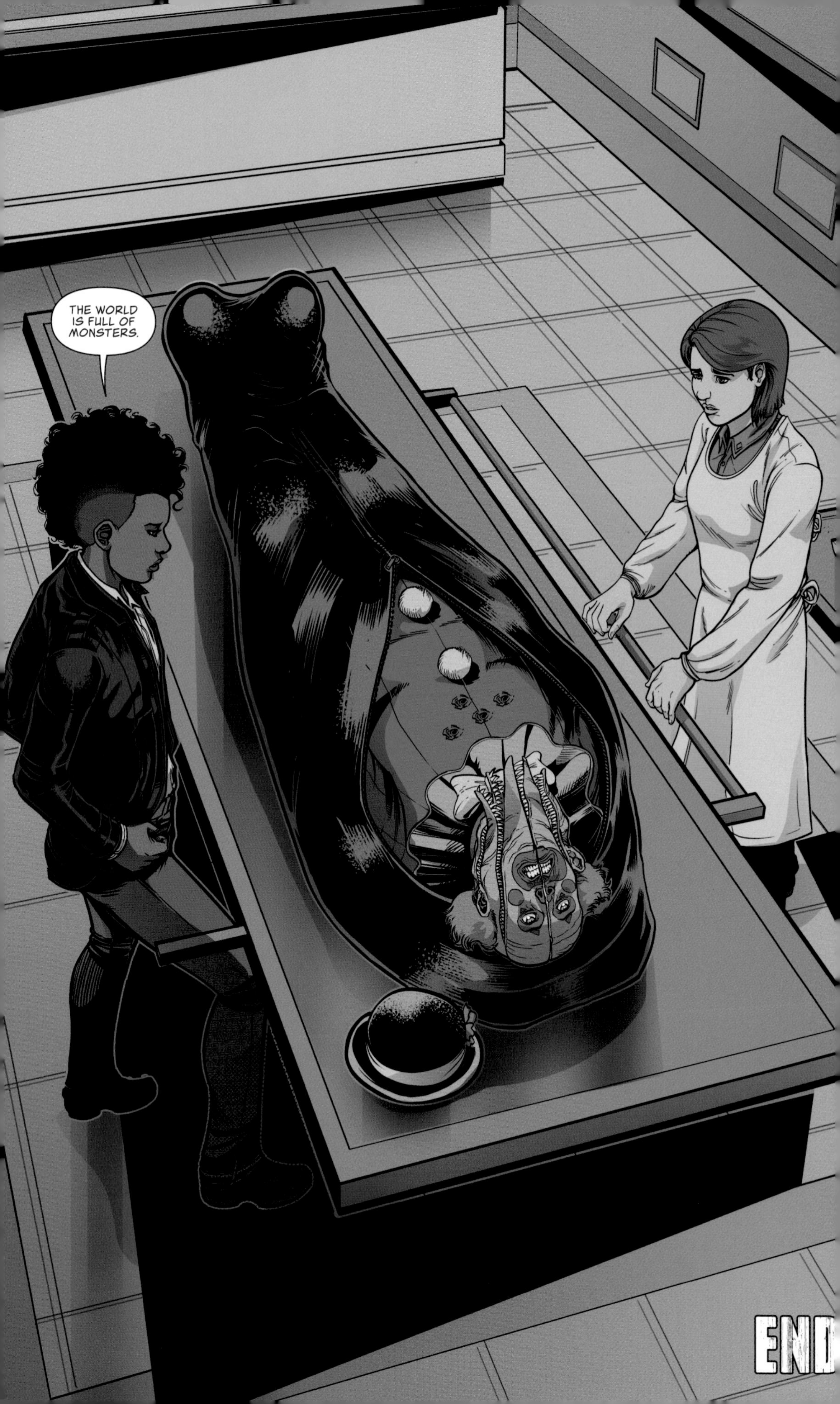
THE WORLD IS FULL OF MONSTERS.
END

covers by: RENZO RODRIGUEZ

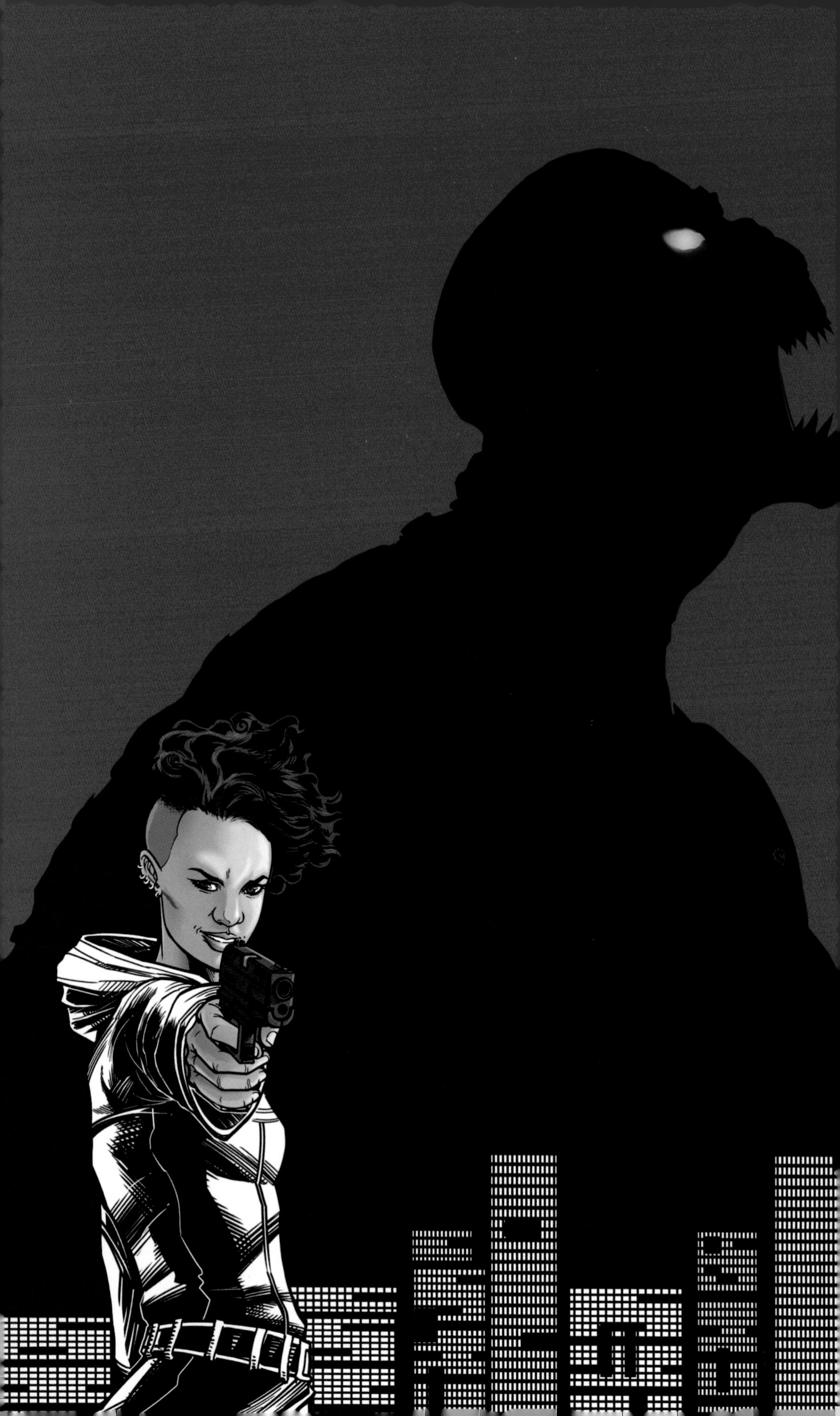

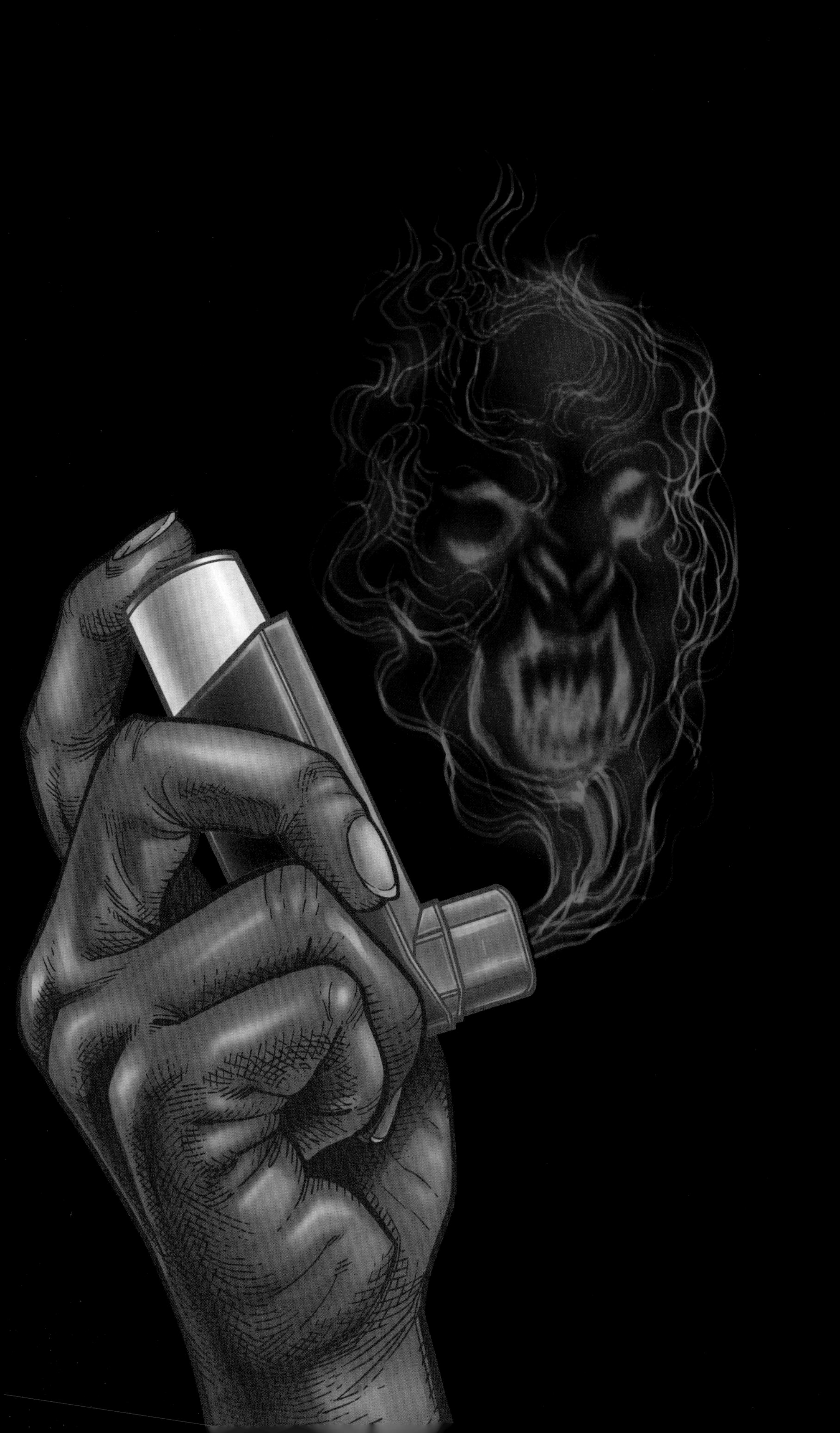

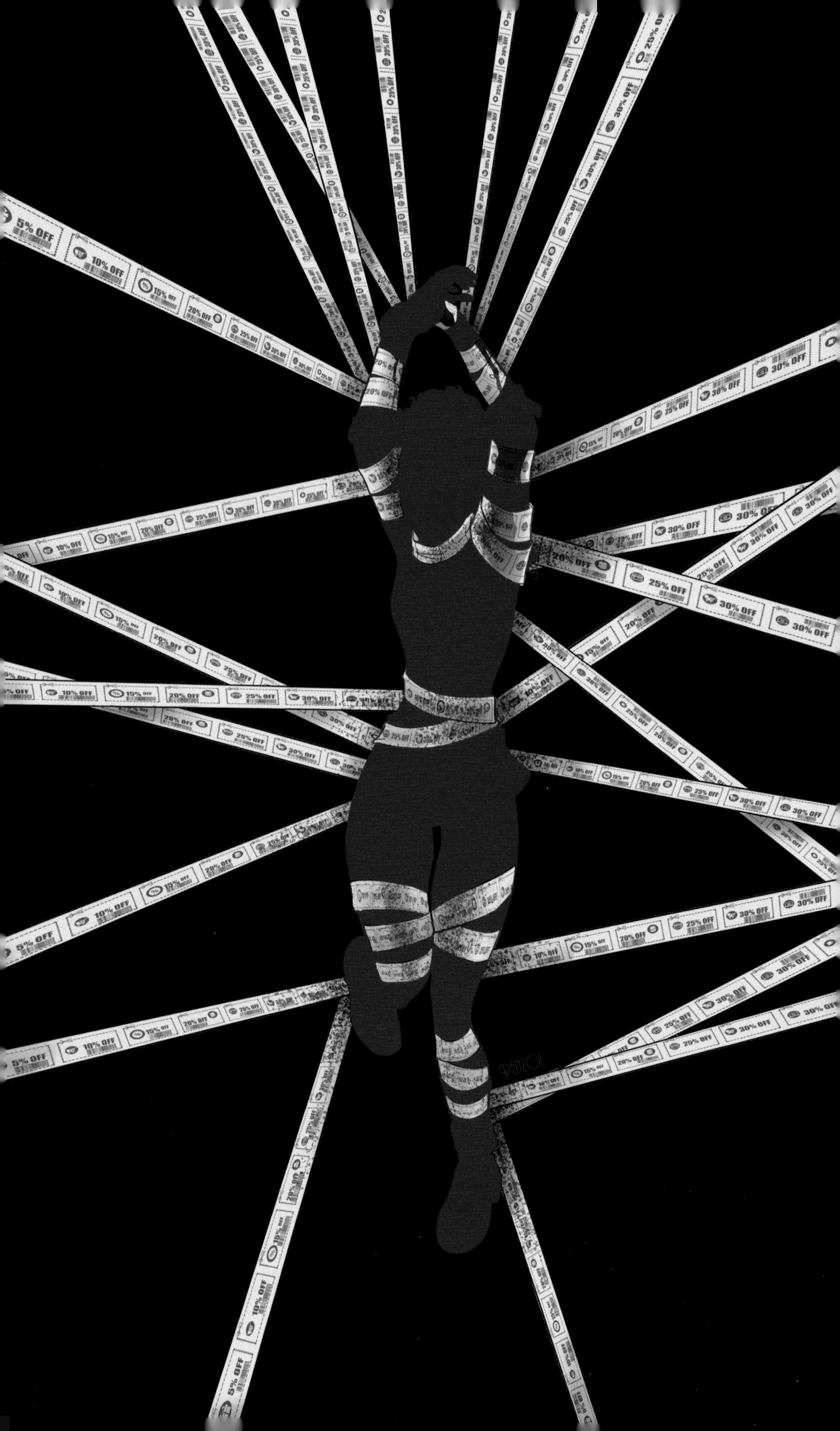
5% OFF
10% OFF
15% OFF
20% OFF
25% OFF
30% OFF

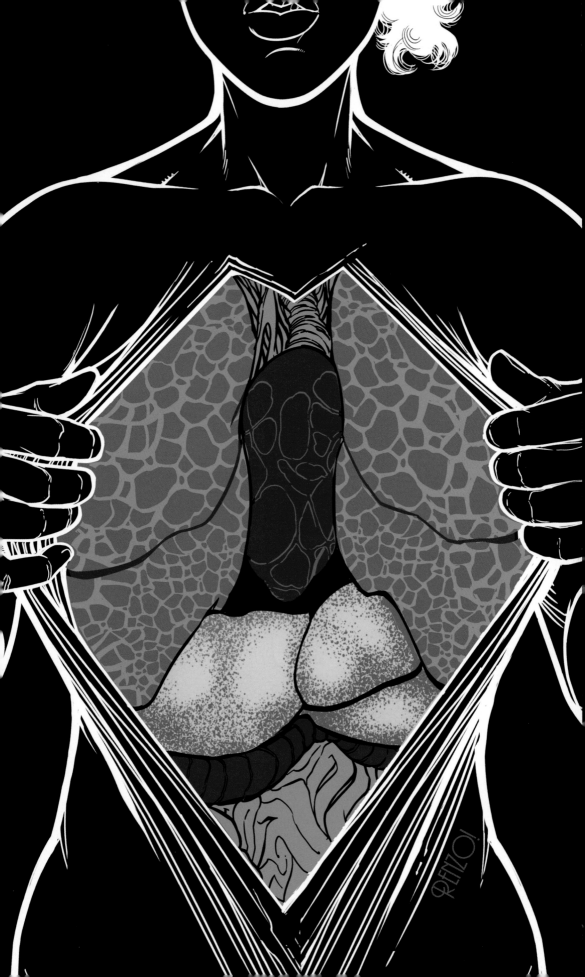

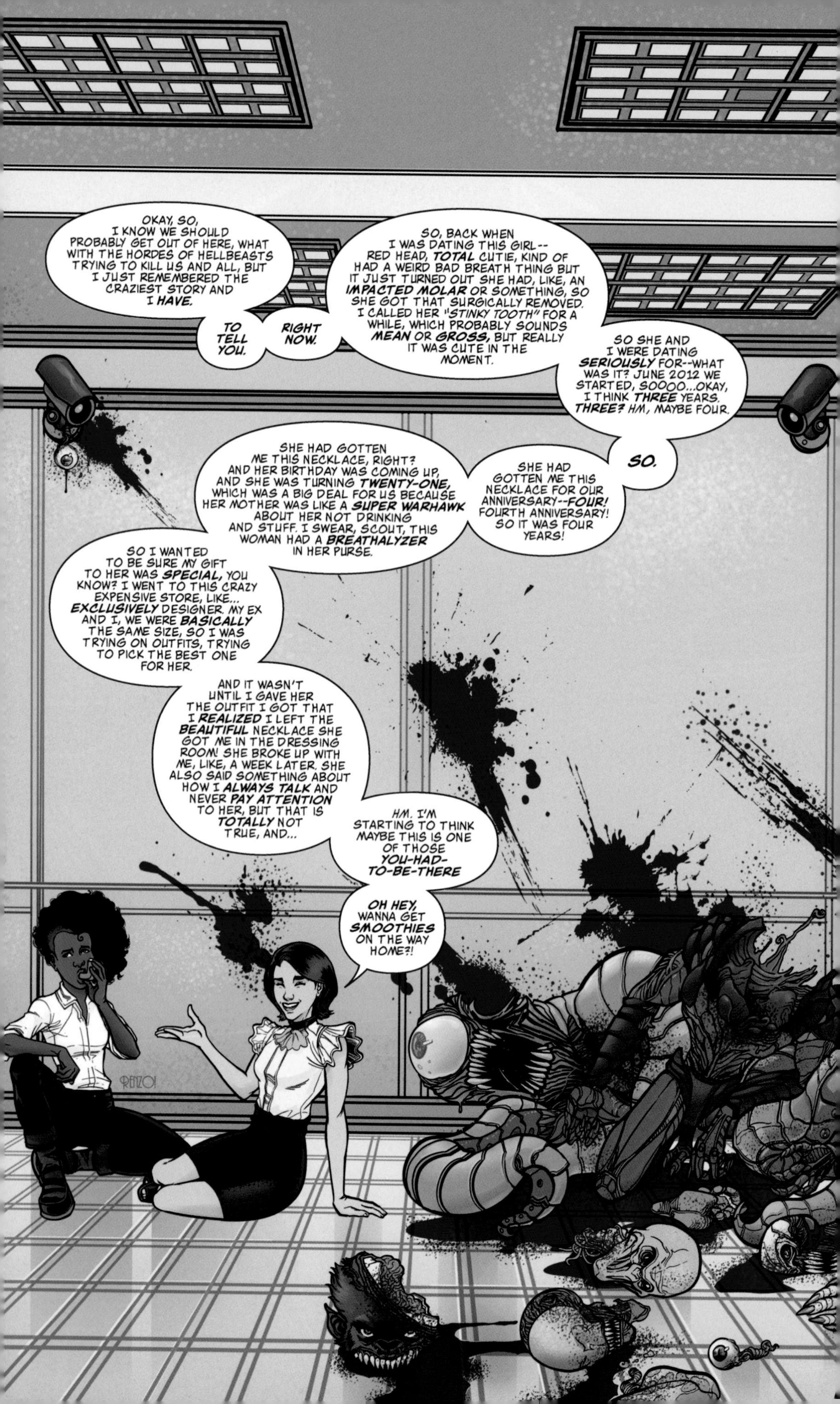
OKAY, SO, I KNOW WE SHOULD PROBABLY GET OUT OF HERE, WHAT WITH THE HORDES OF HELLBEASTS TRYING TO KILL US AND ALL, BUT I JUST REMEMBERED THE CRAZIEST STORY AND I HAVE.
TO TELL YOU.
RIGHT NOW.
SO, BACK WHEN I WAS DATING THIS GIRL-- RED HEAD, TOTAL CUTIE, KIND OF HAD A WEIRD BAD BREATH THING BUT IT JUST TURNED OUT SHE HAD, LIKE, AN IMPACTED MOLAR OR SOMETHING, SO SHE GOT THAT SURGICALLY REMOVED. I CALLED HER "STINKY TOOTH" FOR A WHILE, WHICH PROBABLY SOUNDS MEAN OR GROSS, BUT REALLY IT WAS CUTE IN THE MOMENT.
SO SHE AND I WERE DATING SERIOUSLY FOR--WHAT WAS IT? JUNE 2012 WE STARTED, SOOOO...OKAY, I THINK THREE YEARS. THREE? HM, MAYBE FOUR.
SO.
SHE HAD GOTTEN ME THIS NECKLACE FOR OUR ANNIVERSARY--FOUR! FOURTH ANNIVERSARY! SO IT WAS FOUR YEARS!
SHE HAD GOTTEN ME THIS NECKLACE, RIGHT? AND HER BIRTHDAY WAS COMING UP, AND SHE WAS TURNING TWENTY-ONE, WHICH WAS A BIG DEAL FOR US BECAUSE HER MOTHER WAS LIKE A SUPER WARHAWK ABOUT HER NOT DRINKING AND STUFF. I SWEAR, SCOUT, THIS WOMAN HAD A BREATHALYZER IN HER PURSE.
SO I WANTED TO BE SURE MY GIFT TO HER WAS SPECIAL, YOU KNOW? I WENT TO THIS CRAZY EXPENSIVE STORE, LIKE... EXCLUSIVELY DESIGNER. MY EX AND I, WE WERE BASICALLY THE SAME SIZE, SO I WAS TRYING ON OUTFITS, TRYING TO PICK THE BEST ONE FOR HER.
AND IT WASN'T UNTIL I GAVE HER THE OUTFIT I GOT THAT I REALIZED I LEFT THE BEAUTIFUL NECKLACE SHE GOT ME IN THE DRESSING ROOM! SHE BROKE UP WITH ME, LIKE, A WEEK LATER. SHE ALSO SAID SOMETHING ABOUT HOW I ALWAYS TALK AND NEVER PAY ATTENTION TO HER, BUT THAT IS TOTALLY NOT TRUE, AND...
HM. I'M STARTING TO THINK MAYBE THIS IS ONE OF THOSE YOU-HAD-TO-BE-THERE
OH HEY, WANNA GET SMOOTHIES ON THE WAY HOME?!
RENZO!

BREATHLESS

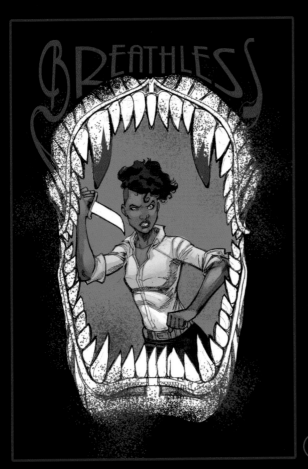

#1

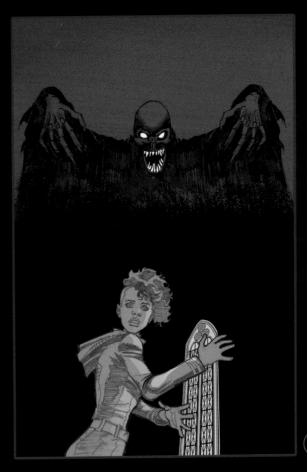

#2

PAT SHAND is a writer. He has created/co-created the comic books *Breathless*, *Snap Flash Hustle*, *Little Girl*, *Family Pets*, *Prison Witch*, *Afterglow*, and *Destiny, NY* as well as writing for established properties, such as *Charmed*, *Adventure Time*, *Disney Princess*, and Joss Whedon's *Angel*. In addition to his work as a comic book creator, he has produced off-off Broadway theatre and worked as a novelist on original stories for Marvel, including *Guardians of the Galaxy: Space Riot*, *Iron Man: Mutually Assured Destruction*, *Avengers: The Serpent Society*, *Spider-Man: Spideyography*, and *Thor: Crusade of the Forgotten*. He runs the independent publisher Space Between Entertainment in New York, where he lives with his wife Amy and their army of cats.

RENZO RODRIGUEZ is a comic book artist from Mexico. In 2012, he started his first indie comic collaboration, *Toxic Storm*, with the writer Adam Cheal, released by Markosia Publisher. In 2015, he worked on *Puppet Master: Halloween Special* from Action Lab Comics. In 2016, Renzo paired with Pat Shand on the series *Hellchild: The Unholy* from Zenescope Entertainment, which led to work on *Grimm Tales of Terror*, *Ripley's Believe it or Not*, and *Grimm Fairy Tales*. He has also done work on *Modern Dread* and *Gangster Ass Barista* for Space Between Entertainment. *Breathless* is his first creator-owned comic.

MARA JAYNE CARPENTER is a professional colorist & cartoonist, whose favorite stories to work on are the kind with blood & magic. She has worked in comics for over 5 years with Black Mask, Action Lab, and other independent creators. She lives in New England with a gay scientist and two spooky cats.

JIM CAMPBELL has been lettering professionally for a decade, following the realization that his previous career as a graphic designer gave him a lot of skills that were completely transferrable to a job that was more fun! In addition to Black Mask, his work can regularly be found in books from Aftershock, BOOM! Studios, Devil's Due, Image, Lion Forge, Titan and Vault. He lives with his wife in a small English market town with a pub at the end of the road. Mostly, he works at home and not in the pub. Honest.